Pernille Hughes (pronounced Pernilla) has previously had three novels published, *Ten Years*, *Probably The Best Kiss In The World* and *Punch-Drunk Love*. Her writing has also been printed in the *Sunday Times*.

She lives in Buckinghamshire, with her ever-patient husband and four kids when they're home.

pernillehughes.com

CW01507626

Also by Pernille Hughes

Ten Years

Probably The Best Kiss In The World

Punch-Drunk Love

A COPENHAGEN SNOWMANCE

PERNILLE HUGHES

One More Chapter
a division of HarperCollins*Publishers* Ltd
1 London Bridge Street
London SE1 9GF
www.harpercollins.co.uk
HarperCollins*Publishers*
Macken House, 39/40 Mayor Street Upper,
Dublin 1, D01 C9W8
This paperback edition 2025

1

First published in Great Britain in ebook format
by HarperCollins*Publishers* 2025
Copyright © Pernille Hughes 2025
Pernille Hughes asserts the moral right to be identified
as the author of this work
A catalogue record of this book is available from the British Library
ISBN: 978-0-00-878598-7

Printed and bound in the UK using 100% Renewable Electricity
by CPI Group (UK) Ltd

To the Knappe Clan

Loons, the lot of you,
but my *lovely loons*
xxx

Chapter One

Ind og ud. Ind og ud.

It repeats in her head and under her breath. In and out. A mantra to get her through the day, supported by a steady tap of her passport drumming on her bag.

The man in front of Anna, tall and broad, turns to look where the tapping sound is coming from, and scowls. He must be having a bad day. It's hardly a crime, or loud for that matter. And she really isn't doing it on purpose. More of a nervous tic. But she does cease and desist as per his scowl as she doesn't want to cause a scene. Instead, she pages through the passport, pausing only to shuffle closer to the control booth and the policewoman inside it. Each of the many stamps brings her joy. So many trips, and adventures. She won't get one here, though. This will just be a cursory glance.

Anna gazes to the side, but there are no windows overlooking the planes in this part of Copenhagen airport. Being able to see the planes, parked and readying to leave

1

again, would make her feel better. In and out, she chants again in her head. That's all this is.

The guy moves to the booth while she stands behind the yellow line on the beautiful floor. Copenhagen airport has the most beautiful cherry-wood floor – all part of the Danish design aesthetic; its building is modern throughout, and if viewed from the sky, the shape of a paper aeroplane. Anna used to love passing through, window-shopping in the modern jewellery design of Georg Jensen and Ole Lynggaard, the homeware of Illum, or having a last-second hot dog from a *pølsevogn* stall or grabbing a cinnamon pastry in Ole & Steen. But not now. Now, she feels anxious and her eyes dart about in case she sees someone she knows, because Denmark is a small country, and Copenhagen is a very small capital city.

"In and out, Anna," she breathes quietly, "in and out." The ticket on her phone will have her back out this evening.

The scowly guy exits around the side of the booth and it's her turn.

"*Hej*," she says, reaching the desk and handing over the battered burgundy passport.

"*Hej*," the policewoman responds, only looking up to check Anna's face matches the photo.

It won't be the "carefree, almost smiling, but not quite because The Rules" face in the photo. That photo was taken five years earlier and Anna imagines the face before the policewoman now carries The Weight of Experience. Far more savvy and no way as naïve. Worldly. Clued up. But it probably just translates as wrinkles.

And yet, it must satisfy her, as a second later she shoots

Anna a warm smile as she hands the passport back. *"Velkommen hjem og God Jul."* Welcome home and merry Christmas.

Baggage reclaim is rammed, not that Anna has a suitcase to collect. She's not staying. Strictly *in and out*. No, she's here for the *pølsevogn* – to buy a hot dog. She's always thought it a clever move to have one positioned here, where waiting travellers can grab a bite and returners, Anna for example, can immediately get their hot dog fix. She orders a red boiled sausage rather than the grilled alternative – because that's what she's in the mood for, it could have gone either way – with *all* the trimmings. Three parallel lines of ketchup, mustard and yellow remoulade are squeezed along the long sausage in its small finger bun, before loose spoonfuls of chopped raw onion, crispy onions and pickled cucumber are added on top. This. This is the real deal. Danish through and through. And while, yes, she's on a tightly timed mission, a girl has to eat, so.

Anna forgets to quell her groan as she horses the first mouthful, the flavours stimulating senses and evoking memories all in one hit. Her eyes being closed during her foodgasm doesn't help, as she is bumped from behind in the mêlée of harried travellers, and she's propelled into someone waiting by the carousel, the hot dog mashing between them.

"Hey!" the figure says, turning. Anna's eyes are frozen

to the red, yellow and brown stripes down the back of his coat. She whips the hot dog behind her.

"*Undskyld*," she apologises and looks up. Bugger. It's him, Scowly Guy. His annoyance has definitely ramped up. In spite of his scowl, Anna feels the need to mention the mess on his back, to try to wipe it away. She starts to explain that she was shoved, but he simply turns his back on her, facing the carousel, then moves forward with a start as his suitcase comes around. He's grabbed it and gone before she can say anything more, apologise further, or remove the slice of pickled cucumber that's glued with ketchup to his back.

She's feeling worse now as she wanders through the customs corridor into the Arrivals hall; guilty about the man's coat, annoyed at his rudeness, gutted about her mauled hot dog, all on top of not wanting to be here at all. The hall is busy. Relatives stand in throngs, with Danish flags – as is the custom – waiting for their loved ones. No one is waiting for Anna. No one knows she's here except for the people at the clinic and they might be doubtful about her turning up. It's taken some cajoling. Keeping her head down, Anna steers towards the end of the hall where the metro waits to take her into the city. Despite trying to keep her eyes front and centre, they're drawn to the large glass windowpanes. The air outside is moving. Snow. Not dainty, confetti flakes, but large fluffy tufts against the dove-grey sky.

Well, that shows how out of practice she is. She hadn't checked the weather before coming. The Nordics know how to dress for the weather, and although she's wearing her

4

large woollen coat and leather boots, that's simply because it's December and London is chilly, not because she's checked. It hadn't occurred to her, in her reluctant prepping for this trip, to consult the forecast. Her plan of landing, making the pick-up and leaving, had somewhat missed all the exterior and contextual detail. Which is ludicrous for a travel specialist. Now, looking about at her fellow metro-users, she sees that even coat and boots allowing, she is still underdressed for Copenhagen. Others wear hats, scarves, gloves and proper winter boots, while the children are in padded one-pieces and earmuffs or balaclavas. She realises her transition is possibly now complete; she's become *a tourist*. In the city where she was born. She isn't quite sure how she feels about that. A small joy, perhaps, that she's properly severed a tie, but also a deep-seated embarrassment that she hasn't got this right. *There is no bad weather*, states the Danish saying, *only poor clothes choices*. She's on the wrong side of that today. Oh my God, she thinks, what an amateur.

She delves into her bag, the one Maiken always said she could live out of for a fortnight, if marooned, with a "Come on. Pleeease," muttered under her breath. And there, in the depths, Anna gets the first win of the day, which she celebrates with a resounding "*Ja!*" – scaring the Chinese tourist walking next to her. Her knitted hat – squashed and lightly covered in the smaller detritus of her bag: dust, paper fragments, and … a boiled sweet stuck to the pompom – is gripped in her hand. Encouraged, she checks her coat pockets, hoping she'll find some gloves, primed to congratulate herself on having some innate, Nordic preservation skills after all, but is disappointed. No matter, she consoles herself, she can stuff her hands in her pockets, unlike her head, so this is the better outcome. Given the size of the snowflakes and the rate they're falling, this is definitely the better way around.

"*Ind og ud*," she repeats. Into the city, make the collection, back on the metro, back on the plane, back to London. Bish bash bosh. Done. One day and it's over. One single day she'll sign off and box up in the back of her mind. Provided no one sees her, it will be as if it never happened.

In her hopes, mashed hot dog aside, everything will be smooth today; no hold-ups, no delays, no chance meetings with people she doesn't want to see. Or even those she might want to see, as they'll come with recriminations. Why hasn't she called? Why doesn't she *ever* call? And they'll invite her to stop for a coffee, as they always have, and she'll say no and then she'll feel bad. Plucking the sweet, a mint hexagon with a chocolate inner, from the not-so-tufty pompom, she tucks the hat on her head. Better she keeps her head down and merges into the behatted crowds.

In and out, it comes as a determined mutter, now. She'll get through the day, and as a reward, just before she heads to her gate, she'll treat herself to a little moment of nostalgia. Not *longing*. Of course not. She left Copenhagen of her own volition. But another hot dog – uninterrupted this time – along with a bottle of Cocio chocolate milk, will be just the pick-me-up she'll need.

❄

The metro, a two-carriage driverless shuttle, is crammed with passengers heading into the city, who chat as they look out of the large windows at the island suburb of Amager as they pass. Not so Anna, who keeps her eyes on her phone, resisting the call to fill her vision with the arrival into the city. Before, she would have tried for a front seat with its big pane and savoured the journey, but not now. Now, standing, she checks emails and tries to ignore the fact that with each stop, there seems to be more and more snow falling, much of it being carried into the carriage on passengers' boots. And more and more passengers come with each stop, too, pushing her further and further in, until they're squashed like herring in a barrel, as the Danes would say. At this latest surge, Anna finds herself crushed up against someone's chest. She feels a breath exhale above her head. What strikes her is the tone of the sigh; not a physical reaction to the squeeze of the crowd, but more … dismay? Anna looks up through her lashes at the face above her. And is met by a rigid visage, with steely, blue eyes, which do not look in any way pleased to see her again. She suspects he knows about the cucumber. There's the slightest scent of ketchup about, too. Casting her eyes quickly down again, Anna acts as if none of this is happening, that she isn't rubbing against him with every shift of the train, thankful he's choosing to ignore her and allowing her to do the same, though there's little room for doubt between them – physically or figuratively – that he doesn't like her.

It's an enormous relief, then, when the train reaches Kongens Nytorv, where many of the passengers spill out to move above ground or connect to other lines. Just as the city is small, so too is the metro network, with just four lines, but Anna hopes this is where she and Scowly Guy now go their separate ways, never to cross paths again.

But no. Connecting to the other set of lines, she spies him up ahead. It's clearly him, the enormous mess on the back of his coat unmissable. He glances back and spots her, which of course garners her another scowl. She wants to march up to him to tell him that obviously she's not following him, she's just heading in the same direction, which is totally different. But she doesn't, because Anna doesn't do things like that. And she's trying to fly under the radar. Instead, she fakes adjusting something on her boot, to expand the space between them.

And yet, they end up on the same train, nonetheless. He moves up the carriage, none too subtly, away from her. Anna focuses on her emails, keen for him to see he's of no interest to her whatsoever, so he can keep his scowls to himself. As the train reaches Østerport station, Anna jumps off as fast as she can, primarily to demonstrate she truly isn't following him, but secretly also to be in front, should he get off, too. Which he does. Of course he does. Sighing, she keeps her eyes front and centre as they ride up the escalator, but she can't help but catch a glimpse of his stony face. It's a shame, she thinks, that he's such a miserable git, scowly and cross, because by all metrics, that would be an enviable face for a guy to have, objectively speaking; strong cheekbones, striking eyes and a razor-sharp jaw under perfect stubble. And as such, she's relieved when he takes his face in a different direction when they reach the street. Thank fuck for that.

Everywhere is covered in snow, with more falling, thick and fast. The clinic is two streets from Østerport station and Anna negotiates the walk quickly and with minimal engagement with the scenery and buildings, which is tricky, as her traitorous eyes want to drink it all in. However, as the pavements are already slippy with the snow, attention is needed. Snowflakes keep catching on her eyelashes, which, much as Anna normally loves snow, is annoying. She keeps her hands firmly wedged in her pockets, hoping the wool coat won't soak up too much meltwater, knowing that naturally it will, and that the locals will be judging.

The banner across the front window says Farvel & Tak, wishing customers "Goodbye and Thanks" as the generations-old clinic is closing for good. Walking in, Anna's glad of the warmth, although she's more trying not to think of the last time she was here. She'd been in tears then, and about to have a shedload more crap heaped on her in the following days. Crap she'd not had a single inkling of.

Waiting in reception, she notes the boxes behind the desk. The clinic officially closes tomorrow, but they've been quite stern with her about not leaving it until then.

"*Hej*," says a woman in scrubs passing through on the other side of the reception desk. Anna can't help but notice the woman's gaze sweep over her more-than-damp state. *Judgey*.

"*Hej*. Anna Lundholm. I'm here to pick up—"

"*Ja*," the woman cuts her off and runs her eye to the desk. "It's good you came. It's the only one left, and it's been a while." There's an admonishment in there. Anna mumbles something contrite about living in London. The clinician places a brown cardboard cylinder on the counter. It's plain, but for a label with a name and then Anna's details below.

Anna feels a pang in her heart. The sticker reads *Pølse*. Sausage. Her grandparents' cat, and hers after they died; a moody old thing but beloved nonetheless, and absolutely the only reason that could bring her back to Copenhagen, as everything else save for weddings and funerals can be done digitally here. She's missed him. Very much. But in the madness of the last eighteen months, she's never had the chance to properly mourn him. Or collect him. Hence the trip.

Placing the cylinder carefully in her bag and saying goodbye and thanks, and good luck and also merry Christmas, she leaves the veterinary clinic. The cold smacks her in the face, and the snow serves a follow-up slap. The wind has picked up and the flurries mean business. Anna's quick to rebutton her coat and cross her arms in front of her as she dips her head and steers directly across the street and in through a gate. She has one more stop before she turns her nose back towards the metro, the airport and London. And then that'll be it. The Bosh to the Bish and the Bash. One more stop, and she'll finally be properly done with this city, its bad memories and scowly men.

Chapter Two

On the little list in her head, Anna has four points.

- Arrive
- Collect ashes
- Scatter ashes
- Leave

And she's already managed the first two, so yay, Anna! She gives herself a mental pat on the back.

Through the gate, Holmens Kirkegaard, the cemetery which lies between the vet and her old home, where she lived with her grandparents and later with Carl, is where her grandparents now lie. Since the vet first called (OK, called for the *eighth* time, but she's been busy), Anna's been thinking what to do with Pølse's ashes. Her grandparents, Vivi and Mads, had had him since he was a kitten, and they all doted on each other. When Anna had inherited him, he'd done his best to come across as aloof and too cool for her, but she'd already seen his true colours and he soon gave it up. He came for cuddles as much for himself as for her, the two of them mourning her grandparents together. It makes complete sense to leave the ashes with Vivi and Mads. The three of them belong together.

Anna soon finds the path she has walked many times before, between the low-hedged plots that cover the cemetery. Danish graveyards are some of the best kept in the world, from her experience of exploring cities on foot. In her mind's eye, she thinks of the cemetery in spring or summer, or occasionally in the autumn when the leaves are golden and russet, but always with radiant light shafts. But those images in her head aren't what meet her now, as the snowflakes and wind are dancing together to form the beginnings of a snowstorm. The snow is resting on the boughs of the fir trees, and it would look positively festive if it wasn't for the biting wind whipping her face, making her squeeze her eyes as closed as she can while still affording her some vision. The weight of the moisture in the wool of her coat is now considerable and it's no longer the warm item it was when she left the airport.

"*Hej, Mormor. Hej, Morfar*," she wheezes out as the snow flies in her face, greeting her grandmother and grandfather in turn. She'd got used to chatting to them over the five years they'd been gone, before she left, using their shared headstone as a sounding board for ideas. Sometimes it just helped to say things aloud, to feel it was shared. And they were very good at keeping confidences. She should stay for a longer chat, to update them on what's happened and where she's living, but she can feel now that her boots aren't waterproof, and she's beginning to shiver with the cold. She tells them she's brought Pølse to join them. Unzipping her bag, however, she hears sounds behind her and turning, she sees a large party of people heading towards her through the snow. Of course they are bundled up in proper winter clothing, but there's no disguising the priest, in her long black robe and white ruff collar, at the front. (Anna bets she's got lots of lovely merino-wool base layers under that, as will the mourners probably … and almost everyone else in the entire city, with the exception of herself.) There's no disguising the coffin being carried behind her, either. Anna can't think of worse weather to be doing this in. Rain is one thing; the snow, cold and wind another. She scans the ground around her and sees the prepared grave just three plots along. She'd been so targeted through her squinting eyes, she'd missed it completely.

Standing very still, Anna lowers her head as the cortège reaches and passes her, telling herself it's in respect, which it absolutely is, but it's also in a vague attempt at anonymity. There's bound to be someone in this group who knows her or knew her grandparents. Instinctively, she pulls her bobble hat further down over her ears to hide herself as much as she can. While she's loved her hat for years, just this minute she wishes it was a nondescript colour, rather than bright red with a white pompom.

She deliberates on the next course of action. Scattering the ashes while there are others who would see is a no-go. It's just not done. And she'd want to do it gracefully and slowly, with the respect Pølse deserves, and in this wind and trying to be surreptitious, that's not going to happen. There's every chance Pølse might blow over them all. Equally, she doesn't think she can stand waiting for the entire duration of a burial without seeming noticeably odd. Or perishing. Moving stealthily from one foot to the other, she tries to generate some heat, but quickly accepts that without breaking into actual star jumps this is a nonstarter.

Anna's shoulders sink as she sees she's missed her moment. Carefully, she re-zips her bag, Pølse safely dry inside – unlike herself – and judging it respectfully safe to withdraw, swiftly does so while trying to lower the volume of her chattering teeth.

Muttering apologies to Pølse and promises to find somewhere equally lovely in London, Anna's trip back across the graveyard is as brisk as she can manage, given her limbs are beginning to seize up with the cold and wet of her clothes. Her back-patting mood has dropped considerably, and now she's simply focused on getting back to the airport and onto her nice warm, toasty plane. A quick look at her Apple watch tells her it leaves in three hours. That's fine. There's just time for a speedy mooch through the airport shops and definitely for that hot dog and Cocio. And a *kanelsnegl*. Probably an extra one for tomorrow, too. There are comforts only cinnamon swirls can truly offer.

Descending into the shelter of the metro is a deep relief. She appreciates the plain grey stone walls and floor; there's literally nothing to tell her she's in Copenhagen, no litter to remind her of everyday foods, no posters for sites or events. The anonymity aids her tunnel vision to get out and away. Scarred from earlier, she checks that Scowly

Guy isn't about, which thankfully he isn't. The awkwardness would have been horrific. Anna pops in her AirPods on the platform to drown out all the Danish conversations. It's different from when she overhears Danes on the London Underground. She's pleased to detect fellow countrymen who are travelling like she is, but here it's overwhelming and the everyday-ness of the conversations too raw. But she lets herself look out of the window this time as the train comes above ground, expecting to see the Blue Planet aquarium and Kastrup Fort, but only seeing white as the air is full of falling snow.

Reaching the terminus, she almost bursts off the train and sprints into the airport hall, desperate to get through security and airside, where she can face away from the city and mentally be on her way. In less than six hours she'll be back in her rented apartment, in front of the TV, watching something, *anything*, rendering today a simple blip in her life and soon to be forgotten. OK, she'll still have Pølse to scatter, but then ... then she can fully move on.

Weirdly, staff are meeting the arriving passengers in the main hall, and at first Anna thinks it might be some kind of Christmas shenanigans. The hall is decorated with white star-shaped Christmas lights. But registering the dropping shoulders and faces of the passengers in front of her, she comes to suspect not. Pulling out an AirPod, she hears the words "cancelled" and "snow" and "closed".

Anna reaches a man in staff uniform. He looks weary already.

"*Hvad sker der?*" she asks. What's happening?

"All flights are cancelled. Grounded due to the snowstorm."

"For how long?" she asks, panic beginning to rise in her. This was not in her plan.

"No idea. The weather is worse across the rest of the country and there's more to come."

This is not what she wants to hear. "OK, OK," she says, more to herself than him. She will just need to revise and adjust her plan. "But I'll just wait here in the airport, yes?" She can totally manage that. Sleeping on one of the designer chairs, living off hot dogs and cinnamon swirls for as long as it takes, is absolutely within her skill set. Her cavernous bag probably has most of everything else she'll need and there's bound to be a toothbrush – designer probably, but needs must – to buy somewhere in the building. Dry clothes might go on the shopping list, too. Anna feels a small spark of pride at her survival thinking.

"I'm sorry, no. We've no idea when flights will resume and we're emptying the airport. No one else comes in. Everyone is being urged back home or to hotels."

That panic? It ramps up several notches. It's not just that she can't leave Copenhagen, although that is the most immediate thing making her breath come in short painful pants, but beneath it, the hidden part of the iceberg, is a dread that she can't leave full stop, that escape is impossible. And it almost brings her to her knees.

"Really?" she asks, in a pathetic whisper. Can this really be true? Nowadays and at a Nordic airport, which knows about snow, that owns twenty-six snow ploughs? "Really, really?"

A vibration on her wrist demands her attention. *Flight SK642 is cancelled. Further information to follow*, her watch confirms.

The official looks at her with pity. "We can't send planes out in snowstorms. Nature decides sometimes."

Much as she'd like to – very, very much in fact – Anna can't argue with that.

Chapter Three

Both hotels at the airport are full. Of course they are. Huddled for warmth in the reception area of the second, Anna calls the five next nearest, with the same result.

It seems many, many planes have been cancelled, and while Anna was oblivious and chilling her bones in the snow, all the world's passengers have raced to the hotels and bagsied the rooms, so there isn't one for her. She's even enquired about the sofas in the reception, but the clerk said "*Nej.*" Harsh. So much for people pulling together in the face of adversity. And she hopes, like in a Hallmark movie, one of the guests might offer her the pull-out in their room or, if a dish, then the other half of their just-one-bed, but none of that has been forthcoming yet. Anna is left bedless, warming her fingers at the three lit candles on the reception desk.

"Perhaps you should try back in the city?" the clerk suggests, but kindly offers her a paper cup of coffee. Anna's hands are around it in a second, not about to pass up a direct heat source. Yes, she supposes, she could. But maaaan she doesn't want to. She wants to stay out here, near the terminal, so she can be away as soon as the flights reopen. She doesn't want to go back in there.

"Or maybe you know someone in Copenhagen? They might have a sofa?" Now, she gets it. He wants the vagrant lady to leave. The coffee is just to assuage his guilt about casting her out into nature's wrath.

"Thanks," she mutters, ignoring the hint, but savouring the warmth of the steam and the glorious smell of coffee that wraps around her slowly defrosting face.

"*God Jul,*" he says. Happy Christmas, indeed. She feels her hand clench into a fist at that. Really. Mocking is a poor look on hotel staff and she'll be telling Tripadvisor as much, once she gets home. And to a charging point. Her phone is down to the last twenty per cent of juice.

She wolfs the coffee, relishing the heat as it snakes down her insides. Mmm, Danish coffee; strong, thick and not necessarily appreciated by other nationalities. Pulling her stuff together, she braces herself and with a couple of silent words of encouragement, gets up from the now damp sofa. She absolutely, one hundred per cent, does not want to put her sodden coat back on, but has little choice. Leaning her forehead against the glass of the doors, she's not quite ready to venture out in the snow. But what are her options?

In the old days she would automatically have called Maiken when anything bad happened, but that's not an option, now or ever again.

All the hotels she calls from the train are full. All of

them. Transport plans have been banjaxed for everyone, whether the intercity trains, the motorways or the planes. People, it would seem, have simply dug in, extending their existing hotel bookings, which must please the hotels no end, as no one is arriving in the city now, either. There's only the less salubrious hotels on the back side of the central station left … but she's loath to think about what's gone on on those mattresses, frankly.

Starving now as she surfaces at Kongens Nytorv, she navigates the dilemma of a hot dog from a *pølsevogn* on the street or cake in a café. Head wins over heart as the café offers her warmth. She orders a coffee and a *honninghjerte*, a heart-shaped cake of honey and Christmas spices, which is pure nostalgia for Vivi's kitchen, in cake form. Yes, she could have picked something fancier, but sometimes you just need as close to Mormor's baking as you can get. Her tastebuds are assaulted with memories, of Christmases with Mormor and Morfar, sometimes with her mother, sometimes not, but also of Christmas afternoons with friends at Christmas markets, the spices rich in the air around the stalls, and nibbling on the hearts as they walked.

It prompts her to scroll through her contacts, like the hotel receptionist had suggested. She has friends. Really, she has. Or rather she has had. All good women who had called and texted her when she'd left the city so abruptly, but who she'd sort of not responded to more than a cursory, *Don't worry I'm fine.*

A sense of shame washes over her. They've repeatedly reached out to her, and she's brushed them away until they finally stopped. She wants to think they've decided to give her space, but then perhaps they've given up on her. She certainly hasn't checked in on them like a good friend would.

She wonders which of them would be most forgiving. Signe, perhaps, an old colleague from her first job. She lives in the city rather than the suburbs, which clinches it.

Anna takes a deep breath, prepares the first line of her humble pie, hits dial. There's a long time before the dialling tone sounds and it definitely isn't the Danish one. Anna ends the call quickly. Signe and her husband Jonas have a liking for travelling to hot places to dose up on vitamin D during the darkest month. The thought of their empty apartment in Christianshavn is almost enough to make Anna weep. Had she kept in touch with her friends, nurtured those relationships as she'd once done, had she actually let them know she was coming, she might be safely sat in Signe's apartment in the blink of an eye, dry and feet warming up on Signe's heated floor. If only.

Thoughts of the fun she's had with her friends seep into her mind. The way they'd laughed and had a short-hand language, how easy things had been. How *honest*. (Or so she'd thought.) If she'd told them she was coming, if she'd arrived a couple of days early, she could have caught up with them, seen their lovely children, laughed. Instead, she'd sat alone in her London apartment, the one she is paying waaay too much for just to get a view. A new view. A replacement view.

So Signe is off the table. Katrine, then, her long-time friend and boss at the e-publishing house. They've kept in touch mainly via text, but she's one of the few who knows what went down eighteen months ago. Anna calls but is met with the engaged beeps. Katrine doesn't believe in voicemail, because writers can be needy things and it'd always be full.

Everyone else lives too far out of the city and the overground trains are suspended. Her options are looking few and bleak.

Anna weighs things up. She can go door-to-door at the questionable hotels behind the station, but it's getting dark now and she might be mistaken for a sex worker. It would have to be the very, very last resort. Or she can chance the one place she's been studiously trying to ignore all day. A place which technically she has a right to, but morally doesn't. A place which would soundly rely on the kindness of a stranger.

She digs about in the secret pocket of her bag for the key, which has lain untouched there all these months. She won't use it, that would be wrong when someone else lives there now, a paying tenant. But she can at least use it to prove she's the landlord. And the little key which hangs on the ring with it, next to the wooden Viking key fob, will give her access past the padlock, to everything she's left behind, including a bed and a wardrobe full of dry, weather-appropriate clothes.

Her frozen feet make the decision.

Kartoffelrækkerne are eleven streets of houses between the water of Sortedams Sø and the ramparts of Østre Anlæg park in central Copenhagen. Dubbed the "Potato Rows" for their linear formation, the triple-floored terrace houses were built around 1889. Anna's *morfar* had been born to this house, which his parents had inherited from his *farfar*. Anna had lived in it from her teenage years and been left it when Morfar died. The small streets are tight knit both physically and metaphorically, the neighbours looking out for each other in a way that is not perhaps typical for capital cities. Anna wonders briefly what her neighbours Niels-Christian and Dorte, and Anne-Grete on the other side, had made of her vanishing and a stranger moving in. There's that twist of shame again. She should have called them, told them personally what was going on. But then they probably hadn't missed her throwing Carl's belongings out of the door into the front yard. That hadn't been her finest hour.

Just as one never forgets how to ride a bike, apparently walking from Østerport station to her street is still a matter of muscle memory. Which is a good thing, given the now blizzard and her having to squint the entire way. She can barely move, she's so cold. Her hands have cramped into fists inside her coat and while her hat is still on her head, it's not because it's warm, but because it's soaked through, partially frozen, and she doesn't want it to get anything in her bag – particularly Pølse – wet. Before she commits to entering the street, she tries to call Katrine again, barely able to hold the phone in her cramping hand and hit the buttons. Still engaged.

She takes the plunge.

Cold or not, Anna takes a moment outside the cherry-red door halfway up. The little yard is much the same as she left it, albeit with a couple of inches of snow covering the cobblestones and the bench. There's no sign of the plants that run around the edges, save for the bulges of some pots. A Christiania cargo bike is parked to one side, it, too, bearing a thick layer of snowflakes. The streetlight makes it all glisten in the winter darkness, and Anna feels a pang at the beauty of it. Another reason to pause at the door is to rehearse what to say when the door is answered. She's praying there'll be someone home.

A deep breath and she knocks, before quickly ramming her hand back into her wet pocket. There's a pretty wreath on the door, which appears to be made out of ... paper. *Quirky.* She stamps her boots, trying to get the blood back into her toes, but that's a pointless exercise. She'll be surprised if they aren't frostbitten in there.

Not hearing any plodding on the sanded wooden floor, or anything on the stairs beyond the door, she hopes it's the weather muffling the sound. There is definitely a lack of door answering. She knocks again, more loudly this time, in case the wind-muffling goes both ways. What she *can* hear is her heart pounding, louder and louder as the seconds pass and the prospect of having to walk away gains traction in her head.

Anna feels her nose begin to twitch at the notion of there not being anyone home. That would be the perfect end to the day; her crying on her own doorstep, sodden to her knickers and frozen to her bones. Just the thought of it increases her panic and she hammers on the wood this time.

"Yes, yes. *Jeg kommer!*" shouts a voice from inside. Male and possibly not Danish, given the mixed language, but you never really know, given the way the Danes often mix words.

The door opens and before her stands a man, tall and broad, filling the doorway, wearing just a tiny towel around his waist.

He has a face she recognises.

And it forms a scowl she knows.

To which, knowing her hopes for shelter are scuppered, Anna bursts into tears.

Chapter Four

"**D**id you follow me?" he growls.

The situation is bizarre, neither of them knowing quite what to do. He doesn't seem to be the kind of man who slams doors in the face of distressed women. On the other hand, and quite fairly, he doesn't seem inclined to let such women into his home either, especially when he only has a tiny towel to defend himself.

"Absolutely not," she manages, in something she wishes was less sobby, but it's out of her control. The snot isn't helping. The burr of his English tells her he's a Scot. She suspects he'll recognise her accented English as being that of a local. "This is just a weird coincidence."

The arch of his right brow says he does not believe her.

He waits, silent. And glowering.

"I wasn't following you before, either," she adds, her earlier wish to set him straight coming back to her. "We were just heading in the same direction." She spots his big Nordic parka hanging behind him in the hallway, the condiment apocalypse wiped off it, but a dark stain remaining. "The coat thing was an accident." That scowl of his is back. His eyes look behind her now, to see if he is being pranked. "I did apologise," she reminds him. It is hard to stay focused on stemming her tears and also being contrite, when his cold, and thus very hard, nipples are right in her eye line. That said, the animosity vibrating off him is helping.

Looking back at her now, presumably satisfied he isn't about to be rushed by thieves, he gruffly asks, "What is it you want?"

Now, now she knows it's *him* in the house, she isn't so sure. Does she want to go into the house with someone who thinks she's a stalker and clearly dislikes her? Anna half turns back to the street. Could she knock on a neighbour's door instead? She'd have so much explaining to do.

Some cold meltwater from her hat drips down her forehead and catches in her eye, making her blink even more than in her efforts to stem the hot tears.

"Do I know you?" he prompts.

"No. Yes. Sort of. But no," she rambles, turning back, possibly a little delirious now with the cold, and looking beyond him again, through the sliver of the doorway he doesn't naturally fill. She wants to see what it looks like. She wants to be inside in the warmth.

His eyebrows draw together. She isn't making any sense. And of course, she isn't; this entire day has been nonsense. "I'm Anna. Anna Lundholm. I own this house. Your landlord, I guess."

"Really?" The frown remains. "My landlord lives in

London." He folds his arms across his chest in a show of strength or to preserve warmth, she supposes, then remembers the towel, and swiftly moves his hand down again to hold onto the knot.

"Yes, true, but we met at the airport, remember?" she can't help but point out. "I was in town for the day, and the weather happened, and I can't fly home, and I can't get a hotel room anywhere." Thankfully, in the one well-timed occurrence of the day, her teeth start chattering again. "And I am so wet and cold, I couldn't think of what else to do but come home and knock." So, OK, her use of the word *home* is deliberate and an intentional pull of the heartstrings, though whether he even has any remains undetermined. Anna feels she's getting a grip of things.

He still doesn't look convinced.

"What colour is the bathroom?" he demands.

"Which one?" she counters, drawing the back of her hand across her nose to wipe the snot. It's not pretty, but needs must, and it comes across as feisty, which she'll take, having just sobbed on a stranger's doorstep.

"Main."

"White. But there's a mosaic on the wall that's shades of blue." She'd done it herself. It had seemed a good idea at the time, copied from something she'd seen in Greece, but very quickly used up all her patience and had taken months for her to complete.

"Kitchen?"

"White. But the accessories are grey." She sees his intention, but she's flipping cold and doesn't have time for this. "Look, either of those things I could have seen on old lettings ad pictures. But I *can* tell you the third step on the second staircase squeaks like a bitch."

His face relaxes. Fractionally.

"Anna, did you say?" She nods. He sighs. Deeply. "I'm freezing my tits off here." Yes, she can see. And *Same*, she thinks, but keeps it to herself. "Come in, warm up and we'll work out what to do with you." The delivery is slightly begrudging, but Anna graciously chooses to overlook it.

She waits in her own entrance hall, as the guy sprints back up the stairs then re-emerges in under two minutes in joggers and pulling a sweatshirt down over his chest. She averts her eyes from the last sliver of skin, but she's surprised herself at how much she's ogled. Ogling has been soundly off the cards lately.

"Give me your coat," he says. She unpeels the dripping coat from her body. "That's what you've been wearing?" he asks incredulously. "I thought you Danes knew how to dress for the weather." She resists the urge to snarl.

She hands him the coat and he obviously regrets his offer the moment his hand comes into contact with the wet wool. His is no poker face; it's virtually subtitled. He hangs it on a peg, though.

"I … forgot," is the only real excuse she has. "And it was just supposed to be a quick in-and-out trip." That mantra has not worked. She also hands him her sopping hat, its pompom a sorry state.

He looks critically at her. "Your clothes are wet, too." He makes it sound like she's done it on purpose, to annoy him.

"I am aware," she mumbles.

His eyes move towards the open kitchen-diner living room, and she senses his reluctance. But his manners are stronger, it seems.

"Tea?" he asks, ushering her further in. "Or are you still mainlining coffee at this hour, like a true Dane?"

She's been drinking tea in the evening since she'd been away at *efterskole*, between the end of her senior school and college.

"Tea would be great, thank you." Just the thought of hot tea is almost enough to bring her to tears again. She's still feeling stupid about the over-clothes and very aware of the wet remaining clothes, every movement clammy and cold.

The room is mainly as she remembers it, the pale wood dining table and chairs and pendant lights. It was a great space for dinner parties. Today, one end of the table is covered by piles of work papers and the other a space where she supposes he eats. The room is lived in without being messy, orderly in its daily use. Her *mormor*'s Swiss cheese plant is still going in one corner, which makes her smile. The kitchen has way fewer things cluttering the tops than when she lived here. It's tidier than her London kitchen, so she supposes it must be a "her" thing. A large rechargeable candle flickers in the window. That's his and she likes it, what it represents. But best of all, it's the memories the room offers that have her staring for a long moment, memories of being here with Vivi and Mads, but also with Carl and the life they had here. Lounging on the sofa at the far wall, basking in the morning sunshine with cups of coffee, stroking a purring Pølse, and watching the birds in the courtyard garden. There's a knitted throw hanging over the arm of the sofa, and Anna has to rein in the overwhelming desire to wrap her sodden body in it.

"Do you need some dry clothes?" he prompts, knocking her out of her reverie. "Something while you tumble yours?" Her black merino-wool V-neck and black trousers are dry-clean only. Neither of them are going near the tumble dryer.

"Thank you … er…" She's standing in the kitchen with a man whose name she doesn't know. Or at least she can't remember. She'd digi-signed the lease documents the agent had sent her in a hurry, keen to get it out of her head. Was his surname MacKinlay?

He takes the hint, with a grunt. "James. Jamie MacDonald." He doesn't look at her as he makes the tea. He uses loose leaves and a strainer, the tea leaves having been spooned from a small brown paper bag. He's either been gifted it or self-selected the blend in a shop. She likes the idea of him assessing the scents before making his choice. It's something she'd always done, too.

"Jamie, thank you. But I'm thinking I can maybe change into some of my clothes stored in the room upstairs."

He frowns for a second, then understands. "You mean the sex room?" he asks and Anna has to cough her caught breath. Her mind spins through the rooms upstairs and wonders what he's done to one of them. Surely there were terms and conditions in the lease about that kind of redecorating?

Jamie places a steaming cup in front of her. Her hands are around the ceramic cup in a short second.

"The room with the padlock. That's what my friends call it. No one knows what's behind the door." He's not laughing as such, not at her, certainly, but she senses amusement there. Like he *is* capable of humour.

"Oh." Now she sees.

"The estate agent said it was your stuff, but it put other viewers off. They were expecting a body or something torturous behind it. They've been reading too much Nordic Noir. But their loss was my gain, so…" This is the most he's spoken to her so far, so she suspects he's genuinely pleased with his luck. To be fair, he's got a great house here, in a central location. The houses are much sought-after, which is ironic, given they were built as lowly workers' terraces, three families to each house. She hadn't been aware of viewers not taking to the house, she'd left the agent to it.

"Trust me, there's just my personal items in there. No bodies. I just didn't have time to arrange storage when I left. Piling everything into the one room and locking it seemed the best idea. That and the storeroom in the basement." She sees now that it is … irregular, but she hadn't been thinking too straight at the time. All she'd thought about was getting the hell out of town. "I have the key. If it's OK with you, I could grab some dry clothes?"

"Sure." Back to the minimal sentences then. They drink their tea in relative silence, Jamie busying himself tidying his paperwork away, in what she suspects is an effort not to engage her further in conversation – or to hide his notes just in case this is an elaborate ruse of industrial espionage.

Either way, Anna can't see how she's going to get to a point of asking whether she can stay the night. Her eyes skitter to the courtyard, wondering whether she can at least slyly scatter Pølse's ashes somewhere out there in one of his beloved sunspots. Unlikely.

Eventually, she digs out the Viking keyring and heads for the staircase. He follows. She's not surprised. He's already not happy about her being there, so there's no way he'll let her roam about his possessions upstairs unchecked. Understanding, she stays quiet, thinking, too, that it must be strange living with a mystery room in your home. She looks about as she goes, trying to see all the differences. It's strange; her home, but not her home. She recognises the basic layer of walls, floor, simple furniture and rugs, but then there's a top layer, of things which aren't hers; a guitar on a stand in a corner, a couple of framed photos on the sideboard. It's strange, but she finds she likes it. Her house is still a home, and it deserves to be loved.

Something suddenly dawns on her. "Do you live here alone?" What she really means is: *Is your wife about to come home and find another woman getting dressed in your house?* Anna wouldn't wish that on anyone. She's astounded she hasn't thought of it until now. She really hasn't thought coming here through. The intrusion. She only thought about getting warm, somewhere she felt safe.

"Aye," he says. His tone is wary. Maybe he's feeling uncomfortable being alone here with her? He hadn't really had much choice in the matter. Anna tries to put him at ease with more chatter as she scales the stairs.

"And you've been in Copenhagen long?" He'd known

to shout *Jeg kommer* at the door. He's obviously picking up the language or actively learning it.

"Two years, give or take." She stays quiet, hoping he'll elaborate and surprisingly he does. "I lived in Nordhavn first, but I wanted more room nearer work and somewhere central. This place was a dream."

She can't help smiling at that. A sense of joy that this house, which she's grown up in, is something he values. It's pride and it surprises her, given the last time she was here she was fuelled by a need to be anywhere but here, its walls tainted by what she'd found, the secrets they'd kept.

"Where's work?" she asks, then realises she's asking all the questions and interrogating him. "I'm a travel specialist," she offers in exchange, moving along the corridor, passing two bedrooms, to the second flight of stairs. "I write for travel blogs and I devise city tours. Hence the living away." True, but not quite true. It doesn't matter, she'll be out of his life soon enough, back to London. The third step gives a loud squeak. "Ha!" she exclaims and instinctively looks back at him. There's a ghost of a smile on his mouth, but it fades as soon as he sees her notice. All the same, Anna doesn't give away how moved she is to hear the squeak again.

"Do you travel much?" she asks. It's a question she asks everyone she meets, always keen to hear about new places or suggest some.

"I used to."

"You make it sound like you've outgrown it," she says with a laugh. That can't be a thing.

"No, just priorities change. And I live 'abroad' now.

There's still lots to be discovered, so I'm not feeling the wanderlust so much. If I do leave, it's either to see my dad on Skye or on business."

Priorities change. She can't argue with that. Only his seem to be the opposite of hers, which are to be away from here.

"Which was it today?" she asks, keen to get him talking more, to relax, to perhaps not be so grumpy with her.

It takes him a moment to remember that they'd met at the airport. "One of those." Right.

As they reach the top floor, she sees the open den space, once her *hyggekrog*, and a door with a padlock on it beyond.

This secluded snug is her favourite room. It homes her low coffee table, a flea-market find in Frederiksberg, where she'd spent many weekends, pottering around the stalls, picking small pre-loved bits with which to decorate. Under it is a soft grey rug and around it are a small sofa and an armchair, each with cushions, and a standing lamp. There are wooden shelves at the wall, which she remembers clearing, but are now covered with novels, photos, knick-knacks, beach finds, and more rechargeable candles. On the table is a work-in-progress jigsaw. Still very much the cosy nook she remembers.

"I used to do jigsaws here with my grandfather. Always the hard ones. Only, *his* coffee table was very ugly, dark brown wood with brown ceramic tiles on the top. Very 1970s." She'd happily sold that to someone who'd valued the style more than her.

"The seventies was a strong decade in Denmark."

"You're a style enthusiast?" He still hasn't shared what he does with her.

"No, but I have eyes." It makes her laugh. His mouth doesn't crack a smile, but he's more willing to talk, it seems. "I see the difference between the designer styling of every single office and younger people's décor and then their parents'. People take pity on me as a single Scotsman here in the city. My colleagues invite me to their family parties, so I get to see their time-warp family homes. Not all, but the majority."

"They do?"

"I'm their novelty Scottish friend who owns a kilt. That's the deal; party with drink and food in exchange for my wearing it. Sometimes it's playing my bagpipes."

"Really?!"

"No. Don't be daft. Not all Scots play the pipes."

She doesn't know how to react to that, whether he's taking the mickey as a joke, or to admonish her for stereotyping. This is hard.

She turns her attention instead back to the nook and a closer look at the shelves. The books are interspersed with small Scottish highland cows, photos of rugged landscapes and seascapes, plus a couple of bottles of whisky. All very tasteful. Home for him, but still in keeping with the white walls she'd scrupulously painted when she'd taken over from her grandfather. She doesn't tell Jamie this house had been exactly the time warp he's mentioned. A brown corduroy sofa and mustard yellow curtains. The ceramics had been brown and orange and she hadn't missed them one bit since she'd passed them on to the charity shop. She missed her grandparents. Constantly. But their styling? Not so much.

He clears his throat behind her, and she realises she's been blatantly assessing his home, which considering she was uninvited, is highly rude.

"You've made it very *hyggeligt*," she says, hoping the commendation makes up for her manners. "I have the same Kay Bojesen monkey and bird in my apartment," she adds, pointing to the designer wooden ornaments on the shelf. "And my Hoptimist is yellow," she says, noting the iconic dome-headed spring figure, his a wooden one, which is supposed to instil optimism and good mood when bounced. She resists the urge to suggest he bounce it more often.

"You left me with a blank canvas, and the modern Danish furniture is quite easy to blend with," he says with a shrug. "A few accents here and there and a father who likes to photograph his surroundings and is proud of our tartan." He nods at the soft tartan throw on this sofa.

"Sounds like a keeper," she says, to which he gives her a simple noncommittal, "Aye."

Anna heads for the door at the end of the landing, pulling the keyring from her pocket.

The padlock which hangs on the door is shiny and new. Considering the state she'd been in when she'd screwed it into the doorframe, Anna doesn't think she did too bad a job of it, although her *morfar* would have disagreed, but he was a perfectionist with his handiwork. Not that he would ever have thought to screw into the doorframe in the first place: *A doorframe built in 1889 should be respected, Anna!* — she'd heard that plenty of times when she slammed a door as a teen.

The U-bar pings out with ease and a satisfying click as she unlocks it. Anna suddenly feels self-conscious, given Jamie's standing right behind her. There could be dirty clothes in there. But that isn't her usual way. And she'd be surprised if she'd left any food in there – that isn't her way, either; but those had been dark and unhinged times, fuelled purely by the notion to pack up and leave. And while she still stands by that decision as being the right one, she does accept her thinking had perhaps been on the more deranged side of organised. She's better now. Much better. She hopes Jamie can see that when he sees what's on the other side of the door, or she might be out on her ear.

Chapter Five

As the door stops at halfway open, most of the drama is lost. Anna figures something might have slipped or shifted when she'd closed the door, but edging her way in, she sees she'd rammed so much into the room, things stacked on other things, others wedged into tiny spaces, like some psychotic Tetris, that she must have contorted herself back out those eighteen months ago. It's a minor miracle there hasn't been a landslide at some point, and that she could get in the door at all. In stark contrast to the nook they've just passed, it is the exact opposite of *hyggeligt*.

There's very little space in which to move within the room, and she imagines unpacking it will be a game of strategy.

A light whistle comes from behind her, where Jamie's peering round the doorjamb, his hand gripping its edge.

"Wow," he says.

"Don't judge."

"There's more furniture in here than in the entire rest of the house." Oh, so now he wants to talk...

"Once more for the cheap seats, no judging."

But he isn't letting up, his eyes scanning the spectacle of the room. "I mean, I thought Scandies inherently had this sleek minimalism thing going on, but now I see they're as much hoarders as the rest of us. You just hid yours."

Following his gaze, her shoulders sag as she accepts the judgement. Somewhere in this small room, her teen room which she'd made into a dressing room when she'd moved into the main bedroom, there's a wall of wardrobes, a bed, another sofa, a bookcase full of novels. They're camouflaged by boxes of more books, her research files, her writing files with old drafts, her university notes and all the extra furniture she couldn't part with, but knew had no place in a rented home.

"Sometimes, when you're in a rush, your choices aren't too smart," Anna tries.

She pushes a box aside, nearly bringing a chair down on her head, allowing the door to move enough so he can scrape himself in.

"Is there a bed under there?" he asks, bending at the waist to try to see through things to what might be supporting it all.

"Yep," she says with dismay, looking towards where the window is but can't really be seen. It's dark out there and she suddenly feels bone-tired.

His sigh is reminiscent of the one he gave her when deciding to let her in. "You can sleep in the guest bedroom."

She gapes at him.

"You think I'm the kind of guy who shoves a person out into a snowstorm? Nice." He rubs an eye, weary. "See this light beard? It says I'm kind and decent." Jamie looks at her, deadpan, then gives a single slow bat of his eyelashes. She doesn't know if he is taking the piss.

"I could google 'serial killers with beards' and have a list in five seconds." She holds his gaze, her attention snared by those lashes. Long, soot-black and deeply unfair. And the eyes they frame? Steely blue. With his dark brown hair, the contrast is striking.

He isn't budging. "Look at these walls. Completely impractical for blood spatter. No serial killer would rent a house with so many white walls. The Scandi aesthetic is completely wrong for that. So, not guilty." He looks away from her now. "Use the guest room while you get sorted."

Anna is speechless, because the simplicity of his offer is close to making her weepy. Gahd, it's been an exhausting day.

It seems now he's decided she can stay, he's willing to talk more, but she wouldn't class it as relaxed. "Remind me what it is you're hoping to do in here?" he asks. He can obviously see she's having a little wobble and is polite enough not to make a deal of it – or simply doesn't want her full-on sobbing again.

She points vaguely at the far corner.

"There's some warmer clothes in there, or just, you know, dry clothes."

"Good luck with that," he murmurs.

Anna looks about, slightly overwhelmed by the task. She hadn't remembered it like this at all. In her memory, she'd been far more systematic and smart with her packing. Just being back among her things is making her emotional, too.

"Look, move some of the boxes into the hall," he says, seeing her at a loss. "That'll be the start you need."

Jamie grabs her mug and heads downstairs, and she finds herself wondering whether he is just stunned by the madness that's been hiding in his home for so long, or whether he's being tactful and allowing her a few minutes to get her head around her former life. Because it might take more than a few minutes, to be honest, both physically and mentally.

Pulling herself together, she stacks the nearest boxes in the hall. And then some more, freeing up more floor space inside the room. By the time he reappears, fanfared by the squeak of the step, and with two more steaming mugs of what turns out to be a winter-blend tea, Anna's calm enough to say, "That took you a bit. Were you having a little cry because it wasn't a sex room in here?"

An hour later she's made excellent headway. Anna has to admit, Jamie's strength has been a boon; he'd quietly moved all the boxes to one wall and the space is no longer a Health and Safety avalanche waiting to happen. There's a clear path to her wardrobes and a thin space to move along them all, but the bed is still piled with things, so it'll definitely be the guest room for her tonight. But best of all, which actually made her whoop, is that she's changed into dry clothes.

"OK, so it doesn't really match," she excuses, as she walks back from the bathroom, "but it is dry, so hurrah!"

Jamie scoffs from his slouched position on the snug's sofa. "The standard black/grey/white/beige palette of a Copenhagener's wardrobe means, to a normal person's eye, everything matches."

Anna thinks about this for all of five seconds. "I don't think that's true. But you're a man, blessed with a world of clothes which miraculously all go together, or you all live in a culture that doesn't really care."

Still, her clothes are warm, she's not going out and so she chooses not to care either about her mismatching. She doesn't mention that her bra and knickers, as well as being wildly mismatched, are from an aged selection with now questionable elastic robustness. But at least they too are dry.

Looking at the wardrobes, she wonders what she'd planned to do with the clothes. Was she intending to come back? No. She'd known that much eighteen months ago. But she hadn't had time to sort or sell it all and in the end it became too much, and in her teary haze and manic flurry, she'd simply slid the doors shut and parked the whole problem. But (hurraaaah again!) her arctic coat is there and her Nordic winter boots, which just goes to show the state she was in when she left, stuffing mainly summer clothes in her case, as that was the current season. Her weather-prepping skills had clearly gone out of the window with the shock.

Jamie has pulled himself up to upright sitting, his focus

on the jigsaw pieces on the coffee table. He's been lightly scanning it, which Anna feels he might have been doing to give her space. Now his hand suddenly swoops on a piece and equally swiftly has it up and clicked into place. Anna drifts towards the table and considers the pieces. He's already long into it, a vista of the colourful quayside at Nyhavn.

"Where's the box lid?" she asks. She can see it's Nyhavn, because it's iconic and she's a native, but she'd still like the cover picture to work from.

Jamie tuts at her. "We don't cheat here. No pictures allowed."

"That makes it double as hard."

"Double the achievement," he says, glancing up at her, through his fringe.

"Crazy," she says, but picks up a piece, the apex of a roof she'd recognise anywhere, and fits it.

"*Tak*," he says in thanks. He obviously doesn't mind sharing. But then he stands, picks up their empty mugs and walks to the stairs.

"Take your time, do more of the puzzle if you like. I'll make us some dinner."

"You don't have to do that," she starts, but he cuts her off.

"Don't get too excited, I haven't got much in. It might be fridge tapas. I'll see what I can forage." His manner is still frosty, but she senses he's lowering his guard now, fractionally, given her story has proven true.

Anna watches as Jamie's head disappears from sight. Uncomfortable as this is, she's been lucky; he could have been out. He could have slammed the door in her face. He could have been creepy. But he wasn't and he didn't, and he absolutely isn't. Frosty, yes, creepy, no. And like the light beard says, he *has* been kind. And she thanks her lucky stars for that.

Feeling she should give him some space in his own home, Anna kicks around upstairs for a little while, then, when she feels she can't hide any longer, joins him in the kitchen, to sit on a barstool overlooking his prepping. He has a glass of Merlot on the go, and he pours her one, too. It's good and she's glad for it.

Assessing the materials he's working with, she hazards a guess. "*Biksemad?*"

"It's leftovers, I know, but I had the potatoes, onions and meat from yesterday, and I can make it stretch for two."

Anna lifts her hand to still him. "I love *biksemad*. Especially with a fried egg on top, if you have one? But to be honest I'm grateful for anything you make me."

He slides an egg box into view. "Runny yolk or nah?"

"Runny. Always," she says, and can tell he's the same.

He picks up his glass, and for a second she thinks he'll clink with her, but, on reflection he simply says "*Skål*," and moves to the hob.

"So, what brings you to Copenhagen, Jamie MacDonald?" she asks, watching him moving around the kitchen preparing to fry the potato hash. He seems to glide about the space, closing cupboard doors gently, pushing drawers in quietly, which is in stark contrast to the way Carl used to slam around. It always felt like a protest, and he was under duress. Anna shakes off the thoughts of Carl, keen to stay in this moment and not tarnish being here with thoughts of her ex.

He pauses before he says, "Work."

"Which is...?" She'd asked him before and he swerved it. Maybe it's something top secret, but probably he doesn't want to let her in any further. His long pause makes her think it's the latter. If it was secret, he'd have a cover story, surely?

"I'm a sustainability consultant and work in a think-tank for city-sustainability initiatives. Denmark and Copenhagen are frontrunners for environmental issues, and it's the perfect place for me to be." Intriguingly, his tone is adamant about that last bit. Like it's a statement. She wasn't about to question it. Weird.

"And you've been here two years?"

"I have. And I love it here. It's got a bit of everything I need." For all his initial frostiness, now he sounds impassioned. Anna is finding him quite mercurial.

Her thoughts go to the photos upstairs of the Highland landscapes.

"Bit low on mountains here," she points out. Denmark is predominantly flat, which has allowed for cycling to become the main mode of transport.

"True, but I come from the Highlands *and Islands*. Personally, it's the water that draws me more than the heights."

Anna nods and drinks. "Where's your office?"

"Here most of the time, unless I'm meeting companies to advise them on initiatives, projects and collaborations, which can be all over the city, or into Sweden on occasion. The bridge makes that easy."

"No office?"

"We have an office in Christianshavn, in an old *pakhus*. I show my face there a few times a week, or if I'm passing. Everything's close here though, isn't it?"

"It is indeed," says Anna, although she wants to say, "sometimes too close."

Jamie serves what will be the best *biksemad* her exhausted body thinks it has ever tasted, although her head will tell her she's disloyal to her *mormor*. He turns on a few more candles around the room before he sits and tops up their glasses. Anna feels like she's a guest a colleague has cajoled him into entertaining. It's polite and gradually more and more open – perhaps due to the wine – but it isn't quite friendly or truly comfortable.

Anna takes the moment to look about the room some more. He has illuminated paper stars hanging in the glass doorways to the garden. She hadn't noticed them earlier. They're both festive and cosy.

"Aren't you supposed to be against frivolous use of energy?"

He takes a swig of his wine and considers the question. "I spend my days trying to come up with helpful sustainability ideas, things we can all manage and can help in the long run, but I don't begrudge people wanting their *hygge*. I don't strive to make people miserable." Good to know, Anna thinks, as he's had his less-than-charming moments with her. "Because then they won't bother. And I'm not looking to dismantle an entire culture. In a land like this, where winter is long, the need for lights and cosiness is vital. So, I don't consider it frivolous.

"If I spun Christmas lights around the entire house and needed a generator to power it all, you should probably have a frank chat with me, but this? No. The candles are rechargeable, as that's better than the wax, and the bulbs in the stars there use the lowest wattage bulbs. And I feed my guests leftovers, so I'm doing my bit." He'd have to wrestle real candles out of Denmark's cold dead hands, so thank goodness he isn't on a crusade for that. Anna, a little stunned from him speaking so many words, raises her glass to him, then sips. They still aren't at a clinking stage.

"And you?" he asks. "Travel specialist, you said."

"I'm freelance, so I have various income streams. I used to work full-time here for a travel e-publisher and devised a series called *Romancity*, looking at cities through a romantic lens. That's franchised now. I still write for their website, though. I'm based in London but spend time in the cities I'm writing about. I go by train when I can," she adds at the end, not wanting to come across as solely responsible for climate change. "To be honest, arriving by train can be a very romantic way to enter a city, but sometimes, I have to confess, the timings require a flight."

Thankfully he doesn't tell her off. She is, after all, encouraging people to do things that make his job harder. She sees the conflict. "Meanwhile," she carries on to divert him, "I write articles for the glossy magazines on specific places, depending on where they want a feature, but my favourite job is coming up with niche tours around European cities: food tours of Lisbon, or Vespa tours of Rome, that kind of thing. I put them together with the local vendors and sell them to travel and cruise companies."

Jamie nods, but doesn't ask more. Instead, he clears the plates.

"Out of interest," he asks from the other side of the kitchen island, "your things upstairs in the room, and I'm guessing in the locked room in the basement…"

Anna holds her hands up. "It's my bike and outdoor things like ice-skates, definitely no bodies, or a sex dungeon." Her face heats when she realises what she's said. She does not need to be bringing sex to the table. Her inhibitions and manners have disappeared with the wine and the tiredness that's creeping up on her.

"I'll be sure to inform my friends," he says. "I was actually going to ask what you had planned to do with them. Are you coming back to Copenhagen?"

"Oh, no," she says immediately. "You don't need to worry about that, Jamie. I'm not about to end your tenancy and turf you out."

"Not what I meant," he says, "but good to know."

"I left in a hurry and hadn't quite thought it through, but I have absolutely no plans to move back here. Ever. Copenhagen and I are finished with each other. Full stop. Done."

She watches his eyebrows rise at her vehemence. Bloody wine. It is definitely getting to her. "I suppose I'll have to come back to sort it at some point, maybe between tenancies if you choose to leave one day, but not for the foreseeable."

There's a prospect she's going to safely leave for Future Anna. The planes will be back up and flying as soon as the snow stops, and her bum will be firmly in a seat out of here.

Jamie watches her quietly, his mouth pressed in a pensive line. She wants to know what he's thinking, but also, she doesn't want to know, because she worries she'll be found lacking. And as worryingly, she's not sure why that would matter to her.

In the quiet and to her horror, a huge yawn ambushes her. The mortification on her face makes the side of his mouth twitch.

"You should go to bed." She's not sure if she is being dismissed, but the idea is welcome.

Thanking him for dinner with the customary, "*Tak for mad*," Anna offers to wash up. It seems only fair, but she's relieved when he refuses. "The bed's made and there's towels in the bathroom," he adds. "Go and sleep."

Anna manages a simple "*God nat*," to which he returns a soft "*Sov godt*."

His wishes for her to sleep well clearly work, as she's out the instant her head hits the pillow.

Chapter Six

"*God morgen*," Jamie says as she walks gingerly into her-but-not kitchen. His pronunciation is good and sounds exactly like the "*G'morn*" she returns.

"Is it still morning?" She's slept like the dead and straight through, which hasn't happened in a long, long while.

He looks at his watch. "Just." He's dressed in jeans and a black Henley, and working at the table. He doesn't hide his papers away, which she takes as an advancement between them.

"Are you going into work today?" she asks. He just points to the window. Anna doesn't really need to look. She understands the different light that comes with snow; part of the Nordic upbringing. Although Anna spent much of her childhood in warmer climes, she learned about snow when visiting her grandparents and loved its arrival every year when she'd come to live with them. Before she left, she was delighted by most aspects of the Danish winter; the crisp cold, the long nights, which encourage being at home and *hygge*, the ice-skating, the snowmen, the sheer prettiness of it all. And from a distance she had thought about it in a nostalgic way or with pride when London came to a halt at a mere dusting. Today, however, Anna has deliberately not looked out of her window, because denial is her friend right now.

"Snow day?" Danes are not put off by snow, so it must be quite extreme out there. Once snow has stopped, pavements need, by law, to be cleared by the homeowners or shopkeepers by eight a.m., allowing the city to keep functioning and safely.

"Should stop this afternoon. They're saying to only venture out if necessary."

"I need to call the airline."

"According to the internet, the airport's closed until they can clear the runways."

Anna wishes he hadn't said it out loud. And she's not sure what it means that he's checked. Is he being kind, or checking how soon she'll leave?

"I'll just give them a quick ring, see what they're saying."

He shrugs, seemingly unbothered by her not taking his word for it, and points at the coffee percolator. She'd almost glided down the stairs to the scent of the brew.

"*Ja, tak.*"

"Sleep?" he asks as she pours herself a cup. Hmm. He seems a little more amenable today. Perhaps he was knackered from travelling.

"Perfectly. Exhaustedly." She's not sure that's a word, but he doesn't pick her up on it.

She'd thought she'd lie awake for hours, churning over the strangeness of being back in her old home, in her old city, next to a room in which a man she doesn't know was sleeping – a man who could be a serial killer, but claims he isn't, and she hasn't told anyone where she is. And yet instead she'd been out like a light, only waking to the squeak of the third step and a whispered "Fuck", which made her smile.

She offers him a refill.

"Other than harassing the airlines, got any plans?" he asks, lifting his mug to accept. She takes a sip of her own before she answers, relishing the taste.

"I could sort through some of the boxes and turf a load of the stuff out, and then I'll try to combine the storage, so perhaps you could have the room back."

His brow contracts.

"What?" she asks.

"Will you increase the rent?"

"What? No."

"I can only afford a place like this because it has a mysterious padlocked room in it," he says, his wariness of her returning. "A three-bed is out of my price range, and I don't really need it, so…"

"I'm not going to up the rent, Jamie. I mean, if you ever leave and I rent to someone else, I might, but I'm not doing that for you. That'd be quite unfair, don't you think?" She'll also be forever grateful that he let her in.

Jamie's expression changes to embarrassment. Not

something she's thought possible. Yesterday he'd come across as mainly bolshy. "Sorry. I didn't mean to imply you were like that. You just don't know with some people, and I don't always get it right."

"What, reading people?"

He studies her for a long beat, then nods. Anna feels Jamie is showing something of himself here, something quite raw in him and she's touched he feels he can.

"Easily done," she says, lightly. "Sometimes you think you have the measure of people, you trust them, give them all of you, and then they stab you in the back instead, ripping out your heart and tearing it into pieces in front of you."

"Oh," says Jamie, eyes widening. "Not quite my experience, but fair enough. It's disconcerting, isn't it?"

"It makes you question everything," she agrees, quietly. She hasn't really spoken about it. She hasn't wanted to tell anyone in London. All they know is she's a travel writer. "You start wondering whether you read it wrong or assumed too much, and how much is too much and how low a bar should you expect? We generally assume relationships – whether friends or lovers – are reciprocal in value, until something happens, and you realise that the balance in your head was wrong. It's a bit soul destroying, to be honest."

Anna stares into her mug, losing herself in the depth of the midnight-black liquid.

"Bad break-up?"

"The worst." She hopes he won't ask more and she gets her wish. Ridiculously, she feels ever so slightly put out, but then he's perfectly within his rights to keep things aloof. And besides, she doesn't want to bring bad juju into the space by spilling her guts about Carl.

"Look, I have some work to do. Why don't you work on the room. Then this afternoon we can go for groceries. It'll be good to get out." The thought of them shopping together sounds bizarre to her, but he probably doesn't want to leave her alone in his home.

"I don't know if I'll be here this afternoon, Jamie," Anna says. "The flight?"

He gives her a tilted look, like, *really?*

She refuses to accept she might not be heading back by this evening, but an eye-flick to the window doesn't bolster her hopes.

However, she knows an olive branch when she sees one. He might be a grump, but he's willing to spend time with her. "I do appreciate the offer, though. If I'm still here, then yes, let's find something to do." She means indoors, because she has no intention of being out and about in the city doing recreational things. No sirree. There's a perfectly good, unfinished jigsaw upstairs and a television. While none of this has been part of her plan, she's going to be staunch with her "no engaging with the city" strategy. She doesn't want to see it or risk seeing people she knows. The chances are too high, even in weather like this.

As the opening to her *Romancity: Copenhagen* guide details, Copenhagen is a small capital city, perfect for a city break, crossable on foot and explorable in a long weekend. But more to the point, there's only just over six-hundred-thousand inhabitants, which makes it nearly impossible not to see people you at least recognise. (And yet possible, as it turns out, for your partner to conduct an affair for a year with your best friend, without you stumbling across them, or on the two occasions that you do, it's totally plausible that they've just bumped into each other, as they claim. That part isn't detailed in the guide, but fact nonetheless.)

Jamie nods and dips his head back to his paperwork.

Anna decides the first thing she'll do is ready her bag in case the airline says to come straight away. That could happen, right? They might want planes locked and loaded for the minute the snow stops, and the runways are cleared. Once the bag is packed, she'll call the airline and check others on the internet, if need be, before trying to make more headway with the room.

The idea of being gone again prompts a thought.

"I forgot to ask last night, how long are you in Denmark for?"

"Worried about the tenancy?" he asks, writing something in a moleskin notebook.

She rolls her eyes at him and his table-turning. "No. I mean it's none of my business, but I think we have a three-year contract, no? I just wondered whether you're here for a longer working period."

"Actually, I'm here for the foreseeable. I like it here; I intend to stay."

She waits and he takes the hint. "My work excites me, Denmark's stance regarding that work lifts me, the working conditions are great. Your taxes are something to stomach, but I see the pay-off. It's nice to go back to Scotland when I have to, but I like coming back here more."

His speech sounds genuine to Anna, but she feels there's something not being said. Well, she's not elaborated on her heartbreak, so it's fair if he doesn't want to tell her. They clearly aren't in a trading-personal-secrets kind of place. It's unlikely they ever will be.

With a nod of understanding Anna stands, picking up her mug to refill and take with her. She's going to need all the reinforcement she can get to face the cull upstairs.

"Send a search party if you hear boxes toppling, or I haven't resurfaced by the time you finish. I'll try to keep the noise down."

"No worries about the noise," he says, but doesn't look up. She's rooted to the spot for a moment, watching him, the glow of the wax advent candle on the table in front of his work casting a golden light across his concentrating face. Finally, she turns on her heel for the stairs.

Sometimes Anna doesn't want honesty. She realises that now. When speaking to the airline, she actually just wants them to say, very convincingly, that it's all in hand, that we have a plan to get you home, Ms Lundholm, don't worry. Instead, they're honest, damn them, and freely admit they have no idea when the airport will be functioning again and that there is, in fact, no plan for Ms Lundholm. And of course, it's Christmas, so everything is already sold out before and after for days and days. Would she like them to put her on a waiting list…?

The long and short of it is she's there for at least another day. She decides she'll ring every four hours to see if anyone's cancelled their tickets and she can move up the waiting list. She considers it being proactive, which must count for something in the universal scheme of luck. She has to be "in it to win it", and if she isn't manifesting her need, then how can the universe know what to send her way? She glances at her bag at the door, primed and ready. She could be on the metro in fifteen minutes, sprinting into the departures hall twenty-two minutes after that. Anna boxes the air to show she's "got" this.

"Is that to frighten me?" Jamie stands leaning against the doorframe, arms folded and watching her.

God, he's good-looking. For so long she's not looked at another man in any kind of appreciative light, and now it's no effort at all.

She whips her hands behind herself, feeling a rush of heat to her face.

"Noooo. You know, just keeping limber. Can't get my step count in, thought I should do something else."

The singular eyebrow that rises on his face is a perfect blend of poise and disbelief.

She busies herself at the nearest box, one for the Red Cross shop nearby.

He lets her off. "The room's looking better."

"I know, right?" It looks like a bedroom again, with actual space around the bed, as opposed to the earlier furniture Jenga. "I've pulled out a suitcase and some more clothes I'll take back with me. The rest I'm packing down into the basement storage room."

He nods.

"Finished your job for today?"

"Aye."

"Solved climate change?"

"Ah, not quite," he says with a slow shake of the head, "but working towards."

Anna wonders what it must be like, working at the coalface of such a monumental task. Especially when a lot of what people classify as having fun, and indeed she encourages in her work, is detrimental to his cause.

"Any luck with the flights?" he asks, changing the subject.

"No," she says sullenly. "It's all fucked out there. And in the UK. Snow everywhere. They don't know when I'll be able to fly out, and my ticket won't leapfrog anyone who has the ticket the day they reopen. I'm sorry to have to ask but—"

Jamie instantly holds up a hand. "Just assume it's fine. It's your house. Consider us housemates."

She finds him very confusing. He seems determined to remain aloof, but also seems happy enough for her to stay. Well, maybe not *happy*, but accepting.

"Time to go out," he states, cutting through the awkwardness.

She spins towards the window, now reachable and fully functioning again. Big flakes float down past the pane, though not blustering like before. He wants to go out?

"Why?!"

A sound comes out of his head, and it takes her a moment to recognise that it's a bark of laughter. It's the first proper sign of amusement he's shown in her presence. He's laughing at her panic. It's her turn to scowl at him.

"Aren't Danes supposed to love the *Friluftsliv*?" he asks, resetting his face.

"That's the Norwegians. Masochists. Danes are more sensible. Outdoor living is only fun when it's dry. Even better when it's warm, but we can always wear outer layers. I don't think we're DNA-bound to love the rain and being wet. That might be you Celts."

"Get a grip, Anna. We need food, and I have umbrellas, so let's go."

She wants to ask whether he can't go by himself, but it feels rude.

Supermarkets appear to bring out the happy in Jamie. He peruses the shelves with interest, as opposed to her method of storming through. "Remoulade?" he asks, holding up the yellow squeezy bottle across the aisle in Netto. "Initially, I had no idea what this was. I was challenging myself to eat something new every week to expand my Danish repertoire, and this was one of the weirder ones, but it rocks." Anna has a dealer for this in London. She won't eat fish and chips without the garish yellow pickle-based condiment, which she finds superior to tartare sauce, and which is a household staple in Denmark. He holds up a glass jar of pickled herring. "These on the other hand, are a big no, especially the curry sauce one."

That makes her laugh. "If you didn't like one kind, why

did you try more?" To be fair, she's with him on the herring thing, but her *morfar* was a firm believer.

"Because you never know. I might have liked one and not the other, so I didn't want to sign off the entire genre without trying."

"You've tried *all* the herring?" she asks, astounded, pointing to the row of different types, such as dill, mustard and the current Christmas marinaded variant. They each have a trolley, his with sensible things, hers with mainly snacks, sweets and cinnamon *gifflar*.

"Aye. Now I definitely know." Clearly a loon.

"This thoroughness, with things you don't like, is that normal for you?" She doesn't know whether what she's experienced is Normal Jamie. It's been a bit of a rollercoaster, so far; frosty and guarded, then more open and chatty, then not, and repeat.

He stops and thinks about it. Anna watches him, under the guise of waiting for a response.

Then he simply shrugs and says, "I don't know," before walking off into the next aisle, obviously on a mission, leaving Anna watching him some more.

A laugh from a little way off catches her attention and it's like a cold bucket of water has been thrown onto her. She ducks her head down into the trolley as if checking the goods. She would know that laugh anywhere. So many evenings out, and evenings *in* for that matter, laughing together as if they were sisters, not just the best friends they used to be.

Anna feels her head become hot and her heart's

beginning to race, too, but not in a good way. Alarm bells are ringing in her head.

Here it is. Exactly the reason she hadn't wanted to come out. Still trying to hide amid the snacks in her trolley, she also pulls the hood back up over her head. Yes, she looks like a mad woman, but she has to get out of here ASAP, and unseen.

Turning away from the laughing woman, dreading she'll be spotted, and more so that the woman isn't alone, Anna sprints for the cashier, pausing only to pull a packet out of a freezer cupboard. There's a queue, but Anna keeps her head down, loading the food onto the conveyor belt, and then bagging it all at the other end, making no eye contact with the spotty, teen cashier. Jamie will just have to work out she's left. It's either that or she had to abandon the trolley in the aisle, but she really wants to contribute to their food supply. Not that any of her things would particularly count as nutrition. But it's been over eighteen months since she was faced with these treats, so sue her.

Bill paid, she's out of the door into the snow and gone, not stopping until she's back at the house, in the front door – a panicked struggle with her key – shrugging off her coat in a heap and leaning her forehead against the warm wall of the hall. This! This was why she didn't want to come back. It's played out precisely as she's expected and dreaded, and it shows she's been right all along to stay away.

Chapter Seven

When the door opens and closes Anna already has the kettle boiled, tea leaves in the strainer and the oven heating for the *æbleskiver*. Small round pancake dumplings, they're some of her favourite things about Christmas. Perfect treats for a winter afternoon. She also has every candle in the living room switched on and music playing low, for maximum *hygge*.

She waits in the kitchen, opening the raspberry jam and some icing sugar to dip the *æbleskiver* into. She hopes it'll serve as an apology but knows there'll be some explaining to do.

Jamie takes his time in the hall, which is little wonder with the number of layers everyone has on. Eventually he appears in the doorway, that stony expression back on his face as he gazes at her. Anna, in response, simply puts both hands on the top of the kitchen counter and gazes back.

He tilts his head at her, asking.

She's not sure how to begin, not really wanting to at all.

Had the tables been turned she would find his behaviour bizarre. He must, too.

"You vanished," he says. The contrast to Supermarket Jamie is stark. His defences are back up, she can feel it.

"I did. I'm sorry."

He looks at the countertop and the shopping, which she's been sorting while waiting for the oven to heat.

"I bought everything in my basket," she feels the need to say.

"Good job. That would have been one hell of a shoplift."

He's making light of it, but it's clear he's annoyed. He's keeping a distance, too, like he can't work out where he stands, but he could equally be thinking she's deranged.

"I looked about for ages and then it dawned on me you'd gone." She's made him look silly and that makes her feel awful. "I asked the cashier, who said you'd paid and left. And I couldn't work out why you'd do that, not let me know."

The steeliness in his eyes has returned and she cannot bear it. It's like they're back to square one. No. Worse. He's been letting his guard down little by little and now he thinks he's misread her.

"Sit down," she says, pointing to the bar stool. "I'll explain." Then she adds, "Please." She's got better at saying *please* while living in London, the word not existing in Danish.

He does as he's asked, but she can see he's uneasy.

"I'm making some *æbleskiver*."

He briefly flicks his eyes at the jam and the icing sugar on the two small plates, and the dumplings sitting ready to heat on a baking tray. He nods but waits for her to get to the point.

"It's a small city. I saw someone I didn't want to see. I panicked. I should have come to find you, to tell you I had to leave, but I just had to get away. I figured I'd call you when I got out onto the street, but I don't actually have your number. I couldn't go back in after that. So, I could only come home and wait. I am sorry, Jamie. It was rude and wrong." The kettle boils and she pours the hot water onto the tea leaves, before popping the *æbleskiver* into the heat of the oven, with the remaining hot water into a tray beneath for steam.

"They stay fluffier that way," she explains, just trying to fill the silence, but Jamie doesn't look like he currently gives a shit about dumpling fluffiness.

He evaluates her explanation.

"Why didn't you want to see them?"

It's a fair question, though not one she wants to answer, but she feels she owes him something.

"They're part of the reason I moved away. I didn't want to drag up those memories. I don't want to now." She tries to be as polite about it as she can, aware that Danes sometimes come across as brusque or rude, but she also wants to be clear about not talking about it.

Jamie's lips purse in thought and the look makes her hope he can get past this.

Eventually, he reaches out and pushes her telephone across to her over the countertop. "Open your contacts," he says.

Done, she looks at him, waiting.

He dictates his number, which she dutifully adds.

"Next time, please call and I won't be standing talking to myself in the fruit aisle."

"I'm sorry, really."

He mulls her apology then gives her a nod.

"Just a thought, Anna; you might find facing things rather than running from them more cathartic."

"I'm not looking for catharsis," she says, but it comes out slightly snappy. He doesn't know the score, so she doesn't appreciate his opining on it.

"Beneficial, then?"

"Nope. Really." She turns and busies herself cleaning the dusting of icing sugar that's settled on the opposite counter.

Jamie doesn't say anything, and she feels not that he's judging her, but trying to get a read on her. She doesn't mind that so much. Something makes her want him to get it right, another something fears him doing so. Either way, it intrigues her.

The oven beeps and she removes the baking tray, to fill a bowl with the hot pancakey dumplingy goodness.

He picks up the mugs and both plates and heads towards the stairs.

"There's a jigsaw that needs progressing," he says, and jerks his head for her to follow. She takes it her olive branch has been accepted. But if she follows, then she doesn't know where the conversation will go, and that's uncomfortable. On the other hand, she doesn't want to walk away from him. At the very least she's still mid-apology with the *æbleskiver*; she can't just grab her plate and bugger off to her room, although part of her is tempted. More to the point, doing so will give him more ammo in his pseudo-psychology that she runs from things. So.

Anna picks up the bowl and teapot and follows.

Jamie dips one of the dumplings first into the jam and then into the icing sugar before taking a bite. They sit at either end of the sofa, his faux candles lit in the windowsill and on the shelves opposite them, the tartan throw over her lap, Snow Patrol playing low on the speaker pod. She watches him as he chews, getting the flavours; first of the sugar and raspberry jam, but then the subtler flavours of the pancake batter with the added hint of cardamom and lemon zest. It's a flavour she hasn't realised how much she's missed. A true flavour of her childhood, when Mormor made them for her and Morfar, turning the half-cooked batter in the funny seven-holed frying pan. After Mormor died, they'd bought them ready-made from the shop to remind them of her, and because neither of them could turn the dumplings properly in the pan. Giving up after a couple of attempts, they'd decided shop-bought would do. The taste brings Anna right back to the memories.

"Delicious," she hears him murmur. He shoves another one in his mouth. Shoving is perfectly acceptable etiquette when it comes to *æbleskiver*.

"Perfect for a winter day, right? Hot and sweet. Nom." She shoves one in her own mouth, savouring it, then licks the remaining icing sugar off her fingertips.

When she looks up, he's watching her. His Adam's apple bobs as he swallows.

"Have I got icing sugar on my face?" she asks, self-conscious, and paws at her cheek.

His nose twitches for a second, then he says, "Mmm-hmm, but you got it." He sits up straight then to look at the coffee table. "Right. It's not often I have a jigsaw partner, so here are the rules. One: no looking at the picture, which you already know. Two: first person to correctly place five pieces, wins."

"Competitive jigsawing?"

"Aye," he says, and she realises he's already scanning the pieces. Cheat!

Anna is, and always has been, competitive and shifts forward to get in the game. "What's the prize?"

"Glory and bragging rights." He doesn't look at her, but she's dismayed to see him pick up a piece and click it into place.

"Lame," she states. Bragging rights between two people is pointless.

Jamie pauses and does now look at her. She deliberately shifts her eyes to the pieces, wishing she can find something quick. The manifesting must work, as she finds the next part of a boat's mast.

"That's fighting talk. OK, increased stakes. Winner chooses dinner and decides what we do this evening."

"Can't be outside," she negotiates, manically looking for another piece.

"No restrictions, Lundholm. You either want stakes or

you don't." Damn him. "Come on, ya feartie. It'll be properly dark soon, anyway."

Her eyes flick to the window. It's true, the light has faded, the candles giving off more of a glow. Then Anna finds the next two pieces of the mast. Only two bits to go. Confidence surges through her and so she finds herself actually agreeing.

The words are just out of her mouth when Jamie places a piece onto the mast – her mast! Rude! – and then a piece of half a porthole, swiftly followed by a second to complete it. Within fifteen seconds she's gone from winning to losing. He only needs one and she needs two.

There follows a period of deeply invested concentration, their silence loud with the determination to find the next piece.

"Yes!" she shouts and fixes a piece of a green-painted house. They're level. The *æbleskiver* have been forgotten. And then she sees it: a white, low triangle of a quayside restaurant sunbrella, which she snatches up with a whoop, wishing now that she'd kept the bragging rights, too, as she's going to win. She presses it next to a similar triangle. Only it doesn't click into place. She tries again, but still, it won't.

"Oh dear, Anna," Jamie says, "what a shame," as he slowly and decisively moves her hand aside to deftly click a very similar and correct piece into the space. He lets out a very satisfied and over-exaggerated groan of pleasure, while Anna's gaze is stuck on her hand where he'd touched it, and the feel of his skin that remains. Apparently oblivious to this, Jamie neatly dips another *æbleskive* and pops it smugly in his mouth. "Bad luck."

She wants to tell him speaking with his mouth full is very ill-mannered, but she's still swayed by how close she was, and how she now might have to go outside. Dejected, she self-soothes by horsing another four dumplings on the trot. It's very hard to be a gracious loser right now, but she eventually manages a mumbled, "Well done."

She holds the bowl out to him to snag the last one, which he does. She regrets her generosity. She'd hoped he'd decline. But then he pulls the *æbleskive* apart and gives her half.

"So," he says, sitting back again, "tell me where you've travelled to." Jamie is opening the conversation, Anna notes. This is new. And this she is happy to talk about.

"It's a bit of a list. By the time I was sixteen I'd lived in ten different countries, often more than once though never in the same place, mainly within Europe except for a stint in Thailand. You can imagine how consistent my schooling was. Then I came back here to live with my grandparents with a view to getting the education under control. After uni I took an extra journalism qualification in Aarhus and became a travel writer. The subsequent list is a lot longer." She's relaxed into the sofa now, belly full of pancake and jam. Bliss. "I had said I curate tours too, hadn't I?" she asks, not sure.

"Twice already. And I checked."

"What?"

"I googled you," he says, unabashed.

Her eyebrows shoot up.

"Oh, come on," he says, "I might take in bedraggled strangers, but I check their details on my phone before I invite them to stay. I watch crime shows. I'm not a complete idiot."

"There I was, worrying you were a serial killer, and you *mocked* me." What really narks Anna is she hadn't thought to google him *at all* before accepting. What a muppet. One handsome face and all her survival instincts go out of the window.

"And being a travel specialist told you I was a safe and good human?" she asks, wanting his efforts to be as flimsy as hers.

"No, I was just starting a trail for the police to follow if I go missing." The possibility in the "go" is not lost on Anna. Good. Seems she still has an ounce of agency left in this.

"So where have you travelled to, Jamie?"

This starts a game of Travel Snap, as he reels off places he's visited and she matches them, both chipping in what they'd loved and hated.

"And you said you travel on business?" she asks.

"A little. Conferences, etc. It's mainly Copenhagen-based, though."

What Anna particularly loves when travelling, is the flux of people; the coming and the going. Stations where people get on trains as you alight, or airports with planes landing as you take off. And she loves being part of that moving energy. And, presumably Jamie has too, in his extensive travelling, yet here he is, having … well, stopped.

"But one day, you'll be back out there, right?" She wants him to be having the joy of travel, the thing that had them both buzzing moments ago as they swapped stories and shared memories of the places they'd been.

His face seems to cloud, and then he stands and picks up their plates and mugs.

"I've got no plans to leave. It's my home now. Or at least I'm working on it."

Again, there's something in the way he says it that reinforces her thought that there's more to this. Something central to his being here, when, given his history, she can see he's a traveller at heart. Like her.

Whatever it is, it's not something he intends to share with her.

"Right," he says, descending the stairs. "Dinner's out. Winner's prerogative. The shopping can wait 'til tomorrow. Get your coat on, Anna."

Her jaw drops. Serial killer or not. The man is cruel.

Chapter Eight

"What are you doing?" Jamie's stopped walking to turn and look at her.

Anna peeps out from the doorway she's hidden in, one of many she's scurried between to stay out of view.

"Sheltering."

Jamie looks up towards the glow of the streetlight. "It's hardly snowing at all. Mere flakes."

"It accumulates."

He tilts his head at her. "Don't be ridiculous." Then he walks back towards her. "Come out. It's dark, you have your hat on, your hood up and no one is looking for you."

Her face tells him she disagrees.

"It's not far now."

"Where are we going, anyway?" It comes out whiny. She's not proud of it.

"No clues."

"Oh, come on." She knows they're heading down Gothersgade, plodding through the path previous feet have made through the snow, but that could still take them to any number of places. Worry and curiosity aside, Anna is enjoying being wrapped up in her big coat and her feet are toasty in her winter boots. It's a world apart from the state she was in yesterday. And today she's more willing to look around her, taking in all the apartments above the shops and offices, each of them with candles burning next to poinsettias in the windows and with white fairy lights strung on balcony ironwork.

Jamie relents. "Fine. What day is it?"

"Sunday."

"Date?"

"December thirteenth."

"Which is…?"

Ah. "*Sankt Lucia*?" St Lucy's Day, bringer of lights.

"Points to the lady in the hat."

"Everyone is wearing hats," she points out. Jamie is wearing a navy beanie of his own.

"Not *that* hat, though."

"True."

"OK. Points to the lady in the red hat with the white bobble."

"Are you taking me to church?" There will be processions in churches all over the land, with a young woman, dressed in a white gown, a fir wreath crown on her head with four lit candles. She and a troupe of children, also dressed in white, will process up the aisle, holding candles and singing. A true Scandinavian custom, Anna has always found it very moving in the dark of winter. She's taken part in plenty, too.

"Nope," he says. In spite of his passive face, Anna is sure he is enjoying this, the keeping her in the dark.

Piqued, she takes better stock of where they are. "You know, Tivoli is up that way, right?" And quite a way off, she thinks in her head. The iconic pleasure garden has its own annual procession, all amid the thousands of lights that fill the park every Christmas.

He gives her an indignant look. "I might not be a local, but I know where Tivoli is. Not a complete noob."

Reaching the end of Gothersgade, they cross to skirt the edge of Krinsen, the ice-skating loop at Kongens Nytorv square.

"Are we skating?"

"Nope." They keep walking, past the many skaters, and the small stalls at its edge. Children laugh on the ice or in the snow, dressed in their brightly coloured one-piece snowsuits, balaclavas and mittens. This is what Anna loves about snow; the instinctive delight it can bring.

Then the realisation hits her. "Why are we going to Nyhavn?" It's fine to see it on his jigsaw picture, but she has no desire to be there.

"I have a friend who has access to somewhere special." She huffs, not entertained by his mysteriousness. "Relax," Jamie says. "You'll like it." Quite how he thinks he can make this statement, Anna has no idea, because he barely knows her.

Nyhavn, the colourfully painted old harbour, has always been one of her favourite places in the city. She has, on occasion, been known to sit at a table of one of the quayside restaurants for an entire afternoon, just because she loves the vibrancy and the history and the colours of the old buildings. But all that has been tarnished for her, now she knows Carl and Maiken would meet here. Hardly discreet and hardly worrying about being seen. Anna has, since the discovery of the affair and her dissection of all the signs she missed, felt certain locations in the city were, if not complicit in the subterfuge and betrayal, at least involved, and so she's fastidiously stayed away.

"Have you been to the Tivoli procession?" she asks, her heart rate increasing as they get closer to the harbour.

"Aye. Last year." His broad frame, just behind her, though not touching her, herds her along. She can't turn and bolt home. She'd be met by his chest and she'd have no chance of getting through him.

"You don't want to go again?" she tries.

"Not today," he says. He is completely unbothered by her clearly being bothered. Infuriating man. She huffs again, frustrated.

"Need I remind you, Anna, that I won the rights to decide this evening. A wager you willingly entered into, of your own volition, quite keenly in fact, and so there really shouldn't be any objection or push-back, from you, The Loser." She resists the urge to stamp on his toes with her toasty boots.

They reach the bulwark end of the harbour basin, where the tour boats start and finish. She always advises visitors to Copenhagen to start with a canal tour, to get a feel of the city before they start their foot tours. The entire area is teeming with people, well wrapped up, hands clasped around cups of steaming *gløgg* from the nearby stalls.

The air is heady with the spiced scent of the mulled wine. It's pure Christmas.

"This way," Jamie says, steering them not to the restaurant side to the left, but down the right-hand side, which leads to the cycle bridge.

"Are we heading to Reffen or Christianshavn?" she asks. Both the street food and entertainment island, and the old part of the city lie across the main harbour.

"Nope," he says and then, "We're. Here… Now." He guides them through a cluster of people standing along the pavement and onto the gangplank of an old, moored boat. The wheelhouse roof carries both a thick snow layer and a festive weave of party lights, to charming effect. Anna feels her braced shoulders sink; she has no chance of resisting Nyhavn's loveliness in the face of this.

There are numerous people milling around on the deck already and a man appears from inside, having spotted them. "James! *Velkommen til.*"

They shake 'n' hug in that way men do, and Anna stands behind. The man looks to her. "And this is your guest."

"Anna, Mikkel. Mikkel, Anna," Jamie introduces.

Mikkel bids her welcome and tells them there's a vat of *gløgg* further around the deck and they should help themselves to any of the *småkager* they'd like. Anna has never needed asking twice when it comes to cookies, Christmas or otherwise, and she leads them around the light-spun wheelhouse to the other side of the boat.

A roar from the crowd across on the other quayside draws them to the rail. They're just in time to look down towards the mouth of the basin, where there on the water, a flotilla of lights has rounded the corner and is coming towards them. Hundreds of kayaks, all adorned with fairy lights, are floating up the quay through the dark, the kayakers wearing head torches, Santa hats and even more strings of fairy lights around their bodies, all reflecting in the ripples of the inky water. It is *utterly* magical.

"Oh…" she sighs.

"Exactly," Jamie concurs.

"I've written about it, but never actually been to one. It's quite a new tradition. The one year we did try, we screwed up the timing and the crowd along the Christianshavn canal was so huge, we couldn't see a thing." *We.* Carl had been late home for some reason, and they'd simply arrived too late. That and, unlike some, they didn't have a friend who had access to a boat in Nyhavn.

The flotilla glides to a halt, clustering together in a fairy-lit mass. From somewhere, a voice starts to sing, soon joined first by the other kayakers, and then from all three sides of the quay. Anna knows the carol by heart, so joining in is instinctive. The lights, the water, the unity of voice move her in a way she hasn't experienced since she left. Mikkel appears, singing in a rich baritone, with cups of *gløgg* for them both, hot and secretly hiding the rum-and-port-steeped raisins and almonds at the bottom. There's a spoon handily placed in the cup to scoop them out, and Anna knows these are the bits that really get people drunk. Spirits by stealth. Jamie has tucked in already, but he doesn't know the words to the carol, so fair enough. Mikkel has also left them a small paper bowl of cookies, and Anna snaffles herself a *brunkage*, a brittle brown disc with gingerbread-like flavours, a couple of *pebernødder*, small, sweet biscuit nuggets, and a *vaniljekrans*, a vanilla-spiced wreath, which she sticks her finger through and eats like that – just as she did as a kid.

As the song comes to an end, a huge cheer goes up, and the kayakers slowly negotiate their way to turn and extract themselves from the floating cluster, before heading back out of the harbour.

"Danes do like their singing," Jamie notes.

"It's integral to the national culture, I think. *Fællessang*. Not sure what you would call it – community singing, maybe? 'United singing'. I honestly believe singing's good for the soul, and coming together with others, strangers even, to sing together … well, I think it's a cornerstone of our society and community. Danish society," she corrects herself. It's not her society anymore.

"I've been to a wedding here," Jamie says. "The guests wrote songs for the wedding couple. Known melodies, personalised funny lyrics. Everyone really got into it."

"Oh, yes, and not just weddings. Literally *any* party. And during Covid there was daily *Fællessang* on the television throughout the lockdowns. It helped people feel less isolated. It's a big thing. And tonight, it was beautiful."

"Totally," agrees Jamie. "Who's glad they came out, now?"

"Shut it, MacDonald. Smugness is not pretty."

"Where do they kayak to next, do you know?"

"Kayak Bar," Anna replies, thinking of the canal-side bar near the parliament building, where she has spent many summer evenings drinking by the water. "I believe they normally serve cups of bouillabaisse and bread rolls tonight."

"Fancy that for dinner?" asks Jamie.

Her smile tells him she does.

The night is clear, the stars pricking the ink-black sky, so they take a circuitous route, walking over the cycle bridge then through Christianshavn, passing the houseboats which are gloriously decorated for Christmas. Then they cross back over the harbour via Knippelsbro almost as far as Børsen, the stock-exchange, but dropping down steps just before, to the bar which perches against the water. They talk as they walk, Jamie explaining how he knows Mikkel from work, whose grandfather owns the boat. He tells her about the wedding he'd been to, plus a few others, and Anna is impressed.

"You don't seem to have any problem making friends," she says.

"What do you mean?" he asks. "I'm a friendly guy."

Anna snorts.

"What?" he demands, offended.

Anna rights her face. Should she poke this wasp nest? She's leaving soon, she reasons, egged on by the *gløgg*. Why not?

"Mikkel seems to like you, so OK. But my first experience of you wasn't overly friendly."

"I let you in," he states.

"Before that," she clarifies.

Jamie's lips chew this over as they walk, his hands stuffed squarely in his pockets.

"Yesterday was … challenging," he finally says. "The *entire* trip had been challenging. You caught the tail end of it. Last straws and that."

"Difficult business meeting?"

He sighs. "Difficult parent. Five days of nonstop badgering to move back to Skye. Yesterday I just wanted to get home, to some peace."

Well, Anna sees now that context has its place. "And being assaulted by a hot dog didn't help?"

"Not so much."

"If you'd hung around for the rest of my apology I would have offered to pay for some dry cleaning."

Jamie's eyebrow raises. "I don't remember you offering during your other stalker moments."

"Again, *not* stalking, just going the same way," she says firmly, "and you'd been rude to me by then, so I'd retracted my offer. In my head."

He rolls his eyes at her. Which makes her laugh. His is not a rolly-eyes face.

"I *am* friendly," he says, grumpily.

"Let's say that, then," she says, deliberately making it sound like she's placating him. Mean, but he'd called her a stalker, so fair is fair. "But Danes are a reserved people, and not always quick to let new people into their social circles," she says, returning to the subject. "I don't think it's meant to be rude, it might be more a wariness, but that's what I've heard from many non-Danes who come to live here. That said, once you're in, you're in – and you seem to have fast-tracked the selection process." Anna thinks of her first sixteen years, constantly moving, just managing to make friends before her mother uprooted her again. She stopped bothering by her early teens, and while she might have played the education card in her case to stay with her grandparents, wanting friends was a large part of her motivation.

"I reckon you get what you put in. I'm normally friendly."

"Even though you say you don't always read people correctly?" She wants to know more.

He wrinkles his nose. "Sometimes I get it wrong. But I don't want that to change me too much. I don't want to be that person who assumes the worst of people up front. If that means I get disappointed sometimes, so be it."

He managed to think the worst of *her* up front, she thinks, but bites her tongue. Bad day and all that. Instead, "Hmm" is all she says as she considers his point. If she's honest, that's how she's come at most new people she's met in the last year and a half. That might explain why there's no one she needs to phone in London to let them know she's delayed. Now she thinks of it, if anything happened to her – staying with a serial killer, for example – there wouldn't be many people who would come and check on her. Maybe her mother, when Ida eventually noticed the radio silence…

"You OK?"

"Fine," she says with a forced smile and briskness. "Super."

He doesn't look fully convinced, but they've reached the soup station and ordering two bowls of hot fish soup with what looks like freshly baked bread rolls, is a welcome treat and subject-changer.

"It's still my winner's evening," Jamie states. The soup vanished in minutes, but then there were a few more cups of *gløgg* consumed and Anna thinks he might be buzzed. The bar serves them stronger than the street vendors. She's certainly feeling the effects herself, in that pleasantly tipsy way. The happy mood in the bar is infectious. The kayakers have made it back, to another rendition of the carol, plus further traditional songs once back on the solid ground of the bar deck. Anna and Jamie have managed to get a table and, as well as their being warm in their bulky outwear, are wrapped in the blankets all the bars have to loan. There are candles on every table, and strings of pastel-coloured lights the full length of the quayside bar, all of which is reflected in the harbour water, creating a nocturnal glow around them all.

Anna checks her watch to see if it's gone midnight, but not even close. It's only half eight. The darkness feels much darker here, thicker even, than back in London. Her concept of time is skewed. Or maybe that's the *gløgg*.

"What now?" she asks, hoping he'll say "Home." She's been lucky so far. She's seen only a single person she recognised, an old colleague, but they were on the other side of the canal and didn't see her. Probably because she pulled her hood back over her head.

"Last stop for the night," he says. "Tivoli." She should say no, that she's fulfilled her part of the bet and been out – or *exposed*, as she sees it – enough already, and more would be pushing her luck. And yet. The *gløgg* has done a good job; the mood in the city is bouncing and Tivoli's Christmas lights have always been something special. Thousands of lights in all the trees around the park in addition to all the Christmas trees they add for the season. Christmas market stalls and the scent of hot, cinnamon-coated almonds. And the screams and laughter from the rides – all this adds to the ambience and right now, the temptation.

"No rides," she finds herself saying.

"Not even the Starflyer?" Just the thought of being spun in a swing round and round eighty metres above the city makes her stomach twist. "The view of all the Christmas lights across the city will be amazing from up there."

"Not tonight, Jamie. Too much soup and *gløgg*. I know my limits." She doesn't mind a ride, but not on a bellyful of fish soup. Barfing on tourists doesn't feel very festive or welcoming, for that matter.

"Just the walk, then," he concedes.

"Just the walk," she says, and follows.

Chapter Nine

As Kayak Bar has provided the dinner, Tivoli apparently stands for dessert. Having grabbed another *gløgg* at the Christmas market at Thorvaldsens Plads, they've walked on to the famous pleasure garden. Once they've passed under the sparkling entry arch and into the park, they both suddenly crave all things sweet. And more *gløgg*. Anna's logic is simple; she's leaving, she won't be back in the foreseeable future, so she needs to taste every single thing for memory's sake. Jamie seems to be along for the ride and happy to try new things. They scoff caramelised almonds and hot chestnuts, more *æbleskiver* (they share a plate; they aren't complete gluttons, they tell themselves) and some *jødekager* cookies. She also introduces him to *klejner*, deep-fried dough cookies, which are an instant hit.

Lulled by the alcohol, Anna dares to lower her hood. The hat is donned instead because being surrounded by thousands of lights doesn't make it less December; there's still snow on the ground and it's dog-cold, as the Danes would say. It's the dry, crisp cold, not the damp kind that seeps into your bones, but cold nonetheless, and so the hat is pulled firmly down over her ears.

"Tell me about the hat. I mean I like it, it's ridiculously cute," now-definitely-tipsy Jamie says, flicking the pompom with his finger, "but it's not the normal Copenhagen wear." The *gløgg* has lowered his guard and oiled his jaw.

"What do you mean?"

"Copenhageners are far more subtle in their colourings."

"Do you mean stylish?"

"Like I said earlier, there seems to be a basic colour palette with little deviation after puberty. This hat does not follow that palette, although I do appreciate it's the colours of the Danish flag, which, knowing how passionate Danes are about their flag, might be the answer in itself."

"You think I wear this to show everyone I love the flag?"

"Maybe?" He offers her a *klejne* from his bag as a peace offering, not sure whether he's insulted her.

"I've had this hat since I was one," she says.

"Toddler Anna clearly had an enormous head."

She bumps him with her hip and an "Oi." Yes, so Anna is squiffy, too, otherwise she would never have instigated actual physical contact.

"My *mormor* knitted the original for my first winter. I loved it and wore it all the time, even in summer and sometimes when I slept. It was mine, and consistent, I suppose. I can tell you it looked far odder when we lived in Malta. As I grew out of one, she would knit me another. At first my mother just subbed them, and I didn't really understand it wasn't the same one, and no doubt I would have thrown a hooley had I realised, but later I did, and I appreciated it. It was something from her, and something she knew I valued. This was the last one she made me. She knew she was dying, and she wanted to make sure I had a fresh one."

Jamie looks somewhat chastened. "I wasn't taking the piss out of the hat."

"I know. I get that it might sound a bit strange, but if you grow up without much consistency, and find it hard to create your identity because you have few foundations to build it on, you hang onto the small things, *your* things. Do you see?"

"I do."

They walk past a willow which seems to have every single bough strung with lights. It's exquisite. And how unlucky that they happen to pass yet another *gløgg* stall. Jamie suggests another cup each, "to stave off the cold", although their rosy cheeks are more from the drink, as opposed to the low temperature. Anna doesn't say no. As much as she doesn't want to be in Denmark, or in Copenhagen, she is very much enjoying being back in Tivoli. It feels like a light-spun dream world. Or, again, maybe that's the alcohol.

"OK, then," she says, "One for the road."

It's getting late now, and tomorrow she intends to call the airline early. The snow has stopped and she assumes the twenty-six snow ploughs are caning it up and down the runways.

Jamie has a steaming cup in front of her face in less than a minute. She appreciates the skill.

"So, Jamie," she asks. "Why no girlfriend? You said there isn't a wife, and I can't see any sign of a girlfriend. I'm not sensing you're gay and I'm usually good at that. Am I right?" The alcohol is definitely in action.

"There was a long-term girlfriend from university, but it fizzled out. I was too focused on my work, apparently. I wanted to get as far as I could, I wanted to give my dad some financial stability."

"But not live near him?"

"I love my dad, but it was just him and me when I was young and it's quite stifling. So, this works better for me. I earn enough now to help him out but also, I think it's better that we can live without giving as much thought to each other as we did. Does that make sense?"

Anna sees this as another version of her childhood and teen years. She likes that they have had similar-ish childhoods; one parent, no siblings.

"My mum saw me more as a mini-me and so encouraged me to be as free a spirit as she is. She had no time for any neediness and actively discouraged me being dependent on her, which frankly is mad for a child."

Jamie can only nod but then adds, "My dad was very happy for me to be dependent on him. He wanted me to take over the farm. Still wants, I mean."

"Mine wasn't happy when I wanted to stay! But then I threw her own beliefs of self-determination and autonomy at her, and she couldn't really argue with that."

"I bet young Anna was quite smug about that win."

Anna laughs. "You have no idea!" She thinks about those first years away from her mother, having somewhere permanent to call home, and how much she savoured the stability of her grandparents.

They naturally follow the pathways up through the park, almost drawn by the scents of Christmas, past more snow-covered stalls, and finally out through the arch, this year a big yellow illuminated star hanging above their heads. As they reach the street, Anna catches a flash of red hair, long and bushy. She feels her stomach drop. It's Maiken, her hair unmistakable, and with her is Carl, taller than the usual Scandi tall. He has his arm wrapped around her shoulders as they walk and specifically, they're walking towards Anna. She KNEW she was pushing her luck! Of course she was. The absolute last thing she wants on this earth is for them to see her. She doesn't want them to know she's in town. She certainly doesn't want to talk to them or have any interaction, for that matter. She looks around to see where she can hide, or maybe a tourist group she can infiltrate and camouflage herself with. Her dignity is not a commodity she's precious about right now. A quick look tells her they're closing in on her very fast, and she turns to Jamie to yelp "help me", but instead an idea grasps her boozy brain, and she runs with it.

Anna reaches her hands to the sides of his face, clasping his jaw and then, raising up on her toes, places her lips firmly on his, hiding her face in his.

Oh. My. God.

It takes her an extra second to recognise the reality of what she's done, of what she's currently doing, because so far Jamie hasn't pushed her away in shock or disgust or offence. In fact, and she does give this proper consideration, his lips are responding to hers. And that is also an arm wrapping itself around her waist and pulling her into him, making her back curve and a foot raise from the ground. Their breaths are warm and spicy from the mulled wine, their rubbing noses are chilled from the cold, and all of it's a heady mix in their tipsy states. It doesn't take much for one of her hands to slide from his jaw around the back of his neck, as they pull each other tighter, combining themselves in each other's many warm layers to become one faceless statue of kissing.

Someone passing bumps them, bringing Anna back to her more sensible senses, and she draws away, to look at the ground and regulate her breathing. Oh, crap. Things just got a whole load more complicated.

A quick look along the pavement shows her the back of Maiken's head further along, so complications aside, her subterfuge worked. Yay for that, at least. Pressing her lips in on themselves, Anna looks up into Jamie's face. He stands very still and his eyes are as wide as she feels her own to be.

"I ... um ... I..." she starts and steps away, just enough for his hand to slide off her hip to drop to his side.

She needs to sort this, immediately, but the face-to-face thing is too much. Instead, she pulls at his sleeve, towards home, employing the side-by-side talking technique. Eye contact right now would take her right back to that kiss, which she has to admit is still buzzing on her lips.

Neither of them speak until they're a street away, the crowds now thinner. She's been trying to sort out her apology, but it's been loopy in her *gløgg*-head, so she'll have to wing it.

"Jamie," she says, eyes front and centre, hands clasped in front of her. "I'm so sorry about that. The kiss. That was…" What's the word? Rude? Assaulty? Unforgivable? She can't sort out what to call it. She leapt on him, didn't wait for any sign of consent before she closed in on his face and it was wrong. But after he responded – she *knows* he did – it felt good. How do you describe that? She tries again. "I didn't check with you that it was fine, or wanted, and I'm sorry. I don't normally behave like that." She could tell him her motive, the wanting to hide, but she doesn't think that will make it better.

He says nothing, but she knows he's mulling her words. The awkwardness she's feeling is excruciating. If he's worried about misreading women, then she's just given him a shit-ton of mixed messages.

His silence is understandable but makes her go on. "Can we just forget it? Act like it didn't happen? Let's put it down to the *gløgg*. You have to admit there's been plenty of that this evening. And also, the magic of Tivoli?" It wouldn't be the first time she's snogged a boy in Tivoli, far from it, to be honest, but she decides not to add that either. TMI. "I really don't want this to be awkward between us. If I'm here for longer, then I don't want things to be weird in the house and if I am gone again soon then I don't want you to think badly of me. It was just a thing that happened."

Anna crimps her lips shut. All of that came out in one swoop. She stops now to face him. Jamie keeps walking until he realises she's stopped, upon which he walks back a couple of steps to look her in the face.

"It's fine. All good. No worries."

Anna releases an enormous breath she was very conscious of holding. "Really?"

"Really." Then he nods her on towards home.

"Decent kiss though," he says as he turns and moves off.

Just like the kiss itself, it leaves her rather speechless.

Chapter Ten

Anna is awakened by her phone's persistent ringing. And a pounding in her head. The *gløgg* has a lot to answer for. Not least her actions of the night before. Which she lay awake replaying and worrying about for much of the night before finally passing out. Embarrassment can be very exhausting apparently. She hadn't hung about when they got in, making her excuses and beelining for her room, thankfully a floor above him now, rather than on the other side of the wall, having moved her things up.

Having stressed about it most of the night, she's decided she'll take Jamie at his word and relax about The Kiss. He seemed OK about it being a drunken thing.

That kiss though… Anna's fingertips drift to her lips, not for the first time, either, as she recalls the way he nipped at them, and parted them and—

The phone starts ringing. Again. With a groan, Anna reaches for it and with a single eye looks to see who it is.

Katrine, her commissioning editor and friend. Strange. She normally texts.

"*God morgen*," Anna says, trying to sound bright and as if she's been up for hours working on an article Katrine's expecting.

"Anna? *Er det dig?*" Is it you?

"Of course it's me, Katrine. You rang my phone."

"Noooo, is it *you*? In the news?"

What is she talking about? Both of her eyes are open now. A crack in the curtains tells her it's snowing again. Seriously? More?

"What do you mean?"

"Check BT-online. It looks like you. Are you in town?"

"Hang on," Anna says, deliberately not answering that last part. Katrine will string her up if she's in town and hasn't let her know.

Anna opens the Copenhagen newspaper's app on her phone. She's only kept it on there to cross-check any news she hears about Denmark in the UK press. That's all. She only checks it now and again. Ish.

As she opens the app, and the lead stories come up, Anna takes a second to compute before having a little choke. Oh nonononono.

For once, the paper is leading with a feel-good story. The headline reads "Copenhagen Snowmance". The rest of the screen is filled with a photo. The background is the Tivoli arch, lit up with its tiny lights, and its big, shiny Christmas star hanging under it, right over the heads of a couple. He has his arm wrapped around her waist pulling her in, she has her hand on route from jaw to neck, her foot lifted in the moment. Their faces aren't clear as they are firmly fixed to one another in their kiss.

Anna's eyeballs are popping out of her head and her stomach has slid down to her arse area. This is a nightmare. So much for forgetting it happened, or for staying incognito.

"Anna?" Katrine's voice comes from the phone.

"Errr," is all she can manage in response, but Katrine is happy to do the talking. "I saw it this morning when I woke up and I said to Rune, that profile looks like Anna, and she wears a hat just like it. And I keep looking at it and I'm sure it's you, with your blonde bob. Are you here?"

She has no choice but to be honest. "Sort of, but only fleetingly, sort of fly-in-fly-out, no time to see anyone, and then snowmageddon started and I got stuck, so here I am."

Thankfully, Katrine takes this at face value and doesn't hold it against her, at least not at this point. This, it turns out, is because she has far bigger fish to fry. "And who, Anna, is that that your face is stuck to?"

Anna really doesn't know how to explain this away, either, so can only go with the truth. "He's the guy who rents my house here. We had too much *gløgg* at the kayak parade and in Tivoli, and this happened. It was an accident."

"An accident?" Anna completely understands why Katrine is sounding sceptical.

After a deep sigh, she confesses to her friend, one of the very few people she has ever told what happened. "I saw Carl and Maiken and had no escape. And the *gløgg* made me think this was a smart way to hide, which in my defence did work, they didn't spot me... But this"—she looks back the photo—"rather screws that up a bit."

"Does Carl read BT?"

"Daily."

"Yep, you're screwed," Katrine says.

"Not what I was wanting to hear."

"What now?"

"I'll keep hiding now until I get a flight back out and then I'll vanish, and it'll all blow over," she says, far more confident than she feels.

"The paper is trying to trace you. They want to know who the couple is," Katrine tells her, then adds, "I wonder if there's a reward?"

"Trine! If you dob me in, I will never write another word for you."

"OK, OK, *da*!" Katrine says with a laugh. "Your secret is safe with me, but good luck. I'm looking at the other media outlets on my laptop and they're running with it, too. Copenhagen Tourism wants to know who you are."

"Nononono," Anna chants under her breath. This cannot be happening. If it goes too far Maiken will know she's here, too. That's if Carl doesn't turn to her in bed to show her. Anna has no idea if they live together now, but they looked like a couple last night.

Anna feels a knot tighten in her stomach. Seeing them had made her panic. The knot in her stomach now isn't due to missing him. It's the hurt of the betrayal giving her another kicking. Even after eighteen months, it pains her, what they did. And that she hadn't spotted it makes her toes curl in humiliation. It all adds a sheen of sweat to her forehead.

"But coming back to your tenant," Katrine insists. "Dish it."

"Nope. Accident, remember," Anna insists, trying to sound stern.

"That's the most passionate accident I've seen in a long time. It reminds me of that photo of the sailor and nurse kissing in Times Square on VJ Day? You know the one. An iconic moment in time."

"Stop. It."

Katrine laughs. "OK, I'll stop, but now you've snuck into the country without letting me know, here's the deal: the department *Julefrokost* is coming up and I want you to be there."

"I'm not leaving the house again, unless it's to go to the airport," Anna states, in spite of having missed Christmas lunches last year. Danes love their month of boozy lunches, whether with work, clubs, or friends – any excuse, frankly.

Katrine makes a *Pffff* sound and says, "Good luck with that. We're booked for the twenty-first at Sankt Annæ, at one o'clock. If you make it back to London then let me know, but if you're still here, then I'll see you there." Katrine can be very bossy sometimes.

Anna mutters an OK, but crosses her fingers she'll be long gone, away from that photo and any media search.

"*Vi ses! Hej, hej,*" Katrine says signing off, and hangs up without waiting for Anna's response. Within seconds a calendar reminder pops up on her screen for the lunch.

Anna drops her hand and phone onto the bed and stares at the ceiling. This is so far removed from her original plan, and she has very little idea of how to get things back on track.

Heading for the kitchen and a strengthening cup of coffee, Anna's sure Jamie will be as appalled as she is. Admittedly, his face isn't as clear in the photo as hers given the photographer's angle, but still. He's a professional person in the city; he certainly won't want to have a schmaltzy picture like that doing the rounds.

And it *is* schmaltzy. There's an inky sky and fairy lights, a huge, illuminated star hanging over what looks like two oblivious lovers clinched with snow around their feet. It couldn't have been set up better and the photographer has framed it so perfectly, they must be a professional. What a snoop! Sneaking around the streets, taking shots of innocent individuals. Anna feels a little rage brewing inside her. Later, she'll see if she can find the photo credit, hunt them down and blast off a sternly-worded email about privacy and the invasion thereof.

Jamie is at the dining table already engrossed in his work. He's on a call, but it sounds like it's winding up. Reaching the coffee machine, she raises the jug to him in offer of a refill, to which he gives her a slow nod. He looks well-slept and alert, not like her, strung out from beating herself up about her actions. Well, maybe his hair looks a bit dishevelled, but that's about the sum of it.

"Go' morgen," he says, ending the call and pulling AirPods from his ears.

"Hmm," she humpfs. She's not sure it is.

Jamie tilts his head for her to expound.

She may as well hit him with it. Placing the coffee jug on one of his journals to protect the table, she points to his open laptop. "May I?"

He spins it towards her with a "Sure."

"This happened," she says after hitting the keys and bringing up the site. "Like I said last night, I am very sorry, Jamie." And she turns the screen back to him.

She waits.

Jamie moves his face nearer the screen.

And then back out again.

And then back to check again.

"Wow."

"I know, right? Nightmare. I've already had someone I know ring me about it. So, my cover is blown."

"Your cover?" he says, that right brow rising.

"OK, maybe that's a bit drama llama, but you know what I mean. People know I'm here now. But thankfully it isn't as clear that it's you, so I think your reputation should be safe."

He sits back in his seat, and crosses his arms. His sleeves are pushed up to his elbows and Anna can't help but glance at his forearms, lean and sinewy. "My reputation?" For some reason this amuses him. It makes his eyes twinkle, which she vastly prefers to the steely look she is more often on the receiving end of.

"I mean your professional reputation. I don't know

about your … personal reputation." She feels herself getting flustered and also distracted from her point. "What I mean is, I really hope this won't be difficult for you at work and with regards to your standing in the sustainability field."

Jamie thinks about this. "I am pretty sure this won't negatively affect my reputation at work, Anna. In fact, it might just elevate it. And my ego, for that matter."

Strangely, he does not seem as shocked, appalled, or outraged as Anna is. Far from it.

He keeps looking at the image, angling his head to look at it from various angles.

"It's a great shot."

"Jamie!" Impulsively, she slaps him on the shoulder. Wow, solid.

"What? It *is*. I bet Tivoli is delighted."

Had it been anyone else in the shot than her, Anna would agree with him, it's a perfect advert for the park. But it *is* her, so that's not happening.

"Do you think I can get the paper to take it down?" she asks, taking a seat opposite him. She picks up a box of matches and lights the advent candle for him.

"Unlikely. And probably too late. This'll be all over the place by now."

Opening his phone, he swipes about before holding the smaller screen up to her face.

"Instagram. The VisitCopenhagen account. And there it is again, with the same 'Copenhagen Snowmance' caption. And beneath it *'Hvem er de?'* Who are they?"

"Oh, no." Anna groans, putting her palm to her forehead. "Nooooo. They can't make a quest out of it."

"Like I said, too late," says Jamie.

"Not helping." She sinks further into the chair, dejected, and surrounds her mug with her hands for the comfort of the warmth.

"Don't worry about it. Not on my part anyway."

"You really don't mind?" she asks quietly.

"Nope. And as for you, if you have your way, you'll be back in England as soon as the snow thaws and you can forget about it."

That's true, but in the meantime, there's things Jamie doesn't understand.

"Here's the thing, Jamie. I have an ex." It makes sense now to give him the topline, so he's prepared. "We lived here together. I threw him out when he had an affair and he hasn't seen me since, because I left. But now he might know I'm back, he might turn up."

Jamie's face turns stony in an instant. "Was he violent towards you?"

"No," Anna says quickly. "No. Nothing like that and I don't expect him to be, either. But he is the kind who wants to discuss things to the nth degree, even though there's nothing to be said and I really, really don't want to."

Jamie's face relaxes a little, but not much. He gives her a concerned look, but says carefully, "And you don't think it might be a useful thing to have this conversation where he apologises to you, and you get to tell him what a shit he's been, because that might make you feel better?"

"No thanks."

"Anna."

"Really," she says quite primly. "I don't need any of that."

"What, closure? That widely regarded thing most therapists will guide you towards, if the TV shows are anything to go by?"

"Yeah, no. I'm happier walking away. After what he did, he doesn't deserve my time, attention or forgiveness, if that's what he's looking for."

"I was more thinking about you, actually. Being able to draw a line under it—"

"I have! The line is drawn," she cuts in.

"—having addressed it and being able to make peace with it," he continues.

"Who says I haven't made peace with it?"

"Just at a guess – and as I've admitted, I'm no therapist – but hiding in a house and stressing about being in the paper is not a sign of being at peace with your path."

Anna busies herself with staring into her mug.

"Back to the kiss, though," he suddenly says in an alarming segue. "It's had me thinking."

Anna's face is instantly hot with shame. Given he now knows about Carl, she's better off confessing all. "Jamie. Here's another thing; I was avoiding Carl. That's why I kissed you. He was walking towards me, and I had nowhere to hide. Which was stupid, I know. But here's the even stupider thing; given the photo, it's had the reverse effect." She waves her hand at the laptop screen. "Again, I'm sorry, it was shocking behaviour on my part. My thinking was iffy."

Something shoots across Jamie's face, but she can't read

it and it's gone within a second. "So, it wasn't that you were unstoppably attracted to me?" he says, deadpan.

Anna doesn't know quite what to say.

"I… Er… Look, Jamie…" she starts, flustered.

Jamie's mouth pulls up to one side. "I'm messing with you. We covered that last night, right? *Gløgg* and Tivoli magic, etc., etc.?"

Anna, wide-eyed and out of sorts, just nods slowly, then asks, "Am I forgiven? For using you as a shield?"

He fixes her gaze and she forces herself to keep the contact, deserving everything she gets. "Aye," he gives her.

Anna lets out a slow breath.

Jamie leans towards her, those toned forearms flat on the table between them, his hands clasped. "And on that foundation, I have a proposal for you."

Chapter Eleven

Anna can't believe she's doing this. It's absolutely not what she's here for.

The wind is rushing through her hair, which for once is not under her hat, due to her being worried about being seen in it. It's stuffed in her pocket, though, just in case. Thankfully the snow has stopped again. The on–off nature of … uh, nature, is adding to the frustration of being here, but right at this moment, Anna is rather enjoying herself.

"Are you warm enough?" Jamie asks loudly, from the bike seat. "There's another blanket in the big bag."

Anna is currently sitting in the front of Jamie's Christiania bicycle, a cargo bike with a box on the front, which can carry multiple bags, children or an adult – in this case, Anna. She's well wrapped up in her big coat, but she won't say no to a blanket around her legs, so delves into the bag Jamie put together as she searched her wardrobe for the required attire.

She had noticed the bike in the front yard when she arrived, but not thought much of it.

"You really are getting the full Copenhagen experience with this for transport," she calls back to him as he pedals hard, the slush spraying after them.

"My company car," he says. "I don't need an actual car living here, but I do sometimes have to transport presentation materials and prototypes to clients, so we thought this was the best thing."

Anna thinks of her old bike in the basement. She's missed it. London is not nearly the biking city Copenhagen is – to be honest, the idea frightens her, as the drivers don't consider cyclists in the same way, if at all – so she stays safely on the Tube. That said, there's something very lovely about being ferried around under someone else's steam, while she sits like a princess in a wooden box. It makes her think back to Signe's wedding, where her friend arrived at the Town Hall in a Christiania bicycle festooned with gypsophila, white gerberas and strings of Danish flags. Her husband-to-be was riding the bike, followed by an entourage of family members on their own decorated bicycles. It was a gorgeous sight, happy and romantic. Not that that is anything like her current position, she reminds herself. This is simply Jamie driving them to meet his colleagues for their monthly social. Totally normal. Except that she is faking being his girlfriend. *That* kind of "totally normal".

"It's like this," Jamie had started. "I'd like a certain woman to think I'm involved with someone else, and therefore not romantically interested in her. Which for the record, I'm not. Not in any way. We work in the same field, so if word gets about, which it invariably will, then hopefully it'll make things less awkward between us."

Anna had stared at him.

"You want us to fake-date?"

"Um… Yes. I think that's what it's called."

"Outside of this house."

He slow blinked at her. "Well, obviously. Fake-dating inside isn't really going to have the desired effect." No, she could see that. "Look, you've already been outed. People will know you're here, and maybe it can work in your favour, too, with regards to your ex. If he thinks you've moved on, with me, then he might leave you alone."

That sounded far more positive.

"And you'll be gone soon," he'd added, "so no harm done."

There was that, too. She'd just walk away from it.

Jamie had watched for her answer.

Could she fake being his girlfriend and loved-up? Gazing at him, his jawline, his rumpled hair, his forearms, she'd suspected this would not be too much of a hardship. They'd already got a trial kiss out of the way, and boy-howdy, what a kiss that had been. They were clearly attuned in that department.

Amid her gazing and contemplating, he'd still said nothing. He'd explained and she felt it wasn't the hugest of asks, considering he'd let her stay. Refusing felt mean in light of his generosity. And he hadn't kicked off about her using him, and his face, outside Tivoli. Aaand she appreciated him not pressing her to agree, and that's what had convinced her to croak out an "OK, then." Like he said, what harm could it do?

Then he'd said, "Great. Dig out some swim kit from upstairs. We're going out later."

Which is why she now finds herself swaddled in the bike crate, heading back towards Nyhavn and the bicycle bridge that will take them to Refshaleøen, or Reffen as the island's known, where they're meeting some of his workmates. The bottles of beer sticking out of the bag, previously hidden by the blanket, are a welcome sight. She suspects she's going to need a little Dutch courage.

"They're nice guys," Jamie says, perhaps sensing she needs reassuring.

"I've told you, Jamie, it's a small city, I probably know them already. We might even be related." This most likely isn't true – her family is small – but in a city of six-hundred-thousand, who knows.

Jamie scoffs. "I think you exaggerate the danger there."

She turns to shoot him an admonishing look. "Need I remind you that twice yesterday, I was forced to dodge people I know." She doesn't mention the kiss, although she's suddenly replaying it in her head. Again. "This city is exactly as small as I say."

Jamie pedals on, over the slim bridge, furiously ringing his bell like a native at pedestrians who've strayed onto the cycle path, until they reach Little Siberia, thus known for being the coldest part of this island, previously home to shipbuilding. Night is setting in and the lights of shipping and wind turbines glow in the Øresund sound. Jamie parks the bike and offers Anna a hand out of the crate. In front of them is Copenhot, a complex of outdoor hot tubs and rows of saunas, positioned to look out over the water.

Jamie slings the bag over his shoulder and gives her a "Ready?" as they walk towards the hot tubs and his friends. Coming into view, Jamie sweeps his arm around her. His hand on the curve of her waist would be warm, if she could feel it through her multiple layers, but just knowing that makes her self-conscious. She's been aware of his scent around the house, but now, this close, against the clear, cold night air, it's more potent, its masculine notes dancing around her nose.

"Anna?" she hears him ask through the smile he's sending his waving friends. Her brain catches up; she has a role to play. She knows these moves, she's been a girlfriend before, after all. Awkwardly, she slides her hand around his waist and leans into him as they walk on. Anna thinks she must be better than this. Looking up at him, she supplies him a wide smile, like they know each other well, like they have just come from home, where they live, laugh and make love. Nonstop.

"On it."

She notices his pupils widen as he catches on to her role-playing and then he plants a kiss on her temple. The deal is sealed.

"Unbelievable!" says Jamie, with a shake of his head.

"I told you so," Anna says, feeling smug. Which is daft, as it's exactly what she's been worrying about.

There are six of them in the wooden tub, the wood-burner heating it just by their side. The water is gloriously hot, in beautiful contrast to the frigid air and also the cold beers they are holding at the tub's edge.

Jamie's colleagues, three men and a woman, had already been submerged when they arrived and introductions were swift, to get them into the water without freezing to death in the interim. The others are Danes, and all of the men Copenhageners like Anna. It only takes a couple of questions of where they live, work or went to school to shock Jamie. As it turns out, Stefan is a grandson of Anna's erstwhile and retiring vet; she's worked with Anders' photographer brother, and to top it all, Emil's mother taught her at high school. Anna and the three men clink their bottles in an alliance of linked Danes.

Smilla, who Jamie says joined the company at the same time as him, is apparently from Jutland, the mainland, but has come to Sjælland, or as she calls it the "Devil's Island", to experience the bright lights of the big city. Really, she's well aware Copenhagen is far from being a big city as capitals go and they all share stories of crossing the city several times in one night for parties, bars or clubs.

They're a welcoming bunch, although she suspects that's down to the way Jamie's behaving around her. He offered her his hand to get up the steps into the hot tub and sinking in beside her, draped a relaxed arm around her immediately. If the others spotted her immediate blush

Anna thinks they'll have put it down to the heat of the water shocking her skin after their cold ride in. Fingers crossed.

After that, there's a couple of minutes where Anna is uber-conscious of sitting close to Jamie, him in just his swim shorts and her in, well, not a lot.

Having been sent to the wardrobe to find some swimwear, Anna had been pleased to find a black one-piece she'd obviously chosen not to take with her to London. Changing into it before they left, planning to don her clothes straight back over it, she had the dismay of discovering the elastic at the leg holes had given up the ghost and now flapped around her bum-cheeks. Not the look she was going for. Jamie had given her a shout and she'd had no choice but to panic rummage through the drawer to find the only other swimwear present. An itsy-bitsy teeny-weeny red polka-dot bikini; perfect for sunbathing at Nordhavn quayside, or in her own back yard, not so much for meeting colleagues of one's fake boyfriend for the first time. Or sitting in such close proximity to said fake boyfriend himself, as it turns out.

The tub is small, and they have the maximum number of people in it, which means every time one of them turns to grab another beer, or wants a change of view, everyone shuffles and Anna finds herself sliding skin-on-skin with Jamie. Her bare thigh is constantly slipping against his equally bare thigh. When he speaks and she turns to listen, she's gazing straight up into his face from her position tucked under his arm. His bicep makes for a comfortable pillow when she's looking the other way, too. Had she been with Carl she would have landed a small kiss on his pec. So that's what she does now. She feels him tense for a fraction of a second, all hidden under the steaming water, then the light squeeze of his hand on the curve of her exposed shoulder. It is all so very different from the way they have navigated around each other in the house; both at home, but as individuals. And it puts her in a strange position; she's hyper aware that that's what's happening, then she remembers they're supposedly a couple, so it isn't weird, and then she recalls they're only temporary housemates – virtually strangers – which *does* make it weird, but then she also can't deny that she kind of likes it. It's very, very confusing. Plus, she notices Jamie doesn't budge. At all. Which can only mean he doesn't find it awful. In fact, as they get more into the chat with the others, he runs his thumb up and down the top of her arm. It gives her goosebumps. It has nothing to do with the cold.

"So how did you two meet?" Smilla asks. "Jamie only mentioned you today." She doesn't look suspicious as such, but there is something enquiring about her curiosity.

Oh, bugger. They hadn't thought to work out their origin story. They can't say she's snowed in, as that would date their established relationship to all of two days ago.

But Jamie, it seems, is on it. He turns to look Anna deeply in the eyes, which makes a weight suddenly descend in her tummy. His normally steely, blue eyes are soft tonight, and the pupils blown wide. The others could simply vanish with the steam for all that look cares. It's the stuff of Anna's younger dreams, before they got dashed.

Without taking his eyes from her, Jamie says to the

others, "She turned up on my doorstep one day. Like she'd been delivered to me."

Damn, he's good at the faking, Anna thinks, as she wants to respond "aww" just as Smilla is doing right now. Good job, Jamie.

"Was she lost?" asks Anders, which makes Emil snort and the two of them fist-bump. But Jamie ignores them, finally breaking eye contact to say to Smilla, "Turns out she's my landlady. Came to check out the house … and me."

Now Anna's blush is undeniable. Jamie notices and, with a glint in his eye, lifts her hand and places a kiss on the inside of her wrist. It makes her clench inside her itsy-bitsy teeny-weeny red polka-dot bikini bottoms. Though she hides it, she's shocked by her physical reaction to him. And she'll be having words with him about deliberately trying to make her blush more.

"Knock it off, you two," says Stefan. He stretches his empty beer bottle towards Jamie. "Your round."

Grinning, Jamie gets out of the tub, leaving Anna feeling the loss of his skin against hers, and she realises that while her mind might know this is fake, her body has not received the memo. She hasn't felt anything like this in a long time. That she can still feel that sort of thing warms her. She'd assumed the entire endeavour extinct, but no, apparently not. Good to know, even if it isn't something that can go anywhere. She'll be gone soon, not to return and most likely their paths will never cross again, but she'll leave knowing she can be attracted to someone again, that she still has a scintilla of sexual appetite left. She might not be as broken as she'd thought. It's pleasing.

A gust of wind comes in from Øresund, and Anna's hair flies about her face. Despite the hot water, it makes her shiver, too.

"Here," she hears, warm breath at her ear. The skin immediately rises in reaction. Then she feels her hat being slid onto her head. Lots of the other hot tub users have hats on, too, as does Emil because as Anders and Stefan keep joking, he has no hair under it. While she's glad of the extra warmth, it's Jamie's thoughtfulness that makes Anna glow. Getting back in beside her, he hands out the new round of beers and they clink the bottles with a resounding chorus of "*Skål!*"

Finishing her swig, Anna realises Smilla is looking at her, head cocked.

"It's you," Smilla accuses, and then looking at Jamie, "Oh my god, it's you *two*!"

Anna sits very still, clueless as to what to do about this.

Smilla turns to the guys and continues, "The Tivoli couple, the Copenhagen Snowmance couple. That's the hat." She rounds back on Anna. "That's the *nisse* hat, isn't it? It's you."

Anna feels Jamie's arm slide back around her shoulders and this time it feels protective, like he's got her, he's got this.

"Busted, Smilla. Good spot," he concedes. "But do me a favour, don't tell anyone. We didn't know the picture was being taken and we don't really want the publicity."

"But it's amazing," Smilla protests. "It's all over the socials."

Jamie shrugs as if it doesn't mean anything to him, though he gives Anna's shoulder a little squeeze, like he knows that's not the same for her. "Like I said, we didn't pose for it, so keep it quiet, yeah?"

The others all nod, even Smilla who is clearly bursting with questions, but unfortunately needing to be respectful towards Jamie, who Anna is now fairly certain is more senior in the company.

Thankfully, Anders and Emil aren't romance spotters and switch the conversation to Denmark's current football form and then their Christmas plans, the latter of which Anna manages to enthusiastically fib her way through, keen to keep the conversation off certain photographs.

As their booked time comes to an end and they all climb out, Jamie helps Anna down, pausing to push an errant lock back under her hat, before doing a great job of swaddling her in her towel. Then he pulls her in and tentatively plants a kiss on her lips. It's cold in the night air and out of the water, so Anna leans in, at which Jamie wraps his arms around her further, the kiss blossoming to something deeper, and she rises to her toes, keen to give his colleagues the show she'd agreed to, but deep down wanting a replay of last night. She's not disappointed.

"That's enough, you two," Anders scolds again. "Some of us are lonely singles and this is just cruel."

Anna extricates herself with a genuine "Sorry." She knows what it's like to be newly single and have loved-up people flouting their loved-upness right in front of her.

Once dressed they ride as a cluster back into town, chatting as they go, unlike the concentrated speed-ride of a rush-hour commute. Beyond Nyhavn they all scatter in different directions, with waves and the standard "*Vi ses*" and "*Hej, hej!*"

There's a moment of quiet as Jamie pedals them alongside Kongens Have, the king's gardens, Anna relaxing back into her carriage, feeling rather floppy from the hot tub and frankly, from that kiss.

"Did we do OK?" she asks, hoping so.

"Perfect," says Jamie.

"Good job they promised to keep the photo thing quiet," she adds. All in all, she isn't sure what their fakery will really achieve. Smilla clearly isn't the woman he's wanting to redirect.

Jamie laughs. A proper, deep laugh. It's a beautiful sound. "Ah bless you, Anna. Smilla'll be texting all her contacts the moment she gets home. The whole company will know by tomorrow and by my calculations the person I want to get the message will be aware by end of play. Mission accomplished, I'd say."

Chapter Twelve

Eckersbergsgade, right in the middle of Kartoffelrækkerne, is a very social street. Permanent picnic benches down the middle and a children's playhouse make for homemade traffic calming, though there are numerous cars parked along the house fences. The trees all house fairy lights, probably there since early November, if past years are anything to go by. Candles glow in most windows, below hanging star- and heart-themed Christmas decorations. In the darkness, the lights are not quite Tivoli, but are still gorgeous in their own way. Right at the end of the road lies Sortedams Sø, the jet-black lake currently reflecting the lights of Østerbro on the other side. Pulling into the street is a wonderful welcome back, though this might be down to Anna still being a little squiffy from all the beers.

What's not such a wonderful sight is the figure, pacing in the street in front of her house, illuminated by the streetlight.

She'd know that silhouette anywhere. Carl.

"Fuck," Anna sighs, keenly aware she's trapped in her crate with an oblivious chauffeur, who blithely bypasses her ex, to park in the front yard, and then extends his hand to help her out with a "Mi'lady." She'd give more thought to the feel of her hand in his if she wasn't freaking out. Hustling herself out as quickly and tidily as possible, which isn't much, she tells him in a low voice, "Carl is here."

Jamie immediately tenses. "What do you want to do?"

There's no time for that, though, as Carl is standing just inside the boundary and calls, "Anna."

"Fuck *igen*," she mumbles. She wishes she'd told Jamie to keep cycling. They could have simply completed circuits around the streets all night or until Carl gave up and left.

"I have nothing to say to you," she says, and tries to head for the doorstep.

"That's as may be, but I have things to say to you," Carl snaps back. He's cross, it's clear. Maybe standing about in the cold for however long has done that.

Anna turns to look at him.

"What can you possibly have to say to me? Other than you're a shithead, which I already know, and that you're sorry, which I don't care about."

The security light above next door's entrance has flicked on, Carl being within the sensor's range. It leaves her in the shadows, which she likes. He's not changed much, his hair perhaps a little longer, but still wavy from boyhood curls, and while not the white-blond he was as a boy, it's still golden. His shape is more basketball player than Jamie's rugby player; taller and leaner, some might say lanky.

Carl shakes his head with a scoff. "Had you not run off, we could have talked about it."

Anna shrugs. "What for? You did what you did. You betrayed me. With Maiken, of all people. Did you particularly want to talk about what an arsehole you are?"

"We could have discussed why it happened. Things weren't good between us."

This has Anna seeing red. As she recalled it, they were fine. Better than fine.

"What we had was good," she manages through her fury.

"You weren't looking."

"Clearly!" she says, but it's a bit more like a shout. "Had I been looking I would have spotted the two of you fucking about around the city. I would have seen you for the snakes you are."

She turns again towards the door, noticing Jamie standing quietly behind her. What must he be making of this?

Carl tries another tack. "I have tried calling you, texting you, coming here, emailing you, ringing your editor to get a message to you, but none of it works."

"I blocked you, told Katrine to ignore you, and I don't live here anymore. For someone who was always so sure of how bright he was, you are very slow to take a hint."

"Seeing you in the paper, though, tells me you're back. We should talk." He nods towards the door.

Not. A. Chance.

"As I said, there's nothing to say. I've moved on and so have you and Maiken." She hopes, as soon as she's said it, that he doesn't realise she must have seen them to know this.

"You threw my stuff out on the street, Anna. Valuable stuff. You changed the locks." Yes. Yes, she had done that.

"So what? I didn't want you in my house. Then or now. You gave up that right when you got in Maiken's knickers. And as for your things, you should have thought about that before you trashed our life."

"You are so unreasonable. And a chicken. We could have discussed it like adults!" His fury is rising and Anna senses Jamie step closer to her.

Finally, Carl registers him properly.

"Who's this?"

Anna snaps, "None of your business," just as Jamie says, "The boyfriend." Bollocks. The entire conversation has been in rapid Danish, but Jamie can clearly pick out "Who's this?"

Carl's eyes widen a bit at that, but he has the sense not to ask for details. She just wants him gone and this to be over.

"Go home, Carl. You've said you're unhappy about me throwing your stuff out. Noted. Don't expect an apology."

She really hopes he'll go. This is excruciating. She's praying none of the neighbours have caught wind of what's going on.

Jamie lays his hand on her shoulder, which she takes as a show of strength to Carl.

Carl's lips are pursed in anger, his eyes blazing, though

she doesn't know what he was expecting to achieve. Unless it was to make her feel uncomfortable, and she must give him that. Bullseye, there.

"Maiken wants her locket back," he suddenly says to her, staunchly ignoring Jamie.

"What?"

Carl looks less assured, like he's been tasked with an unwanted job. He switches to English. It's a tactical move to pressure her. "You took her necklace, and she wants it back. The big locket. The one she always wore. Her mother's."

"I am aware of her locket, Carl," Anna says indignantly. "I don't have it, and I don't know why you'd think I do. So, you can take your accusations and … and … stuff them up your bum." OK, so that didn't come out as eviscerating as she'd hoped.

Anna shoves her hand in her pocket to dig out her keys. "You should go. There's nothing to say here," she reiterates and heads up the stairs, not looking back, to wrestle with the key for much longer than helps her badass stance, until Jamie's hand settles on hers and takes over.

"Tell me about Carl," Jamie says, the two of them having resumed normal housemates-mode the moment the front door closed behind them. He hands her a mug of tea and places a bowl of *brunkager* on the coffee table, before taking a seat in the chair opposite the sofa, giving her space. She's not sure she wants it. The space, that is. The tea is welcome. She's still shaking.

Anna sinks back in the sofa, pulls up her feet and wraps the throw around her, with a sigh. Where to start?

"I really thought it was The Big Love, you know? We met at twenty-four and we were sure it was forever. We were just in tune with each other, or so I thought. I thought…" Anna feels ridiculous saying this now, and keeps her eyes squarely on the flickers of the trio of candles on the coffee table. "I thought we were a team; invincible. That there was nothing we couldn't overcome or withstand. Because we talked about things, discussed them and knew each other." A bitter laugh bursts out of her now. "I was so naïve! Turns out we only talked about *some* things and actually were far from untouchable, and were felled by the most common, tawdry of events. We weren't special at all. He slept with someone else. Turns out it wasn't something I could withstand or overcome. Or forgive. So, I threw out his things and it was over."

"And you ran?"

Putting it like that makes her wince.

"I *removed myself* from all that was painful. Being here in the house was agonising. And the whole city felt tainted; everywhere we'd been, they'd probably been. I couldn't, *can't* believe that people we know, friends, hadn't seen them out, too, and *knew*. The humiliation was savage. Still is."

"OK," he ventures carefully, "and having 'removed' yourself, did the pain go away?"

Anna scowls at him. Is he making a point?

"I'm just hypothesising that perhaps, the pain is in you, and travels, too," he says, "and that removing yourself from somewhere you love, hasn't made that better."

She takes a breath to interject but he leans forward and offers her a *brunkage,* to cut her off.

"You love this city, Anna, and the country. The things you crave when you get here, the food, the sights, the memories – and from how you've described your new place, you've made a little shrine to your homeland. You might not see it, but it's obvious to me. You're homesick and at some point, that might be worth recognising.

"But back to my hypothesising about your pain. It isn't going to go away, no matter where you remove yourself to, it needs dealing with. At the source. You need to say what you need to say, to the people who hurt you. And they need a chance to explain themselves."

Well, that's not a thing. "I have zero interest in hearing a single word either of them has to say. I don't want to see them or hear their lies. I don't want the conflict of the arguing, like just now," she gives a shudder at the thought of what just happened in the street, "and I don't need more humiliation on top of what I've already had. Can you hypothesise on that?"

She's getting defensive and she can hear her voice becoming shriller. Conflict and drama are something she avoids as much as possible. Having grown up with Ida, drama usually heralded her life was about to go sideways. Her experience with Carl, showed her she was right. All she really wants is calm and a simple life of respect and trust. Is that too much to ask?

A silent stand-off ensues. Anna snaffles another *brunkage,* unrelenting.

"Can I ask you something? Something else. Something personal?" he asks, finally giving up.

"Sure." She figures she can always lie if needs be.

"Upstairs, on your bedside table, there's a tube labelled, *Pølse*. Sausage, right? What's that about?"

"Oh! Right. Yeah, that must look weird. It's why I came back."

"For a tube of sausage?" It must be testament to how deranged everything about her has been in the last few days that Jamie doesn't look more alarmed.

"Pølse was my cat," she starts, and realising that that doesn't clear things up much, adds, "He died. His ashes are in the tube. The vet was shutting, and I had to collect them. One of the few things that can't be done digitally or through an embassy, as it turns out. Weddings, funerals and cat-ashes collection. That's it."

Jamie's mouth lifts at one side. "Who knew?"

"Who knew, indeed."

"What's the plan for them now?"

Anna explains her thwarted plan to scatter them with her grandparents.

"We'll go tomorrow," he says, looking at her over the top of his mug. "Weather should be better tomorrow."

Something about that "we" pleases her immensely. She tells herself it's simply that two people will make it more of a ceremony, as opposed to the "scatter and dash" event it would have been the last time she tried. He's a thoughtful guy. She has to give him that – reserved and guarded, perhaps, or maybe just towards her – but under that she's seeing kindness and consideration. After what happened with Carl, she gets a glimmer of hope that some men can be trusted.

"Can I ask you something?" she echoes back at him.

"Sure." Now Jamie has seen the source of her odd behaviour, knows she isn't a stalker, perhaps he'll be more open with her.

"What's the story with the woman we're faking for?"

Jamie's eyes settle on the faux flame of the candle. Finally, he says, "We had a misunderstanding. By which I mean, I got things wrong, and now she'd like me to not be here, but I want to stay." Anna is stunned to see him blush. Blushing isn't something she'd expect on a face like his. He's generally so assured.

"And you think if she believes you have a girlfriend," Anna points at herself and pulls a face to lighten his mood, "that she'll think she's safe from you?"

His mood doesn't lighten, though.

"She's *completely* safe from me," he snaps, his tone rough, but he takes a breath and goes on. "I hate that she thinks I'm any kind of threat to her, because I'm not. I'd just like to be on speaking terms. Just two regular people, you know?"

Anna's not so sure about this. "You know, you can't be friends with everyone, Jamie. Not all friendships are meant to last."

The look on his face says he disagrees.

She presses her point. "We can't possibly know everyone we ever interact with for always. I don't think there's capacity for that." She's dipped in and out of lives all through her childhood, she couldn't possibly have retained all those friendships. "Not enough head-space or heart-space, to be honest, and in many cases it's not healthy. I've jettisoned Carl for my own health and self-respect, because he didn't treat me well. Maybe, you just aren't supposed to keep knowing this woman?"

She can see he's thinking about this, but the thinking is very deep and Anna sees it's deeper than he'll let her in.

"Do you think people really think like that?" he asks.

"Well, *I* clearly do. And my mum does. She's walked away from every relationship she's ever had as soon as it doesn't serve her any longer. She thinks life's too short to tie yourself to what makes you unhappy."

All he says is "Hmmm," and then he finishes his tea. She hasn't convinced him, but she thinks she's given him food for thought.

He stands, which makes her want to protest. She's been enjoying the discussion, and simply having company. "I'm exhausted from the hot tub and the cycling. I'm turning in." Fair enough, he was transporting her across town at a fair clip. He calls for her to *"Sov godt"* as he reaches the stairs. She's sure she will sleep well. The hot tub and the fresh air have been soporific. Or maybe it's the stress of seeing Carl again. That was exactly what she'd wanted to avoid. Thank God it's over.

"Tak for idag," Anna says, thanking him for today in typical Danish fashion, but she isn't sure he hears her. She sits for a while, watching the glow of the candle in front of her. It's the first time she's seen Jamie properly

uncomfortable, and there's clearly lots more going on there. It dawns on her that maybe she shouldn't be in a rush to be trusting again.

Chapter Thirteen

There's been a lot of progress made on the jigsaw, Anna notices, when leaving her room the following morning. He must have been up early, and he must also have been moving around like a ninja as she didn't hear him at all. He'd certainly skipped the third step. Maybe he uses the jigsaw to clear his head, she supposes, as when she makes it to the kitchen, he's at work; the coffee is on as normal and he's on the telephone. They go through their now ritual of mouthing "*God morgen*" to each other, as she pours herself a mugful, then comes to refill his. He's also been out to the baker, as there's a plate of pastries on the kitchen counter for breakfast. She helps herself to a *spandauer*, with its custard centre and white-icing drizzle, commonly known as "the baker's bad eye", and scoffs it in a flat minute.

It's only now, coffee in hand and pastry in gob, that Anna registers the call is contentious.

"No, Dad," Jamie says, insistent and weary at the same

time. "We've been through this. My life is here. It's everything I want. I'm sorry."

Anna makes herself busy, trying not to listen in, but it's hard when she's hearing the mix of frustration and guilt in Jamie's voice.

She sits at the table when the call comes to an uncomfortable end.

"Still wants you back on Skye?" she asks. There's no point acting oblivious.

He gives a long exhale. "Aye. Same conversation over and over. He doesn't get it, or he doesn't want to hear it."

"He doesn't want you to be happy?"

Jamie looks her in the eyes. "He can't see how I wouldn't be happy on Skye. An island he loves and has never left, and a farm he was born to and wants to pass on to his only son. In his eyes, it's a gift I'm passing up, for something he has no experience of." He gives her a flat smile, then changes the subject with a more upbeat, "What's the plan?"

"Well, I've already had my daily chat with my friends at the airline. We all know each other by name now," she says, holding out the plate to him. He takes a *kanelsnegl*, some of the pastry flaking onto his work. "Copenhagen is clear and flights are going again, provided you live east of here and didn't have the snowstorm. British airports are still stuffed and all UK flights still cancelled. So, no news, to be honest." She's almost resigned to it now. Maybe getting the fear of seeing Carl out of the way, has doused some of the urgency? Anna lifts up the laptop she's brought down.

"Can I work here? It's all research, not calls, so I won't disturb you."

"Of course," he says. "Unless my calls will disturb you?"

"Nope. It's nice to have other voices around." She's used to working alone in her apartment. Often, she'll move to a café just to hear other human beings.

And so, they sit together, each hammering away at their respective keyboards. It's a comfortable silence, even as Jamie refills their coffee cups, or Anna brings a plate of *småkager* to the table to go with it. Now and again, Jamie takes a call, and Anna tries to ignore it, but it's intriguing to see and hear him being his professional self. Carl always had his work persona – more bolshy and demanding – because that's how he got his way. Jamie's persona isn't too different, from what she's seen of him, from his home self, listening rather than demanding, considering, standing firm in some cases, compromising when he's shown a better way. It makes for a far more relaxed environment and Anna imagines his office must be the same. When she isn't actively travelling or devising and discussing her tour ideas, she doesn't have much face-to-face interaction. It's mostly the subsequent online research, emailing vendors or cruise lines, or her staple of writing articles for Katrine's website.

It's during a pause in the hammering that Anna hears Jamie's breath hitch. He's been checking something on his phone.

"What?" she asks, naturally intrigued.

Jamie's eyes meet hers across the screen.

"Nothing."

Something feels off. Anna might work in travel, but she's still a journalist by training and she can sense there's something here.

"You gasped."

"I don't gasp," states Jamie. "Maiden aunts and Regency heroines gasp."

She rolls her eyes. "Your breath distinctly hitched. It suggested shock or disgust."

His brow furrows at that. "I grew up on a farm. Takes a lot to disgust me."

"Shock then," she says, taking it as an admission. She makes a "gimme" gesture at his phone. He places it screen down on the table instead.

"Trade secrets?" she asks. Fair enough if it is, but he hasn't suggested there's anything clandestine or competitive in his work.

"It's nothing," he says again, smoother this time, but it's too late. Something is going on.

"Jamie? If it isn't a business thing, then just show me? Is it Carl, did he put something on the street Facebook group? I bet he's still on there." She isn't. That was a tie she had to cut early on.

Something is battling on his face. Anna crosses her arms.

"I've been a teenage girl, Jamie. I can out-stare you, out-mood you and out-stubborn you. Give it up." She repeats the hand gesture.

He scratches his cheek, then finally sighs, before opening his phone and sliding it across, with a "You asked for it. Remember that."

The sound that comes from Anna is somewhere between

a scream and a yowl. Jamie sits back and rides it out. He's crossed his own arms, mirroring her, but it appears more like a "told you, but you wouldn't listen" gesture.

"Oh my God!" she manages once the sound has abated. She cannot believe what she's seeing. "What is the matter with people?!"

There on the screen is a new photo of her and Jamie, gazing at each other like smitten kittens. The sky is dark behind them, there's steam rising around them from the tubs, their skin is glistening from the water. Jamie is holding the towel, seconds from swaddling her in it. Some other hot-tubber has snapped this of Jamie and Anna. Or rather Jamie and Anna in the teeny-weeny bikini.

"I look like some bloody *nisse*-nymph!" The red hat and red bikini does make her look like a Christmas elf. "Did you see anyone with their phone?" she snaps, cross, appalled, distressed, all of that.

"Um, I was just looking at you," he says, pointing to the phone as proof, keen to show he was in no way complicit. "I would have made them delete it if I had." She would have dunked the photographer and their phone.

Anna's own phone pings. Her eyes skitter to the message. Katrine. It's a "starry-eyed" emoji with a photo attached. Anna doesn't need to open it.

"That's it," she says, flopping back into the seat. "I am not leaving this house until I'm heading for the airport."

"Yeah, no," states Jamie. "We have an arrangement for this afternoon."

"What?"

"Just get your work done," he says. "We leave in about an hour."

"Not leaving," she says crossly. She sounds like a toddler, she knows.

"Anna, stop. I'm not going to blow sunshine up you by pointing out that it's a hot photo. You'll see that yourself when you calm the hell down. But I *am* telling you not to let it get in the way of your life. Ignore it."

"Easy for you to say, you aren't in a miniscule bikini," she seethes.

"I am, in fact, topless, if you look," he points out. "I'm wearing half the amount of garments you are. So, I should command the majority of the outrage here. But I know there's nothing I can do about this, and to be honest, this suits my purpose brilliantly. Smilla will have something for her show and tell."

Anna's jaw drops. "You're happy with this?!"

"It's a blatant infringement of privacy. Aye. I get it. But it's out there already and we aren't doing anything indecent, and as such I'm going to see it as serving a purpose in our fake-dating. Great job there, fake girlfriend."

His own stubbornness is well on show and outraged as she is, she can't help but be impressed by his reframing. Again, if it had been anyone but herself she would have thought it a romantic shot, probably commissioned by Copenhot themselves. Perhaps she should reflect on what she finds acceptable for others but not herself, but that can wait for another day. Another day when she is safely away from this city.

Jamie's expression says he isn't going to be budged on

this. With a cross huff, she goes back to her own work, hammering more aggressively on the keyboard and ignoring him for the following hour.

At noon precisely, Jamie slaps down the lid on his laptop.

"Time's up. Let's go." His tone is bossier than normal, like he's expecting resistance.

She hadn't planned on a half day, but then she's her own boss. The thought of bunking off with decent company is appealing. She'll eventually be back in London with plenty of alone-time to fill. And yet, she says, "I really don't want to go out."

"I know," he says, his voice softer, "but you can't live like that. Hiding. And we had a plan. So, go get Pølse, and your big coat. I've got the rest."

Oh. She hasn't given much thought to his mentioning the ashes last night. But apparently this is happening.

The walk to Holmens Kirkegaard from the house is only ten minutes, but Anna revels in it. She's fully wrapped up in a hat under her hood, coat, scarf, gloves, winter boots and a thick layer of lip balm. It's a blue-sky day, but the cold is bitter out there. Jamie is equally wrapped up and carrying a rucksack that he's refusing to reveal the contents of. Mysterious. Anna is not averse to this.

The dry crispness of the air is perfect winter weather. She's not missing the perpetual damp cold of the London winter. Bundled into her layers here, the cold makes her cheeks rosy, but otherwise she's toasty and, in spite of her earlier livid state, happy. Which is in stark contrast to the last time she walked this route, albeit in the opposite direction, bedraggled in the relentless snow and praying someone would be at home in the house. Anna sends a glance to Jamie as they walk side by side. How lucky she's been. He can be aloof, but there's still no signs of serial killer tendencies, and this excursion is so thoughtful.

They pass the wooden chapel at the gate and then Anna leads the way along the paths, finally coming to stop in the little plot where Mads and Vivi now reside. Compared to some, it is simple; no ostentatious, grand headstones for them. Just one matt, granite stone with both their names and dates engraved. The rest of the plot, within the low, perfectly-kempt box hedge is laid with small grey gravel, but speckled with many bigger rounded stones, with little messages of love. A trip to the beach with a bag had allowed for a little cairn in Anna's back yard, where she would take a stone to write a message on for when she would go to visit. Not that any of this is visible today, of course, because Snow.

"Cute birds," says Jamie behind her. On the top edge of the headstone sit two brass birds, as if in chatter.

"This was exactly as Mads and Vivi were. They always had a conversation on the go." Each bird currently bears a little snow hat.

"I forgot to bring a stone," she says.

"Danish tradition?" he asks.

"No, just mine. Shows how out of practice I am," she says, feeling bad about it. She'd left Mads and Vivi, too.

Jamie knocks her side with his, his hands firmly stuffed

into his pockets. "Today you've brought them something else."

Ah, yes.

Anna removes the tube from her pocket, having clutched it all the way, and has a quick check around them.

"Worried about incoming funerals?"

It makes her laugh. "No. I checked this time."

"Then why the worry?"

"I'm not sure you're supposed to scatter pet ashes on graves."

"I'd be surprised if there were written rules anywhere." He most likely has a point. From some of the graves they've passed, it looks like people are free to decorate as they see fit. "I'm sure we can make a case for Pølse being some sort of sustainable glitter or something."

Again, with the "we" there. Something about that…

Satisfied there's a defence plan, Anna brushes the snow aside with her boot, near the headstone, before pulling the top off the tube and letting the ash fall on the gravel beneath. Then she pushes the snow back. It feels like she's accomplished something, finished a job. OK, so she still hasn't made it back to the UK, but doing right by her cat had been the objective, so.

"Going to say something?" Jamie asks.

"Oh, right. Yes. *Farvel og Tak, kære Pølse*," she says solemnly. Farewell and thank you, dear Pølse. Then she can't help but add, "You were a grumpy old thing, but we loved you and I know you loved us really."

Something suddenly catches in the space between the back of her mouth and nose. It makes her eyes start to sting and in the shock of it, Anna doesn't quite know what to do. Before she knows it tears have welled in her eyes and one spills over, to roll down her cheek.

"Anna?" Jamie asks from her side, but stunned at her own body, she cannot look at him or answer him. Instead, her head fills with images of herself and Mads and Vivi and Pølse in their house and memories of them together, the good times they had. How she misses them, so very much. How there are times when she simply cannot understand that they do not exist anymore, when they had had such a presence in her life. How there are times when she'll catch a white-haired glimpse of someone and think it's one of them, or even a cat laying on a wall in London and she'll think of her own lazy boy. And now they lie here, in another land, slowly fading in her memories. She feels herself shudder at the concept of forgetting them completely, now she's away from them, and at that a fully-blown sob escapes her.

It opens a dam and before she knows it she's holding onto her sides, bent almost double, wracked with sobs, so deep and out of control they make her shake. This is all too much, being here is too much. Not the grave as such, but the city with all its memories and emotions. She'd known this was a poor decision coming, but what choice did she have?

Gradually, she becomes aware of him, as he moves behind her and, wrapping his arms around her, raises her back up from her stoop. The sobs slowly morph to weeping, but they continue as he turns her to hold her properly, tight and safe, and simply lets her cry herself out. He doesn't say a word, or make any sounds, refusing to lull her or soothe her, knowing these are things she needs to do for herself, as he gives her the space she needs to mourn them all.

Whether they stand for minutes or hours, she has little idea, but eventually, Anna finds herself able to staunch the flow of the tears. She chooses to stay right where she is, though, tucked under his chin, wrapped in his woody-leathery scent, hidden from the world. And it seems Jamie is in no hurry to move, waiting for her to make hers first. She swears if anyone takes a photo of this, she'll hunt them down, with a bat.

"Got a tissue?" she finally asks, her voice rather claggy from the tears and the rasping of the sobbing. Her face feels sticky and hot, and no doubt she'll look blotchy and rough. Pulling away just a little, she sees her face has left a mess on his coat. Ah, crap. In an effort to disguise it, she wipes her hand over it, but makes it worse. The dry cleaning is definitely going to be on her.

Slowly he moves them apart, and having checked she's steady on her feet, he delves in his backpack for a pack of tissues.

"Sorry. I should have had these ready in my pocket," he says, his voice unexpectedly gruff. Rising, he pulls a tissue out of a packet, and after a beat where she thinks he'll hand it to her, instead chucks her chin and gently wipes her eyes, without a word. Then he hands it to her and with a small thank you, Anna blows her nose, which, of course, is as loud as a clown horn. Doesn't matter, though; it's not as if she has any dignity left anyway.

"What's in there?" she asks, pointing at the bag, seeking

some distraction. She doesn't look at him, though, fearing that seeing any pity will set her off again.

"I brought a libation," he says simply. "I don't know if you want to—"

"Yes." She needs something else to focus on, while she pulls it together.

Jamie pulls out two plastic cups then a can of Tuborg Julebryg, the Christmas beer.

She holds the cups as he pours, and hands him his. "Pølse," Jamie says, sounding duly morose, "I never knew you, much to my loss I'm sure, but I wish you well in your onward journey." Anna emits a sniff, but has control now.

Jamie pours some of the beer onto the grave. It makes her smile. A small smile, but a welcome one.

"Godspeed, Pølse," she says, and does the same, feeling joyously ridiculous. Then she turns to him, to clink their plastics, toasting the grumpy cat, and they drink. She can't help smiling at him, a sad, watery smile.

"Better?" he asks gently.

And she nods, because as much as she feels exhausted and fragile, she also feels like this was cathartic. It was so unexpected. Would this have also happened, she wonders, if she hadn't been interrupted the other day? Would she have broken here, alone in the snowstorm? What she does know, with absolute certainty, is that she's glad Jamie was here to hold her up.

Chapter Fourteen

Jamie has further plans to stay out. Much as she's inclined to go home, curl up and sleep as one does after a big cry, the house suddenly feels too raw a place to be. She'll be seeing Pølse's beloved sunspots and imagining Vivi and Mads' voices telling him what a lovely creature he is, to his purring agreement. Plus, she's feeling too fragile to protest. There's an element of self-preservation in simply letting Jamie make the decisions today. It leaves her free to focus on herself a little, and bring herself back from her graveside breakdown. A weight's definitely been lifted from her there though, or else it's the rest of the 5.6 per cent beer that they've finished off as they walked through Holmens.

Kindly taking control of the conversation, Jamie tells her about the first time he walked through the cemetery during the summer and was surprised to see people of all ages on picnic blankets, using the area as a park, drinks and all. She'd not quite considered that that might look strange to others, but she'd spent many a summer evening chilling with friends or a weekend afternoon reading a book amid the graves. Totally accepted and normal. She suggests he heads up to Bispebjerg Cemetery in May, for their cherry-blossom festival.

"It's beautiful," she says, "almost Japan," which makes him chuckle. It's the first chuckle she's had from him, and it raises her spirits.

"Lunch!" Jamie states, pointing in the direction of Nørrebro. She's not saying no to that. Her stomach is rumbling under the down of her big coat.

It's still a good fifty-minute walk to where he has planned, but the route is pretty, especially with the snow. Walking side by side, close but not quite touching, they meander through Østre Anlæg, the park created from the city's old fortifications, complete with a flooded moat, the lake now frozen over and glistening in the early afternoon sun. They pass the State Museum of Art and the Botanical Garden with its iconic Palm House, Jamie finally steering them to Torvehallerne, two glass food halls blending stalls and eateries. There are cheesemongers, French pâté stalls, a butcher, amid porridge vendors, poke-bowl cafés and many others. Jamie and Anna um and ah whether to go for open sandwiches at one shop, but a Spanish tapas eatery wins out, as Jamie is, it turns out, a sucker for a deep-fried croquette. Minutes later they're installed on two yellow metal barstools by a window, with a plate each of three baguette slices topped with different toppings, a glass of Spanish wine each and a side plate of molten croquettes.

The smoked-salmon-and-mayonnaise-salad-topped slice

doesn't stay on the plate long, with a tuna one following quickly after. The meatballs in tomato sauce actually make her moan aloud.

"OK," says Jamie, "that's clearly your fav—" And then he stops. Anna sips from her wine, waiting, realising just how hungry she was and how the wine is hitting the spot, but his attention is firmly caught by something on the other side of the pane. Anna turns, but whoever it is has walked in through the glass doors just behind her and Jamie is still entranced. Anna turns to the other side to get a proper look.

It's a tall, Nordic blonde woman and a small child. Both are warmly dressed, the little girl in a floral snowsuit and a purple balaclava that rounds her face and rosy cheeks. The woman takes a moment to pull back the head part of the balaclava to become a neck warmer, releasing a wealth of light brown hair. It's as she rights herself that she sees she's being watched, and her focus moves from Anna to Jamie. Her expression then changes from relaxed to very tense. Whatever Anna's sitting in the middle of, it doesn't feel comfortable and she doesn't know what to do. At a loss, she moves her eyes down to the little girl and gives her a smile, which is enthusiastically returned.

"*Hej, Lajla,*" Jamie says. His voice sounds careful and tense. Not the Jamie voice Anna's used to.

"Um… *Hej,*" Lajla responds and Anna looks back up to see her looking about, perhaps for escape.

"How are you?" he asks in English, although Anna is sure he normally ventures the initial pleasantries in his best Danish when he meets friends.

"Fine." Her tone is tight. Anna looks at Jamie for direction, but his attention is now on the little girl.

"*Hej,*" he says to her, a big smile on his face, and again the little girl smiles back. Is it Anna's imagination or is Lajla moving between them?

Jamie snaps his attention back to Lajla. "This is my girlfriend," he introduces Anna. It comes out oddly, not natural, but then she supposes that as a fake couple, it would. The way he drops his hand on top of hers across the table is clumsy, too. Jamie is clearly out of sorts here. He was much smoother with his colleagues, but she knows a "we're on" sign when she's being given it. Knowing her role, she holds out her other hand to Lajla.

"Anna," she says, in the way Danes do.

Seeing scant option, Lajla shakes her hand and gives her name, too. There's no smile coming back at Anna, but there's less of an edge to her expression.

"I have to go," she says quickly. "I'm meeting friends." Anna suspects this isn't true, and she notes Lajla only refers to herself, as if her daughter isn't there.

"Good to see you both," Jamie says, but Lajla just nods and draws the girl away by her hand.

Jamie looks back out of the window and takes a long swig of his wine. Anna simply observes him, waiting for an explanation as to what that was, but as she does so, sees Lajla and her daughter leave again from one of the side doors behind Jamie's back. Weird.

The little girl looks back at the food hall as they go and Anna can't help thinking there is something about her that's familiar.

Jamie takes another of the croquettes, and then another.

"You really like those," she says, for want of something to say.

"Comfort food," he mumbles. Clearly something about the exchange has made him need it. And something about *that* gives Anna a clue.

She hazards a guess. "Was that who we're fake dating for?"

He looks down at the table. "Aye. It took me by surprise. It was a bit—"

"Clunky?"

He gives her a wry smile.

"Can we talk about it? I'd like to understand."

Jamie's face says there's a million other things he'd far prefer to talk about, but she knows she has some credit here, having told him more about Carl last night.

"Come on," she coaxes. "You might feel better, and I can definitely fake-girlfriend better if I know what I'm dealing with." Lajla and Jamie would make a striking couple. Anna needs all the ammo she can get.

He still doesn't look convinced.

"I can see why she caught your eye, Jamie. She's gorgeous." Anna doesn't know why she feels the need to say this, although it's true, Lajla had something almost regal about her, the way she held herself and just her put-togetherness. Anna can't remember when she last felt she looked put together, her life seems far more like random things thrown at each other in the hope something will stick.

He nods his head from side to side, "Aye, she's *something*." He pauses, then makes a decision.

"I met her in Edinburgh; she was over for a week-long conference, and we hit it off. At least, I thought we did. We spent the entire time together," he goes on after another sip of wine, "obviously hiding that there was anything going on. I guess the subterfuge was fun, but I think I got wrapped up in her attention. I mean, she was totally out of my league; she was a super-confident professional during the day and in the evenings, she simply took control and ... I dunno, when I look back at it now, I was like a puppy. She took the lead, and I happily went along."

Considering the aloofness Anna's experienced, she cannot imagine Puppy-Jamie. But then, what she's been through with Carl has totally changed her, too; she's wiser now, more guarded and uninterested in another relationship. There's no way she'd take that risk again or trust like that again. And she didn't know there were leagues above the one Jamie's in...

"After the conference she ghosted me. Which, if you haven't experienced it before, is truly shite." Anna thinks for a moment that he could be making a point about her blocking Carl, but decides not. He's too lost in the memory of what was clearly a painful experience. "But coincidentally, I was headhunted off the back of the conference by a company in Copenhagen. I ... I sort of took it as a sign. I was ready for a change, too, and so I accepted."

He shifts his eyes back to Anna. "I see, with hindsight, it could look dodgy. Stalkerish," he mutters the word, ashamed. "I *do* get that, but I thought she and I clicked. So, when I'd settled in, I thought I'd see if it was worth a shot. Fortune favours the brave and all that. I waited outside her work, to surprise her." The more he tells, the more Anna can see he's cringing at his own actions. And rightly so. If Lajla had cut ties with him then he should have taken it as the No it was. But Anna gets why being ghosted screwed with his head.

"And I succeeded," he goes on, after another sip of wine. "I properly surprised her. And she was really pissed off with me. Told me she didn't want me, she didn't want to speak to me or see me and I should leave. She said we were just a conference fling and that I'd read far too much into it. Which obviously I had, and I won't make that mistake again."

The expression on his face leaves no doubt of whether that had hurt.

"Why didn't she want more? I mean, you're a catch, Jamie. You're smart, solvent, kind and … you know," Anna waves a hand in the direction of his face and physique because it bears saying, "you. So, I don't get it."

His face reddens even more. If he didn't look so pained, she would have been loving being able to do this to him.

"Oh, come on," she says with a smile. "You know you're fit. Don't get bashful on me now."

Jamie drinks from his glass and once he's swallowed, the bob of his Adam's apple slightly mesmerising Anna, he says, "It's not that. It's embarrassment. About the coming here. I just got things wrong. I misread things, which is completely on me. But like I said, I love it here and my job, so don't want to leave, even though she'd prefer me to."

"And you didn't know she had a kid?" Anna asks. "Oh my God, is she married?" If that's the case, then Anna has even more understanding of where he's at.

It takes Jamie a moment to answer before he says, "I didn't know. To be fair, I never asked. Anyways," he says, sitting up straight from his gradual slouch, "I couldn't leave the job I'd just started, or rather I didn't want to, nor should I have to. I'd like to speak to her, have things out for my own peace of mind, but she won't. So, I'm hoping meeting you might make her feel more open to the idea. See? *You* might not need closure with Carl, but I would prefer some with Lajla."

At that he drains the rest of his glass.

"Let's finish up here and head into town," he says, drawing a line under the conversation. "Let's see the lights. Maybe we'll see some more of my friends-slash-probably-your-relatives."

He's clearly in need of distraction, and having just had his support in the cemetery, who is Anna to say no to that?

Chapter Fifteen

"Your ears look cold," he says, leaning against the shop window. This seems to have been deemed a foodie day, as having walked through the shopping streets, Jamie has steered them to Conditori La Glace, the generations-old cake shop. Behind the glass, there's a range of decadent gateaux, Christmas cakes and cookies. There are a host of *nisser* positioned around the cakes, the little Christmas elves making the entire window look very festive. Not that passers-by can really appreciate it as the queue to get in is long and thick. Anna had suggested they go to A.C. Perch's instead for the afternoon tea, but it seems Jamie's heart is set on hot chocolate, which La Glace will serve him bottomlessly, and A.C. Perch's won't. To convince her, Jamie actually pouts, which makes Anna laugh, seeing the young boy in him.

Then he rubs the top of her one ear between his forefinger and thumb. "They're freezing, Anna. Where's your hat?"

"Yeah, I'm not wearing it anymore. At least not here." She'd stuffed it in her pocket as they got further into the city.

"Why? You're cold."

"Why do you think? Everyone will know it's us. In the pictures."

"So what?"

She has to think about this, because it technically isn't a problem; Carl knows she's here. The damage is done. And it is helping Jamie's cause, but that doesn't mean she wants to become the poster girl for the city. The hurt is still there.

"If I wear the hat, then my life suddenly becomes Where's Holger? You know how social media works." He looks confused and she explains the reference.

"Oh! You mean *Where's Wally*?"

"Huh. OK." She hasn't seen the English version before. "But my point still stands."

"Come on, give the world a little fun."

"Nope." She shakes her head, shifting forward as a group of four ahead of them are shown in. She can smell the coffee inside, tantalising on the cold air. The light is beginning to fade now. The day is short as they approach the winter equinox, but the lights suspended across the street, boughs of fir, with a big red heart illuminated in the middle, now come into their own.

The move brings them to a new window and an array of more cakes.

"Which one have you got your eye on?" he asks, and she can almost hear him salivating. He might be buff and fit, but Jamie has a sweet tooth. He's happy to put away his fair share of treats. She likes that.

"Othello cake for me," she states, looking at the macaroon-based cake, with layers of custard and thin vanilla sponge, topped with chocolate icing, with a marzipan collar. "Or maybe a Karen Blixen." The cake with its coffee mousse and mocha truffle with roasted hazelnuts, all on a chocolate sponge base, looks to die for. Now she's in a dilemma.

He leans in to look closer at the window, too, his body alongside hers. Anna doesn't move away. In fact, she might lean a fraction closer in. Well, like he said, her ears are cold...

"I think I'm having the *Sportskage*, simply because "Sports Cake" feels like an oxymoron. Whoever called it that was having a laugh."

At last, it's their turn to be seated, and they are led into the vintage room, with its dark wood furniture, green upholstery and pink walls. Anna is sure it's looked the same since it opened in 1870. Jamie, behind her, places his hand on her shoulder as they steer through the room.

"*Hej*, Anna," someone says as they pass a table, and she draws up short. The couple at the table are Carl's colleagues. They've been guests in Anna's house for dinner many times, and Anna realises there's a whole extra layer of people she hadn't even thought of, on her list of people she wants to avoid.

"Rasmus, Mette, *hej*," she says weakly as the couple gaze up at her, then to Jamie and back to her.

"It's been a while," Mette says with a smile, then it fades

as she remembers why. Maybe she doesn't know the ins and outs of what happened, but she knows about the split.

"*Ja*," agrees Anna with a flat smile. She suddenly imagines them gossiping between themselves as to why Carl moved out. It's the same image she's played many many times in her head, with various permutations of friend groups, all speculating at first then getting wind of the truth – or Carl's version of it – and discussing that, too. The pain in her chest from eighteen months ago is suddenly back. It's just the tight cringing pain, though – it isn't the additional debilitating ache of heartbreak, which came with missing and longing. She definitely doesn't long for Carl anymore. So, this is pure shame and humiliation. Is that progress?

"*Hej*. Jamie," she hears him say next to her, and sees him stretch out his hand to Rasmus and Mette, who introduce themselves in return. Anna sees what he's doing and leans into him. Well, it's more of a slow slump, but the effect is enough for Mette, who is now looking at Jamie with renewed interest.

Right, thinks Anna, let's do this. She slides her hand into Jamie's. He gives a light squeeze to confirm they're "on".

"It was good to see you," she says, summoning up a big smile, "*God Jul*." Turning, she beams at Jamie. "Shall we sit, *skat*?" It's been a long time since she's called anyone her treasure.

In her head, they'll now walk away into the back of the café, far away from Rasmus and Mette, but to her dismay, the waitress is standing at a vacant table just on the other side of them, talking distance, in fact. Bugger.

They sit and unpeel themselves from their many layers.

"OK?" Jamie says under the guise of wedging coats onto a spare seat.

"Carl's colleagues," she fills him in.

"Excellent," says Jamie. There is something in his expression, something new. Mischief? He offers his hands to her across the table, palms up. Looking at him, she sees he's gazing lovingly at her. *Right.* She places her hands in his and he clasps them, running both his thumbs over her skin.

"All right?" he asks, still doing the gazing thing.

"Sure," she says. His hands are warm and just that right blend of soft but worn enough to have seen some graft.

"I think they need something to talk about when they report back to Carl."

It makes Anna gulp.

It makes Jamie grin. It is quite … devastating.

"Trust me?" he clarifies and all she can do is nod.

The waitress comes and takes their order, and as she leaves, Jamie moves his chair around to sit closer to Anna. They have their backs to Rasmus and Mette but are perfectly in their eyeline.

Jamie is back to looking at her and Anna chooses to bask in it. Why not? She lifts her chin to meet his gaze, affording Rasmus and Mette a perfect view of their profiles.

He tucks a lock of hair behind her ear, then trails his fingertips back down to her jaw and along to her chin, all the while Anna feeling the heat rise in her skin to his touch and also between her thighs. She sees his pupils widen. Bloody hell, how does he do that on command? She'll have to ask him later, but in the meantime, she focuses on softening her gaze at him. It isn't hard. It comes quite naturally, in fact. Maybe she's a better actress than she thinks, too.

He tips her chin up even more, his eyes releasing hers and gliding down her face to her lips. Her eyes immediately follow suit to his.

They are good lips, she thinks and not for the first time. Neither too wide nor too thin, plump but not rubbery, just right. And right now they make for a fabulous all-in smile. Nothing measly there.

"Hold on tight," he whispers to her, which makes heat shoot up through her body.

And then, fingertips at her chin, he settles his lips on hers, and she's right back to Tivoli again; the scent of his skin wrapping around her own face, the soft notes of cedar, patchouli and leather; the warmth of his breath mingling with hers; the softness of his lips; the teasing of the tip of his tongue as he spreads her lips, and they begin a light but short dance. He pulls away far too soon, but it's enough to leave her feeling quite heady and she has to tear her eyes away from his mouth.

"Anna?" he asks, under his breath, as he gives her hair a light stroke.

"Ooof" is all she can manage at first, then blushes for being such a doofus. She remembers they're on show and leans her head onto his shoulder.

"Too much?" he asks, wary. Not enough, she thinks. "I decided there's probably some café etiquette to follow," he says into her hair, before giving the top of her head an additional kiss.

He probably has a point. If that had gone much further, she might have crawled into his lap and that would never do. She would hate to be blacklisted from La Glace, even if she doesn't live here anymore. That would make her soul sad.

Not living here brings her thoughts back to that thing he said, about her being homesick. She doesn't think that can be true. She's engaging with London life. OK, so making new friends is tricky when you work by yourself, but that's more loneliness than homesickness. No, she spends a lot of her week seeking out new spots in London to write about; sights, venues and places to eat. She has places who invite her to come now. She's engaged with *them*. She doesn't think she was pining for Copenhagen. What would make him say that? So, maybe her shopping included a regular stop in at ScandiKitchen, the Scandinavian grocer, but that's just including food she's used to in her diet. And perhaps her apartment is decorated with Scandi things, things she'd scoured Etsy and second-hand stores for, but that's simply about taste and it's completely normal for hers to have been shaped by her years living in Denmark. She has plenty of other souvenirs from her travels about the apartment, perhaps just not as prominently on display. And the Danish news apps she has on her phone are just there to keep her informed if anything bad happens in the city, so she can check her friends are OK. Everyone does that, she's sure. Jamie most likely has a Scottish news app or maybe even the shipping forecast on his phone for exactly the same reason. She'll ask him at some point, but for now she's quite sure he's off the point with that observation.

Their drinks and cakes arrive, and Jamie lets out a deep groan of pleasure. That, in and of itself, does things to her. It's such an intimate sound, and she knows exactly what he'll sound like in bed. His serving of Sports Cake is a big slice of white decadence, with the whipped cream covering layers of crushed nougat and caramel choux buns to garnish. In stark contrast, Anna switched at the last second to a Lucky You cake. It's a base of pumpkin meringue, mascarpone, caramelised and salted pumpkin seeds with a chocolate mousse on top, filled with raspberries, covered with chocolate ganache, decorated with more pumpkin seeds, which, frankly she'd like to plant her face in, it looks so good. Instead, and keen to take some lead in their ruse for Rasmus and Mette, she scoops a forkful and feeds it to Jamie. He gets no say in this, but he's invested in the game – or simply the cake – so doesn't protest.

"'S'amazing," he groans again, savouring his mouthful. "You're not hoping for me to share mine, are you?"

Anna pouts. "Not even for our audience?"

Jamie pouts right back and they both laugh.

"I could do the *When Harry Met Sally* reaction," she suggests.

Jamie's eyes bug a little at that, which makes her laugh more.

"Tempting to watch, but maybe too much," he replies, but he does feed her some. A smaller morsel than she fed him, and not as willingly. It's the first time he's been anything less than generous, and Anna feels she's learned something about Jamie and his catnip.

The hot chocolate clearly meets his approval, too, and

Anna wonders whether La Glace have really thought carefully about their free refills policy. He finishes his cupful quickly and Anna's delighted to see the chocolate moustache it's left. Emboldened, she reaches a hand to his face, cups his jaw and then wipes the chocolate away with her thumb. Jamie's eyes glaze as she does so, and then in a move that seems to come from nowhere, she draws her hand back and gives the tip of her thumb a slow suck.

She gives him a loud, long, "Mmmm," for good measure.

Jamie is still gazing at her, his mouth fractionally parted. She does believe she's left him speechless.

"*Vi ses*, you two," says a voice from behind them. Rasmus and Mette are leaving, and Anna watches as Mette gives Jamie a proper check-over, garnering as many facts as she can to make her report. Well, check away, Mette, love. Fill your boots.

"*Hej igen*," says Anna, with the biggest smile she can fit on her face, "*og God Jul.*"

The couple depart and Anna feels both she and Jamie relax, though neither of them moves away. In fact, they stay close to each other for the rest of the cake and the four cups of hot chocolate Jamie manages through the next cosy hour, where they chat amiably about all and nothing, looking to all and sundry like a firmly established couple.

Chapter Sixteen

K ongens Nytorv is buzzing. A large square, between the end of Strøget, the world's longest shopping street and the top of Nyhavn, it's surrounded by baroque-style embassies, hotels, a theatre and a department store. Currently, the square is filled with Krinsen, the enormous circular loop of an ice-rink, which Jamie and Anna have already passed a couple of times in their excursions. It's milling with skaters and surrounded by Christmas market stalls. Not being tourists, they're smart and buy their *gløgg* just off the main drag; it's better and it's cheaper.

"You need to do a *gløgg* guide, Anna. Tourists need to know about spots like this," he says, having taken a sip.

"Krinsen?" she asks, nodding at the ice-rink. "Pretty sure all tourists will know about that."

"No, the secret *gløgg* sellers, the top tips for not paying quite so much in an expensive city. An article on the website." Maybe something for next winter, she thinks, then parks it. It'll take far more in-situ research and she isn't going to be here to do it.

"Right. Time for selfies," Jamie says, turning 360 degrees to look about them and taking her with him. He comes to a stop with Hotel D'Angleterre behind them, which has been draped in a curtain of tiny white lights, above a Christmas tree of lights on its front balcony.

"Let's cause a stir," he says, that look of mischief back on his face. It's like she's seeing the younger Jamie. Of course, this mischief could also simply be him high on cake and chocolate. "Put your hat on," he says.

"Stop it, MacDonald."

"Get it on, Lundholm, let's see if anyone notices."

Anna is sure someone will.

"It's good for tourism," he tries.

"You're supposed to be against that."

"Nope, my job is to *harness* it for the climate cause."

He sticks his hand into her pocket and finds the hat, which he hamfistedly pulls over her head. Sure it will look appalling, she slaps his hands away and takes it off again to redo it. She does this all with an air of annoyance, but there's something about the idea of a selfie with him that she likes.

Hat donned, she stands in front of him, her back to his chest. Jamie slings one arm around her collarbone and pulls her in, before holding up his phone with the other hand. Anna can see both of their grinning faces in the screen and feels a warmth that isn't just their close proximity.

A couple of young women nearby have noticed them.

Anna can see they've made the connection, but it seems best to ignore them.

"One more, smile, Anna," he says, and she looks up at the phone again and gives it her best.

"Perfect," he says, without even looking at it.

Anna is about to remove the hat when one of the women comes across. "You're the Tivoli Couple, aren't you?"

Jamie says "Yes," before Anna can come up with something else. At least they didn't mention the bikini.

The woman turns to her friend. "See? I said it was." Then back to Anna she asks, "Can we take a picture?"

Having her photo taken with Jamie for a selfie is one thing, but Anna doesn't feel happy about having her face saved in someone else's camera.

"Not sure about this, Jamie," she says quietly. "I don't want my face plastered everywhere."

Jamie thinks about it for a second. "I've got this." He takes her *gløgg* and places both cups by their feet.

He looks at the woman. "Ready?"

Before Anna knows what's happening, he swings her around and dips her, so she's side-on to the hotel and its lights and... Oh, her lips are connected to his. What with the whirling and the surprise dip, it takes her a moment to get a fix on things, unlike her lips it seems, which are well ahead of her and engaged with Jamie's, as per earlier. Some things simply come naturally apparently.

"*Tusind tak*," says the woman, and Anna is righted to see three other people have taken a photo of them kissing, too. She ducks her head to shield her face.

"Ashamed to be seen with me?" Jamie asks, reuniting

them with their cups before moving them on, towards the lights covering the Magasin du Nord department store. White lights edge every window and the outline of the building.

"Very," she says.

He gets another selfie of them, more discreet this time, and Anna's intrigued by him wanting to record this. Unless he plans to send these to Lajla as proof, these are for him.

Heading home, they take a meandering route through Kongens Have, the royal gardens. They stop at a street vendor to buy more sugar-roasted almonds, but really, it's the smell that seduces them as they're both still stuffed from their cakes. Walking in amiable silence for the first part, they smile at the range of snowmen and the snow angels in the park's blanket of snow.

Anna secretly replays today's kissing in her head. She has, it must be said, very much enjoyed it, in spite of it being fake. It occurs to her that she has perhaps been suffering from lack of physical contact in the last long while. The times she and Jamie have touched? She's been aware of all of them. When he chucked her chin in the cemetery, she felt an incredible pull to lean into it. When he held her hands in La Glace, she didn't want him to let them go. She can only conclude that her skin is craving touch. It might be something to consider once she's back in London; the dating apps maybe, to find someone. Not a relationship, absolutely not, not again, but something casual, to meet that need.

Either way, she's grateful Jamie's reminded her she can still feel this. "Airdrop me those selfies at some point, yes?"

"Of course," he says, and she can't tell if he's pleased by the request.

"That kiss at D'Angleterre?" she asks. "Lajla wasn't around. Or are you hoping to go viral again and she'll see it?"

"That hadn't really occurred to me, to be honest. It was more that the woman wanted a pic, and you didn't want your face in it, and as we've already established, kisses mean we can hide our faces, so everyone's happy."

"That's important to you, isn't it?" Anna says, thinking about it. "You like to make things work for people, to fix situations."

"Erm… I dunno. I don't feel I'm succeeding in my job where that's concerned."

"My God, Jamie. Managing climate change is more than a one-man task, don't you think? Cut yourself some slack."

"OK, fair enough. So, yeah, I like people to be happy, sometimes that needs some arranging, or fixing, or small pushes in certain directions. I like to facilitate that. When it works it's satisfying."

It brings to mind his suggesting she talk to Carl and Maiken.

"You do see, though, that not all things can be fixed, right?" she asks, carefully.

"I like a challenge," he says with bravado, clearly in too good a mood for her to bait him with this. "Sometimes people just need to give things a try, even if they think they don't want to."

She's not going to change his mind in this mood, she can

see that. She's about to let it drop when he then says, "Tell me why you chose to run from things."

Bugged, Anna pauses to look at the Kongens Have café, closed now, the snow-topped tables and chairs empty. It buzzes with people in the summer. Right now, however, there's only a couple of robins hopping around.

"Why do you keep saying I run from things?"

"Don't you?"

"Not in the way I see it."

"Ahh … a difference of perspective."

"Precisely," she says firmly.

Jamie simply presses his lips together and nods in a "well, you could put it like that if you really want to, but the rest of the world might not agree" kind of way. Rude.

Anna tries to stand taller than she is.

"Jamie, if you're being burned by a fire, do you, a) stay put, or b) move away?"

"Obviously I would move away."

"There," she says, victorious.

"I might however return to douse the fire," he says, "and stay around to examine how the fire got lit and find the answers. I might discuss with people what led to it, what can be salvaged, what lessons can be learned?"

Anna's face pulls together, indignant, which makes him smirk. "Not the perspective you wanted?"

She starts walking again. "So maybe that was the wrong example. If someone punches you in the face, in front of all your friends and they all laugh at you, do you hang around?"

Jamie's brow rises at that.

"OK," Anna adjusts, "I'll admit such a person would have to be very tall to do that to you, but imagine the pain and then the humiliation. *That.* Do you hang around to see what you can learn? No, you move aside, sensibly, to check your bruises, and administer some self-care, and try to forget about the person who punched you unexpectedly and without reason."

"So, no lessons to be learned?"

Anna laughs wryly. "Of course. Don't trust anyone ever again. Not with your heart, at least."

Jamie's smile drops at that. "That's really what you've taken from this? To never venture your heart again?"

"Well, duh," Anna says. "I'm not a complete idiot. You get burned once, you don't stand near the fire again." She's back to the fire thing.

Jamie shakes his head, wraps an arm around her shoulder and propels her along. "Lundholm, that is so sad. You should still stand by the fire. It warms you."

"No thanks. I'll wear an extra jumper instead," she says, distracted by that arm. They aren't on show, so he needn't. Not that she minds, actually.

"Not as exciting," he says.

"It can be plenty exciting," she insists. "I've removed myself from the danger and now I can navigate the world without fear of further pain."

"Lonely."

"No. I have friends." Suddenly Anna feels the need to convince him. She doesn't want him thinking of her as a saddo loner. Not that it really matters as she'll be out of his life soon enough, but she'd still rather he didn't think of her that way for some reason. "Jamie, I grew up in the same way. As soon as my mother became uncomfortable for whatever reason somewhere, we upped and left. She ... *we* saw it as a freedom. We just packed up and found somewhere new and exciting."

Now, if Anna is being truly honest about this, then this description would be quite off centre. She had not, in fact, seen it as a freedom, more an annoyance every time Ida suddenly announced they were off. But the fact was that they *could* up and leave, which is what she's trying to get across to him now. Nor was everywhere Ida took her exciting. Some places were godawful and she'd been pleased when they moved on again – but *again*, they had, and had exercised, the option to move on. That was a privilege. And Ida could become uncomfortable at many things; a disagreeable neighbour, unreliable plumbing, a shoplifting accusation on the one occasion (Ida, not Anna), but often, in fact mostly, it was down to a man.

Ida was quite free with those, too. In hindsight Anna had to admit Ida had both good taste and good fortune; the men she'd got to know had all been decent. To both of them. And yet, every time, when it felt like there was a chance they might settle into something more permanent, Ida suddenly felt the need to see somewhere else, to spread her wings again, saying, "Pack your bags, Anna, the world is calling." Anna wished many times that it wouldn't. Couldn't the world just leave a message, and they'd get back to it later?

When she looks at it like that, she sees a disjointed childhood tied to the churlish whims of a flighty mother –

and she's surprised it took her as long as it did to summon the courage to ask her grandparents if she could stay with them. But then hindsight is a bitch, isn't it?

"And it didn't bother you?"

"No," she lies. "Like I said, it was exciting. New places, new people."

"For a little kid? Sounds like it would have been a nightmare placing roots."

"No, I had roots here with my grandparents, who we visited regularly. And it made me really good at making friends quickly. And when I needed more permanent schooling, I stayed put in Copenhagen."

"Which you didn't leave again when you could." Anna opens her mouth to contest this, given she literally lives in another country now, but he holds up a hand. "Until now. You didn't carry on these exciting travels as soon as you were out of school."

"I moved to Jutland for uni."

"Doesn't count, it's still Denmark and you came back."

"My grandparents were really old, so they liked the help." Morfar was absolutely the sprightliest old man you could imagine, and Mormor would still cycle everywhere even in spite of the cancer. But Jamie does not need to know this. He doesn't need to know how she savoured living in their home, with a room of her own, year on year on year. How she could accumulate things she got to keep, too. Sure, she knows how to travel light, it runs in her blood or at least in her synapses, but she likes to have small tokens around her and collectables, all things her mother's always scoffed at, and on more than one occasion "accidentally" disposed of.

Thinking about it makes Anna's eyebrows draw together. Which Jamie notices. He stops them and places a light finger on the crease between the brows.

"One day, Anna, you might acknowledge that it may not have been quite as idyllic as you're choosing to remember it. If you do, then you should know I'll be happy to listen to you tell me about it as it is, in a way that doesn't make you frown or wear a smile that doesn't reach your eyes."

She feels her jaw drop. He's calling her out on her fibbing, and she is outraged. The un-gentlemanliness of it is astonishing, and yet he does it with such grace she almost – *almost* – feels the compulsion to do what he suggests.

"It's exactly as I'm saying," she grinds out.

Jamie starts walking again, heading in the direction of home. "Sure, you tell yourself that," he casts back at her. "But you can't kid a kidder."

Chapter Seventeen

Anna's still pondering Jamie's words as they near Eckersbergsgade. He's been kidding her? How? Which bits? All of it? The serial killer bit? She really doesn't think so, but women can never really know, can they? The walk has been quiet, perhaps both thinking about each other's words. She feels out of sorts but isn't sure why. And he hasn't replaced his arm around her shoulder. Now they walk separately, hands in pockets.

"Shall I get a bottle of *gløgg* for home?" he asks. Home. She supposes it is home to both of them but in different ways. Something about that, teamed with the way they are walking, makes her feel … melancholic? What is that about?

She casts him a sideways glance as she says she'd rather have tea. His profile is determined as he faces the direction of the house, but she scans the rest of him; his unruly hair that could really do with a hat on it, and the knitted scarf wound around his neck. Her eyes pause at his nape, currently covered by multiple thick layers and she has a raging desire to slide her fingers in and over the skin. Anna gives herself a mental slap. Jamie is her tenant, not someone she should be having lusty ideas about. This day has been a flurry of emotions, she must be exhausted and hence unruly in her thoughts.

He might feel her gazing, as his face flicks to her.

"Look, I didn't mean to upset you. With what I said before," he says, but not fully contrite. More appeasing. "Everyone's entitled to live as they see fit, you and your mother included. If moving whenever you like works for you then … as you wish."

He stops there, but Anna feels he was about to add more.

"But?" she supplies.

"I guess I don't understand it," he says, somewhat unwillingly. He wants to be honest with her, apparently. "I don't talk about it much, but I suppose it might inform my thinking and judgements. My mother left my dad and I, when I was young. I never got to ask her why or have any kind of explanation that made sense to me or allowed me to make things better or prevent her going. So, I think I was judging you when I said you run away. I might still think it's better to face things, and fix them, or at least try to, but if you feel it's better for you to remove yourself, then I guess I should see that that might be valid for you."

"Not quite an acceptance there," Anna notes.

"I can't say I get it, but I can admit to why I don't get it. Does that make sense?"

"Sure." It sloughs off any umbrage she's been carrying. She imagines now a young boy without his mother and with a lonely dad, and it makes sense that he wants some kind of closure for Anna when he's had none, and why he can't see that it might not matter to her.

She saw a Charlie Brown cartoon once where Linus says there's no problem too big or complex that it couldn't be run away from, and while she'll stick by her guns that she isn't running, she'd always understood the message: You can always move on. However, she suspects Jamie would suggest the cartoon was saying you can always bury your head in the sand. Tom-ay-to tom-ah-to.

"Did you ever find out where your mother went?"

Jamie pulls his mouth together, deliberating. Does he trust her? That's what it looks like to Anna. Turns out he does and Anna feels a glow, but only for a fraction of a second, because he says, "When I said she left us, what I should have said was she took her own life." He moves into their front yard without waiting for her reaction.

"I am so sorry, Jamie." It feels so inadequate a response, but it's all she has in the shock.

She gives him the space to pick up the topic, or let it go.

"She was a good mum, but she suffered from depression. Always had," he says, head bowed, as he stands on the doorstep. "And when she fell pregnant when I was nine, she chose to come off her industrial strength anti-depressants without discussing it with my dad, or her doctor. She didn't want the baby affected by the drugs, I think. Anyway, it's all supposition. Gradually, she sank lower and lower, which, being only nine, I thought was due to the pregnancy, and my dad hardly noticed as it was a really busy farming season, and he was rarely home."

She wants to tell him it isn't strange that a little boy wouldn't have been able to spot signs of an illness he probably didn't even know she had. But Jamie seems to be working something through, and instinctively she knows to simply let him.

"One morning, she waited until I had left for school, took a cottage pie out of the freezer to defrost for us, then took herself out to a small copse away from the house where she swaddled herself in a blanket and swallowed a shit-ton of sleeping tablets. I came home, put the pie in the oven, ate it, watched some TV, and eventually went to bed. My dad came in, ate the leftovers, and only when he went to bed realised she wasn't there and woke me. It took a day before we found her and that was only because the dog tracked her."

"Oh, Jamie, that's awful," Anna says, putting her hand on his arm. Not touching him right now feels all kinds of wrong.

His voice sounds thicker. "I never thought to look for her around the house. Maybe I could have run for my dad earlier and we could have found her in time."

"Don't," Anna says, her heart bleeding for the little Jamie. "You were only nine, and nothing looked amiss to you."

"Yeah, logically that makes sense, but I'll always wonder. And while some people were judgemental about her having done this to us, I see that even through her illness, which convinced her we would truly be better off without her and that she should take the baby with her, she still cared enough to take herself away from the house and keep it as a safe space for us. She didn't take a messy route, and above all … she left us the bloody cottage pie, so we'd eat."

Anna simply doesn't know what to say to him. This poor man, caught in the crux of his mother making such a devastating decision and yet still doing so in a way that showed she cared about them. How did you square that?

Instead, she throws her arms around him in the biggest hug she can manage.

"She was ill, Jamie, but she was clearly kind."

He is still for a long time, until she feels him nod against her head.

"She was. But I would give anything to have one minute with her."

"What would you say?"

"I'm tied," he says, clearly having thought about it infinite times before. "Do I use the minute to beg her not to go, or do I use it to make her help me understand her need to remove herself?"

The use of the word *remove* scratches at her, but she lets it. It's nothing in comparison to the pain he's experienced.

"Thank you for telling me, Jamie," she says, releasing him.

He shakes himself and nods towards the door. "I need chocolate. And maybe some cookies. Turns out I crave comfort food when coughing up my past." And as she casts him yet another sideways glance, she senses she might just be the first person he's ever voiced this to.

❄

Anna follows Jamie quietly up the stairs, him with the teapot and mugs, her with the plate of *pebernødder*. She senses he's a little raw from having bared his history, and she wants to give him the space to come back to them. The jigsaw seems the perfect way, and without conversation, they each move around the *hyggekrog* space, lighting the candles, creating a gorgeous glow, both around the room and in the dormer window, the raised sill holding more candles, and Jamie's mementoes. The light from the streetlamp outside shows snow beginning again. The flakes fall leisurely, in time with the piano music Jamie has arranged to play low on the speaker pod. This, Anna thinks, is what he needs; the comfort and low demand to bring him back. Each claiming a throw to wrap around themselves, they sit side by side on the little Hans Wegner sofa, perusing the jigsaw in comfortable silence. Every so often they'll give each other a "Well done" for having placed a piece, or hand each other another, which might work on their respective sides.

Small as the sofa may be, they aren't quite touching, but the space between their thighs is close. Anna can't help looking at it. She senses the warmth that lies there. She wonders what would happen if the space were to close. Would there be sparks? It would be so easy to slide her hand onto his knee, to give him comfort, she tells herself, but really it's because her fingers are twitching to. And the flat of her palm wants to slide slowly across the solidity of his thigh and sense the heat of his skin beneath.

"Ah, shit." Jamie jolts her out of her ruminating and she gives her head a light shake to dispel the thoughts.

The cosiness is doing strange things to her. "We're a piece missing," he says.

Gradually, they've connected all the pieces and just as he says, there is a space just off centre and no corresponding piece.

"Nooo," she says, disappointed, not least because these jigsaws had been her *morfar*'s and he was meticulous in putting things away properly, but also as this was a something she and Jamie were working on together.

"We have the victory," he says. "We completed it. It's enough."

But Anna isn't happy about it. She pushes the throw aside and gets down onto the floor, searching through the pile of the rug. She looks up to see Jamie watching her on her hands and knees, his pupils huge. Putting it down to the low lighting, Anna searches on. Ducking lower, she moves in under the frame of the sofa, its legs raising the seat off the ground enough for her to get in under there.

The light beneath is even worse.

"Jamie? Your phone. Can you shine the torch under here?" She supposes they could just move the sofa away for a better look, but she's down here now and she doesn't want to move him out of his comfiness.

Jamie has other ideas it seems, and in the blink of an eye, he's on the floor next to her, lying on his stomach, like she is. He shines his phone torch about and Anna tries to keep her eyes on the rug pile, her mind on the task. It is hard. His measured breathing is loud in her ear, the closeness of him warming the entire length of her side.

Eventually, she admits defeat, dropping her cheek onto the rug, facing him.

"'S'gone."

Jamie lowers his face to the floor, too, mirroring her. "Doesn't matter, Anna." And in their little den, under the sofa, on top of the shaggy rug, it does suddenly feel like nothing really matters. It's safe and snug and perfect. They gaze at each other in agreement.

His eyes drop to her lips and she can't help but follow suit. And from there, there is only a synchronised tilt of their bodies, for their faces to come even closer and their lips to touch.

It's a light kiss – really just a long, slow touch, a sharing of breath almost, no parting of lips, no advancing, no exploring. A tentative trial, to connect, here in this hidden space, as the rest of the world continues turning, oblivious. The tenderness of it is exquisite, and when Jamie pulls back, it takes Anna a longer beat to open her eyes, hanging onto the moment.

Neither of them move, but their gazes hold.

"I—" he says, but stops.

"You…?" she prompts lightly.

"I've come to understand I can misread things. Not exterior things, those I'm quite good at, but internal things. Like thoughts, particularly other people's." He looks embarrassed and Anna wishes he didn't because his misreading Lajla sounds like a mix of over-enthusiasm, lust and hope, which to her feels simply human. "So, I prefer people just to say what's on their minds, blunt and to the point. It's one of the things I love about being in Denmark, to be honest, there's so much less pussyfooting about and softening truths when it's the truths you need to hear." She wonders if he felt the same way when Lajla turned him down flat, but opts not to ask.

"I know we're fake-dating, but I find I'm wanting it to be real." He's looking her right in the eye with his declaration and she thinks he's a braver soul than her. "Like right now," he goes on, his voice low, making her want to lean closer in again, but resisting, "I want to touch your face and slide my hand into your hair as I kiss you. But there's no one here to be faking for, it's simply because I want to.

"But I won't press it beyond the faking if you aren't interested. I'm just putting it out there that I'd like to see if this might be something more, because my gut tells me it is."

Anna says nothing. There are so many thoughts that come to her: that she wants to touch his face and thread her fingers through his hair too; that she finds his kisses intoxicating; that rolling into him, under him, would be so easy; that she'd be starting something she knows she can't finish; that he's had enough abrupt endings in his life already; that she's absolutely not risking "something more" ever again... but she can't work out which to put first.

"Ah," he says, his tone somewhere between disappointment and understanding. "It's OK. You don't feel the same. I guess I got that wrong."

"You're not wrong," she says low, but suddenly she can't hold the gaze any longer and her eyes are wanting to look anywhere but at him.

"What?"

Anna shifts, to push herself up onto her knees, away from their cocoon. And still she won't meet his gaze.

"I said, you aren't wrong," she says, feeling that having trusted her with his past, he deserves the truth, but her thoughts are ordering themselves now. She senses his relief, but knows it's to no good. "But it's not something I can pursue, Jamie."

Chapter Eighteen

"And then what happened?" asks an enthralled Katrine across her office desk. Work is soundly being ignored as they drink coffee and work their way through Anna's gift of a *smørstang*, an oblong of yeast pastry, with *remonce crème* and *vaniljecrème*, and alternating circles of white and chocolate icing on top. Anna hadn't realised just how much she'd missed yeast cakes. She pledges to make herself more cakes in the new year. She'll just have to go running more, to compensate.

"Then we had a very awkward Sunday, pottering around the house, with this big awkward thing between us. Totally amicable, but treading on eggshells. He disappeared to the gym for some hours and I spent a lot of the time sorting my storage project."

There had been far more to it. Of course there had.

She'd had to watch the disappointment on his face deepen, and then him rein it in, because he respected her choice and he wasn't the kind of guy to push. Not when he'd fallen foul of that before. It hurt in her chest to watch it play out on his face and see his defences slide back up.

"Just to be clear," he'd said, "you're not interested in more, or it's something else?"

"I'm leaving, Jamie. My staying here isn't on the cards. I don't want to mess with your feelings, so it seems better not to start."

"Shouldn't I be the one worrying about that?"

She shook her head, unwilling to explain further or be budged.

Jamie rolled onto his back with a sigh of resignation. Or frustration. She couldn't quite tell.

"You definitely don't want to?"

"No," she said. It felt like glass shards in her mouth. She crawled back up onto the sofa and he followed.

"Is it going to be difficult between us, now?" she asked.

"I was honest with you, and you gave me an honest answer in return. I'm not going to be a dick just because it wasn't the answer I wanted. We should just move on, back to where we were."

Which is easier said than done, as with the jigsaw made, they sat in stilted conversation for the next quarter of an hour, then made excuses and went to bed. Their separate beds. And Anna had lain awake for hours replaying it and wondering why, having made the right choice for both of them, she felt so grim about it.

"But you like him!" Katrine exclaims, exasperated. Anna hasn't actually said this, but Katrine can easily read between Anna's lines. Yes, she's attracted to him, of course she is; she has eyes and is sentient. And those kisses will be etched in her psyche until she dies. No one could withstand those.

Anna sighs. "Yes, which I told him, but, once again, I am leaving. Which is why I said no. There's no point."

"I dunno," says Katrine. "I've seen the photos. I'd move on that, if I were you."

"I'm sure Rune would be delighted to hear you say that." Katrine's husband is the best of men.

"*If I were you*," reiterates Katrine, unashamed. "If those kisses are anything like they look, you should fill your boots." She looks dainty and prim, but Katrine's filters are sometimes questionable. Anna wonders whether coming into the office, somewhere she really has no call to be, was a good idea, but then, like she's just told Katrine, she and Jamie are now tiptoeing around each other and she felt the need to talk to someone.

"Unfortunately, they are even better on the receiving end," says Anna, sounding glum.

"Then I don't get it. You're leaving. So what? Have at it. You both know the score. No one gets hurt."

Here is where Anna disagrees. As she'd laid there on the floor, she saw she needed to, *had to*, put a cap on any feelings she had for him. She needs to keep the physical attraction she has towards him, and the physical clinches they're having for show, in two very distant boxes. Because what she can see is this: Jamie's had two important women in his life abandon him. His mother leaving him must feel like a rejection of sorts, and Lajla not wanting more with him must, too, even though he hides it well. He had thought it worth moving to her country for, to give it a go, after all. What Anna refuses to do is to allow what they have to become more, and risk that her leaving – her most definite leaving – could feel like another rejection. He's a decent man. He doesn't deserve to be messed about.

It not being her story to tell, Anna abbreviates it for Katrine to just his being hurt badly before and her not wanting to be the inevitable next.

"Benevolent," commends Katrine, "but very boring."

"You just want to live vicariously through me," Anna chides. "Declining is the right thing to do."

Katrine mouths "Boring" at her and eats more of her pastry. There's a pause in the chatter as they scoff and Katrine watches Anna over the top of her coffee cup.

"How about a Once-and-Done? You know, get it out of your systems?" Katrine pitches.

"Behave, Trine. You've been reading your spicy romances again." Anna refuses to let this idea even germinate in her head.

"Are you sure not hurting Jamie is your only reasoning in this?" Katrine asks lightly.

Anna's brow pulls together. "What do you mean? Of course. What else would it be?"

Katrine's expression is one of angelic innocence. "Nothing. Just wondered if it might be something more about you."

"No," Anna instantly says, confused. "I can't see what

that would be. I mean, maybe aside from not hurting someone who has done me a good turn, which I think is plenty, maybe I'm also being practical. Long-distance is a nightmare, I'm not moving back here and Jamie just got here and loves it. So really, no." Anna feels quite adamant about this.

Katrine shrugs with an "OK, *da*." Which doesn't sound like she's convinced, more that she's sensing Anna getting het up. She then spots something on her messy desk, under the cake plate. "Here, small job for you," she says, pulling out a printed email.

"A commission?"

"Yep. Day after tomorrow. Just a quick report, please."

Anna scans it. Rundetårnet, a cylindrical church tower in the middle of the city, with an observatory at the top, is offering stargazing nights. "The sky's set to be clear, so do me a quick write-up, yes? In by end of play the next day, please." Cake break is over, Anna senses, and Katrine has clearly decided that they are agreeing to disagree on Anna's choices about Jamie.

Rundetårnet is somewhere she always suggests tourists go for its views across the city. Stargazing there is new to her, though, and sounds rather … romantic. Eyeing the detail, and then Katrine's vaguely smug face over the top of the page, Anna wonders whether it's coincidence that the invite is for two people.

One of her favourite parts of Eckersbergsgade is the picnic bench in the middle, right outside her house. If it's sunny, there'll often be someone sitting out at it, and other neighbours will join them with a cup of coffee for a quick chat. Or if it's a birthday, they might bring a cake and anyone could appear to congratulate them and share the cake. Currently, the table and seats are under a layer of snow, but as Anna enters the street, she sees that on one end sits a hunched figure she recognises. As she gets closer a smile spreads across her face.

"*Hej*, Anne-Grete," she says. The tiny, ancient woman has cleared just enough space for herself on the end, and now sits, wrapped up, on a plastic bag, so she doesn't get wet. In front of her is a huge cup of coffee and a plate of two cinnamon *gifflar* plus a large gap that suggests it once held several more.

"*Jaaa, jeg syntes nok det var dig*," says her old neighbour and Vivi's best friend. *I thought it was you.* She holds out the plate and offers Anna a cinnamon roll, in exactly the same way she did when Anna was a child. Also like then, Anna does not need asking twice. Scoffing it, in spite of already having a belly full of *smørstang*, she feels extra guilty for not having knocked to say hello, but Anne-Grete doesn't look too cross.

"I was only supposed to be in the city for the day and got snowed in. Jamie is letting me stay."

The old lady's eyes light up at that. "*Han er vel nok en flink ung mand*," she says, to which Anna can only agree, he *is* a nice young man. "*Og et skår*," Anne-Grete adds with a naughty smile, sending Anna into a little coughing fit. She cannot wait to tell Jamie, the octogenarian next door thinks he's hot.

Anne-Grete asks Anna how she is, and she tells her a little about her life in London, making it sound as shiny and exciting as she can.

"And Ida?" she asks of her mother.

"Still moving around. I added a tracker to her phone so I could know where she is," Anna confides.

The old lady chuckles, though Anna doubts she knows what a tracker is.

"*Hun har altid haft ild i rumpen,*" says Anne-Grete. She's always had fire in her bottom is a fairly apt assessment, thinks Anna. "She could never settle as a child," Anne-Grete goes on. "Always a handful for Vivi and Mads."

Anna's well aware that teen-Ida was a challenge to her *mormor* and *morfar*.

Anne-Grete looks at her with a sad expression at the mention of Vivi and Mads, clearly missing them. "They were such good people, gave her such a stable childhood, but it was like she saw it as a prison."

"Yeah, she's not good with permanence," is all Anna can really say to this, unkeen to dwell on her grandparents too much, lest she should burst into tears again. The cemetery incident had really caught her by surprise. And also, because she can't explain why Ida is as she is. She doesn't truly understand it. Anna never saw stability as a prison. She relished living here as a teen, and also as an adult, but then, that was before she saw stability was really just an illusion; Vivi and Mads died, and Carl cheated. She's long concluded you can't see what's beneath stability, what foundations are truly there, and eventually it crumbles. So, maybe Ida is right in her outlook. She shudders at that thought.

"You're cold," says Anne-Grete. "Go in."

Anna bends to give her a hug, feeling how bony and frail the woman has become in the last year and a half.

"Take good care of yourself," she says with genuine affection and a kiss to the cheek. Anne-Grete could have used this moment to delve into what happened with Carl, or harangue her for not visiting, but she hasn't. She's always been kind like that.

Anna, on the other hand, is not above a little gossip and bounds towards her door to tell Jamie that Anne-Grete thinks he's a hottie. It might at least lessen the awkward politeness between them.

Chapter Nineteen

There's a note from Jamie on the table when Anna makes it inside house, saying he'll be back before dinner. She's touched he's inclined to let her know, but gutted she can't tease him immediately.

She tidies the living room and then the kitchen, filling the time. Finally, taking a leaf out of Anne-Grete's book, she makes herself a coffee, grabs a blanket and sits outside on the bench in her front yard, enjoying the afternoon sun on her face and the sounds of the city.

The coffee aroma wends its way up around her nose and she's grateful for it. This, the crisp Copenhagen air, coffee and a warm coat and warm feet, this is what she sees when she envisages her birth city in winter. And she *has* envisaged it. Much as she's decided to relegate the city to her past, shun it for new, Carl-and-Maiken-free pastures, it's impossible to always keep her mind on track. Her heart has some say, too, and every so often an image will appear in her mind's eye of something she's once loved. Or she'll see something Copenhagen-based in her Instagram feed, even though she'd been on an unfollowing spree for all those accounts once she moved. Or someone will tell her they're off to Copenhagen for a long weekend or on business and every instinct will fire to tell them where to visit and what to see, while revelling in her memories of doing exactly what she describes. Now, she has a Word document she offers to email them, to divert the conversation elsewhere.

She closes her eyes and lets the afternoon light drape her face, her chin resting on one hand. She's not meditating, she's never had the patience or self-discipline for that, but she is trying to calm her thoughts, to just be here, in the moment, in her front yard, alone save for a robin who is busying himself around the snow piles. Every so often she'll sip the coffee, but it's an automatic motion, as she focuses on the sounds around her; the chirp of the robin, the hum of a car passing at the end of the street and the scent of snowy air. It brings a light smile to her face.

Her pocket buzzes and Anna pulls out her phone to see a notification from an airline, for their incoming New Year sale. It makes her growl. They should be concentrating on their backlog, by which she means her, not teeing up customers for next year's travel. Prompted, though, she swipes through the site and some others, now on autopilot, after several days of scouring them.

And there, on the last site she tries, is a ticket. They must have had a cancellation. For Christmas Eve. The price is eye-watering, and it is still days off, but it's the only ticket she's seen given the backlog. The cursor blinks impatiently at her. She could forgo food for a couple of days to afford it, she supposes. And turn her heating off, too. The thought of it makes her shudder. It wouldn't be so bad in the summer, but over Christmas, that's a nightmare. But she needs to get home, and she's been checking every day for exactly this, so agreeing with herself she can spend the days huddled under her duvet, living off cheap popcorn, she'll make the sacrifice. She fills in her credit card details and hits confirm. The dial spins in front of her. On and on, nothing happening.

She waits and eventually her patience runs out. She hits refresh and tries again. Only now the ticket is gone, and the plane is sold out.

Anna lets out a yowl of indignation and frustration at having lost out on the ticket she really couldn't afford.

"How is this happening?!" she whines to the robin. But she knows full well. It's Christmas. People are travelling home and back, and there's a backlog from the cancellations and she appears simply to be at the back of the queue.

The last of her coffee has grown cold and she stretches to tip it out into an old plant pot behind her in a corner, half-filled with soil, old autumn leaves and now snow. She gives it a hard look, wondering why she'd left it like that. Searching back through her memory she has some inkling of repotting something indoors the weekend before things went sideways, perhaps Mormor's Swiss cheese plant in the living room? The pot must be its own little biosphere by now, and a sodden mush under the layer of snow on it, save for the small brown hole from the coffee dregs.

Gazing at it, an odd feeling creeps over her, as some memories connect, something about the day things had gone shitwards, something Anna had done in the haze of it all.

The smile slips off her face as she pieces it together and hopes that it isn't, in fact, true. A quick check of her forehead is disappointing; no fever there to be giving her hallucinations. Bugger. Reluctantly, she finds a stick and starts having a drag around in the pot and pulling it up every so often until she finds what she's hoping she won't.

"Fuck," she sighs. "Anna, you idiot."

Full-on recollections pop into her head now and she feels shame fill the rest of her body. She takes a quick squiz out towards the street and the houses that overlook the yard, in case anyone's watching. Satisfied she's unobserved, but feeling very shifty, she lifts the item from the end of the stick. Grubby and wet with coffee, meltwater and eighteen months of plant decay and insect excretions, it's a long chain, attached to a large golden locket.

Mondays were always busy days for Anna and Carl. They tended to front-load the week, so things could wind down towards the weekend, where they could spend time together around the house or away with friends. Anna carefully closed the front door this Monday morning, having spent her Sunday painting it cherry red. The oil-based paint had required her full attention, which was perfect as she needed something to take her mind off missing Pølse. It had been a week since she'd taken him to the vet for the last time and his absence in the house was palpable, which was impressive for a grumpy cat who saw it as his sole purpose in life to lie in a sunspot.

Her Monday job list consisted of a smear test, shopping and picking up Pølse's ashes, before spending the rest of the day at her keyboard, working. Conversely, Carl had virtual meetings all morning, and further live meetings around the city in the afternoon, leaving her peace and quiet to work in. Just one of the many ways they dovetailed beautifully. He saw her off, kissing her at the door, in just his boxers. They were nearing their six-year anniversary, and she had a surprise for him. Tonight, she thought, I'll tell him tonight.

Three streets away, she realised she'd forgotten her purse on the kitchen counter. She needed her health insurance card for the smear test. If she got a wiggle on, she'd have just enough time to double back.

Turning into Eckersbergsgade, she saw a figure walking into her front yard. At first, she thought she'd judged it wrong, but no, there were a couple of planters outside the fence and the figure definitely walked between them. Anna paused, instinct telling her to hang back. Something was odd about this. Unless she was very much mistaken, the figure had been Maiken. Anna knew that dress, long, billowy and apple-green, and Maiken's red hair was striking. But Maiken *knew* she wasn't home this morning. They'd literally just been texting about the joys of smear tests. Wracking her brain as to why her best friend would be dropping in and not at work herself, Anna walked slowly to the house and her shiny front door. Sliding the key in the lock and opening the front door was conducted with cat-like stealth, for reasons she couldn't, or *wouldn't* put a name to. Same for the uncharacteristic light-footedness she had crossing the hall to the bottom of the stairs. She didn't go further. No need.

Maiken's dress, pooled on the second step, her underwear on the fifth and ninth, and his boxers at the top were an initial indicator of what was afoot. The moans from the bedroom were a confirmation. She could hear them groaning each other's names, so that nixed any chance it was random strangers who'd broken in for a shag. She had almost hoped.

What was the etiquette for such a situation? Anna stood immobile, trying to fathom it out. Walk in on them? No. There were things in life you could never unsee, and she knew in her gut this was one to swerve. And besides, she didn't think her legs would agree to go up the stairs. They were barely holding her up.

Another shout of Maiken's name from above snapped her stunned brain into something more like consciousness. *Her best friend.* Had anyone suggested it, Anna would have laughed in their face. And Carl. She trusted him, with everything. Anger started welling in her, starting in her belly and surging up through her like magma. She wasn't going to burst in and cause a scene – after the initial "Gotcha!" she couldn't imagine anyone, by which right now she exclusively meant herself, coming out of it with any salvageable dignity. She needed time to work out how to approach this properly. She'd do her chores and when she came back, she'd have more of a clue what to do.

In the meantime, she wanted them both to know she knew. Let them sweat, let them recognise their guilt.

She lifted the dress between her thumb and forefinger. She'd been with Maiken when she'd bought it, told her how great it looked. Now it disgusted her. She hung it on a coat peg, so they'd know she'd been there. Turning to look up the stairs again, her eye caught on gold lying on the second step, previously hidden by the dress. Maiken's locket and chain. He must have lifted it over her head, before divesting her of the rest of her things, as they stumbled up the stairs; kissing, no doubt, groping each other, fantasising on how to use the next hours while Anna collected her dead cat's ashes. That anger magma whooshed to her head, and reaching for the locket, the rest was a bit of a red mist…

"Anna?"

Down in the cellar, she shouts a hello from the now unlocked store room. It is filled to the gills with all sorts; boxes, her bike, far more garden tools than the minimal back yard warrants, more boxes, skates hanging by their laces from a hook, the flattened boxes her *morfar* had been obsessed with keeping "just in case", which she'd never binned, *just in case*. The entire far wall is racked out with practical shelves, with yet more boxes, of Christmas decorations, which her *mormor* had packed by colour, allowing for a different palate range each year in a three-year rotation, although one box is marked "All Years" and contains the staples; the real candles and their holders for the tree, the Christmas-tree stand, the star, and strings of Danish flags.

Next to these are stacks of jigsaw boxes. Anna looks at them now and wonders why she hadn't donated them somewhere, but in the years after Morfar died there had been very little of his she'd wanted to discard (apart from the interior design, obviously), always coming up with a reason to hang onto them for now. And rightly so, she tells herself, as now might be one of those "just in case" times, when she and Jamie need a new jigsaw. She runs her fingertip down the stack, perusing the little images on the side. There's a particular one she's looking for, one of the first she'd bought her grandfather, one she considers particularly fiendish. It's at the bottom of the middle stack and she whips it out before tucking it under her arm.

All of this, is to pointedly distract herself from the locket, currently swabbed in kitchen roll, next to the lit advent candle on the kitchen counter. Does it count as thieving if you don't keep, give away or sell the thing you take? Does it? Google might have the answer.

She hears Jamie moving around upstairs, and it occurs to her to hide it. Bounding up the stairs, she's too late.

They pause at first, getting a measure of each other and them remembering they are trying not to be awkward. Anna holds up the box, with a "New jigsaw," and Jamie simultaneously holds up a bag, with a "Pastries." And then there's a silence, neither knowing what to do next and neither of them willing to approach eye contact. Anna's brain, however, is playing through an alternate universe, where he's walked in, said hello, waved his pastries at her (not a euphemism), and strode across the room to embrace her with a proper, extensive, hello kiss. She feels her face heat as she realises what she's doing.

"Tea?" she asks, and spins towards the kettle. She wants to look at him, and yet she can't because her thoughts will go rogue. She wants him to look at her, and also not, because she doesn't want him to be disappointed in what he sees. Why does this have to be so hard? Why can't things go back to how they were?

"What's that?" he asks.

"What's what?" But she knows.

Glancing back, she sees him pointing to the kitchen roll shroud. "Something for me? A gift?"

"'Fraid not," she says with a sigh. "Quite the opposite. It's something I've taken. Not from you," she hastens to add.

Alerted to her dismayed tone, Jamie gives her an enquiring head tilt. "Want to talk about it?"

"No," she says, like a teen.

"*Need* to talk about it?" he tries again.

"Probably." She really doesn't know what to do about it.

Jamie sits on the barstool. "Spill." This sounds more like him. This is Jamie in business mode and being something he knows better how to navigate, his guard comes down.

"Remember when Carl came round?"

Jamie gives an unimpressed grunt.

"He said something just before he left about a locket?"

"Aye. Suggested you'd taken it."

"He did. And I vehemently denied having done so?"

"You did."

Her lips purse together, not wanting to say it, but they

lose the battle. "Funny thing. This morning, I found the locket."

"Where?" he asks, surprised. "In your room?"

"In a pot in the yard."

"By the bench?"

"Yep."

"Weird. Who'd put it there? Do you have magpies here? They steal shiny stuff." She can't work out whether he's being kind, giving her an out.

"I'm the magpie," Anna says glumly. "I put it there."

"Why?"

Good question. "Because that's how unhinged I was by him cheating. Because I was angry. Because I was being spiteful. Because I was in a haze of rage. And then in the tornado of throwing Carl out, packing up and my life imploding, I sort of forgot about it, blocked it out of my head, I suppose, and the locket really shows the state I was in, as I really only just remembered it and what had happened and I looked to see if it could be real, and Oh, yes, it absolutely was, and now I have officially stolen something and am a common thief." She puffs out then turns to raise her eyes to him. "Do you think less of me?" For some reason it matters to her.

Jamie takes a moment to think about it. Harsh, but probably due. "If I'm learning anything as I get older," he finally replies, "it's to try not to judge. We all do mad things when we're emotional. Look at me; I moved to another country. That I love it here is a stroke of luck. But your moment of madness is fixable." He catches her eyes widening. "I mean, if you want to. I'm assuming you can give it back? You haven't actually explained who it belongs to."

It's probably time to share more of her story with him.

"It belongs to the woman Carl was having the affair with. Her name is Maiken. I found it here when I discovered what they were doing, I swept it up because I knew how much it meant to her. I dumped it in the pot as I left, not wanting to actually have it on me."

"Did you know her, then?"

"Oh, yes," Anna says with a mirthless laugh. "She was my best friend from school. We were like sisters."

If he's shocked, he hides it well.

"That's a pretty shit discovery," he says, which Anna feels is kind when he could completely have gone with "Bloody hell, your soulmate and your best mate! Double whammy! Sucks to be you." Which is pretty much what her inner critic was telling her for the first months she'd been away. She'd torn herself apart, both with heartbreak and scorn for not having spotted it, seen some signs, or walked in on them before, and above all else for being such a trusting idiot. She's better now, though. Better and never making that mistake again. Some cuts run too deep.

"I remember her calling and leaving messages, but I blocked her. I didn't want her apologies or explanations or anything and like I said, I'd forgotten about the locket almost immediately. She could just as well have been calling about that."

"And your ex?"

"Same. Blocked."

"You can't block him from his home, though?"

"The house is mine. Always was. I walked around town in a haze for some hours, then came back expecting him to have cancelled his meetings so he could grovel, but he wasn't here. He'd stuck with his timetable and gone to work. I didn't know if he was just putting his work above us or hiding from the fallout. I saw red, redder than the already red and called a locksmith. The locks were changed by the end of the afternoon and all his clothes were in two suitcases standing in the front yard waiting for him, along with some boxes of his things. The rest I sent on to his office when I left. Meanwhile I ignored his pounding on the door and his calls. I think the neighbours might have called the police at one point, he'd got so noisy."

"You really didn't talk to him?" She knows this will be important to Jamie; it is after all what he's trying to do with Lajla. But Anna doesn't have anything to defend herself on this, so she doesn't even try.

"Nope. While he shouted for the next many days, I was stuffing my things into the spare room and booking a flight out of the country."

Jamie pauses to drink some of her coffee, deliberating. Anna follows suit, wondering whether he'll ever answer her question of whether he thinks less of her with a straight yes or no. "Can you imagine every time you see a friend, you keep thinking, 'Did you know? Would you have said?' and then every time you go anywhere in the city you think, 'Did they come here together?' The laughs I'd had with them in these places, with Carl romantically and with Maiken as a best friend – were they also going there and having those laughs together? It drives you nuts. So, I packed up and left.

I could lick my wounds in private and start something new elsewhere, where nobody knew me and my life hadn't just been trashed."

The energy courses through her as she tells it – it feels good to get it out. She's only ever given Katrine the topline of what had happened, she'd never talked about the paranoia it had brought into her head. All of which, at the time, had neatly served to plaster over any memory of lifting a necklace and disposing of it on the way out of the door.

"But now I need to work out how to get rid of it."

"By which you mean return it, yes?" His eyebrow is cocked. So much for not judging…

"Of course," she reluctantly agrees. "But without her ever knowing it was me. Obviously."

"So, no apology?"

She coughs a laugh. "She fucked my partner. Don't be ridiculous."

Chapter Twenty

Anna always appreciates the early daylight hours in a city, before it properly wakes up. In Copenhagen the tourist throngs don't really start until ten when the shops open, and the hours before are the domain of commuters, cycling in droves to their places of work with speed and intent, even in the December darkness, an urgent flow that no tourists have any business being part of anyway. Bumbling sightseers cause accidents on the cycle lanes, and there will be sweary shouts at the very least.

It's gone eight-thirty, the winter sun bleeding its pale yellow into the blue. The air's frigid, but fresh. Recent days aside, she's always been an early riser, often venturing out in cities when researching, enjoying the sounds of communities waking up, sniffing at the air which always feels fresher. She's curated tours of dawn activities; watching catches being brought in and auctioned in small fishing ports, seeing flower markets bloom to life or her favourite – the pre-opening bakery tour. This one was born from nostalgia, Morfar having taken her, when she woke stupidly early, along to the baker for the freshly baked bread, treating her to a *rosinbolle*, or a *tebirkes*, for the walk back. A raisin bun or the flat poppy-seeded pastry with *remonce* filling was her favourite way to start the day. When she's not researching, she'll often use the time for a run, like this morning, because it clears her head.

Anna's walked or run around the lakes more times in her life than she can count. Three narrow, manmade lakes, running in a line from Gammel Kongevej to Østerbrogade, forming the western edge of the inner city, they lie just at the end of her road and across Øster Søgade.

Her *mormor* would take her around them when she was little and visiting with Ida. When she moved in with them, she would either walk around them of her own accord, or if Morfar sent her to do so when in a teenage snit. She'd harrumpf out of the house but secretly be pleased with the idea. She'd pop on her headphones and walk the 6.35 km, letting the wind slough off her mood. Just as her grandparents knew it would, because they had done exactly the same at various points in their own lives.

Scanning the edge of the lakes as far as she can see, Anna checks Carl isn't out running, too, then does a quick stretch before starting her route. Guided by today's wind direction, she chooses to run clockwise around, heading towards the planetarium at the far end, to run along Svineryggen, the "swine's back", and then Peblinge Dossering on the far side to cross back over at Fredensgade. She could shorten it at two points, with bridges in between, but feels she needs the longer run. Still, it's always good to have options if she sees someone she doesn't want to see.

She tries to keep her eyes front and centre as she runs, wanting to be focused, but is constantly distracted by familiar sights as she passes; small, mundane things she hasn't thought of in a year and a half, but which are embedded in the tapestry of her memories of this route. A kiosk on a corner, a closed-for-winter pedalo-rental booth, a particular bench she and Maiken would hang around on. Anna pushes the thought of Maiken away, but it simply moves her on to the locket and what she should do with it. Posting it would feel like an admission of guilt. Anna has zero desire to admit any guilt. She imagines Jamie giving her a raised brow. He's really blessed with that brow, she thinks, her feet pounding the shore path. In fact, he's pretty blessed with the entire face.

And just like that her head is filled with him. His height, his hair, his voice, his eyes, his jaw, the stubble on that jaw, his lips, his nose at her ear and his breath on her skin, the warmth of his embrace, the dance of his tongue with hers. Just thinking about all of it brings a smile to her face and heat to her belly, which is stupid, she tells herself, when she's resolved that he is not to be pursued. These thoughts aren't helping her. They won't help her when it comes to leaving. She ups her speed as punishment, hoping it will take her out of these intrusive thoughts. She was supposed to be clearing her head, not compacting it with more thoughts about him. On she runs, counting her footfall just to keep her brain in check, regretting taking the longer route now, as it doesn't seem to be working, storming across the bridge to pound her way back, wondering whether Jamie will be in when she gets there, maybe with tea, perhaps with cake, or at the jigsaw – dammit! Back to the counting…

The sun shines pale against the blue sky, a welcome reminder of what Spring will bring, but the crisp cold of the air says there's a way to go yet. It's beautiful as it shines through the naked trees, casting them in silhouette, highlighted by the snow blanket on the lake shores. The lakes haven't fully frozen this year, not yet at least and not enough for the police to allow skating, but there's enough of an ice layer for the winter birds to have a rink for themselves. The sun also silhouettes the people coming her way, as Anna hasn't had the foresight to bring her sunglasses. Which is why she doesn't at first recognise the blonde woman who passes her, then halts and says her name.

Anna, possibly glad of the excuse, has stopped before she can remember there's a list of friends she's ghosted since she left. Too late now. It's not a friend, though. Shuffling the face and the context around in her head takes a moment, which the woman clearly spots.

"Lajla," she reintroduces herself. "We met the other day." Oh, yes. Her long blonde hair is up today in the loose topknot favoured by so many Copenhageners, but now Anna knows, of course she can see it's her – those high cheekbones are remarkable. She's beautiful. Not quite Ice Queen – tricky when your face is rosy from the chill – but still regal, as Anna had first thought, and she feels like a bumpkin in contrast. The hotch-potch of running clothes foraged from her "leftovers" wardrobe is not helping. Jamie might think he was out of Lajla's league, but Anna disagrees, at least on a visual level. Lajla may be a little older than him, but while Anna and Jamie are being heralded as adorable in their internet pics, he and Lajla would be the stuff of magazines.

"You were with Jamie," Lajla adds somewhat awkwardly. Considering it was Lajla who stopped *her*, not the other way around, it strikes Anna as strange that she comes across as discomfited.

"*Hej*," she says, for some reason wanting to put her at ease. Which is odd, as she should be suspicious. This is the woman who shut Jamie down and now won't talk to him, despite him turning out to be one of the nicest guys Anna knows.

Anna looks about her. "Little girl at nursery?" she asks, assuming Lajla is on her way to work.

Lajla's brow draws in. "No, she's with her *mormor*." It makes Anna smile.

"Lucky her. The best times!"

And that makes Lajla smile. "Of course. She'll be eating lots of *småkager* and never being told no. But it gets me a couple of hours to myself. I have the morning off and some Christmas shopping to do."

Anna nods understanding but can't quite think what to say next. They don't actually know each other, and she doesn't quite think it's her place to ask her about Jamie.

As it turns out, Lajla has that covered.

"I want to ask you. What do you think about Jamie?"

This puts Anna on edge. In Lajla's eyes, she's Jamie's new girlfriend. But given Lajla's his ex, this means they're standing in what could be a catfight. "In what way?" she asks carefully.

"Do you think he's a good man?" That must be one of the weirdest questions. Either she's genuinely asking, in which case Anna thinks Lajla should have made up her own opinion before hooking up with him at that conference, *or* she's sounding Anna out in a "Are you aware that your boyfriend is Satan?" kind of way. Is she warning Anna of something?

Lajla looks away at the lake, deliberating. "He wants to meet with me, to discuss … well, to talk about things, and I have refused. I didn't expect him to show up here. I didn't really expect to ever see him again."

"He has mentioned it," Anna says, partly wanting to prompt her on, but also wanting to show that her relationship with Jamie, *the fake one*, is one where they share things. Like grown-ups, sound and comfortable in their firmly-founded, unrockable relationship. Having been cheated on by Carl, Anna is also finding the concept of Jamie asking to see his ex troubling, when in reality it isn't – Anna has no claim on him. He isn't cheating on her or trying to. Good lord, you'd think she was feeling vaguely jealous. She needs to keep things in those distinct boxes.

"He *is* a good man," she states, determined. She wants to fight Jamie's corner. She owes him and she's agreed to his fake-dating plan. She needs to convince Lajla he isn't interested in her anymore, just like he says. "He's dependable, funny and honest. I adore him." She adds in for good measure, "He adores me, too." OK. She regrets that popping out. It sounds rather twee, but she's on the spot and improv was never her thing.

For some reason this still doesn't make Lajla relax.

"He wants to know Nikoline," Lajla suddenly says and Anna is hit by the feeling she's supposed to know who Nikoline is. Ah yes – because she and Jamie share everything, being grown-ups, etc., etc.

"And you don't think he should?" Anna ventures, hedging her bets.

Looking back to her, Lajla sighs. "I wanted a child. For so long. But the sperm banks are expensive, and I'd already tried three times." These were not words Anna was expecting to hear next, and she's sure she's missed a chapter, but having started to explain, Lajla's words now come tumbling. "And then I met Jamie in Edinburgh. I was there for work. I had read all his papers, and he was the keynote speaker. He's kind of a big deal in city sustainability. I guess I was a bit starstruck." This almost makes Anna laugh, how they both see themselves, but she holds it in. "I mean we were attracted to each other, so it was a fun week, but also…" She trails off, clearly uncomfortable with what she's about to say. Anna feels her eyes are wide. Lajla pulls herself together, standing straighter and almost indignant. "I got lucky. But it was never my intention to trap him in any way. I've never asked him for money or a minute of his time. I was always going to do this on my own. He wasn't supposed to know about it. After all, he lived in Scotland, and I live here. I didn't see there would be any problem." Lajla's stance is supposed to show Anna she doesn't regret her actions and that she stands by them, yet here she is, defending them. But not to Jamie.

Anna thinks of the little girl she saw the other day. The one Jamie couldn't stop staring at. The one with the familiar face. Anna had quickly let go of the thought, distracted by something she can't even remember now, but now it seems oh-so-obvious. Anna is having difficulty recalling what she is supposed to know, and also how she genuinely feels about it, or fake-ly feels about it.

"And then he turns up outside my office some months later, just as I'm about to go on maternity leave. I'd thought it best simply not to reply to his mails. He wanted to surprise me, but he saw my stomach, did the maths and then he really wanted to get together. I said I didn't want that. I hoped he'd go back to Scotland, but now he has a job here."

Her eyes blaze. "He can't take her away from me. I won't let him. I have custody. He's not even on the birth certificate."

Anna suspects Jamie won't be remotely bothered by paperwork or lack thereof. Nikoline is his child, it's as clear as day now. He knew that when they were all in the food halls and he had chosen not to tell Anna. He had chosen to lie. Anna feels anger rising in her, but with all the who-knows-what confusion, she cannot work out if it's indignation at the way Lajla has used Jamie or at the way Jamie has used her.

Chapter Twenty-One

J amie's in the kitchen when she storms through the front door. She'd hoped he wouldn't be. Her plan has been to pack a bag, call Katrine to see if she could stay and then leave him a strongly worded note. It would be so much easier just to walk away from this. Conflict-free. But there he stands in the middle of the kitchen, a mug of coffee in one hand and the pot in the other.

"Coffee?" he asks.

She takes the visual clues, the words drowned out by the roaring fury she's built up in her head. The smile slides off his face as he registers her less than friendly expression.

"What's the matter?"

Normally, Anna would just say "nothing" and vacate the area. She's also a master of the loaded "I'm fine" when Carl had questioned a bad mood. But for some reason, now, Anna lets loose. "You lied to me, Jamie," she fires out. She's been going through it over and over in her head as she stomped home with such vigour that dog walkers actively crossed the street to give her space.

Jamie takes a second cup and pours it full, maintaining eye contact with her. He isn't shying from it, but he'll clearly approach it under his own terms. And some caution. He walks to the table, places the cups and pulls out a chair for her to sit in. After a moment she reluctantly does so, in spite of really wanting to walk out. He calmly sits down next to her but pulls the chair around so he's facing her. By design, he's got them so they're on the same level and without the table between them. She half expects him to mirror her stance, but he chooses not to tightly cross his arms across his chest as she has.

"Do you want to talk me through this?" he says.

Anna shakes her head crossly. "The only thing I want is the truth," she snaps, contradicting herself.

He spreads his fingers, palms up, in a gesture of supplication.

"I bumped into Lajla," she says, "by the lakes. She told me about Nikoline and about the two of you. The *real* story about the two of you. And, being your fake girlfriend, I had to play along like I knew all about it and hide my shock. But the thing that really really annoys me is that you lied to me, and it feels like I'm complicit in something dubious around a single mum and her little kid. It gives me the ick, Jamie. Which I think you knew, hence why you lied in describing the favour you wanted."

Anna thinks about how she had blithely agreed to his plan, suspecting it was the kisses which had befuddled her and grossly minimised her scrutiny skills. She should have asked him far more than she did. Her lips had overridden her critical mind. Her lust had probably thrown sisterhood under the bus, too. She feels shame, and she wants Jamie to bear it, too.

And judging by the redness of his face and his look of dismay, she's achieving something on that front.

"Were you using me to get closer to her so you can take Nikoline from her?" Anna demands. This has sat like a knot in her since Lajla said it. While, until this revelation, Anna would have put money on Jamie having great dad potential, supportive and kind, now she's scared she's been a pawn in something nefarious.

Jamie's jaw drops. "Absolutely not! Is that what she thinks?"

"Yes, Jamie. That's what she thinks."

Jamie tips his head back and blows out a breath. "If she'd just let me talk to her, I could have told her this. I'm not trying to take anything from her. I would never. I'm sure there are legal routes I could have looked at, if that was the case. But I wouldn't."

His face is the same face she's been living with for days. However closely she stares at it, she can't see a glint of malice there. Is she just bad at spotting deceit? She doesn't know and she can't work it out. What dawns on her, though, is that his concern isn't with Anna being angry at him – he seems to accept that – but more about Lajla's fear.

"If anything I want to help her, Anna. Look, we've both seen Nikoline. She's like a mini me. I've no doubt she's mine. I accepted long ago that Lajla doesn't want anything romantic with me, though I was slower on the uptake that she actually never had – which by the way does wonders for a guy's ego, when he'd thought he was a bit of a stud at that conference, and it turned out to be true but on a very different level." He says it to make her laugh, perhaps, but she can see the hurt there. One day, Lajla might do him a favour and point out he had all the attributes she wanted for her donor.

"I digress. I've no feelings for her romantically, but I *do* want to help. I have money to help her. It isn't easy bringing up a kid on your own. I should know, having been that kid. And if one day she'd trust me to help with the childcare, I'd be up for that, too. More than happy. I know it's not childcare when you're a parent, but I recognise that until Lajla says otherwise, it will never be more than that.

"But here's the thing, Anna. I want to help because I want to know my kid. *And* I want my kid to know me. That's it. That's all I'm steering for. Not to encroach on their life, but at least to take some of the weight off and perhaps even enhance it."

That all seems ... perfectly *not* nefarious, Anna thinks, and it takes some of the wind from her sails, but then she remembers; *he lied*.

"You lied to me, Jamie! Why didn't you tell me the truth?" Why can't men be trustworthy?!

His shoulders sink. "I don't know. I got this idea, and I just ran with it. I figured if I told you the Nikoline part you'd say no. And for various reasons I really didn't want you to say no."

Various reasons. She'd be coming back to that.

"You could have told me how Lajla used you."

His blush has only just subsided from last time and now here it is again. But deeper this time.

"Well, firstly, a lot of my knowledge is supposition. When I saw she was pregnant and she wanted me to go, she was quite blunt about my role being over. I don't have more detail to tell you. I've been angry about it, but that gets me nowhere. Lajla isn't going to communicate with me if I'm angry, so I've let that go."

Anna is confused by this concept. She's been angry for over a year and a half and simply letting it go has never been on her option menu.

"So, I really didn't have much to tell you. But more than that, and my aforementioned bruised ego, I suppose I didn't want you to think badly of Lajla. Or Nikoline for that matter. Some people would be judgey of both."

This nearly blows Anna's mind. "So, let me get this straight. Even after Lajla did what she did and then won't speak to you, you're worried about putting her in a bad light?" Anna would have painted Carl as Beelzebub had she had anyone to talk to about him. Had Maiken not been involved, they would have eviscerated his reputation and thrown it all to the wolves. With delight.

He gives her a flat smile. "Pretty much. I don't gain anything by doing otherwise."

Well, you're missing out on some *Schadenfreude* there, Anna thinks, but keeps it to herself.

The sails of her anger are now positively drooping.

He *is* a decent guy. Exactly the guy she told Lajla he was. Her arms seem to uncross themselves and drop to her lap.

"Exactly how do you see this resolving itself, Jamie?"

she asks, tired. Being angry exhausts her. Facing conflict even more so.

"I don't know, Anna. Look, I'm sorry I wasn't honest with you. I think I justified it as being the truth, just the edited truth. I should have given you more info so you could have made an informed decision. I think the kiss had messed with my brain."

I know, right?! Anna thinks. It isn't just her who's frazzled by them.

She tries to keep a plain face in response to his small smile, but it's hard.

Sensing he's still not forgiven, Jamie lays it all out there. "Can you imagine, Anna, what's it's like to find out you have a kid you didn't know about? I've missed her growing in the womb, I missed her birth, and her growing to be a toddler and all the firsts. I … I didn't even know her name until you just said it. Can you imagine being denied getting to know your child, and them you? I always wanted to know my mother better than I did, warts and all. She's part of who I am and without her I grew up feeling there was a large part of my puzzle missing. I don't want that for Nikoline. If she doesn't like me when she's older, she can choose not to see me. Fair enough. But as a little kid, she has a right to know her dad, too, don't you think? Especially as I want to know her. One day she'll ask about me, and it breaks my heart to think she might believe I didn't want to know her. Because I do. Very much. But until Lajla will talk to me, I can't plead my case. I'm stuck. And I saw a chance to maybe loosen a knot there. You gave me a little in and I took it." He holds his hands out, again the palms-up expression, and Anna sees this for what it is; an ideas-man who is out of good ideas and so followed a duff one.

"I get it," she finally says. "I do." She remembers asking Ida about her not having a dad when other children mostly did. Ida had simply said they didn't need one, that they had Morfar, which had satisfied young Anna. She hadn't missed something she'd never had and Morfar had definitely been enough.

"Thank you," Jamie says quietly.

"Please don't lie to me again," Anna adds, "even by omission. I have some trust issues since Carl."

"Of course." He gives her a nod and they seem to have reached an accord. "Can I ask you what happened with Lajla?"

Anna thinks back to the end of their conversation. "Well, I'd already said you were a good guy and how we adored each other, so I chose not to backtrack on that. I don't know what she'll think, but I gave you a good reference. And after she told me how she'd duped you, I couldn't get out of there fast enough."

"Because of the ick," he says, deadpan.

"Absolutely because of the ick."

"Thank you," he says again in a tone of blended gratitude and contrition. This is a side of Jamie she hasn't seen before. The confounded and the resigned. For a man who has ideas, who shakes things up and makes things happen, who seeks to fix things, she can see the millstone around his neck that this is for him. What's more, she feels a deep-seated desire to help him.

Chapter Twenty-Two

In spite of the city's lights, up from the top of Rundetårnet, Jamie and Anna are gazing at the stars.

Regardless of the eggshelly way they are navigating each other around the house, he was very fast in the uptake for this. All signs now suggest Jamie is someone who constantly says yes to life, which makes more sense to her now she knows his backstory.

Having scaled the spiral walkway to the top – designed for a king who preferred not to get out of his carriage – they've been given a tour of the small observatory and each had a look to see the planets visible tonight.

"I've been here many times," says Anna, "but never in with the actual telescope." And she'd never known her Venus from her Mercury. Nor her Saturn or Jupiter, for that matter.

"And how did we get these tickets?"

"Work," says Anna. "Tomorrow I get to pay with words."

"Well, I'm grateful," Jamie says, stepping back out of the observatory – Europe's oldest functioning observatory, no less – and onto the observation deck.

Together, they move to the side of the circular walkway, which gives them views across the city and as far as the lights of Sweden, but also down into the nearby apartments, lit and cosy, many with Christmas lights. Leaning against the safety fencing, Anna watches the inhabitants sitting down for dinner and others settling into cosy sofas with their thick knitted socks or felt slippers, the glow of flickering candles surrounding them. It gives her a pang of something she doesn't want to put a name to, and she turns quickly back towards the tower door to block it out. Only, Jamie is right there in front of her and he's wearing an expression of concern.

"I'm really sorry," he says, his eyes a little wild.

"For what?" Anna replies, alarmed. He was grateful just a moment ago.

"This," he says and then his hands are cupping her face, tilting it upwards as his own descends to meet it, his lips settling onto hers. There's no nose-bumping in directional confusion, only pure pinpoint accuracy, as though they're made to fit perfectly.

Anna's eyes widen in surprise for just a second, then slide shut, mirroring her mental glide into this kiss. She could be thinking, *WTF?* or *How dare he?* or *What is going on, Jamie?* But, no. Her entire being simply slips under the surface without a thought for survival, which is something she might consider reflecting on later, but not right now. Instead, wrapped up in this kiss – and she can't deny she's become an equal participant, really she can't – Anna's one hand slips to his neck and the other rises to the chain links of the safety fencing behind her, her fingers threading through them. She's hanging on for her own safety, but she doubts this is what the authorities had had in mind.

Jamie backs her up a step, but having nowhere to go, the move simply presses her hips to his. It's a million miles from the tentative, enquiring kiss under the sofa. It's a kiss that says, I know you said we couldn't pursue it, but here's what's on the table.

She'd like him on a table, truth be told. The thought of it, the images and the expected feel of it, suddenly fills Anna's head and her body fills with heat. His thumb rubs softly along the curve of her jaw, which makes her involuntarily sigh. His lips stretch into a smile against hers and a low chuckle rumbles in his chest, pressed against her. Finally, Jamie pulls away, his eyes locked on hers. He does not appear as breathless as she feels, which is, frankly, disappointing, but to save her pride she puts it down to him having larger lung capacity.

"Again, I'm sorry," he says, low. And then he briefly crosses his eyes at her, which is comical.

Anna's jaw flaps in confusion. Was he just swept up in the moment or—

"*Hej!*" The voice comes from behind Jamie. He gives her a faint smile now, as things become clearer. Smilla stands beaming behind him, wrapped up in numerous layers, just as they are. And with her is … Anders. Who is holding her hand. Anna tilts her head at them. Anders' face turns pink.

"Yes. So, it's new. We're trying it out." And now Smilla's

face is turning pink, too. Cute, thinks Anna, well versed in this brand of awkwardness now and enjoying someone else having a turn. Jamie simply gives Anders' shoulder a squeeze.

"I thought it was you," says Smilla to Jamie, "but I wasn't sure as your back was turned and then … you know," she waggles a finger between him and Anna, "and then I knew."

Anna gives Jamie a bug-eyed look. Their making out has become some kind of signature.

"You know how it is," Jamie tries. "It's the stars and the lights." Smilla and Anders look at him, agog.

"Jamie just gets overwhelmed by the romance of it all," Anna can't help but interject. Smilla looks at her, starry-eyed. Jamie looks … less so.

"Right," says Smilla, "we're next into the telescope. It was *hyggeligt* to see you."

Anna sends them a smile and watches them disappear into the observatory. Her eyes track back to Jamie, who's watching her with narrowed eyes.

"You just made my working day harder."

This makes her laugh. "What, for being a swoony romantic? You started this, MacDonald, and that kiss was on you."

His brows knit but he knows he hasn't a leg to stand on.

"Besides," Anna points out, "they were out on an early date. Unless they want to risk you blabbing about it, they'll not tease you too much for your smoochy ways."

He takes a step forward and Anna knows for sure he's

about to show her more of his smoochy ways, as punishment.

She places a palm on his chest, and he halts immediately. He searches her face and she doesn't need to say it. Much as she enjoys it, much as it does things to her and makes her want to scale him, these kisses are just for show, just their deal, and she can't let it become more. It's for his own sake, she reminds herself.

Jamie raises his hand above her head, weaving his fingers into the chain link, caging her. She could easily slide out to the side if she wanted to, but she feels no compulsion to move away at all. Instead she looks up into his face, trying not to look like she's drinking it in, waiting for what he wants to say.

"Is it always like this for you? You feel it, right?"

She's not sure what the best answer is? Honesty should be it, but she doesn't want to encourage him, not when there's no future for them. But maaan, those kisses…

"No," she says, and she sees a muscle twitch in his jaw. "I mean, no it's not always like this. And I do feel it." She feels better for being truthful, but bad for the shine in his eyes. "I'm still leaving, though. And as much as you've made it better being back here, the city still feels like an estranged relative I've just met in the street. Like you're initially pleased to see them, then you remember why you shouldn't be. I've started a new life elsewhere, just as you have here. So I can't help but think our timing is off. Our lifestyle needs are different. And more than anything, I don't want to mess you about. I know my heart is still bruised, and I suspect yours is, too, so what good would it do, acting on this?"

His smile spreads to something rather wolfish. "Well, more of those kisses would be good."

They would be good. So good. Too good.

"I've read a romance or two in my time," Jamie goes on, "by way of small hotels with lousy Wi-Fi and a less than eclectic in-house library, so I understand the concept of Happy For Now. I feel it's only fair to state I'm open to that." He leans down to breathe into her hair, "So if you change your mind, just let me know…"

Her face flushes. The skin at her ear rises with goosebumps, because the thought of throwing all rules and restraint aside and rolling with this has all sorts of heat pooling in her lower belly. It also has her tongue-tied.

Jamie lets go of the chain link and Anna instantly feels colder for it. Then he takes hold of her collars and pulls them to, only skimming her with his fingertips, but it's enough to have an effect and she suspects this is exactly his intention. He takes a breath to speak. Anna, with a sudden knot of anticipation and trepidation, looks up at him with wide eyes, waiting, desperate to know what he'll say next, what words might come out of his mouth to blow her off the edge of her sensible thinking. Because it will, and it will only need to be the lightest of breezes.

"Time to go, Lundholm. I've got an early meeting tomorrow," he says at last.

Oh.

They walk back up Købmagergade, past the closed shops, window-shopping at Arnold Busck the bookstore, and still talking about the magic of the stars above the city. They walk close, hands in pockets, arms almost rubbing, but not quite. Almost as if it's the safest option. Anna's hand twitches to slide between his arm and body, for her to lean in and be close. She keeps shooting him sideways glances, thinking about her confusion of feelings for him. There is this pull – that's the only way she can describe it – but also the push of everything around them; her situation, the city, her break-up with Carl. And now that her head is getting in there, there's still the worry about him having lied to her. She understands why he did it, and he seems genuinely contrite, but it's still a reminder that people lie, about all sorts of things, and Anna doesn't know how to work with that.

That said, she can't deny she's slightly hoping Smilla will appear again, so she'll have the excuse.

"Anna!" She hears her name from behind her and looks over her shoulder. A man is staring at her, at them. It takes a moment to place him, because it's been a while, the context is off and most of his head is swaddled in scarf and hat.

"Morten. *Hej*," she says. He's Carl's cousin. Having known him for many years, he is also, in Anna's estimation, an arse.

Morten does a very good job of being totally unsubtle in sizing Jamie up. Or perhaps he's checking him out. Either is possible if Anna recalls correctly.

"Are you back?" he asks, not taking his eyes off Jamie. Neither he nor Anna move in for a hug.

"Clearly," Anna says. She feels Jamie's hand slide up her back to rest on her shoulder. It's protective rather than possessive. He must recognise she isn't thrilled to see him. But it reminds her of her manners.

"Morten, this is Jamie; Jamie, Morten, Carl's cousin." She deliberately doesn't explain who Jamie is, because she doesn't want to. Nor is it any of Morten's business, now she thinks of it.

"Carl know you're here?" It's a bit of a sneer. He certainly hasn't said, "Nice to see you."

"He does," she says with a tight smile. "No need to ring him." Morten's smile is equally tight at the insinuation. She doesn't know why. He's generally known as a gossip. He rather fancies himself as the fountain of salacious knowledge among his friends, like a walking Popbitch.

"You pulled quite the stunt on him there," he says. She tilts her head at this, not wanting to be drawn. "Throwing his belongings onto the street," he clarifies.

She takes the bait. "I knew what you meant. I was questioning who was pulling the stunts. Cheating doesn't rank highly in your book, then?"

"Maiken? We thought you were OK with it," he says with a shrug. "The two of you had been together so long, opening the relationship sounded like you wanted some variety again." Anna feels like she's been punched. There are various things to address there, although she knows she should walk away. She doesn't want to be arguing in the street, making a scene. And particularly not with Morten. But she has to ask, "We?"

There's delight in his eyes and she knows she's feeding his snidery. Why didn't she just walk away?

"The family. We'd been talking about it for a while. Was it an official throuple? No one quite knew, though Annette didn't think you'd be up for full-time polyamory."

Annette? Carl's mother!

The blood is slowly draining from Anna's face. His family had welcomed her, and she'd embraced them and now she hears they were discussing the affair before she even knew about it. This is worse than her nightmares had painted. It also shows Carl had been less than discreet.

Again, she can't stop herself from asking, because she's never really found out and it's gnawed at her for a long time.

"When was this?"

Morten immediately sees she's fishing for a timeline.

"Ah, probably some party you didn't attend. You missed lots with your travels. You'll have to ask Carl."

He looks at his watch, as if she's been detaining him. Why hadn't he just walked on and ignored her? She wishes he had.

Her entire night will now be spent running through all of the last family events, working out which she'd missed and how far it could have gone back. She thinks of the get-togethers just before she found out, where his family must have known, but chose not to give her even a hint. That the women had sided with Carl over any kind of sisterly tip-off. Perhaps they thought they were minding their own business and shouldn't intrude. Either sucks.

She'll drive herself mad with it, thinking about his

family discussing it behind her back. Even his mother! Lovely Annette whom she thought liked her. Not enough to warn her or give her son a swift boot to the backside, obviously. And then them all dissecting it later after Anna had kicked him to the kerb. She'd always found it strange that Annette hadn't reached out to her in any way. But then again, Anna hadn't reached out to her, either. Oh, and she'd fled the country. Dammit. Not fled. She'd *removed* herself. Anna mentally admonishes herself to stick to her guns. Jamie's not right on this.

As if he's heard her thinking of him, Anna suddenly feels Jamie's lips on her hair as he presses an obvious kiss on her and says, "We've got to go, *skat*." The sound of him calling her "treasure" is like a balm, and it's the easiest thing to lean into his kiss and into his steady frame. The widening of Morten's eyes is a joy to behold. Which is what makes her turn to look up into Jamie's face, with what she hopes is a private smile, as she flicks her eyes from his to his lips, and then letting the smile spread wider, in joy of beholding his gorgeous face. She feels like her own face is shining on his, and she's thrilled to see it reflected back at her. They are so good at this! Morten's getting the full treatment. Perfectly in tune, they lean their faces together and give each other a small soft kiss; subtle and delicate, the kiss of two people at ease with each other, not that of two rampant teens, although Anna wouldn't be averse to trying one of those, too. She restrains herself, though, keen for Morten to have a clear report to share of her moving on and in a sophisticated fashion, not in a hot mess, snogging in the street kind of way. The art is in the execution.

Holding Jamie's "smitten" gaze – so good and swoony, she really does have to give him props for his skills – for a long moment, she turns back to Morten as if she's just remembered he's there.

"*Vi ses*," she says and pulls Jamie away, as if they have only seconds left to get home and into bed. She doesn't say she's pleased to have seen him or send her love to the family, because of course, she wouldn't mean a word of it.

Reaching the end of the street though, still under Jamie's "for show" arm and having checked Morten is long gone, the reality of it hits her. Not so much that this is all fake and that she hasn't in fact moved on, but that the gossip she'd been worried about was true, the humiliation she'd felt was justified. In fact, it's been worse than she thought, and she's thought plenty of wild things. Anna feels her eyes begin to sting, and pulls in a sniff, but it's too late. A tear has started its slow descent down her cheek, echoing the lowering of her mood. She swipes the tear way with her palm, but there's already another in its place.

"Hey," Jamie says, stopping them. "Anna?"

"I'm fine. It's fine. Just the cold wind in my eyes," she tries. The air is still this evening.

He doesn't argue, though. He simply pulls her into him, like he did in the cemetery, and wraps his arms around her, holding tight. She isn't sobbing this time, more weepy, but she feels silly for crying so much around him. He doesn't seem to mind, though, as he sways them slightly back and forth and says, "He was a dick, Anna. I don't even know him and I can see that. Don't let him get to you."

Easier said than done, she thinks, but nods into Jamie's

chest. The smell of him comforts her. Right here, right now, she feels safe and grounded. She hasn't felt that in a long time.

"OK?" he asks after a while.

With an admittedly unattractive sniff, she pulls back and gives him a flat smile in agreement.

"Good," says Jamie, cradling her face, and wiping the tear traces with his thumbs. "Here's what we're going to do. You're going to tell me every embarrassing thing Morten has ever done in your presence, all the way home. We will annihilate him and then I'm going to make us hot chocolate." That sounds quite good, she thinks, keen now to crawl into her bed and sleep.

It's amazing how he knows what she needs right now, Anna notes as he leads her arm in arm down the street, which just makes it sadder that they've met in the wrong place at the wrong time and their planets simply can't align.

Chapter Twenty-Three

The ringing is coming from deep inside her coat pocket, and against the hum of the traffic, it takes Anna a while to realise it's happening. She's spent the last hour in the Hirschsprung Collection, her favourite art museum, trying to distract herself. Much as she'd dished every morsel of dirt she had on Morten the night before, the run-in is still churning in her gut. In her mind it validates every notion she has to leave the city, having confirmed the humiliating gossiping her friends and acquaintances have been up to. Not to mention the word *throuple* is still ringing in her ears. But the museum, a collection of Danish Golden Age artworks on Stockholmsgade, has always been to Anna a place of calm and beauty. Her mother's face appears on the screen. Ida may have been a beauty in her time, but she has never been calm.

"*Hej, Mor,*" she says, sounding lightly surprised. Ida doesn't call her often. Aside from her work as a graphic designer she's always so busy with local events and festivals. For a woman who never stays long in places, Ida is by no means a hermit. She does not keep herself to herself. On all sorts of levels.

"How's London?" she asks. Anna hasn't kept her abreast of the situation. Her trip was supposed to be so fleeting, Anna had deemed it inconsequential to her mother. She's very inclined to lie, but given recent events, she's feeling averse to lying in all its forms, even in keeping her mother's incoming opinions at bay.

"I'm in Copenhagen, actually. Snowed in. Can't get a ticket out yet."

"What?!" Ida's surprise is vastly over-dramatic, but that's Ida for you. "You just can't stay away!" It feels like a criticism.

"I haven't been back for a year and half," Anna says, annoyed that she's sounding surly. "And it was just a short admin trip." She decides not to mention Pølse. Her mother would think her too sentimental. Sentimentality is a poison in Ida's book. Along with Nostalgia and Regret. She believes only in looking forward, she's proud to say. And mainly in Pleasing Oneself, Anna might also add, but only in her head. Ida would absolutely insist she's done a fine job of raising an independent daughter with a broad outlook and strong wanderlust. Ida has never accepted any complaints about her parenting. Anna knows to steer clear there, as she's never even made a dent in Ida's resolve on that. Self-reflection isn't one of Ida's things, either.

"How's the house?" There's no snark, per se, but Anna knows Ida was hurt the house wasn't left to her. But what they all know, particularly Anna's grandparents, is she would have sold the house immediately.

"It's good," Anna says lightly, not wanting to dredge it up. "The tenant is letting me stay, while I'm stuck."

"Interesting," her mother says.

"Stop it."

"What?" Her mother is poor at feigning anything. You can add Subtlety to the list of Ida's non-attributes. She lauds this proudly as being "an open book", but Anna thinks she simply has no filters.

"What's he like?"

"What makes you think it's a man?" She tries a laughing scoff, but it comes out more like a guilty cough.

"You would already have said. Rather than saying 'Stop it.' I know you, Anna and I'm not an idiot, much as you may think so."

Anna sighs. She won't win. She knows she won't. "He's a Scot. Something big in city sustainability. Nice. Kind, obviously, having let a stranger stay."

"In her own house," Ida points out, like it should be a given.

"Which he's renting and has a contract saying I can't just turn up at." Ida doesn't always entertain legalities, but enough said about that.

Anna wants to ask her why she's calling, but figures it rude. Luckily, for once some mother–daughter telepathy kicks in.

"I wanted to say, *God Jul*. I've signed up for a silent retreat for the Christmas days."

Anna quickly thinks through her last calls with Ida to

remember precisely where she is currently. Settling on Skiathos, Anna experiences a twinge of jealousy, given it must be significantly warmer than here. She seems to remember there being a commune involved, and the twinge vanishes. Having been subjected to a couple of those in her childhood, they are safely filed under "not for me". Anna's broad-mindedness has more limits than Ida's.

"Not feeling Christmassy?"

"It's lovely here," Ida says wistfully, "but a few days of avoiding people and not having to talk will be a delight." Anna places a bet inside her head. Ida will be moving on within the next two months. She knows the signs.

"You should come out and visit."

"Sure." She only ever books last-minute when going to see her mother after having once bought a ticket ahead only to have her mother move to an entirely different country before she could use it.

"*Mor*, can I ask you something?" Anna suddenly says, grasping an opportunity. "My father. Did he not want to know me at all?" After Jamie's confession, her thinking has drifted to her own dad. It's pure curiosity, not yearning. Unlike Jamie, whose circumstances were far more tragic, she doesn't feel she's missing part of her life. She feels perhaps she should, but she simply doesn't. Not remotely in the same way as she misses her *morfar*.

"Why on earth are you asking me that?" Ida asks, sounding utterly baffled.

"I was just talking to someone about growing up without a parent, and it dawned on me, that oddly, I didn't really have any opinion on it. I suppose it's because we haven't talked about why he's not in my life."

"This is unhelpful, raking up the past, isn't it?" Ida suggests, not angrily. More like a therapist might, although she's entirely unqualified for such things.

"I don't know if it's unhelpful yet. You're the only one who knows."

"And I might die one day, right?" There. The over-dramatic.

"I didn't say that. But as you mention it… How else would I find out?"

"Well," Ida says, "there's really nothing much to find out. I don't have more details than you already have. I fell pregnant in Ibiza." And there she stops. Like that explains everything.

"And?" Anna prompts. She's passing a bench and, realising this is going to take some concentration herding Ida to the information pen, takes a seat.

"And what? That's it." Again, Ida sounds bewildered by the questioning. Had Anna not known her she'd be astounded by her obtuseness.

"*Mor!* One doesn't just fall pregnant when visiting Ibiza. That kind of phenomenon would be documented. There must have been someone else involved. That's what I'm asking."

"Well, of course. We had that chat when you were ten."

Yes. Yes, they had. And the way Ida had explained it to her had probably left mental scars, liberated Dane as she was or not.

"So, who was he?" she tries very, very hard not to grit it out.

Again, Ida sighs deeply. "It just wasn't that kind of time, Anna. We didn't really give names and details. It was a party, a good one. All very free and fun. Consensual, of course," Ida suddenly adds, lest Anna should think anything untoward. "And afterwards, everyone went on their way. I wouldn't have recognised them in the street."

Anna closes her eyes at the word *them*.

"There was more than one?" Anna says.

Ida tsks her. "Don't you be judgemental, Anna. Like I said, it was a good party. And. It. Was. Consensual." Anna is being schooled. She bites her tongue, though.

"So, no follow-up at all when you knew you were pregnant?" she asks weakly.

Ida laughs at the ridiculousness. "Where would you have had me start?" She's not malicious. Just perhaps utterly thoughtless about how this might sound to Anna's or indeed another human's ears. "I was happy! I was going to share my life with you. You would be my travel companion." The excitement is still there in Ida's voice, and Anna knows it's genuine. Every photo in her grandparents' home was either of a smiling pregnant Ida or Ida and Anna hugging, with their identical face-wide smiles. Her mother might be eccentric, but she is genuine in her love for her daughter. Given how similar they look, Anna has often wondered what genetics she actually has inherited from her father, whoever he is. All she has currently is her enjoyment of running, as Ida wouldn't be seen dead in trainers. "Anna, it wasn't always easy being single with a baby and then a toddler in all those countries, but people are mainly kind, and we did well and had a good life together. I missed you terribly when you decided to stay with Vivi and Mads."

She had. Anna knows she had, but for once Anna had put her own needs first. She'd got that from Ida, too. For all of Ida's happiness of finding herself pregnant, Anna knows she wouldn't have continued the pregnancy if the opposite had been true.

"Do you think your life would have been better with a father in ours?" Ida asks. It's not a loaded question.

Anna takes a moment. Ida would have hated being tied to someone, that much she's sure of. "No? Not better necessarily," she sounds out, trying to pull her thoughts together. "Just different, I suppose, and I don't know what that would look like." She finally gives up. "I don't know."

"Well, I wouldn't change a thing," Ida states. "Not even you staying behind, much as I missed you. Because it told me I'd brought up a woman who could make her own choices. And that's enough for me." Anna is surprised how warm she feels at her mother's obvious pride.

Ida has clearly had enough of this line of enquiry and turns the conversation to tell Anna about the comings and goings at the commune, which further supports Anna's feeling that Ida will be moving on again soon. It's like the wind changing at the beginning of *Mary Poppins*; change is afoot. Anna can feel it in her bones now, having grown up with it.

Eventually the conversation has run its course. They wish each other *Glædelig Jul*, as Ida will be incommunicado on the day, and hang up.

It takes Anna a while to look away from the phone in her hand, the chill being the thing to prompt her on her way. And as she walks, she is heartened to think that while it would be sad for Jamie if Lajla doesn't let him into their lives, Nikoline doesn't have to have a dad in her life, if she has others around her that love her. Perhaps that's what she needs to get across to Jamie, because as far as she can see, this really is out of his hands.

She could probably walk the route between her house and Maiken's apartment on the other side of Sortedams Sø, with her eyes shut, or cycle it, rather, which would be more hazardous given traffic, but still. Easy-peasy. The two of them lived in each other's pockets through their final school years. After a couple of years in casual jobs, they'd both gone to Aarhus University, and journalist college after that, which meant sharing a tiny flat in Denmark's second city.

Returning to Copenhagen, they shared another tiny apartment, until Maiken met Christoffer, whom she thought was The One, but turned out to be less, and Anna inherited Mads and Vivi's house.

The Østerbro apartment lies to the eastern end of the lake, in a pretty block, with a turret to its front. Maiken's apartment incorporates the turret, giving her a circular space to have her tiny dining table, as well as an exquisite view of the water and the city rooftops.

Right now, Anna is skulking behind a snow-covered van, in front of the wood-and-glass double doors, decorated with Christmassy glass stickers, to the front of the building. She's beginning to think coming during the early hours would have been the smarter plan. If she could walk here with her eyes closed, then the darkness would be the same. But the locket has been burning a hole in her pocket, and she wants it gone. Her plan is sketchy at best; get into the building using the key code Maiken never changed, drop the locket in Maiken's letterbox in the entrance hall, and then get the hell out of there. Yes, given her known presence in the city, it would be obvious Anna was the one who had dropped it back, or else a minor miracle that the locket should make its own way back to its owner's letterbox in a city of letterboxes, but having wracked her – and Jamie's – brain, she can't think of an anonymous way to do it. She doesn't think the police would be amused by her handing it in with detailed instructions of its owner's name and address. That had been Jamie's idea, and she pointed out it would be more likely to get her arrested on suspected burglary. She also said she hoped he was a better ideas man at work. Because that was half-arsed.

She glances up at the turret room. The lights aren't on. Good. Maiken might be at her mother's for the Christmas days. Her mother had moved up to a lovely modern summerhouse in Dronningmølle some years ago, a stone's throw from the beach. Anna and Maiken had spent plenty of weekends up there, swimming and picnicking at the beach, and partying with friends. Just a short trip by train, it was a welcome respite from the bustle and summer heat of the city.

An ache in her stomach hits as she feels a sudden

yearning for those days. The relaxed nature of their friendship, the fun they'd had and how they'd understood each other – or so she'd thought. They'd just seemed to flow together at the same rhythm. Carl had joked early on that being with Anna meant accepting Maiken was part of the deal. How they'd laughed at that! Now, it leaves a bad taste in Anna's mouth, given he'd apparently meant it. *Throuple* drifts across her mind and she crossly bats it away. Bloody Morten.

She will never understand how Maiken could have done it to her. The absolute betrayal, not just to pick up with a man she knew was living with someone else, but also not being hindered by that someone being her best friend. Hurting Anna had not stopped her. Either of them in fact. But the hurt felt more coming from Maiken. Carl's betrayal was like her heart had been smashed, but Maiken's was that *plus* a stab to the lungs, which made her breathing painful to boot. She didn't know if she'd ever breathe properly again. She certainly can't imagine sitting in a turret room, finishing another bottle of wine, laughing in the wee hours, looking out over the city's lights, before eventually keeling over next to each other on the double bed, to share hangovers the following morning, with a friend like that again. Now she'll always be guarded around female friends.

As a child she'd been fast to make friends each time Ida moved them on, but constantly saying goodbye – or not even, in a couple of cases – meant she'd come to believe there was little point investing in the friendships. It only made it harder when she left. A couple of times emails had been exchanged, and chat groups established afterwards, but they all waned in time as everyone moved into new phases of schooling and the points of reference were lost. Moving in with Vivi and Mads had given her the chance to make friends she could invest in, nurture and manage for herself. She'd sat next to Maiken on the first day and it was almost as if the "click" could be heard across the babble of the classroom. Simple as that.

Anna drags her eyes away from the turret and its Juliet balcony. They'd loved opening that in the summer, to let in the breeze. (Loved as in *had to*, as the apartment was stiflingly hot.) Nostalgia isn't of any use to her now. She just needs to do the thing and get out, before anyone sees her. Especially not Maiken. Nor Carl, if he's visiting.

Checking the street, she speedwalks across to the door and is about to press the code pad when she realises it isn't there. No punch-key numbers at all. Just a square, which she recognises from her building in London, one which requires a fob pressed against it. A fob she does not have. There are individual doorbells to press, but there's no way that's happening. Anna considers pressing someone else's bell and trying to bluff her way in, but discards the thought, knowing there are many elderly residents who would be spooked by it being a "scammer". Also, she's used to people doing this to her in London and it's bloody annoying.

Digging her hands into her pockets in frustration, her fingers wrap around the locket. She's cleaned it a bit, well, sort of just brushed it off. She may or may not have used spit, too. But no more than that. She certainly wasn't going to polish it. That might be construed as an apology of sorts, and she isn't offering one. No way.

As she ponders what to do, the door suddenly opens from behind her and Anna almost shits herself at the immediate expectation of it being Maiken. It turns out to be a young mother and her buggy, its snowsuited, duvet-covered occupant screaming blue murder as the mother negotiates the vehicle out of the door.

"Here, let me help," Anna says, reaching out to hold the door open. The harried mother thanks her, drops the wheels onto the cobbles outside and is on her way. She doesn't stop to see the door closed safely behind her, nor whether the helpful stranger slides inside, like they do in the movies, and as Anna now does.

A row of letterboxes is mounted on one wall of the entrance hall. Anna's dastardly grin covers her entire face. One flip of a letter flap and she'll be divested of her painful cargo and Maiken can make what she wants of it. Not Anna's problem.

The locket is already in her hand and she's just about to pop it into Maiken's letterbox when her eyes skirt across the name on it. *Anne-Sofie og Frederik Axelsen.* Not Maiken Holm-Olsen. She checks again, in case she hasn't been looking at the "4th-floor flat to the left" letterbox, but the numbers are right. Panicking, she scans the others around it, but no, there's no mention of Maiken at all.

She doesn't live there anymore.

Another couple is enjoying the turret view, and the summer evenings with the bottle of wine and the view of the city. It makes Anna sad all over again, which is ridiculous, as it wouldn't have included her anyway.

The sound of the ancient elevator being activated from one of the floors above shifts her into action. She beelines for the door, not wanting to get caught, or questioned as to why she's staring at the letterboxes like a deranged person. Reaching the slushy street, she can only think of two things; that Maiken has moved on with her life in more ways than just with Carl, and that Anna still has the bloody locket, with even less of a clue how to get rid of the f'ing thing.

Chapter Twenty-Four

Anna eyes the Christiania bike in her yard from the window. The cover across the box on the front is layered with snow, and there are ice crystals across the handlebars. Against the snowy cobbles, it is rather Instagram-worthy. She has her Christmas-lunch date with Katrine and the rest of the team in just over an hour, and as the sky is cloudless, she's feeling the pull of the cycle lanes.

She hears Jamie come into the room and just as she's about to ask him if he'd consider lending it to her, she realises he's on a call, earbuds in. It doesn't take her long to realise it's his dad again. As Jamie said, they seem to be going around in circles on his moving back to Skye. Or not moving back, as Jamie is steadfastly telling him.

Anna sees the problem. His father must be bewildered that his son is turning down the gift of a generational livelihood and land, but having known Jamie for only a short while, he's clearly his own man who chooses his own path, has his own interests and is good at what he does. And of course there are the other ties to Copenhagen…

"Have you told him about Nikoline?" she asks, when he hangs up. "Perhaps that would help. He wants his son with him, but knowing you want to be with your daughter is something he would understand."

Jamie grimaces and scratches his cheek. "I can't tell him about that. It's all a mess, from start to finish. I doubt sperm-fishing is a thing on Skye." He gives her a small smile now, making light of it, and she sees the subject is closed.

"I'm off out," he says. "Need anything from the outside world?" She dwells on the hunter-gatherer vibe for a second, but shakes her head.

"Going on your bike?" she asks as if it's a standard question, not a loaded one, which she will leap on if the answer is no.

"Aye," he says, loading his backpack. "I can pick up some dinner on the way back."

"Hmmm, I've got a lunch, which I know will be long and *snaps*-fuelled. Maybe get something which can be tomorrow's leftovers if I've over-pigged?" She's not even going to deny there'll be shots knocked back throughout the meal. It is tradition, after all. She's also not going to give too much thought to the pleasant glow the domesticity of his question gives her. Perhaps she should think about getting a flatmate when she returns to London. Perhaps it's the company she craves.

He looks up at that. "I can pick you up later."

The thought is lovely, to be ferried home, but there's also

something which makes her want to do this herself. And to keep things on an even keel between them. That Happy For Now offer hangs in the air – and like eye-catching bunting inside her head.

"I'll be fine, but thanks," she insists, not about to tell him of the maaaaany times she's cycled across this city drunk. An idea hits her. "Any chance you'd help me get my bike out of the cellar?"

Two minutes later, they're manhandling a red bicycle, complete with basket, up the stairs and out through the front door to stand next to his. Why hasn't she thought about this earlier? Oh, yeah, she isn't staying...

He offers to pump the wheels up, but looking at his arms, and at the thought of his straining biceps as he uses the pump, she waves him off with more thanks. Morfar had been staunch about the responsibility of bike ownership and maintenance. Anna is trained. She's brought the pump and oil for the chain up from the cellar, too. Although it's biting cold outside and she hasn't put her coat on, Anna gets a buzz putting the air back into her tyres and thirty minutes later, bundled up properly and pedalling along on the cycle path in towards the city centre, she has to admit the grin on her face is pure joy and not a frozen grimace.

Everyone has arrived at Restaurant Sankt Annæ ahead of her. The white building is old in its style, having been established in 1894. All the windows have been trimmed on the outside with green fir, and the yellow glow from inside is a warm contrast to the cold outside. Inside, it's cosy, intimate and today, bouncing with Copenhageners having Christmas lunches, whether with friends, family or business colleagues. The good-natured revelry can be heard from outside the door and given the many bottles of *snaps* on the tables, it is not going to get quieter.

Anna winds her way through the tables to reach Katrine and the team, pausing only once to say hello to someone she used to know from journalism school. He's on television now, and she's flattered he recognised her. Quick *hello!*s and *how are you?*s exchanged, she says she's seeing her editor, with a point to Katrine, because she might not be on the telly, but she's proud of her guides and not above a name-drop. He looks Katrine's way and Anna predicts a LinkedIn search later. He's a journalist, he must be writing a book of some kind.

The hugs she gets from everyone are effusive, and she realises that she has missed this team. The company publishes travel guides in lots of ways, from ebooks and paperbacks to audio and various travel podcasts, to the website Anna contributes to. Whatever the upcoming medium, they find a way to attach travel to it.

"It has been too long, Anna," Katrine scolds.

"I had cake with you just the other day and I saw you in London!" Anna fights back, as she sits down. She takes a deep breath through her nose, taking in all the scents of the Christmassy foods some are having.

"The book fair is so busy. I'm exhausted in the evenings." Katrine pulls a sad face.

Anna laughs and, putting a finger to her chin, says,

"Funny, the way I remember it, you still managed to dance on a table by the end of the evening, so perhaps not so exhausted?" The other team members around them laugh knowingly at Katrine.

Katrine tries to look confused. "I can't quite remember it."

"Exactly," Anna says, and holds up her phone. "But I have the receipts. So."

"Is this blackmail?"

"Not yet. And only if I ever need it."

Anna was Katrine's first signing, and Katrine was Anna's first and only editor, so they have a special fondness for each other. Anna thinks there are times when they think of themselves as toddlers muddling through publishing together, even though both have proven their abilities over the years.

The waiter comes and waits patiently as they order. Anna forgoes the *Julefrokost* buffet, mainly because there are far too many herring, instead picking open sandwiches, which the restaurant is known for, from the regular menu. She plumps for three; roast beef with horseradish, chicken with curried mayonnaise and bacon, and roast pork rib with red cabbage, all served on rye bread. Katrine orders the first round of *snaps* for everyone, a Brøndum.

"So, how's the fame?" Katrine asks, pouring them each a glass of white wine.

"Pfft. I think it's blown over."

The look Katrine sends her says she's certifiably delulu. "Have you not been on social media?"

Her stomach sinks somewhat.

Immediately everyone is scrolling through their phones. Katrine pulls up the Tivoli website and there they are on the home page. Moments later, Josefine opposite her pulls up Facebook where the photo is on not one but three of the Danish tourist pages, and then Søren along from her finds a separate dedicated page named *Copenhagen Snowmance*, where other sightings of Anna and Jamie have been posted including that kiss against the safety fencing at Rundetårnet. Bloody hell! How are people so quick to this? It's there from various angles, plus a later shot of Jamie, arm caging her, gazing down at her. Someone whistles in Anna's direction and she doesn't know if that's what makes her blush, or the look Jamie is giving her in the photo.

"You've become a sport!" Katrine says with delight. Ditte, on Anna's right, tops it off, finding a cut-out of the two of them being widely used as a meme.

Anna sinks down in her seat. It was probably best she hadn't seen all that. "Ah," is all she can say. She takes a long glug of her wine.

"*Skål*," says Katrine with a laugh, lifting her glass to follow suit.

It's joy to catch up on everyone's news, all while tucking into the food and knocking back more *snaps*. Anna's delighted to hear who's got married (Anne-Marie and Malene, though not to each other), and had children (Kasper), more children (Ditte and Jens, again, not together) or adopted (Josefine and Astrid, this time actually together, which had been a surprise as no one had known they were a couple). She's sad to hear about Søren's divorce and Henrik's retirement.

She spends a long time savouring the roast beef sandwich with its layers of thinly cut, perfect pink roast beef, topped with yellow *remoulade*, fried onions, strings of grated horseradish and pickled cucumber. It's an exquisite feat of layering and flavours and it makes her eyelids flutter. Yes, the *snaps* might also be taking its toll, but by now, as soon as one table starts *skål*ing, everyone else does, too. Anna can feel by the loosening of her limbs and eyes, and the fuzziness of her head, this is going to be messy.

Eventually, after much chat, singing and copious laughter, Katrine and Anna find they are the last at their table, the others being more sensible, and in a couple of cases having something else to go on to.

"Now," slurs Katrine, "I want to hear more about your housemate."

Anna feels the smile spread across her face, even though she'd planned to be more poker-faced.

"Look at you," Katrine laughs, and pours them each another *snaps*. "You're all swoony."

"I am not," Anna tries, but it doesn't sound convincing even to herself. "It doesn't matter, anyway," she adds slightly crossly, then clinks Katrine's glass and downs the shot. "Like I said the other day, I'll be leaving, and he'll be my tenant again, and so."

Katrine rolls her eyes. It takes her an extra moment to re-synchronise them. "That's not what it looks like in the photos. It's not how I remember stargazing. I'm sure there is a telescopic gag here somewhere."

"Trine, behave!"

She leans further in, conspiratorially, but with zero

subtlety. "Did you think about the 'Once-and-Done' idea?" she whispers loudly.

"No!" says Anna.

She has.

A lot.

"Though he has suggested a 'Happy For Now' scenario."

Katrine's face lights up. "There you go, then!" she says, as if their similar suggestion is some kind of sealed deal.

"Am I the only one being sensible here? It wouldn't be smart, Trine. Or kind. I don't want him getting hurt."

"What about you? Are you not at risk of being hurt?"

"Yes, well. Of course, there's always that, too," she concedes. She doesn't really want to examine how much she likes him. How she looks forward to seeing him in the living room when she surfaces for breakfast each day; how she hopes he'll ask if she wants to do more jigsaw, sitting side by side, close but not quite touching, focusing on a shared thing, crowing at each other when they place a piece and the other doesn't; hearing him be professional on the phone; his scent, which lingers around his coat and which she may hang around longer than necessary when putting on her own; how they have a teamwork thing going with the cooking and washing up, moving around the kitchen in smooth synchronisation, each busy with tasks without having to check on the other and both finishing at the same time to a completely tidy kitchen; how he seems happy to see her when she surfaces for breakfast (though that could just be because she's beelining for the coffee and offering him a refill); how he sings badly in the shower and seemingly has no idea at all that he can be heard outside the bathroom; the feel of his arms around her when he holds her tight and the way it makes her feel grounded.

"I'm keeping it light," Anna says.

"Mmm-hmm," says Katrine, in a "bullshit" tone. Well yes, there are a shit-ton of internet photos against her statement, Anna sees that.

The thing with having worked together for many years now, on various jobs even before the *Romancity* guides, is Katrine understands how to handle Anna. Not just editing her words, but how best to challenge her or soothe her to get the best out of her.

"Here's what I think," she says, and Anna is tempted to point out she hasn't been asked what she thinks, but Katrine is already in motion. "I think you might be holding back regarding someone you like, because of what happened with Carl." She does not wait for Anna to respond to this. "I think you're frightened, and so even this, which could be a safe little spate of fun, feels scary to you. When, in reality, it could be a brilliant, short moment with a hot guy, who you clearly like. And yes, it might have an end date, but that could be a good thing as the two of you can go into it with your eyes open and make the best of every moment."

Granted, that could make sense, Anna supposes.

"And you never know Anna, he might even follow you back to London."

That douses her feelings a bit. "Not going to happen," Anna says, vigorously shaking her head. "He can't leave Copenhagen."

"Why?" Katrine looks curious.

"OK, it's not that he can't. But he has reasons to stay here." Tipsy as she is, Anna doesn't want to tell her about Nikoline. It's not her story to tell and she doesn't want Jamie's story to be gossip. "He's only been in his job – his dream job – for a short while, so." She hopes that's enough to move Katrine on.

"Then maybe it might be something to draw you back here," proposes Katrine and Anna sees by the delight in her eyes this is where her thinking has been heading all along.

"Also not going to happen, Trine. It's been interesting coming back to visit, but you know…"

"No, not really," Katrine says, a little more gently. "I understand why you left, you needed a change of scene, especially given what happened, but it's been a year and a half, and you still have a home here. And we miss you."

Anna can't think what to say, to explain how the humiliation feels like it is around every corner. Meeting Morten proved that.

"*SKÅÅÅL!*" A roar goes up from the next table – ten bankers, from what they've overheard of their loud conversation. The rest of the room erupts into their own *skål*ing, and more *snaps* is shotted. Katrine and Anna follow along, this time with an Aalborg *snaps* and Anna is thankful for the diversion. It allows her to take back control of the conversation.

"I do like him. He's a great guy," she gives Katrine. "And maybe something while I'm here would be fun, but that really would be the sum of it. Don't think it'll be more,

Trine, because it won't. I don't want anything permanent. I'm happy as I am."

It is deeply annoying to Anna that Katrine can do that eyebrow thing, too, but eventually her dissatisfied editor lets it go. Ish. "Take the short-term fun, Anna. You could do with someone great being good to you, even for a little while. Even if it's just to get you back out there."

Back out there. That feels like a foreign land and has done for a while. The thing is though, the thought which pings into Anna's squiffy mind, is this; she's a travel writer, *an explorer*, which literally means venturing into foreign lands…

Chapter Twenty-Five

Despite not being able to feel her teeth – a state that is, she must admit, due more to the number of shots she's had than the cold – Anna still has the sense to walk her bike home rather than cycle. Katrine shares the same route for half of the way, so they continue their slurring until they finish with a huge hug and go their respective ways. Katrine's parting shot is to "Go get him!" and it's all Anna thinks about as she plods homewards.

The muscle-memory is back as she locks her bike in the yard, but it doesn't extend to getting the key in the lock, which takes a few goes. Fair enough, she thinks, it's dark. Not her fault.

While it is indeed dark, it's only just gone seven, yet her boozy brain tells her she needs to be quiet because Jamie might be asleep. She might even whisper it to herself out loud, but it seems sound advice and so she does her best to tiptoe around the hallway. Removing her chunky boots brings spectacular failure in this.

"Everything OK out there?" comes a voice from the living room. That faint glow of light isn't just to ward off burglars, then.

"'S'fine!" she loudly whispers, from the floor, confused now as to whether she should be quiet or not. "'S'fine, 's'fine, 's'fffff…" she tails off, having difficulty getting her crossbody bag off herself from this angle.

"Need any help?" he asks. His voice is slightly singsong. Not mocking, per se, just knowing.

"All good," she replies, finally dislodging the bag and flinging it in the corner, vaguely near her boot. The one she did get off before keeling over. Flipping onto her back, she unbuttons her coat and slides her arms out of the sleeves, then raising one foot in the air, unzips the remaining boot and sends it to join its mate. Much safer from this position. She takes a moment to stare at the ceiling and work out the next bit. Crawl up the stairs to her bed, or into the living room to say hello? She remembers her mission to explore Jamie's foreign lands, though she's not sure crawling will be the most alluring approach.

It takes her a moment to control her eyes, but when she does, she focuses on the Poul Henningsen pendant lamp, to steady her breathing and thinking. She should probably try her best to disguise her tipsiness. It's possible she might even have surpassed tipsy. Not all men find that attractive. But they'd drunk together the night of The Kisssssssss – she takes a few moments to veer off at a tangent in her thinking, to replay the kiss, a smile bursting across her face – so he can't be too against it, can he? She thinks about what Katrine had said about having some fun and going to get him. Katrine's editing advice has always seen her safe before, why would that not also apply to life advice?

"What are you muttering out there?" Jamie asks, and she realises she's been thinking out loud again. That's probably not a good idea.

Anna turns onto her front, then gets up on her hands and knees. With the help of the banister she's up onto her feet – yay! – where she gives her hair a quick smooth down, only to find she still has her hat on. She drops it onto the coat and re-smooths her hair, giving herself a quick glance in the hallway mirror. She's looking … pink. That's all she's got. Pink. That'll do. And she heads into the living room to go get him and venture into his foreign lands.

Turning into the room, Anna is drawn up short by what she's met with. Any muttering she's been doing lodges in her mouth as she stands stunned. Jamie stands at the far end of the room, with an apprehensive smile.

"I hope this is OK? I took a bit of a chance you'd be fine with it."

Wide-eyed, Anna can only manage a slow mute nod.

The entire room is bedecked with Christmas ornaments. Baubles, *nisser* of all sizes, embroidered wall hangings, hanging paper stars, woven paper hearts, colourful card cones filled with wrapped sweets, little bells, and in the deep windowsill a winter scene of snow-dusted model houses on a cotton-wool "snow" ground. Perhaps they're not quite in the same order as her *mormor* had them, but they're all Vivi's decorations, all the things Anna remembers from her childhood Christmases. Next to Jamie, and equally tall, stands a wooden eco tree, covered with baubles of all colours, strings of Danish flags and live candles in golden holders, which he must have lit just as she stumbled in. Crowning it is a gold star, the sight of which makes her eyes sting, as she and her *morfar* had made it together with golden craft wire.

"When…" she begins, but of course he's been working on this all afternoon. "Why…" she restarts.

"I saw the boxes in the basement when we were getting the bike out and I thought…" He stumbles. "Well, I thought you might enjoy seeing the things again. I guess it's been a while."

Last Christmas, in London, an onlooker would not have been able to tell it was December in her apartment. There was little difference from summer, except the windows were closed and the heating was on. Now, her eyes keep sweeping over the decorations, drinking them in, remembering them like old friends, and her fingers itch to touch them or pick them up.

"Thank you," she says, but the words are still sticking in her throat, so instead she takes the few steps over to him and throws her arms around his neck to hug him. "Thank you," she says again, clear this time. "It's wondrous." That feels like the right word as, of course, it's beautiful, but it's not just what it looks like but also everything invested in the items, the meanings and the memories.

She feels his arms wrap around her back, warm and safe, and he says into her hair. "You're welcome. It was nothing."

But it was far more than nothing, more than she'd expected and far more than she'd realised she needed.

"And besides," he says, "at thirty-five I felt I should own a tree."

"A man of amenities," she confirms into his chest.

Holding on tight to him for some moments, she revels in the closeness, then looks up into his face. With her slurry eyes she savours the depth of his and the prominence of the brows above them. She follows the smooth line of his nose to his lips.

She leans in to place a kiss on them.

Neither of them let go.

It's a shy kiss only for a moment, but then Anna lets herself go, that beat in her head of "go get him" urging her on. She slides her hands up to cup his jaw and leans further into the kiss and then backs him up to the wall behind him. He lets out a low growl as her hips meet his and she presses further, and one of his hands slides up into her hair at her nape, in turn sending a shudder down her spine. She feels life in parts of her that have been dormant for over a year. It makes her tongue glide across his lower lip and then back in to dance with his, in time with each other but taking turns to hold the control. It's heady and intoxicating and Anna wants more.

She drags one hand away from his face, brushing her fingertips down his side where she slides them under the hem of his Henley. The feel of his skin against her palm elicits a small moan from her and escalates her desire. She wants her hands all over him, to feel the differences in his skin in ALL the places; the smooth, the rough, the silky, the strained. She wants to know it all. And she wants to know it now.

Her lips kiss their way down to his neck, where she basks in the scent of his skin below his ear. Cedarwood and leather and lovely. It fills her nose and entices her to linger longer, with more kisses travelling along to his collarbone.

She doesn't really notice at first that he's stilled. That his hands have released her, until they settle again on her upper arms and gently press her to make some space between them. Has he been distracted? She tries to restart things by pressing her hips back into his, because she can feel he's into this, too. That's not an advent candle in his pocket, she's sure of it. But the rest of him is still, save for his thumbs rubbing the top of her arms.

"Anna?" he says carefully.

It's not really conversation she's looking for, to be honest, so she brings her lips up again to his. He accepts the kisses, but there's something missing. *Response.* She swipes her tongue against his lips, hoping he'll let her in, but instead he presses her further away.

"Anna." He's firmer this time.

Her eyes flick to his, and it takes her a second to focus. Her lust is clearly blinding. His expression is an odd mix; his eyes dark, his lips red with use but his smile is gentle and considered.

He steps aside, to uncage himself from her and the wall, though he doesn't let go of her, for which she is thankful. She doesn't really understand what's going on, other than her horniness is being stymied.

"What?" she asks.

He closes his eyes for a beat and takes a deep breath, as if resetting himself. "This. This…"

Yes, she feels it too – the epicness. She takes a step forward again, to show him. His mouth pulls up to one side and she thinks he's on board. Yasss!

"Stay," he says, like she's a puppy, or an unruly toddler. "I mean, wait."

She does so, but is glad for his hands on her arms, as she might just sway. She can't keep her eyes off his lips. His delicious, clever, kissable lips. Why are they wasting time?

"Anna," he says, catching her attention again. "You've been drinking."

"Mmmm," she agrees, thinking of the last shots she and Katrine had had, drinking arms entwined across the table, mirroring everyone else in the room, and singing heartily. "Just a bit."

"Just a bit," he agrees.

She leans in a little and whispers, "Might have been a bit more than a bit."

"I think you're right."

She smiles at him, glad they're so in tune. That they agree with each other, on so many things. Maybe. But definitely this. And that's a good thing, isn't it? That if you want to get close to someone you agree about things…

"Anna? Stay with me. Your eyes are going in opposite directions."

"They do that," she says. "'S'fine." She gives him her best reassuring smile. "I can shut them, if it bothers you. They don't have to take part."

She hears him chuckle, then feels the warmth of his breath at her ear as he whispers, "When we do this, I want your eyes open and on me. I want to see your pupils blown wide as you shout my name."

Anna can't quite get all the words in the right order in her brain to make sense of them – her attention is mostly on the sensation by her ear – but she feels deeper heat in her knickers.

He pulls back and she experiences a base need to stand on her tiptoes to get her ear back to his mouth.

"Here's the plan, Lundholm. I'm going to take you to bed."

Oh yes, back on track! Anna reaches out and places her hand on his crotch. Nope. Not a candle. She gives him a slow stroke and delights in the combination of the deep rumble from his throat and the grimace that shoots across his face.

"Behave." He moves himself from her touch. "I'm going to take you up to bed, *your* bed, and I'm going to tuck you in, and you'll sleep this off."

The cogs of her brain can probably be heard turning in Malmö, so slow and churning are they, and along with them, the crunch of her smile juddering as it drops.

"You don't want to?"

"Not a matter of *want*, Anna." He drops his glance to his waistband and where her empty hand still hangs between them, because she's forgotten about it – the hand, that is. "A matter of good decisions, and *snaps* isn't really a good decision-maker."

"I don't think I had much," she says, shaking her head vehemently. "Katrine had most of it."

"You didn't match her?" he asks.

"I don't think so?" Every shot. All the way.

"Maybe a bit more than a bit, though?"

She scrunches her nose. That sounds familiar. Her brain circles back to the right now, where it dawns on her that he's rejecting her. Her stomach drops and she feels shame beginning to rise in her face.

"Oh, no, you don't," he says. "Look at me. This isn't me saying 'no'. Just 'no for now'. You're drunk—"

"Tipsy," she corrects.

He blows out a *Pffft*, but lets it slide. "You're wearing Eau de Aquavit, my friend. And I prefer my partners to know what's going on."

"I'm pretty sure I know what's going on." Her smile feels filthy, but that's because the images sprinting across her mind are exactly that.

"Aye." He suddenly sweeps her up in his arms. "Sure you do. And if that's the case then you'll be able to describe it to me in tantalising detail tomorrow. And then we can see where we go from there."

He's already got her to the first step, having circumnavigated the discarded coat and hat in the middle of the hall floor.

She leans into his chest, which is warm and toasty and smells all lovely and him-y.

"Hmm," she sighs into his top. "Can I keep this?" she asks, giving the fabric a tug.

"Sure," he says, humouring her.

By magic, it seems to Anna, they're in her room. He must have flown up the stairs, like the beautiful god that he is, and he's gently tipping her into her bed.

She holds fast to the Henley, and chuckling, he slides out of it, leaving her snuggling into it like a blankie. She opens her eyes and sees his bare chest.

"Get in toooo." She is on the brink of begging, her pride a distant speck on the horizon.

"Not tonight, *skat*." He pulls the duvet over her.

"I wanted to know your foreign lands," she mumbles then, and hears him ask, "You what?", but sleep overtakes her and she's out cold before she can explain her exploratory plans.

Chapter Twenty-Six

Her eyeballs are hurty. That's all she can think. She hasn't even used her eyes yet so how can they be hurting already?

Raising up on one elbow, Anna promptly drops down on the bed again. It's not just her eyes. Her entire frontal lobe is being squeezed by gravity. Her mouth feels like something has scrubbed it dry. And then shat in it. Slowly, *so* slowly, she squints at the bedside table to see if there's any water and is gobsmacked to see there is in fact a full glass. How very practical and forward-thinking of Yesterday Anna. Not that she has any recollection of pouring it. Nor of digging out the blister pack of paracetamol that stands propped against it. It dawns on her that it was none of her doing. Yesterday Anna was her usual unpractical self ahead of a *snaps*-fuelled lunch. Which is disappointing. This was not her first *Julefrokost* rodeo. She is old enough to know better, and yet here she is. She rolls onto her back with a pathetic moan. Why is she so weak?

She blames Katrine. She always gets her into trouble. There will be a snippy text later. At the very least, she hopes Katrine's feeling as grim as she is. That's only fair, given it was Katrine's idea.

Eventually, she emerges from her pit of despair, barely able to handle the bright sunlight in the snug. Squinting again – it's the only way, given her sunglasses are downstairs – she almost misses the change on the jigsaw table. It's now complete. Only, the missing piece isn't there, the hole being filled instead by a perfectly made piece of card which "someone" has covered in gold Sharpie. She stares at it for longer than necessary – hiding the fact that getting this far has taken it out of her – before moving on, enticed by the scent of coffee. Such is her current need for a cupful that if anyone or anything gets in her way she might have a full-on breakdown.

"Well, *go' morgen'*," says Jamie, as she rounds the doorframe, now wrapped in the tartan throw from upstairs. He looks at her over the rim of the cup he's holding and the amusement in his eyes does not help. She's found her sunglasses, and they are firmly on her face.

"I think I'm dying, Jamie," she says, dragging her sorry carcass towards the coffee pot. After a moment she points out, "You do not appear to be dispensing sympathy."

"Apologies," he says, still with little sympathy. "Sit down and I'll get you a cup." She waves his offer away. Apparently, she does have some pride left. Not a lot, but in the face of his amusement, she manages a show of indignation.

"How are you doing?" he asks.

"Thanks for the paracetamol and the water," she says, at a low grumble.

"Anytime." His tone is kinder.

Sitting helps. The hot cup in her hands helps. The coffee in her throat, the caffeine gushing towards her veins all helps, and she drops her head back and lets out a deep soul-felt moan. Opening her eyes, she sees he's gazing at her, an expression on his face she can't quite read.

"What?"

"Just pleased to see you alive. The Copenhagen *snaps*-reserves took quite a hit yesterday. It's on the news this morning."

"Shut up." She manages a pathetic smile. He is literally a sight for sore eyes, but she keeps this to herself. "I saw the jigsaw. You made the piece." She thinks of the perfect fit. It must have taken him a while with a scalpel.

"Seemed a shame to leave it incomplete."

"The gold was a nice touch. Like those Japanese Kintsugi vases."

His smile widens. She can see he likes that she's got the reference. *She* quite likes that she's got the reference. The paracetamol and the caffeine must be kicking in.

"I think it's OK to recognise the loss in the jigsaw's story. Recognising its journey," he says in a posh way, like he knows it might sound wanky, then reverts to his normal tone. "Doesn't mean it can't be fixed. Doesn't mean it's only fit for the bin. Now it has a new life."

It's such a Jamie thing to do. Of course, his job is about fixing things, giving them longevity or renewal, but she can see how he can be quite granular about it, seeing it through in his life. She can respect that.

The eco-Christmas tree behind him catches her eye and suddenly the memory of walking in last night is back with her. It spurs her to get up and walk across to it all, taking it all in again, the reunion with all the old pieces giving her a tender ache in her heart. She picks up a small *nisse* from a shelf and moves it to stand in the street scene in the window. That was where she always liked this figure to be. He's a cheeky little chap, bent over double in laughter. As a child, she would make up stories about the source of his mirth, and she sees him now as a long-lost friend.

"Thank you for doing this," she says quietly. "It was so thoughtful."

Jamie doesn't turn towards her, she sees, looking his way; he simply takes a sip from his cup and says, "My pleasure."

Pleasure. That rings a bell somewhere in her tender brain.

Casting her eyes around the room, they settle on the wall on the other side of him. Something about that. Her fingers rise up and touch her lips. Hmm, something about kissing… She looks back towards him just as Jamie raises his right arm to stretch. It lifts the hem of his top and she sees a sliver of soft Jamie skin above his waistband. Her fingertips tingle in further recognition.

Jamie sighs into his stretch … and there it is. It *all* – well, enough significant parts – comes flooding back into her delicate head. Her launching herself at him, his responding, her pressing him against the wall, touching him, stroking him, kissing his neck, wanting to get up inside his Henley, really wanting to get it all off, his stopping things; his declining her, his putting her to bed like a child. Oh. My. God.

Standing statue-still, Anna doesn't quite know what to do. Instinctively, she wants to run from the room. Possibly screaming. Yep, the caffeine is switched on now.

The quiet obviously transmits to him, as from the corner of her eye she sees him turn.

"Anna? You OK?" She's turned a little towards him at the sound of his voice, but her frozen body is very much facing that space at the wall, and his eyes track there as well. He bites his lower lip. Is he remembering, too, or is he just worried about what she'll do next? Well, same, she thinks.

"Are you having an internal scizure?" he asks.

"Is that when your insides contract into a huge knot of embarrassment and self-loathing regarding your behaviour, which hurts right the way down to your toenails and makes you want to punch yourself in the face? That sort of thing?"

Jamie gets up and walks to her.

"That wall is my current favourite place in the house. Do not spoil it for me by feeling in any way sad, bad or embarrassed about what happened there."

Right, so he *was* remembering, too. Good to know.

And like last night, he leans into her, though very deliberately it seems without touching her, and says in a low voice which makes her edge closer, "If you'd been sober last night, your feet wouldn't have touched the ground."

And then he's walking back to his chair, the warmth of

his breath gone, the air between them empty. She holds back a low keening.

"That bikini you wore at the hot tub. Is that dry yet?" he asks from the table, the least expected question ever. Her head is still full of the whisper, her body with its meaning. The change in direction is befuddling. It makes her laugh.

"There's so little fabric in that bikini it was probably dry by the time we got home."

"Good. I have something planned for us."

He has?

"That involves swimwear? It's still December. There's still snow on the ground."

"Sure. But the hot tub was fun, no? And that involved both those things."

It had, to be fair. And so far, he's been very good at both picking things to do and as a companion.

"I don't think I'm up to harbour swimming," she says. In the summer it's fun, dropping off the baking quayside into the frigid water, but she's never quite been up for the winter swimming.

"Might clear the hangover," he suggests.

"Might kill me, too."

"Don't worry, it's not a harbour dip." Thank fuck for that. She's wracking her pathetic brain for what it could be.

"If you'd told me, I would've bought a new swimsuit. Something more sensible."

"Maybe I like that bikini." He doesn't turn around to face her, which is good because her face is heating up. She's not sure she'll be able to stand in front of him in the itsy-bitsy teeny-weeny bikini now without it feeling charged in some way. He's made his thoughts clear.

"If you'd been sober last night, your feet wouldn't have touched the ground." It's still buzzing around her ear. She's trying to parse it. Is last night the key bit and the moment is gone? Or is it just the sober bit, in which case she'd like to state for the record that she is most definitely sober now. She does however consider she might not look her best. Or even smell her best. She is in need of a shower. Quite why she hadn't had this thought before she came downstairs and let his eyes behold her, she is ashamed to say she has no idea. She is clearly very comfortable around him, which feels at odds with her current bashfulness. How does this make sense when she simultaneously has an underlying urge to climb him like a tree, too?

"Go get dressed, Anna. Dig out that bikini, and be back down here in," he checks his watch, his back to her still, "twenty minutes. I'm finishing up here and then we'll go, I'll drive."

Cycling herself will do her good, the physical motion helping to clear the cobwebs, but then she thinks of sitting like a princess on the front of the bike again. She's not going to turn down the treat of being ferried in style. Who knows when she'll ever have an offer like that again? The wind in her face can do the head-clearing.

"On it," she says, trying to sound upbeat, but it's hard. It feels like one of her smarter decisions of the last twenty-four hours to refill her cup on her way.

❄

As it turns out, it is as far from harbour swimming as possible. Jamie has got them into the spa for the afternoon at Manon les Suites. "Called a friend," is all he'll say, as she questions him walking into the swanky hotel.

And as it also turns out, floating in the indoor pool amid hanging vines, feeling like you are truly in "a slice of Bali" as they advertise it, is both an excellent way to clear a hangover, but also a fun step away from the reality of living in a snowscape.

"Not that I don't think it's beautiful outside," Jamie says, as they float around each other, Anna doing her best not to stare at his chest, "but I thought this might mix things up a bit."

Mixing things up a bit sounds good. With him, specifically. Since Katrine gave her the push, and set the Once-and-Done thought racing in her head for real, she's been on the brink of simply saying, "Please can we do this?" He'd recognise the addition of "please", from a Dane, makes this a serious request. Once-and-Done sounds like the most sensible approach to this … this desperate but doomed yearning she apparently has for him.

And it feels like this is back in her court. He's making her take the first step. Which she technically did last night, but she gets why he didn't take it further. Sober Anna making the first move is what he wants. Sober Anna isn't quite so sure. Sober Anna still holds various reasons front of mind as to why this is a folly.

For now, though, and the following hours, she parks the overthinking and the worry. They float and they flirt. They laugh and they lounge. They move around each other, eyes roving over each other, sometimes subtly and sometimes absolutely not, bare-skinned but for the bikini and his shorts, but there is absolutely no touching. Not once.

It almost kills her.

"Best hangover cure ever," she says, getting out of the cargo bike. It's dark again, and the fairy lights in the trees make the street look magical.

"And unlikely to appear on social media tomorrow," he adds.

"Well, I was hatless, so they'd never have suspected."

"That bikini, though," he says, sounding doubtful. She can see he's grinning in the glow of the streetlight.

Instinctively, she scoops up a handful of snow and flings it at him. Her aim is good and it hits him square in the chest.

There's a silence as they both realise what she's done. Jamie's eyebrows slowly rise. A laugh escapes her, at his face and also at the trouble she is now in.

"Oh dear, Anna," Jamie growls dangerously, "you had to go there…"

With a small squeal, she ducks behind the crate of the bike, grabbing more soft snow in her gloved hands as she goes, but not fast enough to avoid a snowball catching her shoulder. It makes her laugh harder. She hasn't done this in years. She sends one flying at Jamie, who is trying to hide on the other side of the low fence, but she's lobbed it in a high arch and it lands on his head. The groan from the fence makes her howl with laughter. In doing so, Jamie is awarded his chance and lands a slushy one right in her face.

"Gotcha!" he shouts and performs a victory dance, which in spite of her giggling, she brings to a halt by pelting him with three in a row.

"Truce!" she shouts after several more minutes of running and ducking and pelting and laughing. Their faces are red with the exertion, their panting breath misting in the streetlight. Their smiles, though, are wide, their eyes bright.

Her gloves are wet through and she pulls them off, to find her fingers icy beneath. Jamie comes to stand in front of her, as she rubs them together.

"Cold?" he asks, approaching tentatively, presumably in case it's a ruse.

She nods and says, "Time to go in, I think." She shakes her hands to try to get some warm blood back into them.

Jamie steps closer, then clasps his hands around hers, pulling them up to his face. Her eyes follow them up until their hands are at his mouth, where he puts his lips to them and blows, long and steady. Her eyes rise to his, fixed on her face, and she almost sways with the intimacy of it. His lips at her thumbs, his breath on her fingers, the warmth spreading across her skin, his eyes locked on hers; it is sensual and caring all rolled into one, and almost more than she can bear.

"Time to go in, Jamie," she says again, but this time her tone is pressing and her voice husky.

Inside, he helps her off with her coat. She's painfully aware of his nearness. Given their afternoon, the soothing warmth of the pool and the balmy air in the room, the awareness of his body, the not-touching, and now the playing, it all has her *thrumming*. She knows what she wants to do, but she cannot work out how to do it in a subtle, but alluring, way. Everything about her wants to leap on him, but her brain, thankfully now back in action, has the last word, and that word is *wait*.

She waits while he hangs the coats on the peg. There is something vibrating in the air between them as he stands behind her and she realises that he too is experiencing The Thrum.

She waits for him to move past her, but he doesn't. Apparently, Jamie, too, is waiting. For her, and that's the sign her head has been needing. Anna takes a step backwards. Small but deliberate, so it isn't confused with any kind of a stumble or hungover sway.

He doesn't say a word. He doesn't move.

At her next breath, she takes another backward step, bringing her spine to his chest.

Wait.

And then, she feels his hands rest lightly at her hips. Or rather at the hem of her jumper, which slowly, oh-so-slowly, he begins to peel up and off her. She raises her arms, noticing the stretch of her breasts as she does, hoping he'll run his hands along that skin soon. She hears the light sound of the jumper landing on the floorboards. It adds to her tremble.

Wait.

He runs his fingertips down her from her wrists, the length of her arms, past her shoulder blades, down her sides, returning his hands to her waist, where the hem of her next layer starts, and he repeats his upward draw. The slowness is both delicious and excruciating. The only way she can handle it is with her eyes closed, focusing on every inch of her skin as it's exposed to the air. Up and over her aloft arms, the top joins the jumper on its heap.

Wait.

He runs his hands all the way back up to her wrists and grasping them, draws her hands slowly down to her sides, before sinking his lips to the curve at her collarbone and neck, sending her eyeballs rolling backwards beneath her eyelids. Instinctively, she leans her neck away to offer him more skin. She lasts all of ten seconds before her resolve is decimated. She turns to face him.

No.

More.

Waiting.

Chapter Twenty-Seven

It takes Anna a moment to realise why the room seems weird. It's not her room. It's Jamie's. It's not her bed, or her white bedding. He favours a navy-blue check, and what's more, it's a double duvet, unlike the Danish standard of two singles. An arm is wrapped about her body, heavy and warm, and he must sense her waking up as he pulls her in to him. Other parts of Jamie are apparently awake, too. She wiggles into his morning glory, with plans. It's all the invitation he needs as she's suddenly swept on top of him, and off they go again.

She had told him, as he carried her up the stairs, her legs wrapped around his hips, their kisses hungry and incessant, that this could only be a one-off. That nothing had changed and that she didn't want to hurt him, so this was it and all it could be. Once-and-Done. He paused for the merest of beats, that eyebrow raised, then pulled her lip lightly with his teeth and growled, "We'll see." Right now, Anna is reasoning that Once-and-Done means one *night*, and it's not fully light outside, so.

The second time she wakes, after an exhausted snooze, she's facing him, her arm now draped over his chest. He's propped up on his pillow, gazing at her.

"Have you been watching me sleep?"

"Like a stalker?" he asks.

"Yep."

"Totally. Who wouldn't?" He drops a kiss onto the crown of her head. "You're gorgeous."

She'll take the flattery, but Anna worries about her sleep face, whether she's dribbled or snored, but as he's neither kicked her out of bed, nor run screaming from it, it can't have been too bad.

"Good morning," he says.

"So far," Anna confirms. She must thank Katrine for her advice at some point. It was excellent advice, expertly dispensed. Last night was … exquisite. Everything she had dreamt of, and round two had been even more. Jamie has not disappointed, it is fair to say. She aches in all the rights places, muscles having been flexed and stretched for the first time in a long time.

She sits up, about to wrap herself in the duvet, to do the coffee run.

"What?" he asks, regarding her creased brow.

"You have a double duvet."

"So?"

"If I take it, you'll have nothing. You'll be cold. Another reason Danish couples favour singles."

"The other reason being?" Jamie looks baffled.

Apparently, Jamie has not been having a lot of sleepovers in the Copenhagen area. Something about that pleases Anna, but she chooses not to examine it too hard. But a celibate Jamie is a loss to the city's women. She'll have to have a word with him about that.

"Danes generally stick to singles," she answers to his question. "Means you aren't fighting over the share of the duvet in the middle of the night, and you don't overheat."

"And that's what you and Carl had?"

"Yes, of course."

"For how many years?"

She's not sure she sees the relevance. "Six."

"Hmm," is all he says.

Anna tweaks his nipple, which makes him yelp. "What does that 'hmm' mean?"

"Nothing."

"There was a judgement there. Tell me, MacDonald." She holds her fingers in pinch-pose above the reddening nipple.

"Well, I've always enjoyed being under a duvet with someone I like. The shared warmth, the closeness, the intimacy. You can pull it over you and be cocooned in your own little world, just the two of you. Who wouldn't want that? I reckon it's good for couples. If you can't share a duvet, how can you share a life? That's what I think. Plus, it halves the chance of getting a cold arse."

She can't fault him on the statistics there.

"I think Danes would say not fighting over duvet share has saved many marriages."

Jamie crosses his arms and shakes his head. "Hard disagree, and this is a hill I'll die on."

Luckily, Anna hasn't minded the double, nor sharing it with him, so she's not inclined to pick this fight. And besides, as per the deal with herself, she won't be doing it again. This, this thing between them, they've explored it now. Surely, that should calm the simmering in her torso. That was the actual point of Once-and-Done. Only, why then is she still thrumming?

Unsettled, she stands and heads for the door, taking the duvet with her and leaving him very naked and presumably cooling rapidly on his hill.

Anna looks out of the kitchen window to the street as she waits for the coffee to pour through the percolator. The street is busy as her neighbours come and go, maybe completing the last of their Christmas shopping or buying food for tomorrow night. It's *Lille Jule Aften*, Little Christmas Eve, or Christmas Eve Eve as she's been amused to hear her London neighbours call it.

She's not going to bother calling the airlines or check online today. This will be one of their busiest days already as people make their final sprints home ahead of Christmas. What would she be doing in London for these next few days anyway? Sitting in her apartment, as everything is closed. Maybe working, but she can do that here, too. And besides, Jamie just gave her a beautiful gift of a nostalgically decorated living room, so it feels rude not to park the exit strategy just for the next few days. If nothing else, it might just be a light relief not to be worrying about it, just for now.

Looking at the Christmas scene at the other end of the room truly does feel like a gift. And it dawns on her that she doesn't have one for him. When she leaves Copenhagen, she'll be taking some earth-moving memories with her, and Anna finds she wants to have left a mark with him, too.

But what do you get for a man who you don't know very well, but well enough to know that in his life of environmental concern, it shouldn't be something disposable, inconsequential or temporary? No joke-gift for Jamie. It needs an actual purpose or, if not functional, then particular beauty. She doesn't know him well enough either to buy him something arty and worthy for its form. This is tough. Looking at the *nisser* and the baubles again, she realises he *did* something deeply thoughtful for her. He had a guess at something she might like, strike that, she might *love*, and he did it.

The coffee scent is working its way around her face and sparking some ideas. Something he hasn't got for himself… Anna's brainstorming brings her attention back into the street and something ignites a big, but perfect, thought. It'll take research, negotiation and luck. But she has the time and most of those skills – her luck has been a little iffy recently, but even that has brought her an experience in Jamie's bed, so eh, it's worth a go.

"Get your coat, Jamie," Anna announces, walking into the living room. "We're going for a ride."

"I can think of a ride we could take and not even leave this room," he says, catching her wrist from his spot in the sofa.

She looks down into his face and feels the pull in the pit of her belly. It would be so easy to let him tug her down into his lap, for them to continue where they left off this morning. She's been replaying last night and sees quite clearly that it would be just as easy to become used to it, and fall for it, for *him*, and she knows this would be the worst thing to happen.

"Come on, Anna," he coaxes, his voice husky, "I haven't seen you for hours." This is true. She's been squirrelled away in her room, under the excuse of an "emergency web post" for Katrine. There is something about a husky-slightly-desperate Jamie, which makes breathing a little painful for her. Her resolve, though, is stronger, not least because she's slightly desperate herself, but to give him her gift.

"Come on," she mimics back, "coat on."

"Bossy," she hears him murmur, sulkily.

"No, just direct. You know the Danes," she calls from the hallway, pulling on her boots.

He stomps lightly across to follow her, then tries to feel her up, which she points out is pointless as she extracts herself, given all the layers. Jamie's mouth purses and he leans against the wall, arms crossed.

"You OK?"

"Sure."

"You aren't freaking out?"

"Freaking out? Me? No. Of course not." She does her best to look him right in the eyes, face open and with a smile.

"You're being weird."

She pulls an offended face. "No, I'm not. I've been working on something and now I want to show you." Why can't he just follow along as instructed?

"OK, not weird. But you *are* being distant," he corrects.

"Because I said no to going at it on the sofa?" she asks. Now Jamie looks offended, that muscle pulsing in his jaw again. Anna feels the mood has shifted. This isn't what she wants. She doesn't want to have a discussion about *them*, not now – not at all, to be honest – and especially when they have somewhere to be.

"I'm not being distant, I just have something up my sleeve, something I've been arranging, and it's time-sensitive, so we need to go."

The look Jamie sends her says he's neither convinced nor letting this go, but willing to pause it for now. She'll take that – The Conversation can be Future Anna's problem.

"You're in the front this time," she throws at him, opening the front door, changing the subject.

"You're driving the chariot?"

"I am," she says, determined. "Today you are the princess."

This turns out to be something Anna regrets by the time they reach the end of the street. Jamie has apparently bought an old Christiania bike, one built before batteries, and each rotation of the pedals is exhausting.

"Do you want to swap?" he asks.

"No," she insists through gritted teeth.

"It saves on the gym membership." Great.

"I do that in London, by not actually joining. Much cheaper."

"I wanted a second-hand one. It's literally recycling." Of course it is, Anna seethes in her head. Her quads are screaming already. His weight in the front is making this far worse, but her pride is calling the shots. She wants her gift to be epic, so delivering him to it under her own steam is part of the parcel.

"What are we doing?"

"Still not telling." He's asked her approximately every two minutes.

"Shall we stop and get a bottle of wine? Or *gløgg*?"

"Definitely not. We need best behaviour for this."

"Are we meeting royalty?"

"Close. Next best thing."

He looks properly confused and it delights her. Turns out doing secret things is pleasing. Edit that: doing *nice* secret things is pleasing. Carl's and Maiken's secret thing had not been pleasing. Not to Anna. She bats that thought out of her head, not wanting those memories to spoil her afternoon.

After much stifled groaning and less stifled panting, Anna pulls into a park, and then on to a play area.

"I might be a bit big for the swings," he says, with a

laugh, but it stills in his throat as his eyes come to rest on a little girl jumping on a sunken trampette, and the woman behind her on the bench.

"Shit."

"Don't panic," Anna urges. "She knows we're coming. She agreed to be here. I'll play with Nikoline and you two can try to talk."

He looks at her, and she sees worry in his eyes.

"Play it cool, Jamie. Just be you. You've got this." Keeping it a surprise was the right way to go.

"Nothing to lose, I suppose."

Anna cups his face with her gloved hands, telling herself it's for Lajla's benefit. "Exactly." Purportedly their entwined hands are also "fake mode", as they walk across to where Lajla is sitting, her own hands clenched between her legs. She's as nervous as he is.

Anna takes the lead and crouches to introduce herself to Nikoline. The little girl is shy at first, but when Anna offers to push her on the swings, and Lajla gives her the nod, she's on board. Once placed within the swing seat frame, Anna deliberately swings Nikoline face-on. In her head she tells herself it's a safety thing, or even familiarising Nikoline with her face, but both are lies. Really, she's watching for all the little signs that she's Jamie's kid. Her smile is his, the way she pulls her brows together is his and her pout is definitely his. This must be weird for Lajla to see, day in day out. The wisps of fringe that peek out from the little girl's balaclava are light brown now, but Anna would bet they'll be more Jamie's colour by Nikoline's teens.

The toddler is charming. She's quick to laugh and not particularly shy around Anna, but then she supposes Nikoline has a dedicated servant here now, pushing the swing faster at her command, so what's not to like?

The downside about this positioning is that she can't watch Jamie and Lajla. She can hear the murmurs of their talking, but nothing distinct, which is frustrating of course. In the meantime, she takes a lack of shouting as a good sign. After a while she convinces Nikoline to try the wobbly horse, a wooden seat on a big spring, where Nikoline can hold onto the horse's head and wobble forwards and backwards, side to side. Once she's settled on that, Anna sits on its neighbour and wobbles herself, much to Nikoline's amusement, mainly to get a view of the couple on the bench. Couple. The thought of it makes something in Anna's stomach twist. If these peace talks are successful, then perhaps Lajla might let Jamie play a role in Nikoline's life, and maybe they might take it further. Anna looks harder at them. Lajla has her arms crossed over her chest, but to be honest that might just be down to the cold. It's minus-five out here, and she's been sitting still for a while. Jamie on the other hand is sitting safely apart from her but turned to face her. His hands are in his pockets, his posture open towards her. It's a very peaceful, non-threatening pose, absolutely the right way to come at this, Anna thinks.

Nikoline tires of the horse quickly, dragging them over

to the parallel trampettes she was on when they arrived. This requires minimum effort from Anna as she bounces up and down next to her new buddy and can assess how it's going over on the bench. Lajla is looking more relaxed, Jamie is upholding his same stance. His nose is redder, as are his ears, and Anna thinks he'll be regretting not wearing his hat with earflaps. Amateur. She's properly wrapped up with her hat and her thick scarf wound multiple times around her neck, as is Lajla. The woman isn't looking as pained as when they arrived. Her eyes still skitter back and forth to Nikoline, but not as much. Anna wants to punch the air as Lajla pulls out her phone and types in something Jamie's telling her. His number. Or his address. Either would make sense. Either would be an enormous step forward.

Nikoline has had enough of playing with the unknown lady and scuttles back to her mother. Lajla scoops her up onto her knee and wraps her arms possessively around her. Fair enough. Jamie doesn't move an inch. It must be taking every ounce of his resolve not to hold a hand out to touch his daughter. Anna doesn't quite know what to do with herself. Join them or wait by the bike, but the latter might bring their discussion to a premature end. So, in her befuddlement she ends up bouncing on the trampette far longer than is normal and it takes Jamie looking to find her, and then to cock his head at her like she's being weird, for her to step off it, which she does with such momentum, she stumbles her dismount. Her face is scarlet as she joins him on the end of the bench.

Lajla whispers something to Nikoline, who looks up at Jamie.

"*Hej*," she says to him.

"*Hej, med dig*," he says back. Hi, you. His first proper words to his child. It makes Anna's eyes sting a bit. His hands are still in his pockets, and she'd bet it's that or sitting on them. Instinctively, she tucks her hand into his elbow, to let him know she's there with him, but it dawns on her it might look possessive. From her end of the bench behind him, she sees the three of them together. Like they could be a family. It makes her bite her lip and slowly, trying not to make anything of it, she withdraws the hand again.

Lajla tells Nikoline it's time to go home and Nikoline suddenly looks like she's about to kick off. Lajla must be used to it, as she fishes a box of raisins out of her pocket and negotiates that Nikoline can have them when she's in the bike seat. The toddler races for the bike. She doesn't hear Jamie call, "Bye Nikoline!" but then she's two and raisins are infinitely more interesting than adults. Lajla stands and looks pensively at Jamie, who looks up at her with as plain a face as Anna's ever seen on him. There's no pressure being applied here.

"I'll think about it," she says.

"That's all I'm asking," he replies quietly. His body is tense. Nothing like the lithe and limber Jamie Anna's experienced in the last twenty-four hours. She thought this was a good thing to arrange, but perhaps she was wrong.

"*God Jul*," Lajla says and turns towards her bike. There is no *"vi ses"* because she isn't promising anything about seeing each other again.

As she walks away, Jamie slowly exhales, and his body deflates with it.

They silently watch Lajla load Nikoline into the bike seat and strap her in, after which the raisins are duly given to her to hold, although Nikoline hasn't been savvy enough to remember her mittens won't allow her to scoff them. For now, though, just holding the little box is enough, and she grasps them like a trophy. Lajla says something to her, and she turns to look at Jamie. Then she smiles his own smile back at him, and gives a mittened wave.

When they are finally out of sight Jamie stops staring after them to look at Anna. He looks … she cannot tell.

"Was that OK?" she asks carefully, worried she might have overstepped. And she watches in wonder as he releases his facial muscles from the mask he's been holding, to let his smile spread across his face.

"That was very OK, Anna."

Then he leans in and kisses her, and she tells herself it's just gratitude, or it's for show in case Lajla doubles back, or that they are simply celebrating a win, but she knows it's not true. She stays though, because she wants it; the softness of his lips on hers, the taste of him, his tongue lightly stroking her tongue, her breath mingling with his. But eventually she brings it to a close.

"Hey," she says, sliding away along the bench. "Kids' playground, family show." It feels like it's more to remind herself. He doesn't release his hand from her waist immediately, instead studying her, his eyes drifting from each of her eyes to the other, seeking answers.

"Want to talk about this?" he asks.

She thinks about bluffing, acting dumb with a "talk about what?" But she knows he deserves better. She's reluctant to spoil the moment, though, so instead pulls him to his feet, and over to the trampettes, where they spend a while, without a word, bouncing side by side, but still hand in hand.

Chapter Twenty-Eight

"**B**loody hell!"

"'S'up?" Jamie asks, setting up the new jigsaw, in what she now thinks of as the jigsaw lounge. It's the one she dug out for him, and it's particularly evil; an aerial photograph of Kartoffelrækkerner, by Nicolas Cosedis. Row upon row of similar roofs. It'll take them days. Him. It'll take *him* days.

"Did you see anyone taking pictures when we were in the playground?" It's only been five hours since they were in the playground and already photos are up. Also, five hours where they've been navigating each other carefully. She can tell Jamie's deliberately giving her space, but she senses him watching her and sees the flex of his hand when he holds back from touching her. She wishes she didn't notice, but the fact is, it simply mirrors her own instincts. She's aware of his presence wherever he is, and her eyes flick to him constantly. All the while, she's trying to behave as if nothing has changed between them, that it was just a night of passion, which has now been sated, and they can go back to how they were. The charge in the room between them suggests otherwise however, moreover that she's an idiot for even thinking it.

Jamie looks up from turning on the candles. "No, but I've got to admit I wasn't looking at other people. My head was kind of full already."

Fair enough. She hadn't, either. She holds the device to his face. It's a photo of them, mid-bounce and holding hands, above the two trampettes. With her hat on and his same coat, it's obvious it's them again. The photo is captioned as such.

"Cute." He pours them each a whisky from the bottle of Torabhaig on the bookshelf, placing the glasses next to a dish of *klejner*.

"It doesn't bother you?" she asks, snaffling one.

"Not really. It's a sweet picture." Then he looks at her properly, with a hint of something in his eye. "I like being in these shots with you. I like other people thinking they're something. Something cute or even iconic. Who wouldn't want that?"

Anna presumably, is who he's suggesting. Does she want that? She likes being cute with him, too. But she can't square it in her head: that it should be her in those gorgeous photos and that it should all be happening here, in this city. She thinks to say, "but it's not real", but the words feel wrong on her tongue. It *was* real. They were together in this very real, spontaneous moment, celebrating something good.

Jamie had been in a jubilant mood for the entire ride

home from the playground (his turn to pedal, she decided), wanting to know how she'd managed it.

"My superhero-skill might be research, Jamie," she'd said primly but secretly ecstatic he liked her gift so much. She imagined he'd felt the same when she saw the decorations in the house. "That's how I started out at the publishing house, the travel writing was later."

"But you literally only had her first name." He looked baffled and supremely impressed. Probably he'd done some research of his own and only ever got as far as her company and then her office building, which considering he'd met her at a conference, where people wore name badges, would have been a cinch.

"OK, so as I may have mentioned, maaany times, it's a small city. I could google using her first name within the sustainability companies in the city and eventually narrow it down to three candidates. Then it's onto the socials to find someone who has her face on Instagram, which she did, because she's a mum with a super-cute kid and she'll want her friends to see. Her account might be private, but her profile pic isn't. So, then I had a confirmed full name, after which it's super easy as the Kraks digital phone book readily hands over people's addresses and phone numbers in Denmark."

He'd looked down at her in the crate seat, sceptically. "It's true," she insisted, "although I don't understand how it gets around the data-protection laws, but in this case, it's to my benefit, so. Then I just called her." She'd deliberately sounded blasé about it, but she was glowing really.

"Oh, my God," he breathed, like a sixteen-year-old girl. "You're like a *spy*."

She flicked his thigh. "Hardly. I just know how to search."

"And all this info was available to me all this time?"

"Yep," Anna had said with a grin. "Only you needed me here as the mastermind." He'd flicked the bobble of her hat in response.

Anna looks again now at the photo of them. It *is* cute. She discreetly saves it to a secret Pinterest board along with the others. Then, leaning over him, she picks out a couple of jigsaw pieces with a flat edge. Given their angle and the image, she places one on the top and the other to the left edge. Jamie moves to the far end of the small sofa making room for her, plus some to give her space. He's back to leaving things in her court, but she can see by his eyes that it's not his natural inclination. She suspects his impulse would have been to catch the curve of her waist and draw her down to him. Anna snares the wistful sigh in her mouth before it escapes.

Instead she sits at her own end of the sofa and he raises his glass in her direction, though without taking his eyes from the table and the pieces. She clinks it with hers and they focus quietly on adding more pieces to the jigsaw frame, working in bursts, building on each other's finds, and then sitting still in the pauses, when the obvious pieces run out, trying to ignore the buzz in the slim gulf between them.

"I've been thinking," he eventually says during one of the pauses.

"Oh dear," she interjects, sure she knows what's coming and wanting to put it off. It earns her a brisk bump to the shoulder.

"I was thinking," he starts again, sounding sterner, "how about we work together on something?"

OK. Not what she was expecting.

"What do you mean?"

"Not sure yet. A book or a guide. A green guide to Copenhagen, or a book of simple things people in cities can do to help the planet and offset tourism. I was thinking about the things my work has already started here in the city and how we can tell more people about them and promote their use in other cities if there's some kind of published guide to show. Ebook, app, paperback, whatever."

"You want to work together?"

"Aye." He turns his face to look at her for the first time in ages, and her heartbeat increases in welcoming it. She loses herself in his eyes, but hauls herself back. His eyes drop to her lips, but he doesn't move any closer. "I have ideas and established initiatives, you have the words and are, of course, the 'research mastermind'." He does the finger quotes and she lightly slaps them down for his lack of due respect.

"And you'd want it to be based on Copenhagen?"

"Initially. It's an ideal place to start, given everything that's already going on. I know you've been away for a while, and obviously it's winter so everyone is hibernating, but come spring there are lots more projects to see. Tourist things. The green kayaks with the litter bins on the back the tourists fill in exchange for free rental? Like that. Meanwhile, we could work on the proposal, maybe talk to your editor to see what she thinks."

There are lots of things about this that have happy bells pealing in her head, but even so, there's a death-knell which overrides them.

"I won't be here, though. I mean we could work on it online, but it's not the same as being on the ground. And I won't be coming back."

She's been feeling the need to say it. For clarity. Her hiatus in calling the airlines *will* come to an end and she *will* get a ticket, and she *will* resume her life in London.

Jamie turns his eyes back to the jigsaw, and it feels like shade on her face. "You wouldn't want to give this a go?" he asks lightly.

"The guide?" she checks.

"Us," he clarifies, and takes a swig of his whisky.

"Move back?" The thought is alien to her. She's finished with the city. In all the years she lived with her mother, they never moved back to anywhere. "Always forward," Ida would say. Holidays back to Copenhagen were always just that, holidays. Now that it got elongated, Anna is sort of seeing this trip as that.

"Maybe." He places another jigsaw piece, now working within the frame.

Her face is not hiding her feelings very well.

"There's the long-distance thing," he suggests, turning back and giving her an easy look. She feels his hand gently stroke her calf. It is non-pressuring and calming, but at the same time heart rate increasing, which confuses her body.

It feels cruel to give him a flat no, though her instincts tell her it's what's needed. Ida would tell her so. Ida would already be packed and halfway out of the door, she corrects herself. But Jamie values talking things out, so Anna tilts her head at him and says, "That wouldn't be very good for the environment, would it? Flying back and forth regularly. Not sure it would look good on your profile."

"There's the train." He's back to the jigsaw, keeping things chill.

"Ha! You'd be returning as soon as you arrived. Weekends aren't long enough for that."

"You've thought about it?" he asks, eyebrow raised. It looks like hope.

"No, not really, Jamie," she says, trying to be gentle. "This was just supposed to be…" She closes her eyes, trying to find the words that won't be too brutal, but sees there's no way around this. "It was just Once-and-Done. Like I said. And it was mind-blowing, unforgettable, but it's done."

His hand stills and she sees the hurt in his eyes, immediately wanting to soothe it.

"I don't mean that in a bad way. This, with you, has been a wonderful thing in what was a bit of a nightmare for me. But look at it from my point of view; I live in London, and I don't want to move back. And you live here, have a great job here and a daughter who you want to be around for. Long-distance wouldn't be great in the long run. It's too hard; never having the hard discussions in case you spoil the short moments you've got, the missing each other in between, not being near when times are tough. I've seen it." Well, she's seen it on TV. Her lived experience never got to that, as Ida always left when things got tricky.

His gaze softens, and his hand resumes stroking her leg. She isn't sure he's aware he's doing it. "You really can't see yourself coming back here?"

"Really not," she says softly. "I've moved on." She pushes away the thought of her apartment and how, now he's brought her attention to it, Danish it is. The furniture, the style, the trinkets, the single duvets on the double bed.

"The city really holds such bad memories for you?"

"They were awful times, Jamie." She rests her head on the back of the sofa. "Some scars don't heal, but that's OK. They can give you the courage to change your life and move."

The look he gives her, his wry smile, tells her he still doesn't agree with her framing. But she doesn't need him to.

"What is it you're so scared of, Anna?" he asks. He's being gentle with her now, his hand stilling, cupping her calf, and the turning of the tables makes her skin prickle.

"Scared? I'm not scared," she says, raising her head back up. "I'm just facing the future."

"But there could be a future here. With me." His face is open and guileless and oh-so-handsome, but that prickling has become a bristle. Anna slides her calf out of his hand, noticing the cooling that immediately settles there. She pulls the throw over her legs, for warmth as well as defence.

It's an offer. Honest and clear. And for many it would a good one, fantastic in fact. He's a catch. But there is no way she can see to make this work. It's a practical thing, it's protecting him, it's certainly not *fear*.

"I'm sorry, but I can't see it," is all she can say.

Jamie studies her face, then gives her a small nod with a flat smile, before pouring them both another measure, and raising the glass in toast. "To happy futures." The separate nature of the futures isn't lost on her.

Anna repeats it, but the words feel empty in her mouth.

Chapter Twenty-Nine

The kilt.

Oh. My. God.

Anna has to hand it to Jamie, he knows how to pull out the big guns. Having purportedly accepted her decision last night, from what she can see, he's switched tactics today. He's not badgering her, or touching her or even venturing near the subject of "them", but he's around her, being charming, thoughtful and wafting that scent of his close to her, causing something to coil in her core.

And now he's just walked into the room, freshly showered, hair tamed – *ish* – in a thin, knitted grey V-neck over a white T and … the kilt.

Anna sinks a visible gulp.

This is a battering ram to her resolve.

"I told you I had a kilt," he says, the smirk on his face saying he knows exactly what he's doing to her and her nether regions. Damn him. He fights dirty – and on Christmas Eve, a time of peace and goodwill, no less.

She ducks her head, focusing on serving up their food, to hide the long, centring breath she's letting out.

Though small, it's the perfect Christmas spread. They've worked on it together all afternoon, having decided that just because it's only the two of them for *Juleaften*, it doesn't mean they can't have a full Danish Christmas dinner on Christmas Eve. On each plate there's a roasted breast of duck, red cabbage, caramelised new potatoes, blanched half-apples with redcurrant jelly in the middle, all swimming in brown gravy.

"Looks great," says Jamie, walking behind her to collect the wine bottle, passing her in the narrow space between the far counter and the kitchen island, which makes her shoulder blades flex. She rolls her neck for inner strength. As he moves away, around the island, she's finding it ridiculously hard to drag her eyes from the kilt. The perfect fall of the worsted wool over his equally perfect bum, the seductive sway of the tartan pleats as he moves. His easy swagger suggests he is absolutely aware. Argh. Her perving is verging on the obscene. Still serving, she stands on her own foot, hoping the pain will snap her out of the ogling.

"The smell alone takes me back to Vivi and Mads' Christmases. Roast duck is Christmas for me," says Anna brightly. She's also dressed for dinner – nothing too fancy but still an upgrade from the leggings she's been walking around in all day. A satin midi skirt and a loose wool sweater on top, both in navy. Yeah, so the thick home-knitted socks don't quite go, but warm feet are always a priority in Anna's book. She's added some make-up – just enough to make it look like she's made an effort.

A playlist with The Three Tenors singing Christmas carols plays low in the background, and outside there's light snow falling. It isn't forecast to get heavier, so there's no anxiety about that. It's just Pretty Snow.

Jamie pours two glasses of red wine and holds one to her. They clink the glasses.

"*Slàinte Mhath*," he says, as she says, "*Skål*." They drink, their eyes locked the whole time.

"What did you do last year for Christmas, Jamie?" Anna asks, as they settle down to their meal, clambering for the safe ground of regular conversation.

"I went home to see my dad. This year, though, what with the planes and everything, it's a good thing we decided I'd stay here. He's having dinner with my uncle's family."

Lucky for her, Anna thinks. He'd have not been home when she'd knocked on his door. She might never have met him. The thought gives her a pang in her gut.

"What's your mother doing?" he asks.

"Well, apparently, she's on some silent retreat. Which is bizarre. Normally, she'd be in a bar somewhere, living it up. She does like a party and on Christmas Eve there's usually revelling of some kind, wherever you are."

"You hadn't planned to join her? Greece would have been warmer than here."

"So true," she says with an overegged sigh. She certainly wouldn't be in knitted socks. And yet, it hadn't even occurred to her to try to get a ticket to Greece rather than back to the UK, when she supposes she could have. Athens airport most likely wasn't snowbound.

"We haven't done Christmas together for years," Anna says. "It works for us to meet up at other times. Ida isn't big on traditional things and rituals, unlike most Danes. There's comfort and reassurance in scheduled events, but Ida feels it hinders freedom and is the 'product of lazy thinking'." Anna rolls her eyes, remembering many of her mother's monologues on the subject.

Jamie's eyes widen. "Wow. I really want to meet her one day. She sounds like a maverick."

Anna laughs. Obviously, it's never going to happen, and even if it did, Anna would be a bundle of nerves as to how Ida would behave.

"So, what *did* you have planned?" he asks, taking another sip of his wine. It's a Barolo, and a good one. He'd overseen the drinks.

"Well, I had thought I'd go to the big *Juleaften* dinner they serve at the Danish Church by Regent's Park. Danes who are in London and away from family at Christmas can come and eat together. I went last year, and it was lovely. Lots of fun. Or else, I guess I would have spent the evening by myself."

Jamie pulls a sad face at her.

"Shut up. I am excellent company and perfectly happy to entertain myself." Binge-watching some murder series might not be overly Christmassy, but there would have been a bottle of port to make up for it.

He holds his hands up. "Not judging. I might have been doing the same."

"Don't give me that. Someone would have invited you to join their dinner. You're ridiculously popular."

He busies himself with his duck. Something clicks in her head.

"Jamie, did you already have an invitation for tonight?" It hadn't occurred to her that he might. She'd simply assumed he was like her, alone, and them having their own Christmas dinner was the obvious, yet only choice.

"Just two," he says. "Three at most."

"And you chose not to go?" She's stunned.

"I'm sure they would have welcomed you, too," he says, "but I didn't actually ask them."

"Why not? You could have gone. Without me, I mean. I would have understood."

He rolls his eyes at her, like she's being a dummy.

"Could it possibly be, Anna, that the idea of spending the evening with you, just us, sounded way more perfect to me?"

His honesty, even in light of her dismissing his offer, is disarming. It makes her blush. "Oh, well, OK. If you put it like that…"

He holds his glass up towards her. "*Glædelig Jul*, Anna," he says in his best Danish. And she returns it with a clink.

They eat, savouring the flavours of the Christmas meal, him as it's something new, Anna as it's pure nostalgia on a plate.

"You look happy," he says, watching her.

"I don't think I could ever be unhappy eating Danish Christmas food."

"Well, they do say Danes are the happiest people on Earth."

"I hear this all over the place whenever I say I'm from

Denmark," she says, one hand propping up her chin and the other running a finger around the rim of her glass. "But I think we've been knocked off that top position by the Finns. Having thought about it, though, I think it depends on your definition of happy."

"How do you mean?" asks Jamie. "Happy is happy, isn't it?"

"The way I see it, here in Denmark if you have what you need you are content. If you are content, then you are happy. But having lived in other places now, I see it's not always the same. Some people feel they need more money, more material things, newer gadgets, always something more than what they have. Never enough. So, it's not the same. Contentment seems like a forgotten state in some places from my observation, but that might just be me."

"I haven't thought about it that way," says Jamie. "But Danes like their material things. I've seen their appetite for the designer furniture." He gives the Carl Hansen chairs on the other side of the Hans Wegner coffee table a nod.

"Beautiful things designed to last," she says of them. "Feathering nests with pleasing things. Part of conjuring *Hygge*, which is part of the contentment.

"Trust is another tenet of the contentment," she goes on. "Danish society functions on trust. 'I will trust people I meet, and they will rise to that trust, and in turn trust others, who will rise to their trust and so on, and as a result society will function with decency.' If you think and live like that, life feels less perilous and less likely to bite you in the arse, which, like tradition, feels reassuring and makes you more content." She believes it, because she's seen the flipside, how broken trust can banish contentment.

"I'm not sure when I last used the word 'content'," he admits.

"Precisely, but maybe because it isn't thought of so much in the UK? Words mean different things to different people," she says. "Take luxury, for example. If you ask people what luxury means, some will say it's swanky hotels or expensive restaurants, exclusive consumer brands, but if you ask, say, new parents 'What is luxury?' I bet many will say that it's waking up of your own accord in the morning followed by leisurely sex and then having a snooze after." *Just like our morning the other day,* she doesn't say. "That's not something they can do with children, not unless the kids are having a sleepover elsewhere. For them that would be luxury."

Jamie laughs. "How have you come about this information?"

"Ahh, that would be Katrine. She's constantly telling me how she'd kill for a lie-in."

They carry on chatting about their friends in both Scotland and Copenhagen, of things they'd like to see in the coming year, of her travel plans, while they polish off their platefuls and seconds – because, of course, in Denmark there's always seconds. The shame of sending someone home hungry would be unbearable.

Jamie's phone suddenly pings. He gives the screen a cursory glance, then double-takes. Anna sees his eyes widen as he opens the text.

"Everything OK?"

"Look." He turns the phone. It's a picture of a little girl by a Christmas tree, opening her presents. "It's from Lajla. It says Merry Christmas."

"Sounds like a bit of a breakthrough, doesn't it?"

"I didn't give her a present," he suddenly says, looking the most worried she's ever seen him.

Anna instinctively puts her hand on his, then instantly removes it again. She can't cope with the spark. He didn't miss it either, and turns his hand over, palm upwards, fingers lightly curved, creating a space for hers. An invite. She looks at it, considers it, then slides her hand into her lap. "Jamie, don't worry about it," she says, reassuring and distracting him. "Lajla won't be expecting anything. You weren't expecting her to send you a photo, were you?"

"No." He moves his offered hand to play with his fork.

"Maybe this is Lajla reaching out. An olive branch, or moving things on a small step at a time. And Nikoline won't notice you haven't given her a gift."

"Right. Right, sure." He's flustered but still gazing at the picture. It's a lovely shot and one where she particularly looks like her father. Anna suspects this will be his screensaver within minutes.

"On the subject of goodwill and olive branches, you should be honest with your dad and tell him the whole story about why you're here." She sees a cloud cross his face, but ploughs on. "Explain about Nikoline, and he'll get it. He'll understand why you're so set on staying. And he might also be delighted to have a granddaughter. You think it's too much of a mess, but life is messy, your dad already knows that. If you won't give him the full picture, then how can he support you?"

Jamie keeps his eyes on the photo, deep in thought. She might have spoiled the evening by overstepping, but it needed to be said. Finally he gives a small grunt and says, "I'll think about it." Then, he takes a sip of the wine, shows her the screen again and asks, "What will they be doing this evening?"

"Pretty much what we've just done," says Anna brightly, feeling the mood lighten again. "Unless they're uber-traditionalists and then they'll have started with a rice pudding, which is what they did in olden times to fill the stomach before the more expensive food, so they didn't have to buy as much. But normally nowadays, they'll have had family dinner, presumably with Lajla's parents, and they'll have had duck, like us, or perhaps goose or roast pork with crackling, with the same sides we've had. Then dessert at the end and when they've finished eating, they'll hold hands and walk around the Christmas tree singing carols."

"Really?" asks Jamie, incredulous, "Singing?"

"Sooo much singing! You've been to parties over here. You've experienced the singing."

"And that spreads to Christmas, does it?"

"Very much. So, you sing carols as you walk around the tree, sometimes slowly, sometimes fast, depending on the song."

"Sounds like a treat," says Jamie with a smirk. She does not believe he means this.

"I cannot imagine doing it with someone who hasn't

grown up like this," says Anna, already feeling the blush creep up her face. "And then after the singing has finished, people open their presents and, again, it depends on the family how they do it. Some will take it in turns, opening one by one, so everyone gets to see what everyone has received, or for some it's a free-for-all and everyone just opens their gifts at the same time. Then they drink lots of port, while the kids play with their things. And there's no need to get up ridiculously early on Christmas morning." Danish Christmas 101 over, Anna stands. "Ready for dessert?"

"Is this the secret thing you were doing when you sent me out this afternoon?"

"Busted. But we did need port and a good red wine, so it wasn't a wasted trip."

She heads into the kitchen and pulls out from the fridge two small glass bowls. Each is full of what looks like tufts of whipped cream.

"Taa-daaaah! *Risalamande*," she says.

"What the what now?"

"It's French. *Riz à l'amande*. Rice with almonds." She explains it like it is totally obvious.

"OK," says Jamie slowly, "and what do we do?"

"Well, you can look at, but not touch, the two bowls while I heat some cherry sauce. Then you get to pick which of these two bowls you'd like. It's rice that's been boiled in milk and vanilla, cooled and mixed with chopped almonds and then folded into whipped cream. Somewhere in one of these bowls is a whole almond and whoever finds it wins the prize."

"Like the sixpence in a Christmas pudding?"

"I guess so. This is going on in every home, but they might have one big bowl and then people scoop out a spoonful. Seeing there's just two of us I did two bowls, and you can pick. But no touching, Jamie, no prodding with a spoon, nothing devious or underhand. I'm going to turn my back and trust you while I heat the cherry sauce."

"Fine. Got it," says Jamie. "But I can look from all angles, right?" He's looking mischievous, so Anna waves a wooden spoon at him in a threatening way, or at least as threatening as a wooden spoon can be.

It must work as he sits peacefully in his chair watching her, swilling the Barolo around in his glass, while she warms the sauce and transfers it to a pretty crystal bowl, all the while hyper-sensitive to his gaze. As she places it on the table, he selects the dessert bowl to the right.

Anna drags a breath through her teeth. "Are you sure about that choice, Jamie?"

"Don't you play mind-games on me, Lundholm. I made my choice."

She brings the bottle of port from the kitchen counter and pours them each a glassful. "This is what goes with it," she says.

"I can totally respect dessert which has its own specified alcoholic accompaniment."

It takes Jamie three mouthfuls to find the almond.

"I win!" he gloats.

"Noooo! You're not supposed to tell me. You need to hide it until the end, so people don't stop eating as soon as it's found." She still has half a bowl left.

"Is that a thing? This is good," he says, eating on. "And you didn't mention that rule, so how was I supposed to know?"

"Fair point," she mutters, a bit gutted she didn't win. There's that competitive streak.

"Um… You mentioned a prize?"

"What are you? Six?" she asks, amused by his keenness. It makes it easier to be a gracious loser. "Right, yes, your *mandelgave*." She heads for a cupboard.

"My almond gift," he says, and she gives him a "well done" for his translation skills, just as she places his prize in front of him. She averts her eyes, drawn as they are to the kilt, the hem brushing the skin above his knees, as he shifts in his seat. If he put his hand on her hip now, warm on the slinky satin of her skirt, she doesn't think she'd be able to withstand sinking onto his lap.

"A pig," he says, staring at it.

"A *marzipan* pig, Jamie," she corrects, and then with her pointy finger she lifts each side of his mouth in turn. "It's the traditional prize." She tries to ignore the residual feel of his skin on her fingertip.

"Traditional. Got it. Well, I won something and that's what counts. It'll sit on my shelf, with my other trophies."

"You have trophies?" she asks. She hasn't seen any, and really, was that the kind of thing he packed when emigrating?

"Not yet, but maybe one day, and this pig will be ready and waiting for them."

❄

As she later lies in her bed, Anna's thumb and fingers rub lightly together, as she imagines the feeling of his wrapping them in that proffered hand. She thinks about the skin at the base of his throat, just above the neckline of his T-shirt, and his corded forearms when he pushed up his sleeves as the evening drew on. She even thinks about his knees, visible thanks to the kilt. His knees! Honestly, who thinks about a man's knees? She needs to get a grip.

Turning crossly onto her side, she wills herself asleep, away from her lusty thoughts, which will do her no good. What *had* felt good, were his hands on her during their Once-and-Done, and in her hair, his steady breath at her ear, his tongue – dammit, her thoughts are off again…

Anna sits up, properly annoyed. This is maddening. She knows this is not something she wants; she doesn't want to hurt him, she doesn't want a relationship again, she doesn't want to let herself fall. But what she cannot deny, is that she wants *him*. What if, she wonders, just to put it out there, what if Once-and-Done was Twice-and-Done? Would that be so bad? She's made her position plain to him. He understands. He'd toasted to their separate futures. Anna's sure he's clear on her position.

Somewhere in her thinking, her feet have slid themselves out of the bed and onto the floor. Life can be mysterious at times, and she's always been "woo-woo open", so chooses not to question this too much. Which means she goes with it, as they carry the rest of her to the door, which she opens veeeery quietly, and tiptoes, on her totally autonomous feet, out into the hallway and to the stairs.

Anna has on occasion during her teen years, snuck out of the house. She knows exactly where to step to avoid the squeaky stair and does so now, more from muscle-memory than design, yet another sign that it's not her head steering this.

And then she's outside his bedroom door.

She listens, not sure what for – snoring perhaps, or deep breathing, at least – but hears nothing. Her hand raises to knock, but hangs there in the air. What if he doesn't answer? How humiliating would that be? Or what if he *is* asleep, and in not answering she'll never know if he was avoiding her or not? Her hand lowers to the handle, pausing just before her fingers reach the metal. Could she just open it and peer in? But what if he discovered her standing in the doorway like some stalker? She shakes her head at that scenario. Or she could slide in and slip into his bed. The thought of holding him, spooning into his warm body, plays across her mind and into her belly. However, her hand drops to her side, as her head shakes itself in shame. What is she thinking?? How intrusive would that be? Jamie hasn't asked her to his bed tonight. He did before, but now he's asking her for more. He's been clear in that; something more, a future, not "another night of epic sex", she would have remembered that, even through the many glasses of port they've drunk this evening, and the rest of the wine, as they stood side by side, him washing up and her drying.

Anna hangs her head, then backs quietly away. Her desire does not override his right to an assault-free night's sleep. Her head back in charge now, she swivels silently on her wayward feet and creeps back up to her room and into bed, where she lies, a mess of feelings; of shame, and embarrassment about her unrelenting want, and what might also be disappointment.

Why is this so hard? She has her plan, she knows her course and it's a sound, well-reasoned one. Anna starts to list the reasons in her head why she has just done the right thing, but only gets as far as reason three, before something suddenly stops her. Her eyes snap open and her breath catches in her throat. She knows that sound, it is very distinct. The squeak of the third step. Jamie's on his way up the stairs. Her heart picks up its beat at the thought of him knocking, or sliding in, she doesn't mind which. He'd be the best Santa ever. She takes a quick moment to smooth her hair and wishes it was longer, just for the night, so it could fan out on the pillow. A panic then ensues as to whether she should feign sleep, or simply watch him cross the room, with a smile, but she settles on the latter as she prefers things honest.

But seconds, then minutes, pass and nothing happens. There is no footfall outside her room or knock on the door, nor body sliding into the bed to spoon hers.

And then she hears the squeak again, as he retreats.

Anna stares at the ceiling and now she's in no doubt about the disappointment. It's crushing.

Chapter Thirty

After two days of mainly hiding in her room, avoiding Jamie under the guise of boxing up her things until it's finally done, Anna feels the need to get out and stretch her limbs. Jamie declines the offer to run with her. As it's "third Christmas day", some businesses are open, but it's generally accepted that little is happening. As he doesn't officially have kids of his own, he's volunteered to check what, if anything, is going on at the office.

So, with music in her AirPods, and wearing her cobbled-together gym kit, Anna is out running, around the lakes. It's freezing cold, but the sky is blue, so her sunglasses go on and she's off, trying to shift some of the calories her Christmas gorging has piled on. She has, she must admit, been a complete pig when faced with all the seasonal food. She forgets she's a grown-up now and if she wants to cook herself Christmas food in July, she could totally do that. She's tempted to post a July reminder in her calendar just to try it out.

The run is what she needs, clearing her head and steering her thoughts to think about what she needs to do. She's better with a plan.

Jamie's idea about an eco-guide is interesting. There's something about possibly working with him on it that appeals. It would be nice to have some contact with him still, not just his monthly rent transfer. But would it be tricky between them? Working together, but not acting on this strong connection they have, might be problematic. Anna doesn't know if she has the strength for problematic yet. And living with Ida, she was only ever used to clean breaks, never hearing from Ida's partners again, even the ones Anna had formed a bond with.

The flight-ticket quest needs to be stepped up. From what the weather reports are saying, the snow is cleared on the UK side now. Now she just has to fight the backlog and see if she can win one UK-bound seat.

Running on, her panting breaths creating puffs of steam in front of her like an ailing dragon, she eventually rounds the corner back into Eckersbergsgade, and makes it to their door. *Her* door, she means. Or maybe it's his door. Whatever.

Wrapped in a fluffy towel, post-shower, she sees Jamie's sent her a text.

> A.C. Perch's tearoom. 1pm. Afternoon tea lunch.

There's no way she's missing that. They do the best scones she's ever tasted, even inside the UK. Apparently, having enquired, the key is obscene amounts of butter, which is something she can buy into.

A.C. Perch's Thehandel, Denmark's oldest tea shop, purveyor to the Royal Court, is situated on Kronprinsensgade. The shop itself is small, smells delightful, and regularly has a queue outside it.

Above the shop is the most charming tearoom, where they serve tea, cakes, and afternoon teas with or without Crémant, depending on how fancy you're feeling. Anna's spent multiple occasions here celebrating birthdays of girlfriends, before heading out on the town. It's the kind of place where you usually need to book, so she wonders how Jamie has managed it, but then he seems to have contacts everywhere. "Called a friend," she can hear him saying. She suspects Jamie's #makingmemories. Like the Snowmance photos aren't doing that already. But fair enough, if that's what he needs then she won't object. Anyway, she'd do almost anything for the scones.

The town is quiet, as people are still home, but some have ventured out to clear the cobwebs. Købmagergade is empty enough for her not to get off her bike, and she pedals slowly down it, passing Rundetårnet, before turning into Kronprinsensgade. Today there's no queue outside the shop.

Having locked her bike, she almost skips up the old staircase to the tearoom, where she's met by a uniformed waitress.

"Booking for Jamie MacDonald."

The waitress nods and leads the way to a table at the end of the room where the tables are lower, with banquet seats on one side, prettily upholstered chairs on the other. The style is more Japanese at this end. Anna's delighted as it's definitely the cosier end of the room, and gives a clear view through to the wall of tea caddies, at the opposite end, waiting for guests to pick their brew from an excessively long menu-card of tea.

The tea-scented room is busy. Obviously, lots of people want a betwixtmas treat. There's a cheerful hum in the air and Anna settles into her wall seat to wait.

Due to her excitement, she's a little early, so pulls out her phone. She's had an idea on the ride over. Replaying her glory moment of explaining to Jamie how she found Lajla, it dawned on her she can do the same for Maiken. She might be in the Kraks directory, too. A quick scoot around the site shows she's not. Probably best for an investigative journo, who exposes baddies. *But* her mother is still in Dronningmølle. The locket is still in Anna's pocket, so she could drop by a post office on the way home and that'll be done and dusted. Another loose end tied. The thought makes her smile.

On reflection, she sees her escape from the city a year and half ago was perhaps a little hasty. Not *wrong*, just hasty. The speed meant she didn't do things in a tidy or considered fashion. Pølse's ashes being one case in point. Not that she could have done anything about the locket, as she probably wouldn't have remembered it if she hadn't sat by the plant pot the other day. But as it stands, it is something she can get off her conscience now. She could also have put her belongings into storage properly before renting the house out, or even sold the house completely.

Anna suddenly shivers. She looks to the near window, but it's closed. There must be a draft from the door, and she pulls her coat up around her sides. Returning to her thoughts, she sees that had she sold the house, she wouldn't have met Jamie. Perhaps, as Ida would say, "Even fuck-ups can turn out for the good. You just have to look at them from the other side, not the midpoint." Ida doesn't always come across as "together", but in this instance Anna might have to agree with her.

Maiken's mother's address is screen-shotted, and the phone popped back in her pocket. Scanning the room again, she registers a figure arriving at the far end, one she recognises, but it's all wrong. It's not Jamie, and she feels the smile slide off her face as she recognises who it is.

Ah, fuck.

It's Maiken.

She's bloody manifested her with her address search! *Shit, shit, shit.*

Looking about, Anna wonders whether she can fit under the low tea table. Not a chance. Bloody hell. What are the chances Maiken would come here the day Anna's here?! *All the bloody chances,* Anna thinks with a scowl. Hasn't she been telling Jamie this all the time she's been here; it's a small city. This is just her luck. She's crossed paths with her two times already, *of course* she was going to pitch up today.

Something niggles in her head about that. The Jamie part. And as she sees the waitress lead Maiken in her direction – which feels like it happens in slow motion – a couple of cogs snap equally slowly but very firmly into place in her head. About how Jamie, the fixer, thinks she should face Maiken. About how it's just possible he's engineered this, an ambush, for her to do just that. Anna feels her entire body seize up in defensiveness. She's completely hemmed in, and escape is not an option.

Maiken arrives at her table, the confusion showing on her face, too, at seeing Anna, and Anna knows she's hit the nail on the head.

Neither of them speak at first, other than Maiken thanking the waitress before taking the chair opposite. Maiken recovers first and slides off her coat before settling back in the chair to study her. She's always had a smart brain, and she seems to get a grip of the situation quicker than Anna does.

"I was supposed to be interviewing Jamie MacDonald. He said he could only do today due to travel commitments. I guess he lied."

Anna stays mute. Her throat's in a knot of panic and anger and general squirminess. Her eyes check again for a way out of this unwanted conversation. She doesn't want to look Maiken in the eyes, or at her at all, for that matter, but from what she saw through her horror at Maiken's approach, she looks pretty much exactly as she used to. Where Anna's life was shattered, Maiken doesn't seem to have aged at all, or changed at all, and she's certainly not wearing a scarlet letter on her chest, which Anna thinks would be apt. Moreover, she doesn't look ashamed, or contrite or embarrassed, all of which are due, but then again

Maiken is used to facing down all sorts of dodgy people in her line of work, so she's cultivated an iron-clad poker face.

"Carl said you had a new man. I'm guessing that's Jamie."

Something makes Anna nod. Pride? That she could be with Jamie, or that she doesn't want Maiken or Carl to think she's alone still after what happened? That their actions have put her off pursuing any kind of relationship since? Or that she's just sticking to her deal of being his girlfriend while she's here? Who knows? She's simply letting her physical head take the lead while her mental head is catching up, still stuck on Jamie, setting this up, orchestrating the thing he knew she least wanted.

"I'm also guessing you didn't plan this."

"You think?" Anna snaps. Ah. Voice has now entered the chat, and it's riding in on Anger.

Maiken's smile is small, but it's there and it piques Anna further.

"If I had my way, we'd never see each other again," she says through gritted teeth.

Their waitress is back, just in time to hear Anna say this, and the air becomes even more awkward.

"Er," the young woman begins, "an afternoon tea for two has been pre-paid for you, I just need to know what tea you'd like." She senses she's on shaky ground and the question comes out more like "Are you staying?"

Anna wonders whether she can ask for hers "to go".

Maiken flicks a quick look at the card and asks for a White Temple tea. Then she looks at Anna and raises her eyebrows just a fraction, which feels like a challenge. Anna hasn't had a cup of Green Cherry Blossom tea for ages and had already planned to buy a large bagful on the way home. That's what she asks for now, not even looking at the card, like she drinks here daily and knows the menu by heart. She's grasping at the small wins. The waitress practically sprints away, leaving Anna to suspect the vibe is "spiky".

"I saw you in the paper," Maiken says, "and across most of the Danish internet. I would have recognised the hat anywhere, though maybe not the pose. That's not the quiet Anna I remember."

Yes, well, it hadn't sat too comfortably with her at the time, nor in the days after, but right at this minute Anna feels a small thrill that she's the woman in the *oh-so romantic* viral photos.

She tries a nonchalant shrug, as if she's spent the last eighteen months being snogged across London in front of iconic sites.

"Why is it, do you think, that your Jamie has set this up?"

Maiken is being the investigative journalist with her. She'll keep asking questions until she has the information she wants. She's seen as quite the Rottweiler in the Danish news world, a guise she's very proud of.

"No idea, but he'll be getting a kick in the arse for it when I get home."

Maiken quirks an eyebrow at her.

"It obviously wasn't my intention to see you, Maiken. If I'd wanted to see you, I would have called." Sounding tough here is what she wants, but inside she's jelly. This whole scenario is making her toes curl.

The tea arrives and they sit in silence, the animosity bristling between them. The waitress has called in reinforcements and their three tiers of scones, finger sandwiches and cakes arrive just behind. Anna wonders whether this was part of Jamie's dastardly plan, that they'd be forced to share the food from the one cake stand. She'll be giving him an extra kick for his poxy symbolism. She is so mad at him, she can almost feel steam wisping from her ears ahead of the eruption there will be when she sees him. But she has more immediate fish to fry, and so she backburners that for now.

She looks long and hard at the woman who knew everything about her, who she would have trusted with anything and everything, and there is only one thing she wants to know. It's on the tip of her tongue, even though she's insisted to Jamie she doesn't care.

"Go on," says Maiken, sensing it, reading her like she would an interviewee. "Ask me." It's a challenge and it's also the last straw Anna needs to tip her over the precipice.

"What did I do that made you hate me that much?"

Maiken looks out of the window, and Anna sees her shoulders slide lower. When she turns back it's with a sigh.

"I didn't hate you. I didn't ever hate you."

"So why would you do that to me?" It bursts out of Anna louder than she's intended and the couple of women two tables over turn to stare at her. She resolutely ignores them.

"You were my best friend," she hisses, in case Maiken had missed it.

Maiken gives a deflating sigh, which Anna decides to read as shame. "I dare say I wasn't really thinking about you at all at the time. When it happened the first time, I felt incredibly guilty. I hadn't expected it, or intended anything, but it just happened."

Anna is itching to ask for the details, every single little thing so she can pick over them later, but her heart pitches up now and nixes that plan. There is obviously only so much it can take. Topline is enough.

"But after that I began to see the cracks in your relationship, the way you treated him and at the same time the way I felt about him changed to something more."

Anna's jaw hits the floor. What cracks in the relationship?

She's outraged.

"Our relationship was sound. It was good." To seal this, she grabs the first of her two scones from the top tier, slices it in half and piles whipped cream onto it followed by the jam. There's lemon curd on offer, too, but it doesn't interest her, though she does lament Brexit having banjaxed clotted-cream deliveries to the country. Such a loss.

Maiken waits for her to sink her teeth into the scone and let out the light moan that is its due.

"Come on, Anna. You know that's not true. If you two were solid, Carl would never have looked at me, and I would never have gone near him."

Anna's mouth is full, but she can shake her head, as this is so preposterous to her.

"I get that this isn't what you want to hear, but if you look at it honestly, you took him for granted, Anna."

Anna really doesn't get this. They were a couple, they'd been together for years. They lived together. Solid.

"You wouldn't marry him," Maiken states. "How many times did you tell me he'd asked you *again*, with a little laugh. Like it was a joke." Maiken picks a ham-and-cheese finger sandwich and polishes it off in a matter of seconds, before sipping her tea.

"It *was* a joke!" Anna says. "It was a running gag. He would ask and I would say no. He knew my stance on marriage. I didn't need it or want it. We lived together."

"Well clearly you missed the signs. He wasn't joking anymore, and he was asking, and you kept refusing him. And in the end, he took you at your word and the relationship was no longer the shiny thing you still seem to think it was." There is a distinct feel of admonishment here.

"Bullshit," Anna says, but her tone isn't as staunch as it might be.

"I don't think you want to hear it. Anyone could see it."

She's bewildered by this. If it's true – and she has very large doubts about Maiken's reliability – then *she* had no idea. Carl had known from the start she didn't want to get married. She never wanted to be tied to someone to that extent. Living with Carl was because she chose to and because she loved him, not because she *had* to, or was tied to him by some paperwork. She'd taken heart in the fact he was there by choice and love, too. Or so she'd thought. If he was unhappy enough to jump on her best friend, then surely, he would have said something. Carl could be verbose enough when it suited him.

"This might be how you choose to let yourself off the hook for being a shit friend, Maiken, but it's bullshit. And if Carl told you we had problems, then it was to get your sympathy, and you fell for it."

Maiken chooses to ignore her in favour of perusing the cakes, opting for a confection with berry mousse and thin sponge. Anna was about to take the same but holds back. She doesn't want to be seen as mirroring.

"Tell yourself what you like." Maiken eats half of it in one swoop. She takes her sweet time chewing and then swallows, which she follows with a long sip of her tea. "But ask yourself this," she says, "if what you had was so strong and so right, then why didn't you stay and fight for him?"

Anna cannot for the life of her think of something to say. But that's fine, as Maiken isn't done.

"You ran away. You showed him you didn't think he was worth it."

Now Anna explodes. "And I was right. He had an affair with my best friend, and you had an affair with my partner. Neither of you were worth it. You betrayed me."

Maiken's face turns a little pink at that. The occupants of several tables are looking at them now. "I might regret how it came about," she says, her voice lower, which forces Anna to lean in, "but I don't regret where we are now, Carl and I. He's far more assured in the relationship with me than he was with you." She stops for a second and then spills out, "We're getting married in the spring. You may as well know. We told his family over Christmas."

Anna should feel devastated, just as she should probably get up now and walk out, but she doesn't, because the overriding feeling she has to this news, is numbness. And also, there's a second scone with her name on it and short of stuffing it in her pocket, she's not going anywhere without it.

They have a stalemate then, because Maiken has dropped her bombshell, and if Anna isn't offering congratulations, which she absolutely isn't about to do, what do you say to news like that? Instead, Anna fills her plate with her half of the remaining food. It gives her something to focus on, while she ignores Maiken.

"Nothing to say?" Maiken asks.

Anna simply shakes her head, as she studiously slices, creams and jams her second scone.

"I suppose you have Jamie now, so it doesn't matter."

Which is true, she supposes. If it were true, but Anna decides she isn't going to let truth get in the way right now. It serves her better, *protects* her better, for Maiken and Carl to believe Jamie and she are for real.

"You're right," she says, looking up. "Carl doesn't matter to me. He showed his true colours and you'll never be one-hundred-per-cent sure he won't do the same to you, when he becomes bored. As for you, you picked him over me, so you weren't the sister I thought you were. You threw me under the bus. I don't know how you look at yourself in the mirror each day. But perhaps every time you do, you'll remember you're the kind of woman who stabs other women in the back."

A flit of something crosses Maiken's face, and if Anna

were to put money on it, she'd say Maiken has most definitely had this thought about Carl. How *will* she ever really trust him? Something about that pleases Anna and she feels it's a suitable punishment, never-ending as long as they both shall live.

A feeling of discomfort hits her. Is she really someone who delights in the insecurity of others? Yes, apparently, she is, but she recognises it isn't a great attribute. Maybe she'll do some self-reflection when she's safely back in London, unlikely ever to lay eyes on Maiken again. Because right now, her wounds have unscabbed themselves, and she feels raw. Does she want Carl back? Nope. She really doesn't, not least because she's seen new things with Jamie. But that pain she experienced all those months ago, the shock, the anguish and loss of self-esteem, has bubbled to the surface, despite her doing everything to disguise it.

She needs to leave. She scopes what is left on the plate. She can live without the cucumber sandwich, but the eclair is a shoo-in. In the spiky silence, she horses the little-finger-sized eclair in one, then drains her tea and folds the cream-and-jammed scone into a napkin.

"I'd say it's been great to see you, but it hasn't."

Maiken, having watched her pack up, gives her a thin smile as Anna stands.

"I'll see you around."

"Unlikely. I'm leaving soon." She doesn't say to where, but it doesn't matter. It's piqued Maiken's interest.

"Oh, Jamie leaving with you?"

This makes Anna stumble. She knows Maiken, she'll check if the notion takes her.

"We're doing the long-distance thing." She doesn't sound as assured as she'd like, and Maiken senses it.

"Doesn't sound like you."

"You don't know me anymore."

"You think? Everything I've seen today has been typical Anna. And I don't believe you'd do long-distance. You're too like Ida. No ties."

Anna can feel her face heating up and giving her away.

Maiken taps her finger to her chin. "Perhaps I could do a story on the Snowmance couple. Show people who you really are, and where you are now, that kind of thing." This is her revenge for Anna delighting in her insecurity. Anna knew it was bad to think like that and here's karma biting her in the bum, within ten minutes. She will definitely be doing some self-reflection. But more important is the threat this would bring to Jamie. Things are too fragile still with Lajla for their ruse to be overlooked. But she won't be blackmailed by Maiken.

"Leave it alone, Maiken. You already messed with one relationship of mine."

Finally, Maiken shows her teeth. "Give me back my locket and we'll call it quits." There. That's what she stayed for, nothing more. Anna could have told Jamie that.

Anna digs into her pocket and drops the locket on the table. "You saved me a trip."

"I knew you had it," Maiken snarks. "Thief."

"Pot, kettle. And I didn't have it. I found it in the garden ten days ago." The tarnish of the metal gives this more credence. "Perhaps you lost it when you were undressing in my house, with my partner." So, yes, she does up the volume of her voice for that bit, enough for the ladies two tables over to be in no doubt regarding what's gone down.

Maiken's hand covers the locket and Anna slams hers on top.

"A deal's a deal. You'll leave Jamie and I alone."

And then Anna leaves, her head held high, sort of, with her scone clenched in her hand. She'll need the calories, as she has a sound kicking to administer.

Chapter Thirty-One

Amazingly, her key hits the lock with sniper precision and she flings herself inside the house with a livid shout of "Jamie!" It's an angry summons, which is her intent. For once, this is not a conflict she wants to avoid. This one she wants to face square on and shout at, nose to nose with barely an inch between, red-faced and probably with some spit flying, but she doesn't care, because she plans to be a loudhailer of ire, a hurricane of fury.

She is met with silence. She tries again, but the result is the same. Looking around, she can't see his boots, his big coat or his work bag. Bugger! Here she is, wound up and ready, and he isn't bloody here to receive it.

Even so, she stomps into the kitchen to check. Who knows, he could be hiding. Anyone with an ounce of sense would know there was at least a percentage chance this could go shitwards, that she might not welcome being ambushed. She had been very clear about not wanting to talk to either Maiken or Carl. More than once. Jamie's an intelligent guy, he couldn't have mistaken her meaning, yet still he went ahead and set her up.

But he isn't hiding. He really isn't there.

There's no message on her phone either. No "Did I do the right thing?" (absolutely not), "Am I safe to come home?" (ditto), "Surprise!" (fuck right off).

Which leaves Anna in the infuriating stance of her anger still being pending, but the adrenaline ebbing, and it's all washed along with a wave of embarrassment and shame she's all too familiar with already.

Her phone pings in her hand. Is it him? Her fingers grip the device more tightly than necessary but it's an instinct thing, given the lack of his throat to grip instead.

A text message from easyJet, flagging their January promotions.

She clicks through to the site and on autopilot, having done this most days for the last fortnight, she taps in today's date. Normally she'd get the "Nothing available for this date" message before she tries the following day, but intriguingly she's taken on to the next field and then the next and there, in front of her eyes is a seat, a seat to take her back to whence she came, away from all this. It's to London Gatwick, not London Heathrow, which is closer to her apartment, but it'll do. And before she knows it, she's clicked a few more buttons including her credit card number, and the order confirmation is right here in front of her face.

She's going home.

❄

Having already finished emptying her room – many things having been moved down into the basement storage, some to charity and more than she's anticipated simply to the bin – within two hours Anna has her handbag sitting against the wall in the hallway, along with a large suitcase of things she's taking with her. Clearly, a year and a half away has given her perspective on what she really needs. The room upstairs is hoovered and ready to hand back to the tenant.

She's looking around at the living room and kitchen, taking it in, memorising it. Her eyes fall on Vivi's decorations, and she takes photos of all of it. Angry as she is, she trusts Jamie to put them away again carefully. The padlock on the storage room is unlocked, so he can reseal it once he's stored the boxes back on the shelves. She's even managed to wrestle her bike back down there, which can only have been fuelled by the rage, which has also carried her through the furious but efficient packing. Her passport's in her pocket, and her ticket is on the phone, so there really is little left to do but lock up and leave.

She glances towards the window, where it's dark again outside. While she's still livid with him, it sits badly with her to just go, without so much as a "Thanks for having me." Regardless of what he did today, he did her an absolute solid by taking her in. Where would she have been for the last fortnight without him allowing her to stay?

She can't wait much longer, as she has a flight to catch, and the airport will be rammed. It'll have to be a note. She can't think of another way to do it, because calling him is out of the question. Hearing his voice will … no. No call.

Having found some paper and a pen, Anna sits at the table, pen poised.

And ten minutes later, she is still sitting there, at a loss. What should this note be? Essentially, she's telling him she's gone, but thanks for the roof over her head. She could let him know she does like him, really really like him, but the circumstances were against them – oh, and thanks for the sexy times. Or she could use it to give him the bollocking he so deserves for his stunt today. But the paper isn't long enough and writing it won't have the gravitas her fury feels it deserves. And her absence will probably give him an inkling of how welcome his plan was. She could always give him an earful if he calls her, to follow up.

Just as she's recognising what a poor writer she's turning out to be, she hears voices outside on the street. Moving to the window at a crouch, she spies. Jamie is parking his bike in the yard and Lajla stands holding hers, complete with Nikoline in the bike seat, on the other side of the fence. Jamie notes Anna's bike isn't there and Anna supposes he assumes she's still having a cosy making-up session with Maiken at A.C. Perch's. He walks back to them and holds out his hand, to tweak Nikoline's nose, which makes her laugh. It's a sweet little scene, two parents watching their daughter.

And Anna recognises her job here is done, the fake-dating is no longer needed. She also sees, with a harsh dawning, that while Jamie seems sure there's nothing between him and Lajla, looking at them now, maybe there *could* be. Having been through a heartbreak already, Anna knows she can't do it again. They deserve to explore whether this could be something, for Nikoline's sake, and Anna deserves not to sit in London, worrying about a long-distance boyfriend having something else on the go. That could totally happen. No. Anna sees it now. Facilitating this reunion was the reason she was stranded here, and her role is over.

Standing up and moving back into the room, she knows any thoughts she's possibly been entertaining, even just a little bit, of there being more for her and Jamie are soundly popped in a mental box and sealed off.

Although part of her wishes she could just vanish, she waits by the table for him to come in. She hears him call "*Hej, hej,*" to Lajla from the step and then bundle through the door as he normally does. He rounds the corner to the living room and jumps when he sees her.

"You're here," he says, rubbing the back of his neck. He looks gorgeous, Anna thinks, and tries to memorise his face just as it is, ruddy from having been out in the cold, his hair a mess having been released from his hat. He's carrying a paper bag from Skt Peders Bageri. Pastries. He places it on the kitchen counter, then slides off his coat, dropping it on the barstool.

Neither of them knows what to say at first. They watch each other from either side of the table, a strange mix of emotions filling the room.

Finally, Anna says, "You saw Lajla and Nikoline?"

"She texted as I was finishing work. Said they were in the park, and we could meet. We chatted a bit more and I played with Nikoline. She's the cutest kid." His eyes are bright with the memory, but his body is more tense.

"I suggested Lajla come to see where I live. I didn't invite her in, I just thought it might help if she knew where I was, that we're not far apart if she wants help. I don't want to put any pressure on her."

"Sounds like a good plan, Jamie." She means it, too, despite a small lump in her throat.

"And I took your advice earlier and told my dad. About Nikoline – a slightly tailored version, but enough for him to understand that I'm not leaving."

"What did he say?"

"He immediately wanted to come and meet her, but I've told him there's some work to be done yet."

Much as that work is still a hill to climb, Jamie looks lighter for having addressed it. Or perhaps he's just relieved to have his father off his back. Either way, Anna's pleased he's done it and gives him a "Well done."

He tilts his head. "You got home early."

Anna looks away, she doesn't quite know where to take this in the time she has. And yet there are some things that need saying. "Jamie, what you did today was completely out of order." She tries to keep her voice calm, but the words are still unsteady. "It was an ambush."

Jamie rests his hands on the back of a dining chair. "I thought … I thought if I could get you to talk, you could maybe have it out with her and say what you needed to say."

"That wasn't your decision to make." He senses her simmering anger, but as always, he faces the argument.

"How is it different from when you surprised me with Lajla?"

"It's all kinds of different! In your case the surprise was a good one because you wanted to connect. You said you wanted to speak to her, and I made it happen. In my case you knew I'd expressly said I didn't want to speak to Maiken and yet you went ahead anyway. I was shocked and humiliated. I didn't want to be there, and you put me in that position without my permission. It was totally beyond your purview and yet you did it anyway. Like you thought you knew better, and my decision really couldn't be right for me. I don't think you're the controlling type, but at the very least it's condescending."

"That was never my intention," he says.

"I don't need you making decisions for me. I grew up like that; Ida's decisions were never a discussion. If she decided she wanted to leave somewhere, we'd be gone. My decisions are my own now."

Something clicks in Jamie's head. She sees the realisation on his face and watches as he looks behind him at the suitcase in the hallway. "You're leaving? Because of this? It was supposed to be a good thing. It was supposed to move you on, not move you *out*."

"There was a flight available. It's time for me to go back to London and get on with my life and it's time for you to have your house back, some peace and some quiet, and you can spend time with Lajla and Nikoline."

His brow pulls even closer in. "Is that what you're thinking? That I want to get back with Lajla? I don't. She and I, we will only ever be co-parents. That's it. *If* I'm lucky. Hopefully she'll let me be part of Nikoline's life, but she could reverse that whenever she likes. So, the best I can hope for going forward is to be good friends and co-parents. And more to the point, that's *all* I want from her. Nothing else. Lajla and I are not going to be a thing."

"Not even for Nikoline? You could be a family." The image of them all outside, a beautiful trio, hangs in her mind's eye.

He shakes his head, his eyes clear. "No, Anna, not even for Nikoline. Lajla used me to have a child and would have kept her existence from me if she'd had her way. I can't get past that kind of deceit. Can I put it aside in getting to know Nikoline? Aye. But never in a relationship. It's about trust, isn't it? But you? With you, Anna, I want us to be something."

That mental box in her head rattles, but unwilling to unseal it, she shakes her head.

Jamie dips his head. "I overstepped. With Maiken. I see that now. You're angry. I see that, too. But I do think it would help you, Anna, to really talk it out with her."

"And, what? Be friends again?"

"Maybe. We can't change things if we won't communicate." She doesn't think he's just talking in general terms here.

"Nor will we if we won't listen," she snaps back, then takes a breath. She appreciates his optimism but in this case she needs to burst his bubble.

"Here's the thing, Jamie: not everything can be fixed. Not everything *should* be fixed. My relationship with Maiken isn't one of those Kintsugi vases. It never will be. Some relationships you have to just let go. Even if we had made up today, Maiken would never be a person I go to with problems, bad news, or to celebrate with, ever again. It's done. Our friendship has no value to me now. I'll only ever be indifferent to her, at best. And, you know what? That's OK. I'm all right with that now I've seen who she is. I don't need her in my life." She gives him a shrug. "Maybe you did move me on, just not how you thought."

"This might just be early days, if you two—"

"You're not listening," she flares, exasperated at this man, who is blinkered in his goal to fix things. "Please *listen*. I know it's totally against your life mission, but you need to see some things are unfixable. They've reached their natural end, as messy as that might look to you. To me, this mess has been sorted. And I need you to respect that decision."

She can see him mulling her words, and how it goes against every grain. "Please listen, Jamie," she says quietly. And she sees his shoulders sink.

"I'm sor—" he starts but cuts off, his eyes resting on the paper and pen on the table. "You were going without saying goodbye?" The instant set of his jaw, the deep contraction of his brow, and the crossing of his arms, expresses his resentment perfectly.

"My plane leaves in a couple of hours. I was out of time and you were out with Lajla." He narrows his eyes at that, batting away any accusation there. "Look, I wanted to say thank you for taking me in."

"That's all you think this has been?" He sounds bitter. And rightly so. It has been more.

"No. Of course not," she admits, "but I want to avoid—"

"Avoid what?" She doesn't answer, and it seems to push him over an edge.

"You want to talk about avoidance, Anna, aside from your hiding in your room for the last two days?" His arms are still crossed, the jaw still tense, but his eyes are quite blazing now. "The moment we happened, and man did we happen, you started freaking out."

"I was not freaking out," she mumbles, but he might have her on the hiding in her room thing.

"You pulled back the very next day," he corrects, but she suspects it's just semantics, he knows how he sees it. Jamie closes his eyes, breathes deeply through his nose, and returns to meet her gaze. "I get it," he says, his tone controlled "You're scared."

"I am not scared."

"You are, though. Because you've had your trust broken, in the worst of ways, and so you don't want to go there again. But here's *my* thing; I'm not Carl, and you can trust me."

His insistence of knowing her mind riles her. "Can I, though? Really, Jamie? A guy who fake-dates to get to the mother of his child?" It's unfair but she feels on the back foot.

"We covered that. I admitted I got that wrong. But you trust me, Anna. If you didn't you wouldn't have stayed here."

"I had nowhere else to go."

"Right," he scoffs. "Katrine doesn't have a spare sofa?"

"It's my house," she points out, grasping at straws.

"Aye, and I've never said otherwise. I was fine with you staying."

"Once you'd googled me."

"Not apologising for survival instincts," he returns, unabashed. "You do trust me, Anna, and I'm asking you to hold onto that, to believe in us."

Anna studies the floor, but it holds no answer for her.

A phone alarm chimes in her pocket. She's out of time.

Raising her eyes to him, she says finally, "I can't."

"You *won't*. Different."

Her eyes widen with exasperation, and frustration at him not understanding this, or not wanting to understand her position. "How can I believe in something that can't work? I am leaving," she spells out. "You always knew that. I backed off because I didn't want to hurt you. I never wanted to be another woman leaving you."

"Surely that's *my* problem, the hurt? That was my risk to take. And I am here for it." His hands have moved from his chest to his hips and Jamie looks ready to take on the world.

"Then you have no sense of self-protection," Anna snaps. "Or you haven't felt what real hurt feels like."

He throws his head back with a "Ha! I know hurt, Anna, trust me, but I won't let it shape me, like it does you. This is about trust. Trusting your own feelings and someone else who sees you and wants you. I've given you space, but god it's tiring, because what I see is you drifting away and not because that's what you really want, but because you're too fucking scared to face the right direction."

They've reached an impasse and she is done, given what

she sees as his inability to listen. She walks around the table towards her bags. She can't bring herself to look at him.

He catches her wrist.

"You won't take a risk," he says hotly. "And little wonder, given your mother never taught you to stick around or work for a relationship." His anger reignites her own.

"Don't you come at my mother," she rages, the stab at Ida being a step too far, and before she can stop herself, she punches back, "at least mine stuck around for me…"

Whatever he was about to say, it catches in his mouth and they stand for a long moment, the awfulness of what she just said hanging spectre-like between them. He releases her wrist, the skin instantly cold.

Then, eyes dull now and shaken, Jamie finally nods towards her bags and says, "You're right. It's time for you to go."

Chapter Thirty-Two

Østerport station is buzzing with people as Anna drags herself in with her case. Walking the fifteen minutes from the house has been a miserable effort, to say the least. She's taken the route through Holmens cemetery to give Vivi and Mads' stone a stroke. And she took a photo of that, too, so she can look at it from wherever in the world she is. It sits, in her phone, next to the picture of the house. The phone that now sits in the depths of her pocket, her ticket ready on the first screen.

All these small things, as well as deliberately noticing shops and signs as she passes, are about being present in the moment, engaging with her surroundings, she tells herself, and nothing at all to do with distraction and taking her mind off the horrendous way things just ended with Jamie. How could she have said that to him? She is deeply ashamed of it, that she could even think it, but she'd been angry and stressed, and ... no, it was inexcusable. She knows that. And she should probably have hammered on the door, and begged his forgiveness. But he'd thrown her out, of her own house, and her plane is leaving, and so she's done as he asked and gone. She'll write to him from London, apologise properly and hope he accepts. She'll feel wretched until he does.

On reaching the station, her AirPods go in, playing a podcast she keeps losing track of, hoping it will divert the hideous feeling in her. As such, it takes her a couple of seconds to realise someone is staring at her as they come up the escalator as she steps onto hers heading down to the platform.

Ah fuck.

It's Carl.

Not today, not now.

Her eyes shift to the passage in front of her in the hope of dashing through, but her case is big and the stairs are rammed. Why are these people not all at home *hygge*-ing?? She deliberately doesn't look behind her, hoping he never actually saw her, but that stare was quite clear. At the bottom, she steps off and is about to make the turn to the next escalator to take her down to the platform, when she feels a hand on her shoulder. She immediately wrenches away.

"Anna."

His large frame crowds her backwards out of the flow of travellers. She doesn't have time for this. Nor the emotional bandwidth. Not now. She just wants to huddle into a seat on the train and shut everything out.

"Go away," she mutters.

Decidedly not going away, he reaches to remove an AirPod from her ear. She slaps his hand away, outraged.

"Don't touch me."

"You can't hear me with those in."

"Well done," she says. Why can't some men take a hint from women wearing their earphones? A neon sign with "do not speak to me" wouldn't have any effect on those men either.

He stands resolute, between her and the escalator.

"Maiken says you saw her."

"Not intentionally," she snaps. "Have you followed me?" Is this why he's here? Why and what for?

"Hardly," he scoffs, making her feel silly. "I live near."

"Then leave me alone. You could just walk by and ignore me." She would have done him the same courtesy, had she seen him first.

"You *did* have the locket," he says, ignoring her and with a tone which Anna can only describe as accusatory.

She squares her shoulders. "I *found* the locket," she says. "Maiken is all about the drama. I found it and I returned it. I did not *have* it." She almost adds, "I didn't steal it," but isn't sure she's on as solid ground there.

He rolls his eyes at her. It astounds her.

"Why is this so important to you? It's like you want some theft story to pin on me." Her eyes narrow as she looks him in the face. Maiken just wanted her heirloom back, but Carl's concern is more than a lover backing his partner. This is... "You want me to look as bad as you in this, don't you?"

"There are two sides to this, Anna," he immediately

says. "Like I said last time, things weren't good between us."

Anna has replayed these words, both his and Maiken's, many times already, and she still can't see it. "Then why didn't you say?"

"Come on," he huffs, "I shouldn't have to say. You should have been able to see I wasn't happy if you loved me—"

"Bullshit," Anna cuts in, startling a passing couple. Normally this would have her adjusting her volume, fearing causing a scene, but not now. She doesn't have the time. "I'm not a mind reader. Nobody is a mind reader. You need to communicate and tell people what's going on in your head if you want them to understand and respond."

Carl looks away, but Anna takes the opportunity to properly look at him and realises how much she misses it. Not him, God no, not *him*, but loving someone. Being someone's person, having a person, living the same love that Vivi and Mads had had, adoring each other. Anna misses that, so much it aches inside her. Yet Carl had shown her how fragile it was, and temporary, and she simply cannot see how she can go there again, when the potential for hurt is now so clear. The anger of what he has spoiled for her, surges up inside her.

"This is about you, Carl. You always want people to think you're a good guy, but in this case you absolutely aren't. This thing with Maiken wasn't a fling, a one-off drunken mistake we could maybe have worked through. It was a long-term affair, calculated, orchestrated and deceitful. It wasn't discreet." Her volume seems to be rising with each sentence, but she doesn't care. He wants to talk about it? Well here it is, and he should buckle up, because she's on a deadline. "You were totally disrespectful in your lack of discretion. Your family thought we were a throuple!" A cluster of tourists turn at that one.

"Keep your voice down," Carl says.

"Piss off. My voice is my own, and you wanted to talk." Something about him wanting her to tone it down makes her stand taller.

"A year, Carl. If things weren't good then you had all that time, and more before, to say. Instead, you're here trying to gaslight me into thinking I was responsible and ignored all the signs you were unhappy, while you were fucking my best friend. In our bed!" More heads turn. It's actually quite thrilling. Carl looks like he's regretting his decision to follow her. Well, good. "And it's all to make you feel better about what you did and to ease the discomfort you feel about it. Which is pathetic, by the way, given you could just have left at any time, been honest and not had any overlap. How *do* you square that with your mother, by the way?"

"When would we have talked?" he asked, brushing off her accusation. "You were never around. All the travel got in the way." Still more excuses.

"It's my job!"

"But it was never a wrench for you to leave. I never felt it was hard for you when you went away."

"Wow? Needy much?"

He winces.

"I didn't feel a wrench because I knew I was coming

340

home, and I trusted you'd be waiting for me; a grown-up, who makes his needs clear, secure and with a social life of his own to keep him busy. Clearly, I was wrong there, given Maiken turned out to be the entertainment you needed, to salve your needy soul."

"It wasn't like that. I meant more to her than I did to you. That was quickly clear. I asked you so many times to marry me and you said no. Every time!"

"It was a running gag, Carl!" This one exasperates her. "We had always joked about it; you asked, I declined, we laughed. Not once did you stop and say, 'I'm serious this time, I really mean it.'"

"You would still have said no," he insists, which she takes as his confirmation of her point.

"But I was committed to you, Carl. If I thought you needed reassuring, if you'd been clear, I would have made sure you understood. I actually had plans in place to show you how committed I was, but you were busy screwing Maiken."

"Like what?" he asks, surprise on his face.

"You'll never know now. And it's beside the point, because again you're trying to put this on me, Carl. This is on you. You could have ended it if you were so sad and neglected, and if you were a decent human being. If you needed more, or something different, you should have said and given me the chance to see if I could meet your needs – the ones I didn't know I was missing.

"Clearly, truth is very difficult for the two of you," she goes on. "Don't gaslight me into thinking I was responsible for your shitty behaviour. A year of cheating will always make you an arsehole and if that makes you feel uncomfortable, then tough."

Anna grabs the handle of her suitcase and looks him right in the face. "You know, you've given no indication of being sorry for what you did. Not a hint. So there's nothing more to say. You need to sit with your own disgrace and shame, Carl, because it isn't mine." Shoving her AirPod back in her ear, hoping her fingers aren't trembling too much, Anna walks away from him, hopefully for the last time.

Sailing down the final escalator, face red for having drawn attention to herself, a small part of her really wishes someone has filmed it, to upload onto the socials. She wouldn't mind *that* going viral.

Chapter Thirty-Three

The adrenaline has plummeted by the time her train comes and she gets a seat, which is when the emotion of it all gets the better of her; seeing Maiken, shouting at Carl and above any of that, the last minutes with Jamie. Her words to him make her feel truly nauseous. Palming away the rolling tears, she stares out of the windscreen, not that there's anything to see, just tunnel. She doesn't even care whether she'll see anyone else she knows, because she's leaving. She'll be gone, they can talk about her behind her back, and she won't have to worry about it.

The train pulls in at Kongens Nytorv. With hitching breaths, she walks the connection between the two train lines and back down with the escalator to stand behind the glass screens on the platform, waiting for the next train towards the airport. Her head is dipped, as she hides her face, with the shame she feels.

"Anna!" She turns to see who's called her name and spots Katrine standing with her two boys, clutching each by the hand. Briskly, she wipes her eyes, and draws a deep breath, to face her friend. Katrine reaches her to give her a hug, then spots her suitcase.

"Leaving?"

"Yeah," Anna says, getting a grip on her voice and plastering on a bright face. "It's time." She shrugs, as if this is completely normal and her eyes aren't red from tears. Katrine is far quicker on the uptake.

"Tough to say goodbye?"

"Definitely. But the right thing to do." This is punctuated with an involuntary sniff. "*Tak for sidst*, by the way." Thanks for last time, as the Danes say, although now she thinks about it, she owes Katrine a slap for the hangover she gifted her. "Where are you off to?"

"The boys are having a sleepover with Farmor in Amager," says Katrine with delight.

"Lucky you and Rune."

"Rune's mother gave us babysitting tokens for Christmas, so we're cashing one tonight for some extra sleep." She looks blissed-out at the thought.

Anna looks at the two boys, one three, the other six. She's met them before and they're cute but extremely energetic.

The train arrives and the boys race for the front of the driverless carriage and its big window. Someone has placed a sticker with fake dials beneath the screen and the boys pretend they are driving as it pulls away through the tunnel. Katrine and Anna sit together and Anna's suddenly comforted to have her friend with her. While she thought she'd be pleased to be leaving the city, something she's been envisaging for so many days, now she's doing it her stomach is leaden. But it *is* the right thing to do. She *knows* that.

"Want to talk about it?" asks Katrine. Anna sighs deeply. In her head she's thinking "not really", but actually, maybe, it would help.

"I finally found a ticket, so I bought it. I need to get back to my old life. My new life, I mean." Katrine tucks her arm through Anna's and pulls her closer.

"And that's making you sad?"

"Oh, you know. Sometimes goodbyes are hard," Anna says, trying to make light of it. She had got hardened to them when she was younger, with all the times she and Ida would up sticks, but this feels different. And the times she'd say goodbye to her grandparents were also sad, but she knew she'd be coming back at some point. This, though … this she doesn't recognise, and it leaves her aching inside. She's worried she's going to start weeping again.

"So, what's happened since I saw you?" Katrine asks.

Anna gives a small laugh. "Should have known you're just here for the gossip."

Katrine laughs, too. "Busted. I have so little gossip in my own life, I need yours." She's watching her boys with a look of love and pride. She has a good family life, and she loves it, but Anna thinks she sometimes finds domesticity restrictive. Fair enough. Then Anna will give her a moment of salacious gossip.

"Well, I took your advice, and I went for it with Jamie." Given how it ended, she cannot impart this nugget with the enthusiasm it really deserves.

"How was it?" Katrine asks, as if this is the most important piece of information ever.

"Incredible," she says sadly. Anna's not going to lie.

Spotting the glumness, Katrine looks at her, concerned. "I take it that's why you're unhappy?"

Her friend's sympathetic tone is too much. She doesn't deserve it. "Oh, Trine, I've just left him and I said the most horrible thing, truly vicious. I'm an awful person and he'll hate me, but I can't go back because my flight is leaving."

Katrine strokes her hair while she weeps, before pulling out a tissue from her bag, handing it to her.

"You could miss the plane, if it's so bad. Go back and fix it?"

Anna is pretty sure this can't be fixed. An apology is due, but it would merely be a plaster, as this feels truly broken. A very red line was crossed there. She shakes her head. "I need to get back to my life in London. My new life." She feels like she's saying it time and again to solidify it in her head. Another mantra. Like the last one had served her so well...

"In my experience, most things can be fixed, Anna, if you talk them out. Rune and I are constantly talking things out." Anna is taken aback. They've always seemed so solid and balanced as a couple.

"I think this is one of the other things," Anna says. "Ultimately, I don't think we were supposed to be more than this snow-in moment." She would just give anything for it to have ended differently.

"What is it that has you scared?" Katrine asks, flat out. Bloody Danish directness.

"Nothing! I'm not scared. I'm being practical." Why do people keep thinking she's scared?!

"Hmmm," says Katrine. "I had an aunt, Elsebet, who always had a new boyfriend and was devastated with each break-up. I asked her why she kept setting herself up for it. She told me 'A broken heart is an open heart.'"

Anna doesn't quite see the link here. Nor the message.

"What does that mean? That my defences are down and I'm easy prey or prone to let the wrong things in?"

"Anna, no!" says Katrine. "That's not how I read it at all. It means that maybe it's a heart that's open to new opportunities, ready to be refilled by the right person. That's how Elsebet saw it. I think her point was, you have to put yourself out there and risk it. You can protect your heart too much. And maybe eighteen months on, Jamie was exactly the right person for you to cross paths with, someone to risk the hurt for. Maybe this is why you snowed-in over here."

Risk the hurt. Katrine says the words as if they are a logical combination, but not to Anna. Katrine has clearly not been hurt as she has. Anna shakes her head. She snowed-in here so she could help this handsome, kind man, who helped her out and definitely didn't deserve what she said to him, to solve a problem he was having. That's what she thinks.

"Talking of broken hearts," she says, easing the subject away from Jamie because frankly, it hurts too much, "I saw Maiken."

"Really?"

"Not willingly, but that's another story. We talked. I told her what a rubbish friend she was."

"Good."

"But she seems to think Carl and I were already on the skids. That's not how I saw it."

Katrine sighs. "I think we all think friendships have to last forever and they don't. We grow in different directions, life takes us to different places. Some relationships and friendships just die out, whether abruptly or petering out and that's probably OK. Maybe you and Carl were petering out, but you didn't spot it in the daily grind, and then the explosion happened. Add to that your relationship with Maiken blew up, too – and bigger – so you probably haven't seen the similarity. Both were ending, just differently."

Anna shrugs. "And I just had a run-in with Carl at Østerport." What a day. "He hit me with Gaslighting 101, trying to tell me it was my fault we split. That he wanted marriage, and I'd just laughed it off, which hurt him and made him look elsewhere."

Katrine snorts. Yes, they both know he'd looked elsewhere without having the courtesy to move out first.

"But here's the thing: that day, I was about to tell him, I'd been speaking to a lawyer. My cat had recently died, and I suppose I'd been thinking about life and mortality etc., and I'd had paperwork drawn up to put him, Carl that is, not Pølse, on the deeds of the house. I couldn't give him marriage because it's just not what I want, but I was going to give him half of the house to show him I was committed. And then I walked into that."

"Oh, Anna. I had no idea."

"So apparently, Carl wasn't content, but if he'd told me, communicated it better to me, rather than assuming I'd pick up on his hint, then things could have been different."

Katrine spins in her seat, alarmed. "Anna. You've spotted the gaslighting already, do not let him mess with your head. Do you really want things with Carl to have been different?"

"Still be with him? Fuck, no. I see who he is now, what he's capable of. Your Elsebet would say he wasn't the one for me." At that, saying it out loud, Anna feels a lightening in her, like she's removed a cloak, one which, rather than protecting her, has dragged her down. That thing Jamie had said about letting things go that don't serve him? Anna thinks she might just have done that.

"It's OK," she says. "I dodged a bullet, and I still have my whole house. Good timing, some would say."

Katrine gives her an amiable knock to her side in agreement. "Luck in bad luck," she says, using the Danish idiom. "Just remember Carl isn't all men, or every man," she adds.

The train has brought them up from the underground out into the open air and Anna is observing the houses as they pass by, knowing this is her leaving the city, heading towards the airport, back into the air and away from Denmark. It really isn't bringing her the joy she'd thought it would. Something feels like it's draining out of her. Craving comfort, she snuggles closer, knowing Katrine's station is coming up soon. The tannoy announces the next stop is Amager and Katrine gives her boys the one-minute warning.

"Anna, I'll be over in March for the London Book Fair. Let's meet up," Katrine says, pulling her bag onto her shoulder.

"Stay at mine."

"Thanks, but work are putting me up in a fancy hotel. Let me have the joy of a sound-proof hotel room, a bathtub and the mini bar. Dinner, though. Definitely."

"Absolutely." Anna gets it, not taking offence.

Katrine turns to her friend. "Anna, you're going to be fine. In a week or two you'll be able to look back on this with some distance. Maybe you'll send him an email or a text, explain why you said whatever it was you said, make the apologies you need to, but meanwhile you know he's looking after your house, and he'll be a good memory." She stands. "We'll text regarding the dinner." She bends to give Anna a hug and whispers to her, "I missed you."

"Me, too," whispers Anna. And then, "*Godt nytår.*" Happy new year.

Anna honestly hopes a new year will move her on.

Chapter Thirty-Four

The flight is delayed. Of course it is. Given this trip, she wonders how she hadn't expected it. There's heavy fog in Gatwick and they're waiting for it to lift. But even before this, her exit has been hampered. First her baggage conveyor-belt broke, with her suitcase inconveniently out of reach so she couldn't transfer it to another. Once she'd been helped and moved on to Security, her bag had failed the X-ray, due to a so-small-it-took-ages-to-locate bottle of hand gel she'd forgotten to transfer out. Some might suggest her resolve is being tested.

As soon as she's through to airside, she bypasses all her favourite shops to find a seat, and pulling out her phone, she takes a deep breath and calls Jamie. She needs to tell him she is sorry, that she didn't mean what she said, that she should never have uttered the words. If she has hope of ever breathing comfortably again, she needs to apologise. She understands that he won't speak to her after, that the damage is done, but she will at least have told him she is sorry.

It rings out. He's not picking up her call. Staring at the screen, she gets it. She understands. She didn't take Carl or Maiken's calls either once.

She starts a text, but no matter what she writes, it's not enough and she deletes it time and again. This apology needs to be spoken; the hurt came from spoken words, the remorse should come that way too.

Dejected, she buys her hot dog and her Cocio chocolate milk, then moves on to Ole & Steen to buy a *kanelsnegl* for tomorrow's breakfast – her usual routine, trying to reassure herself of her course.

She sits by the glass window looking out onto the planes, checking the board now and again, but her flight is still delayed. Airside is milling with people excited to make their flights, but Anna simply isn't one of them. Prompted by a nearby groan of "Mommyyyy," she turns to see a family, some seats along. A girl, about eight years old, slumped in her seat, looks exhausted by it all. Anna gazes at her transfixed. She could be looking at her eight-year-old self. Ida always went into overdrive when they travelled on, trying to make this bit seem exciting. She would gush with facts about whichever new place they were headed for, while Anna would sit with her stuffed backpack, tired and wondering whether her latest set of friends would notice she was missing. In Ida-speak, what Anna is doing now, venturing out in the world, is a sign of her freedom and should be celebrated. The ability to restart and reinvent herself at short notice. But now Anna suspects Ida simply couldn't manage a long-term relationship, ever, and Anna's childhood stability was the collateral damage. Lovely old Anne-Grete had been right when she said Ida had fire in her bottom, and Anna wonders what life would have looked like, and would look like now for herself, if Ida had ever thought to douse it.

It's dark outside, save for the airport lighting, but her gaze is lost in the middle distance as she sorts through her feelings. She takes a big bite of the hot dog and savours it. Outside is a land with many hot dog wagons, but also many other things that she loves and values. So why, really, is she willing to walk away from it?

The humiliation. That's what it is. The bumping into people who knew and didn't say. And those who knew and now rub it into her face. Those things are the things she's removing herself from. Or running from, as Jamie would say. Only now, having been back, she wonders who wins in that situation. Those people don't care whether she comes or goes. She isn't wreaking revenge on them. They don't give a crap either way. But there are people here who *do* care about her, who like to see her, who don't rub a misfortune many months ago in her face. So why is she removing herself from them?

Balancing her hot dog, she tries calling him again, wanting to face this, settle this, before she leaves the country. But again it rings out. He really doesn't want to talk to her. Fair, she thinks. He'd once said being ghosted was horrible – she sees she's about to be schooled. And rightly so. With a small sniff, she pockets the phone, then takes another bite of the hot dog, ruminating as she munches.

She thinks about people who care about her. Katrine had said "not all men and not every man", but how were you supposed to tell the difference? She'd got it so very wrong with Carl. Having just seen him, Anna realises that here, eighteen months on, he didn't seem a better human being for allegedly having found his happiness with Maiken. In fact, if she thinks about men she trusts, until a fortnight ago she would have singularly said her *morfar*, him being the only real male role model she's had in her life. But then there was Jamie…

She takes a swig of the Cocio and then another bite of the hot dog, as deep thinking like this is taxing. Jamie was right, she *had* felt comfortable with him (after the initial serial killer thing). In contrast to Carl, Jamie is a different league; easily more a Morfar than a Carl, on Anna's limited spectrum of reference. And it makes her wonder whether he might be right about other things, too. Could the possibility of fortune supersede her past misfortune? Like Katrine said, the broken heart can be an open heart. Jamie certainly filled hers for the last two weeks. Perhaps it *is* time to put the humiliation behind her, as it's another thing which isn't serving her. It isn't making her feel better holding onto it. Anna blows out a long deep breath in an effort to let it go.

"You really have everything on that hot dog, haven't you?" says a voice from the adjacent chair and she nearly chokes. Staring so hard out of the window, she hasn't sensed anyone take the seat. Her head swings to her right and there he is. Jamie. Sitting there, right next to her, his big coat on and his rucksack at his feet.

"What are you doing here?!" She's shocked, but also elated, but then also fully ashamed. Perhaps he's here to give her an earful. She'd take it. "I mean … Jamie, what I said to you. I absolutely didn't mean that. I should never ever have said it. I am so sorry. Please forgive me." She looks into his beautiful eyes, hoping not to see hate there. Hate would slay her.

"Anna—"

"No, please hear me out. What I said was appalling. So bad. I don't even know why I suddenly felt the need to defend Ida, but to do it like that was awful. I am sorry, and I hope you'll accept my apology."

Jamie studies her, somewhat less angry than she expects and would understand. It's sort of like he's drinking her face in, truth be told. He sighs a deep sigh, then says, "Didn't we already agree that people do mad things when they're emotional?" Yes, they might have discussed that in the last fortnight. "Your apology is accepted." Well, that has gone far better than she has spun in her head. Maybe there is something to this facing things thing after all.

"I called you. To apologise," she adds, wanting him to know she'd tried sooner.

He digs his phone from a pocket and sees the missed calls. "There was a queue at the X-ray machines. You must have rung then."

Which brings her back to her original question.

"Why are you here, Jamie?"

"There's more I needed to say."

"But how did you get in here?" She waves her hand around at the departures lounge in case he still doesn't understand.

"I got a ticket. A return. I'll fly back tomorrow. I'm hoping there's a good Samaritan who'll let me stay." He bats his lashes at her, and she tries very hard not to smile, all the self-loathing easing now.

"There's fog at Gatwick," she says dully. "No flights in at the moment."

"That's OK," he says, upbeat. "My flight's to Heathrow."

This could be the last straw, that he flies to London, and she doesn't.

"How did you even get a ticket, Jamie? It's taken me weeks."

"I … um, called a friend," he says, looking shifty.

"You and your friends!" She barks a laugh, because it's astounding how quickly he has made himself a useful network, but then the laugh stops in her mouth. "Hang on, if you had a friend, then why didn't you call them for me?"

His shiftiness turns to shame.

"At first, I didn't think of it. Honestly. I swear. Izabela's more a friend of a friend. And then when I did, I sort of … didn't want to."

Will she be banned from the airport if she lumps him one right now? It wouldn't be unfitting in this mad chain of events if she lands in a police cell, too. Little would surprise her now.

"So, all this time, you were deliberately not helping me?"

"I think that depends on your point of view." He's sounding quite defensive.

"Really?"

"Absolutely. I think by delaying you I was helping you fall back in love with Copenhagen."

"I don't think you succeeded there." As she says it, it doesn't sound quite right in her mouth.

"You might not realise it yet, but wait until you get back to London and see how your apartment is decorated with Danish things, how you go to Danish events, how you miss it."

"Deluded," she mutters under her breath, knowing he's bang on.

"And can you really blame me for wanting to spend more time with you? I didn't keep you from your work. You had no dependants who needed you."

"It's like I was kidnapped and didn't know," she says to no one in particular.

"Hardly," he scoffs. "You had a door key and went to *Julefrokost*."

"You kept me here under false pretences."

"List them."

"That there were no flights!"

"I don't think even I have the connections to get all the airlines to follow a ruse like that."

"But you could have got me a ticket!"

"We don't know that. I only called just now after you left. It might have been the first return ticket available. Maybe I'm just very lucky. My marzipan piggy suggests this to be the case."

"Can I suggest somewhere you can shove your lucky piggy?"

He turns to her now, his grin dropping to a far more serious face. "Anna. I know I'm lucky, because I rent the door you knocked on. And since I opened the door to you, bedraggled, wet, crying and snotty, I haven't wanted you to leave. But can you honestly say I have at any point stopped or hindered you?"

"No," she mumbles crossly.

"Did you feel at any point that I was keeping you there against your will?"

"No."

"Have we had fun in the meantime?"

"A bit," she concedes sourly.

"A bit. Right. Well, *I've* had a lot of fun. Meanwhile, you got to spend time with Katrine. You did good things regarding me and Nikoline. You laid Pølse to rest properly, let's not forget that. And whether or not you believe it's for the good, like I do, you finally got to face Carl and Maiken. You got to be a poster girl for the city you were born in, and I think you *are* a little less angry at the city. So much good came out of the extra time you had here."

So yes, from such a point of view it might look like that.

"Don't think I'm going to thank you, Jamie."

"I wouldn't dream of it. I'm here to thank *you*, really."

"You are?" Honestly, life seems topsy-turvy to her sometimes. She thought he was here to administer a bollocking.

"Sure. Things just blew up before I got a chance to say it."

She isn't so sure about where this is heading.

"I got to have a lovely Christmas, not alone."

"*Pffft*, you had two invites! *Maybe three*," she mimics him, still miffed he had invites where she had none.

"I got to hang out with you, and kiss you, and become a poster boy for this city which *I* love, and to sleep with you, and to fall in love with you."

Anna's jaw drops.

"Don't look so gobsmacked, Anna. It felt pretty fucking obvious. But obvious or not, I need to tell you. Because the thought of you flying away from me – or by the looks of it, *me* flying away from you – without you properly knowing how I feel, makes me very sad, which we know won't do in the happiest of countries.

"And before you say I haven't been listening to what you said about this being for the best and that I should respect your decision, I have to say I have listened and I do respect it, but you weren't in receipt of all the facts. I hadn't told you yet I'm in love with you, so you were, you know, making decisions on scanty facts."

"Scanty facts?" She's not sure that's even proper English.

"Scanty facts, aye." He nods solemnly. "But here's my question; Do you really, really want to go back to live in London, or are you in fact running?"

Denial is obviously her immediate thought. But it would be a lie. And she's just been shouting at Carl about not being a mind reader and how people should communicate better, so she gives it to Jamie straight. "Part of me feels I have a plan and I'm safer if I stick to it. It's been like that since I discovered Carl and Maiken. It's the only thing that's held me together for the last year and a half. Another part of me tells me how easy it would be to come back, to move back into the house, live here again." With a shy look she adds, "With you. And there's part of that which scares the crap out of me, and I don't know why."

"Could it be because it sounds stable," Jamie ventures, "and you grew up without that? That you grew up seeing constantly moving on as the thing grown-ups do? Life with Ida sounds extraordinary, and I mean her no disrespect, but it doesn't sound like you ever saw that relationships can have longevity, because she never stayed. Staying here with me is the opposite of that. Throw in a bad experience with Carl, where you went against your upbringing, bought into stability, only for him to let you down. Those things, maybe?"

There is so much of that which resonates with her. Ida had always been ready to go at a moment's notice, her big handbag packed with most things they'd need for a speedy exit. A similar bag now sits at Anna's feet, bought as soon as she had enough wages to buy one. And of course, the first thing she'd done when she'd uncovered Carl and Maiken's betrayal was to pack up and leave her own home. Then, today, she'd immediately searched for a ticket. Oh, bloody hell, she's mini-Ida!

"Don't run, Anna," Jamie says, sliding his fingers into hers. "Fly. Fly when you need to – the job, seeing Ida, whatever, but fly back home to me."

That doesn't sound so bad. Birds return, don't they? Homing pigeons, migratory birds, those storks who come back to the exact same nest year after year. She could be a stork.

But a small sniff escapes her. "I don't know if I can trust my own judgement anymore, Jamie. That's what they did to me."

He leans closer and says at her ear, "Then trust *mine*, Anna, just while your head catches up with your heart. I've got you."

Her eyes are filling as she searches his face for signs of why she shouldn't take him at his word and dare. Risk the hurt, Katrine had said. Looking at him, she's filled with an overwhelming feeling that Jamie is worth the risk.

"You're the jigsaw piece that fits with me, Anna. You complete me. You tell me when I'm overstepping and when I'm meddling or trying to fix the unfixable. I need that. I want that. I want *you*. And I want to be the man who completes you, whose job it is to show you your trust is warranted, who has your back in the face of the things you fear." She scrunches her nose. "Without over-pushing you to face them," he quickly adds. "I get it, now. And I am sorry."

"No, you were right," she concedes. "I don't like to face things, but I've seen Carl and Maiken, and even the evil Morten, and it didn't kill me. I might have hated it, but it didn't destroy me. If anything, it's given me the perspective to let the shame go. Because the shame is theirs, not mine. And while I've been sitting here with my hot dog and Cocio, I've been realising something really important."

"What's that then?"

Anna looks up into his eyes. "That without you in my

life, I'll never be content. Simple as that. And so, by my own logic, I won't ever be truly happy. Not without you." She gives him a small smile. "I think I have a Kintsugi heart, and you are the gold."

She watches the smile spread across his face. "It's a beautiful heart," he says. She squeezes his hand.

"And you are here," she goes on, "so here is where I must be, sharing your duvet, even if here is…" The word isn't there for her, but a wince suffices.

Jamie takes her Cocio and points to her phone on her lap.

"Pull up the secret Pinterest board."

She thinks to bluff "What secret board?" but he's trying to show her something, so she complies.

He slides through the photos. Tivoli, the park, Kongens Nytorv, stargazing. Even the bloody *Copenhot* bikini shot. Kisses and smiles all the way. "You've saved these for a reason, and I don't think it's just because it's you and me. It's you and me and Copenhagen. You might feel awkward because of what happened with Carl here, but when *I* look at them, I see you belonging here. I think you will, too, when you let yourself. Saving these photos is part of that."

It makes sense to her. Those photos have been swiped through daily. "I'll work on it," she says.

"And if you really can't, then we'll move," he says lightly.

Anna looks at him agape. "What? No! What about Nikoline?" Would he really move away from her? From the job he loves? He'd have some explaining to do to his dad…

"Anna, my life with Nikoline will for years be at the

whim of Lajla, who I'll never fully trust, given past experience. But if the offer is to be with you, live with you, love you, on a daily basis, then yes, that's what I'd pick. I'll find other ways to be in Nikoline's life. You've given me the in now and the rest is up to what Lajla and I can work out."

Anna is stunned. That he's offering to give up so much for her, so many things which are so important to him, in a city he loves. And frankly, it chastens her; the weight she's put on her home city keeping her away. Having decided to cast off the worries about other people's gossip and ill-will, it feels pig-headed now to hang onto this.

She lifts their clasped hands and kisses the back of his.

"No need, Jamie. I'm coming home."

He pulls their hands across and kisses the back of hers, like they've just sealed a deal.

"For the record, I think you had me at the doorstep, too," she admits, feeling shy.

Jamie places another kiss at her temple. "It was the small towel, wasn't it?"

"So small," she guffaws. "I didn't stand a chance."

There's movement around them as some waiting passengers begin to stand up and walk.

"They've called my flight," Jamie says, looking over her shoulder.

She feels her teeth grind slightly. Her flight information hasn't changed. "You don't need to go to London, Jamie. I'm coming back. I promise."

"I can help you start packing," he says.

She tilts her head.

"No meddling. Got it," he says. "Although it's going to

be harder to get out of the airport from here, than taking the plane to England and returning. Just saying."

"Surely you have a friend who'll help you?" she says with a smile and some snark.

"I'll stay until your flight is called?"

"Could be hours yet. Go home. I'll FaceTime you when I get there."

"Promise?"

"Promise."

Reluctantly he stands, then pulls her up and reels her in to him. She cradles his face and looks deeply into his eyes. "I love you, Jamie MacDonald. I'll be back soon."

And then he kisses her, a culmination of all the first kisses and then the fake kisses and the recent true kisses, a kiss so fine and tender and bespoke for her, that there's seriously no doubt at all she'll be back. She'll swim if she has to. Notice on her apartment will be served first thing in the morning.

"It's them!" says a fellow passenger from behind them. Anna opens one eye to see various people snapping pictures of them, as they stand not fifty metres from a poster of themselves kissing outside Tivoli. Jamie tightens his arms around her and Anna closes her eye again, content and ridiculously happy.

Author's Note

Naturally, I have used some Artistic Licence here and there. (The capital letters there make it legit, right?)

Some real Danish weather events have been blended to make Anna's snowmageddon. (Snow is not only for Christmas.)

Sankt Annæ's Christmas menu may have been tweaked so Anna could swerve the herring. (Sorry, I'm with her on this. And their open sandwiches are excellent, so.) I might have fudged their Juletide opening dates too. But it is too pretty at Christmas not to include.

A.C. Perch's tearoom has moved since 2024, from the Japanese inspired tearoom above the shop to a larger shop on ground level, next door on Kronprinsensgade. I kept the old venue as that's what I saw in my head, after many happy times scoffing scones there.

In recompense for my blending and fudging, and in the spirit of Anna's travel guidery, here are links to the places and things I've included, in case you want to see pictures.

A.C. Perch's Thehandel – https://perchs.dk/en/
A.C. Perch's Tearoom – https://perchstearoom.dk/

Conditori La Glace's cake selection –
https://laglace.dk/en/sortiment/lagkager/

Copenhot – https://copenhot.com/

The Hirschprung Collection – https://hirschsprung.dk/

The fiendish jigsaw is *Kartoffelraekerne* by Nicolas Cosedis.
You can see it in this site along with his other brilliant aerial
shots of Copenhagen –
https://www.welovecph.com/

Kayak Bar – https://kayakbar.dk/en/

Manon les Suites –
https://guldsmedenhotels.com/manon-les-suites/

Rundetårnet (The Round Tower) –
https://www.rundetaarn.dk/en/front-page/

Sankt Annæ – https://restaurantsanktannae.dk/

Tapa del Toro (Torvehallerne) –
https://www.tapadeltoro.dk/

Tivoli – https://www.tivoli.dk/en

If you fancied trying to make or bake any of the Danish Christmas food mentioned in *A Copenhagen Snowmance*, I would point you to Brontë Aurell. Her book *ScandiKitchen Christmas* should have you covered.

https://www.bronteaurell.com/

When Anna's in London, she's a regular customer at ScandiKitchen. There are two ScandiKitchen cafes in London, each with a grocery section if you want to try some of the food I've mentioned.

ScandiKitchen Fitzrovia – 61 Great Titchfield Street
ScandiKitchen Victoria – 42 Buckingham Palace Road
Mail Order – https://www.scandikitchen.co.uk/

Happy exploring!

Acknowledgments

A huge *Thank You* to you, my reader, for picking up this book! I hope you enjoyed it; I have more if you liked it. I know you have a lot of choice out there, so it means a lot that you chose this one. For those of you who have read my other books, thanks for your patience between this one and the last. I had a brain to locate. Bloody perimenopause…

Extra *Thank Yous* to those of you who now leave a review. They are SO helpful to authors – even a short one, even if you didn't buy the book yourself or borrowed it from the library. (Zero thanks to those who downloaded this as a PDF from a pirate site – you know who you are. Stop it, thief. We've all got to eat.) Extra extra thanks to those who follow me on bookbub.com and the socials. And did you know I have a newsletter? Sign up at pernillehughes.com and get a free short story.

Charlotte, lovely Charlotte, Dream Editor, who doesn't seem to mind when I go silent for years and then pop up with a "Hello, remember me? I have this synopsis…" Thank you for having me again, for your help and ideas and comments. Superstar.

And to Sofia, Kara, Helen, Chloe, Grace and the entire team at One More Chapter, who work so hard to make this happen. Your names in the credit roll hardly seems enough but thank you for making this book a reality.

Further *Thank Yous* to:

Emily Thomas for the copy edit – sorry for my playing fast and loose with capital letters. Simon Fox for the proofread and dealing with my erratic comma game.

My wonderful cover team: Lina Hughes for the initial visualisation of what I had in my head, Sophie Melissa for bringing Anna and Jamie to life, and Lucy Bennett for her design brilliance pulling it all together.

Charlotte, bestest seeester and Copenhagen correspondent. Thanks for spotting the glitches and the fifty minute walks I had down as ten. Life is faster in my head. And for disliking Carl as much as you do.

Caroline, for our coffee *cough* writing sessions, dinners and your emergency read and excellent thoughts. You're always on hand with wisdom and ideas.

Signe for your super-speedy Danish edit. *Tusind tak*!

The *Love & Chocolate* coven: Andi Forsythe-Michael, Caroline Hogg, Donna Ashcroft, Jules Wake, Nancy Peach, Olivia Beirne, and Ruby Basu – always a joy to see you for cake lunch and publishing chats. The support and kindness are magnificent.

Cressida McLaughlin, Bella Osborne and Sarah Bennett for laughs along the way.

My *Romance Snowmance* Whatsapp group: Dottie, Majo, Rosa, Enna, Yotti and Signe for your Danish winter id list and speedy responses to my general enquiries. I think I got most of your wishes in.

Suki, as always, for the cheerleading!

Brontë, for all your kindness, wisdom and support throughout the summer of 2024. I'm now going to be on your case regarding your novel!

My lovely cousin Rune, for my Copenhagen airport snow plough facts. 26!!!!

Katia, for your wine recommendations when all I can manage is "red, white, not Chardonnay".

My lovely fellow Hospice of St Francis volunteers and colleagues at Amersham Owned – you got me back out of the house. Thank you for all the laughs and rehabilitation into society. (Did you spot it, Bela?)

Ailsa, for being there (over 30 years, Jim!!!!!) and for helping fill my cultural well. You are the best, SuperJim.

Linda Barnes, for resetting me again and again with her super skills. Apparently, you are the only one who doesn't mind my snoring.

Whoever invented HRT, to the amazing NHS for providing it and Stephane Watteeux for prescribing it. Game changer.

My family, Clan Knappe. What a year and a half, right? We might be muddling through, but still we keep laughing and that's how he would have wanted it.

My cherubs, M, L, M and K – let's face it, you aren't going to read this, so I'm sending you big sloppy kisses and overlong hugs and public *I love yous* and delightedly imagining your squirming. :)

Ian, you (unlike our spawn) might check this bit, and I'm also sending you big sloppy kisses and overlong hugs and public *I love yous*, which you can cash in at any time, in thanks for your constant love and support. My hero. xxx

Becca and Charlie have known each other since university.

They have also hated each other since university.

Until Ally's bucket list. The death of their loved one should mean they can go their separate ways and not look back. But completing the list is something neither of them can walk away from.

And sometimes, those who bring out the worst in you, also bring out the very best…

Over the course of ten years, Becca and Charlie's paths collide as they deal with grief, love and life after Ally.

AVAILABLE IN PAPERBACK, EBOOK AND AUDIO NOW!

Jen Attison likes her life Just So.

But being fished out of a canal in Copenhagen by her knickers is definitely NOT on her to do list.

From cinnamon swirls to a spontaneous night of laughter and fireworks, Jen's city break with the girls takes a turn for the unexpected because of her gorgeous, mystery rescuer.

Back home, Jen faces a choice.

A surprise proposal from her boyfriend, 'boring' Robert, has offered Jen the safety net she always thought she wanted. But with the memories of her Danish adventure proving hard to forget, maybe it's time for Jen to stop listening to her head and start following her heart...

AVAILABLE IN PAPERBACK AND EBOOK NOW!

True love packs a punch…

Tiffanie Trent is not having a great week. Her boyfriend has unceremoniously dumped her on their tenth anniversary, leaving her heartbroken and homeless.

Frank Black, the owner of Blackie's boxing gym where Tiff has been bookkeeper for the last decade, has dropped dead. He's not having a great week either.

And if that wasn't enough, Mike 'The Assassin' Fellner, boxer of international fame and Tiff's first love, is back in town and more gorgeous than ever. Tiff can't seem to go anywhere without bumping into his biceps.

When she discovers Blackie's gym has been left to her, Tiff is certain she'll fail. Can Tiff step up and roll with the punches, or will she be down and out at the first round?

AVAILABLE IN PAPERBACK AND EBOOK NOW!

ONE MORE CHAPTER

The author and One More Chapter would like to thank everyone
who contributed to the publication of this story...

Analytics
Imogen Wolstencroft

Audio
Fionnuala Barrett
Ciara Briggs

Contracts
Laura Amos
Inigo Vyvyan

Design
Lucy Bennett
Fiona Greenway
Liane Payne
Dean Russell

Digital Sales
Laura Daley
Lydia Grainge
Hannah Lismore

eCommerce
Laura Carpenter
Madeline ODonovan
Charlotte Stevens
Christina Storey
Jo Surman
Rachel Ward

Editorial
Kara Daniel
Simon Fox
Charlotte Ledger
Laura McCallen
Jennie Rothwell
Sofia Salazar Studer
Emily Thomas
Helen Williams

Harper360
Emily Gerbner
Ariana Juarez
Jean Marie Kelly
emma sullivan
Sophia Wilhelm

International Sales
Peter Borcsok
Ruth Burrow
Bethan Moore
Colleen Simpson

Inventory
Sarah Callaghan
Kirsty Norman

Marketing & Publicity
Chloe Cummings
Grace Edwards
Katie Sadler

Operations
Melissa Okusanya
Hannah Stamp

Production
Denis Manson
Simon Moore
Francesca Tuzzeo

Rights
Ashton Mucha
Alisah Saghir
Zoe Shine
Aisling Smyth
Lucy Vanderbilt

Trade Marketing
Ben Hurd
Eleanor Slater

**The HarperCollins
Distribution Team**

**The HarperCollins
Finance & Royalties
Team**

**The HarperCollins
Legal Team**

**The HarperCollins
Technology Team**

UK Sales
Isabel Coburn
Jay Cochrane
Sabina Lewis
Holly Martin
Harriet Williams
Leah Woods

**And every other
essential link in the
chain from delivery
drivers to booksellers
to librarians and
beyond!**

ONE MORE CHAPTER

One More Chapter is an
award-winning global
division of HarperCollins.

Subscribe to our newsletter to get our
latest eBook deals and stay up to date
with all our new releases!

signup.harpercollins.co.uk/
join/signup-omc

Meet the team at
www.onemorechapter.com

Follow us!

@onemorechapterhc

Do you write unputdownable fiction?
We love to hear from new voices.
Find out how to submit your novel at
www.onemorechapter.com/submissions